CHASING DREAMS IN EVERSLEY VILLAGE

AN EVERSLEY VILLAGE ROMANCE BOOK 1

SUZANNE FOX

LITTLE ORCHARD PRESS ®

For Iris Loveland

A CHILDHOOD MEMORY

*M*itchell Booth ran up the hill, toy tractor in hand. He preferred planes so this was a plane – a red plane. Dropping down on the thick bouncy grass which grew wild on the fallow field, he heard a voice from over the wall. It was a higgledy-piggledy wall made of various shapes and sizes of grey stone cut from a local Somerset quarry. He got up and peered over. He saw a little girl in a white T-shirt and yellow shorts playing on a blue and white blanket. He guessed she was around the same age as his sister, about four. Still a little girl. He, on the other hand. was a big boy – six years old and going to proper school. He could read and do sums.

Mitchell sneezed as a fly flew up his nose. It was one of those little ones he could breathe in. The little girl jumped up and grinned at him, clutching a bright toy in her hand.

'Hello – I'm Holly.'

Mitchell stepped back. Great-Uncle Sidney had been very clear about this situation. Do not talk to anyone over the wall. Do not go over the wall. Looking back over his shoulder, he checked to see if his uncle was in sight. He was not, so Mitchell turned back to Holly.

'What's that?' She pointed to the red tractor at his feet.

Mitchell rubbed the back of his neck. 'It's a plane.'

Holly peered at the toy and giggled. 'No silly. It's a tractor.' Her tightly-curled white-blonde hair bounced on her head as she jumped up and down. 'Can I see? Can I see?'

Mitchell smiled and picked up his shiny new tractor, passing it over the wall.

A deep voice bellowed on the breeze. 'Mitchell Booth.'

Mitchell jumped and turned to see Sidney stomping up the soft slope towards him. He spun back to Holly, stretching out his hand. 'Give it back.'

Holly put out her other hand, in which she held a pink plastic pony with a blue fluffy mane. 'Swapsies.' Her eyes opened wide as Mitchell heard his uncle panting behind him.

Sidney's hand flew over Mitchell's shoulder towards the little girl. 'Tractor please.'

Holly handed it over and Mitchell felt his uncle's large grip on his arm as they turned and left. Looking over his shoulder, he could see Holly staring after him. She was frowning as she bit her bottom lip, the plastic pony was perched on the wall.

After a few strides, Sidney stopped and crouched down to Mitchell's eye level.

'Never. I say never give anything to a Loveland. Not your tractor, not land – and especially not your heart.'

CHAPTER 1

*H*olly dug her spade into the soft soil and twisted it. Strands of blonde hair escaped from her cap and fluttered in the spring wind. The afternoon sun poked through a cloud, lighting up the day with a warmth that hinted at summer. She gazed at her land as it gradually descended into the valley. There it met the neighbouring farmland, flanked by the smooth limestone hills of the Mendips which dipped into a v shape where the sun always set. Sighing, Holly remembered running down the gentle slopes as a child, with a homemade kite trailing behind her, then trudging back up for one of her mum's scones topped with thick jam and a dollop of cream.

The freshness of the day brought a pink hue to her cheeks as she crouched to break up a clump of earth with her gloved hands. She loved the comforting smell of the soil. It reminded her of her father and the planting they'd done together. Straightening up she removed her fleece, tying it around her waist as she surveyed her garden nursery. It was housed in stone buildings and buzzed with customers. Children, fresh out of school, clambered over a play area she had built out of reclaimed wood. Holly loved talking to customers and showing the children plants. But today she was leaving everything to her staff. She wanted to be alone. Reaching for her water bottle she took a long gulp, there was a sickening feeling inside her stomach – the same feeling she had exactly two years ago, when her parents died.

Holly was brought back to the present by a high-pitched bark. She thrust her spade into the ground and leant on it. A cream and tan dog bounced over, circling her legs until they were wrapped in an extendable lead. Holly's shoulders drooped. *No peace for me today then?* she thought. She could see the owner, head down, repeatedly clicking a button on the lead's plastic handle. Straightening up, he shook his head.

As he got closer, she recognised him. *Oh no, not Mitchell Booth*, she thought. She had not seen him in years – not since they were teenagers – but she would know his ice-blue eyes anywhere. Set against dark hair, they were like none she had ever seen on anyone else. Feeling her cheeks burn, Holly looked down. The dog had settled on her boots, its tongue flapping out the side of its mouth as it panted. As Mitch got closer she pulled the peak of her cap downwards, in an attempt to cover her face. It had been over fifteen years – hopefully he would have forgotten her.

Hunching over, he pointed at the small dog. 'Stay'.

A bit late for that, Holly thought as the musty aroma of wet dog reached her nose.

'Sorry about this. I'll just get her.'

'Okay,' Holly sighed.

Mitch bent down and lifted the dog as he moved anti-clockwise around Holly's legs, unravelling the lead as he went, until he knocked the spade over which fell onto the soft soil with a thud. Holly shut her eyes as he continued circling, mumbling apologies.

She remembered Mitch as the boy who'd appeared annually at the neighbouring farm. The boy she had chatted to over the stone wall when no-one was looking. The boy whose name she had scrawled in her diary and surrounded with hearts. *But he's no boy now,* she thought, as he stood before her as a six-foot-something man. A tingling heat rose up her neck. *I could do without this,* she thought.

Holly raised her voice as the wind whipped up. 'I'm afraid dogs aren't permitted on nursery property, due to the petting area.'

Mitch held his dog between both hands. 'Petting?' He tipped his head back and peered through mussed-up hair.

Holly flushed. 'Yes, a small petting zoo. A few rabbits, guinea pigs ... a goat.'

Mitch's eyes crinkled at the edges and a smile spread slowly across his face.

'So, dogs aren't allowed here,' she said tugging the peak of her cap further downwards.

Mitch shook the hair out of his eyes and lost grip of the dog which wriggled to the ground, giving one yap before it jumped up at Holly, leaving brown paw prints on her cargo trousers.

Mitch lunged forward. 'Trixy, stop.' He grabbed the dog. 'She likes you.'

Holly flushed.

'Sorry.' Mitch pointed at Holly's muddy cargos and moved forward.

Holly stepped back, worried he would try to brush her down. 'It's fine. They're nursery issue, no harm done. Dirt comes with this type of work.'

After unclipping the lead from Trixy, Mitch shoved it

into his pocket. Straightening up he stuffed the dog under his left arm. 'I'm Mitch. I've taken over Booth Farm from my uncle.' He nodded towards the neighbouring land. 'He's too weak to run it now. Where can I find your boss?' He turned to face the nursery and smoothed his hair with his free hand. 'We need to talk about the gate.'

Holly took a deep breath as she removed her work gloves and stuffed them into her back pocket. *Better get this over with*, she thought.

Mitch lowered his voice and turned to face her. 'What's she like now? I heard –'

'Holly Loveland,' she said thrusting out her right hand, looking him straight in the eye. A gust of wind caught the peak of her cap, it flew off and her long hair blew behind her. As Mitch took her hand, she felt his rough skin against hers and a tingle raced up her arm.

He nodded slowly.

Holly forced a smile.

Mitch laughed. 'I thought you seemed too young to be Holly. I'm useless at first impressions. Although we've met before, of course. I used to visit Sid every summer. Remember?'

Holly pulled her hand away. 'No. No I don't,' she lied as she shook her head, searching her mind for a change of subject. Leaning forward she ruffled the soft hair on Trixy's head. 'An interesting breed for a farmer, don't you think?'

Mitch rubbed his throat. 'My wife, she – she chose the dog.'

They were interrupted by the sound of spitting gravel, the vroom of a car and pulsating dance music as a red Audi TT swept into the customer car park. It came to an abrupt halt. The door swung open and out climbed a suited and stilettoed Jaz.

'Yoo-hoo.' Jaz waved, fingers waggling.

Holly glanced at Mitch who had walked to nearby bushes and was returning with her cap in his hand. He passed it to her. 'You've obviously got company. I'll come by tomorrow, without Trixy.'

The dog added a timely yap.

Holly opened her mouth to speak but he turned abruptly and walked off with his pet wriggling underneath his arm.

Jaz, half way up the path, stopped and gazed over her sunglasses as Mitch passed her. Tottering up to Holly, she mock wiped her brow. 'I would, I so would,' she said, nodding her head.

'No you wouldn't. That's Sidney Booth's nephew.'

Jaz's mouth opened wide and she squealed. 'No way. Not Mitchell your childhood crush?'

Holly saw Mitch turn his head. Their eyes met briefly and he grinned.

Holly crossed her arms. 'Thanks for that.'

'Calm down, he never heard.'

Holly watched Mitch taking long strides in the distance. 'He so did.'

'Flippin' heck, love, he's turned out bloody gorgeous.'

'Down, girl. He's married.'

'How do you know? Been checking him out already?'

'No. He said his wife chose the dog.' Holly replaced her cap firmly on her head. 'Anyway, he's not my type.'

Jaz laughed and pushed her sunglasses on top of her head, opening her warm-brown eyes wide. 'Firstly, that man is every woman's type and secondly, he could be divorced. Maybe he got custody of the mutt?'

Holly shook her head. 'You've got it wrong.'

Jaz smoothed her dark, choppy bob as the wind took it.

'Well, a girl can dream, can't she? I'll defo be asking around if you're not going for it.'

'Of course I'm not going for it. I've got Tom.' She lifted her chin. 'Even if I was remotely interested, which I'm not, my parents always told me not to get involved with that family. They spell trouble.'

Jaz raised her eyebrows. 'Yeah, yeah. The whole village knows that Lovelands and Booths don't mix.' Jaz nodded in Mitch's direction. 'But maybe you and yummy Mitchell will be the ones to end the feud.'

'I'm married and I'm not interested in being his friend.'

'What are you like?' Jaz looked at Holly's muddy clothes. 'You need to get out of the dirt, hun – get in touch with your inner prom queen.'

Holly picked up her spade. 'I never was prom queen.'

'Still – the way I remember it – you were the one the boys wanted to snog.'

'When?'

'At the school disco.'

Holly laughed. 'I don't dance anymore. I'm thirty and that's practically middle-aged.'

'You're joking, right? Thirty's prime time.' Jaz flicked her hair.

'For you maybe,' Holly said, smiling with one hand on her hip.

'Anyway, I've come to let you know – I'm taking you out for drinks in Wells tomorrow night.'

Holly drooped her shoulders. 'I'm really not in the mood.'

'Oh, go on. I got a bonus this month – sold the most cars. Anyway, you need to get out and meet people.'

'I'm married.'

'But you're on a breather, got a hall pass.'

'Tom and I haven't split up. we're on a four-week break. In no way is it a pass for whatever you have in mind.'

'I don't think Tom's moping around.' Jaz put a hand on Holly's arm. 'I have to break the news that I heard down the Eversley Arms last night –'

'I'm not taking any notice of village gossip.' Holly picked up her spade, digging hard into the ground, aware of Jaz staring at her.

'Do you want to talk about it?' Jaz's voice softened.

'I've already told you, Tom's on the circuit with the hot tubs, taking time out to think about us starting a family. The least I can do is to give him some space.' Holly bent over to pull up some roots. 'After all, he was there for me, picked me up when I was down.' Her face flushed and her eyes stung. She dare not exhale in case a sob escaped.

'You don't owe him, hun. Yeah, he cheered you up when you lost your parents but you picked him up from the gutter after his career went wrong.'

'It's not his fault they got rid of him.'

'So he says. Didn't win his unfair dismissal claim from the rig though, did he?'

Holly coughed to disguise a sob but couldn't stop the tears.

'Holls.' Jaz stepped into the soft ground with her hands up. 'I'm coming in.'

Holly felt Jaz's arms around her, keeping her hands by her side not wanting to transfer soil onto Jaz's jacket.

'I didn't mean to upset you, chick. I'm just worried. Worried Tom's taking you for a fool. I'm not getting at you. I just –'

Holly blinked and her chest shuddered.

Jaz leaned back. 'And tears? So not like you, hun.'

'It's not just Tom.' Holly wiped away a tear with the back

of her hand. 'For some reason, without him here all I'm thinking about is Mum and Dad.'

'Oh, hun,' Jaz said as she pulled Holly close again. 'You were so strong when they died.' Jaz released Holly and pointed to the nursery building. 'Leaving your exciting life behind at the art gallery in London. Coming back here and taking over the place, just like that. Throwing yourself into it. Bringing the nursery into modern times.'

'It never feels like hard work here.' Holly stepped back and took a deep breath. 'And as Dad used to say – busy hands stop worrying minds.'

'I can see that.' Jaz gestured at the freshly dug soil. 'I know it's been awhile but these things can catch up with you. And you and Tom – it was all a bit whirlwind wasn't it? He did move in proper quick. Not that I blamed you. I thought you two were perfect when you got back together.'

Holly nodded. 'Things were good, really good at the start, just like the first time around before I moved to art school and he went to work on the oil rig.'

'Yeah, he seemed so grown up then, compared to us. I guess five years age difference is a big gap when you're seventeen.'

'When I was in London, I often wondered what would have happened if we'd both stayed in Eversley. I guess I felt it was meant to be – us both coming back at the same time. Maybe I was blinded, being a soppy romantic.' Holly took a deep breath. 'Hopefully this is only a blip. The course of true love never runs smooth, as they say.' She looked down and pointed at Jaz's muddy feet. 'Oh no, your shoes! You're not off anywhere special, are you?'

'It's the regional awards night with work, in Exeter. I'm staying over.'

'On no.'

'No worries, hun. S'only a bit of mud.'

'Let's get them cleaned up. I've got to finish up here, anyway. There's kitchen roll in the studio.'

Picking up her spade, Holly led Jaz down the winding path towards her small art studio, sandwiched between the main nursery building and the cottage with its stone walls and red tiled roof where Holly had been brought up. Leaning her spade against the outside wall, she stamped the mud off her boots. The blue door creaked as she opened it, leaning into the darkness Holly fumbled for the light switch then jumped as the bulb blew.

'Oh, not again. The electrics are on the blink. Hang on, I'll open the blinds.' Holly squinted as she walked towards the window. The sun streamed in as she lifted the blackouts which protected her work.

'Wow, you've been busy.' Jaz scanned the room crammed with colourful paintings.

'I've been sorting through my art, taken photographs of all of the pieces and logged them.' Walking to the sink in the far corner Holly ran the tap, moistening a few sheets of kitchen roll.

'You've loads here, enough for an exhibition,' Jaz said walking around the room. 'You're still planning to convert the old barn into a gallery, right?'

'I've had a better idea.' Holly handed the wet paper towel to Jaz. Walking to the far wall she grabbed a flip chart A-frame, which made a scraping noise as she dragged it across the paint-splattered stone floor. Turning over a few pages of sketches, Holly reached a map she had drawn of the nursery. 'I thought we could extend the café here,' she said pointing to the page, 'and display paintings on the walls. And then the old building could become an art barn, rather than a gallery – with creative activities for visitors, like painting, mosaic, pottery.'

'That's amazing,' Jaz said standing in stockinged feet wiping her shoes.

'It'd be great for the coach parties that stop here and I could attract visits from local schools. Maybe link with other artists and make it into an arts hub.'

'Yeah! Get back on track with your dreams, do what you want to do, rather than stick with plants.'

Holly shook her head. 'The nursery's in my blood, I'll never give it up. All my family memories are here.' Holly stared out of the window. 'But yes, I can diversify and use my hard-earned art degree.' She cocked her head to one side. 'I've realised, these last couple of weeks how much I miss painting. I've not done much since me and Tom ...'

'Well you must have painted something since you two got together.' Jaz pointed to a portrait of a man with rusty, sun-kissed hair and vibrant green eyes.

Holly laughed and walked over to the painting of Tom. Picking it up with both hands she held it at arm's length. 'It was his birthday present.' She looked into the laughing eyes she had captured, sad that they'd stopped smiling at her. *Where's he gone?* she asked herself. 'I should hang it in the house really. I was waiting for him to decorate the lounge.'

Jaz flicked her head in a silent tut.

Holly bent down propping the painting against the wall.

'When's this all happening?' Jaz said, pointing to the flip chart.

'As soon as Tom turns a profit. I had money set aside but leant it to him to buy stock.' Holly heard Jaz's sharp intake of breath and felt the need to elaborate. 'He ordered a few tubs to show at the exhibitions.' Returning to the flip chart, Holly pushed it back against the wall then turned to Jaz who was shaking her head.

'I didn't realise you'd funded the hot tub business, thought he'd actually done something for himself, for a change.' Putting her shoes back on, Jaz placed the dirty paper towels in the bin.

'The stock was expensive. Not forgetting the haulage costs. But he says he's done brilliantly at the exhibitions.' Holly removed her fleece from her waist and placed it over an easel. 'And the country show season starts in a few weeks. It'll only be a short wait until he returns the money to my project pot.'

Jaz took a deep breath. 'You're always waiting on Tom. Waiting for him to decorate the lounge, waiting for him to make his mind up about having kids, waiting for him to make a profit, Waiting for him to –'

Holly folded her arms. 'Jaz.'

Jaz pulled a face, scrunching her petite nose. 'Sorry.'

'Anyway,' Holly picked up her latest piece of work. 'While you're here, what do you think of this?' Holly held the framed watercolour up to the sunlight. It was a view from her favourite bench, perched on the brow of the slope with views across Booth Farm. A patchwork of orange and yellow fields underneath a bright blue sky. With a line of trees and bushes in striking greens and a burnished sun shining through the gap in the hills. 'It's called *Harvest Sunset*. It's for the Wells Beauty of Somerset competition.'

'O-M-G, it's gorgeous. The colours jump out at you.'

'They're somewhat brighter than reality. I was a bit worried about that.'

'Don't be, that's your style. You'll smash it.' Jaz pulled her mobile out of her pocket and glanced at the screen. 'Sorry, gotta go.' Holly felt Jaz touch her arm. 'I don't like leaving you, though, not when you're down like this.'

'I'm fine, really I am.' Holly smiled as broadly as she could.

'Hmm. Well, I'll come by tomorrow morning and we'll go shopping for our night out.'

'But –'

Jaz kissed Holly on the cheek. 'Take care, chick.' She waved her mobile phone as she walked out of the door. 'Just call, anytime.'

As the door closed, Holly shivered and she became aware once more of the lingering nausea. Turning, she saw the stark white walls of the studio as her mind flashed back two years. She had been working at a gallery in London when the call came in from Avon and Somerset police. They had asked her to get to Musgrove Hospital as soon as possible, because her parents had been in an accident on the M5. She had called the hospital on her way. The doctors were doing their best, they had said. *Stop looking back,* she told herself as she glanced at her watch. Holly realised the competition deadline was in forty minutes and that she had better get a move on.

CHAPTER 2

*S*till wearing her nursery uniform of cargos, T-shirt and fleece, Holly hurried into the market place in Wells. She was met by the sound of metal clanging and canvas flapping, as the mid-week traders dismantled their stalls. The day darkened and Holly gazed upwards to see a charcoal cloud roll over the sun. Sighing, she saw the Cathedral ahead which dominated the scene, dwarfing the neighbouring shops. It stood only yards from the Town Hall. She was nearly there. Coming towards her across the cobbled expanse was Val who'd worked part-time at the nursery café since it opened. She was the closest Holly had ever had to a granny, her own grandmothers having died before she was born. Val ambled from side to side towards her wearing a pale blue coat with a yellow headscarf that covered most of her grey hair. She had a pained expression on her face as she carried a bag in each hand. Reaching Holly, she let out a slow groan. Holly leaned forward kissing Val on the cheek before stepping back and smiling down at her.

'That's some breeze. No sign of summer then. Still

wearing a vest, me,' Val said in her broad Somerset accent as she looked down, chin to chest.

'I see you've been shopping.' Holly glanced at her watch. *I haven't much time.* Val was difficult to stop once in conversation.

'They sells it off at silly prices, late in the day. The veg that is,' Val said smiling. 'What's that there?' She nodded at Holly's folio.

'It's the watercolour,' she said lifting the folio. 'Remember? The competition?'

'Oh yes, love. Anyway you heard anything of your Tom?' Val dumped her bags on the cobbles and put her hand up to her mouth and coughed as if she was preparing herself for a speech.

'No.' Holly swallowed and bit her bottom lip. 'It's only been two weeks, the break's for a month, remember?'

'He shouldn't need no break, or time to think. What's got into him? I've never seen such a change in a person.' Val shook her head. 'A girl like you. Me and Len had both boys by the time we was your age.' She gestured over her shoulder with her thumb. 'That one needs to grow up. How old is he now? Thirty-five?'

Holly opened her mouth, but Val continued.

'You gave him some place to live. Some place to work. Some place to keep his stuff. Time to himself, when you was working every hour God sends while he went off doing whatever he pleased. Like them trips to Newquay.'

Holly's shoulders dipped. 'He hasn't been away surfing since autumn – you know that. He's been working hard at the hot tub business.'

'And now he needs a separation just as his own thing's taking off?' Val shook her head.

'It's not a separation.'

Val glanced behind her then back at Holly. 'I need to warn you, love. I just seen –'

'Can't stop. Sorry, the competition deadline. It's in ten minutes.' Holly took Val's hand. 'We'll catch up tomorrow, though. I promise.' She kissed her on the cheek and dashed off.

Holly's boots slipped on the cobbles, she hoped the final remnants of soil would wear off by the time she reached the Town Hall. Making for the shop-lined perimeter of the market where the pavement was slabbed, she glanced back watching Val shaking her head as she lugged her bags towards the bus stop. Holly sighed as a large plop of rain fell on her head, she knew she should have offered Val a lift back to the village. Another raindrop hit her, followed by another. *That's all I need,* she thought.

Taking shelter from the downpour under a bakery canopy, she zipped up her fleece. The sweet aroma of bread and cake drifted out of the shop, but did nothing for her appetite. *I couldn't even manage a slice of that*, she thought, staring through the window at her favourite treat – lemon drizzle cake. It was only a matter of yards to the Town Hall, so she decided to make a run for it.

Holly stepped away from the shelter, running a few paces then stopped. There he was – Tom, wearing his trademark 'smart but casual'. She smiled and filled her lungs assuming he must have popped back. Lifting her arm to wave, she stopped mid-air. *Who's that?* she thought.

A young woman was at Tom's side, wearing a long purple coat with a scarf, a kaleidoscope of pinks, with hair similar to her own, flaying around in the breeze. Holly lowered her arm and looked down at her muddy cargos. Lifting her head to the sound of laughter, she saw Tom grappling with a folded umbrella as his companion giggled at his side. Rain dripped from Holly's eyebrows, as she watched Tom guide the girl to shelter in a shop doorway with an arm around her waist, smiling the smile which she herself had not witnessed for months.

Holly took a sharp intake of breath. 'No!' she gasped – her voice sucked away by the wind. The skin on her face burned. Her heart pounded. Tom had pulled the woman close for a lingering kiss.

The cool rain pelted down, mixing with the hot tears streaming from her eyes, as she remained fixed to the spot, watching Tom as he opened the umbrella. Seeing them walk in her direction she ducked her head, dashing into the nearest shop. The bell shrilled as the door slammed behind her. Standing motionless she clutched her folio to her chest.

'Oh hi, Holly darling, looking for something special?' asked Nina, the owner of the 'Something Special' boutique.

Holly lifted her head, her heart beating at pace as she viewed the rows of silk, lace and taffeta, all in varying shades of white. *Of all the blinking shops,* she thought. Nina was not her favourite person, they'd always clashed since meeting at college and more recently at the breakfast networking meetings she had attended with Tom. A local councillor, Nina was always right and always seemed to know everyone's personal business.

Nina flicked her long dark hair over her shoulder then peered down her nose at Holly's feet.

'I er ...' Holly glanced at the mud-tinged puddle forming around her boots, then up at Nina's enhanced pout.

Nina glanced over Holly's shoulder and her face softened with a smile. 'Ooh, I can see your gorgeous Tom out there.' She gave a short wave towards the window. 'You're not renewing your vows already are you?' Nina pointed to a wedding dress displayed in the window. 'You only got married last year.' Then brought both hands to her cheeks. 'Oh, my goodness. Is that your younger sister? She's beautiful.'

'You know I don't have a sister.' *If there are aliens up there, please beam me up*, Holly thought.

Nina glance at her then back at the window. 'You're so alike, it's uncanny.' She placed one hand on her chest.

Holly turned towards the window. A light from the display shone on her face and all she could see clearly was her own reflection in the pane. Her hair – flat to her head. Her mouth – downturned. Her eyes – puffy. As she squinted, into focus came the perfectly-made-up face of Tom's friend. Stray tendrils blowing across her smooth heart-shaped face with a perfect selfie smile. Turning her head a few degrees, Holly saw Tom as he raked a hand through his hair and his eyes widened as they locked into her gaze. Holly's eyes misted over gradually bringing her reflection back into focus – until she was again, staring into her own eyes.

I've got to get out of here, she thought and turned.

Nina blocked her way, rummaging through a rail of dresses. She lifted up an ivory number with thin diamante straps. 'Is she getting married? Your friend? She'd look stunning in this. And here,' she said, pulling out a garish mother-of-the-bride outfit. 'This would be ideal for you.'

Holly sidestepped Nina and made for the back of the shop, her folio bashing rails as she passed them.

'I guess you want to try it on?'

Holly glanced over her shoulder, Nina followed with the cerise creation in hand, flashing her whitened teeth.

'Toilet,' Holly said. 'I feel sick.'

Nina overtook Holly in a waft of Coco Mademoiselle as the shop door chimed behind them.

'I need air, now,' Holly said panting.

Nina threw open the metal back door. 'I'll get Tom.' She turned away.

'No ...'

Holly stepped into the back yard, closing the door behind her. Tears ran from her eyes and nose as she fumbled in her pocket for a tissue. Whenever she tried to take in a deep breath it was caught in a sob, like an old car false starting. *That's what I am, the old banger and he's got himself a sleek new model.* Mopping her tears, she opened the back gate and marched through the service delivery area towards the carpark. *How could things have changed so quickly?* she asked herself. Reaching her green transit van, she climbed inside, placing her folio and mobile phone on the passenger seats. Taking a succession of deep breaths, she started the engine.

Again, her parents flashed into her mind. At the hospital, when the doctor told her. 'We did all we could, but we lost them.' She had felt numb, a cold nothing. But now, as she swung out of the carpark and headed for home, the uneasy nausea which she had been feeling for days, increased to an intense burning of her solar plexus.

CHAPTER 3

*H*olly sat in her van, in Lovelands' car park, watching her groundsman, Joe, locking up the nursery buildings. She wanted to wait until he was out of sight before going into her cottage. She couldn't face anyone at the moment. Picking up her mobile phone she hovered her thumb over the telephone icon. She could call Jaz, or Val but decided against it. Knowing they would never say, 'I told you so,' she would still hear it in their voices. It wasn't their fault. They had tried to warn her, she knew that. Her chest tightened as she saw Tom's blue Mazda in her wing mirror as he pulled up alongside her. Wiping her tear-stained face, she grabbed the steering wheel with both hands. She took a deep breath and stared straight ahead, her knuckles white and her lips pursed as he appeared at her right-hand window.

Tom rapped on the glass. 'We need to talk.'

Holly opened the door and he stepped back to avoid being knocked over.

'You're damn right we do. Who is she?'

'Let's go inside.' Tom walked towards the cottage, his hands in his trouser pockets.

Holly slammed the van door shut, her hands sweaty, her heart pounding, as she told herself to stay calm. The gravel crunched under her feet as she overtook Tom and opened the varnished front door.

Once inside she removed her boots and padded in her thick socks along the rug-covered, wooden floors, through to the kitchen. Tom followed. All she could hear from him was the tap of his brogues on the kitchen tiles. It was a large room, a mish-mash of units and dressers collected by her ancestors. The cottage had been in the family for four generations. Pulling a chair from her large oak table, she sat down and Tom took the seat opposite.

'Well then?' Holly said with a quiver in her voice. 'What's going on?'

'I er ...'

'Who is she?'

'Grace.' Tom put his fist to his mouth and coughed.

The aroma of tobacco and mints filled the room as he spoke.'We met at an exhibition.'

'A customer?'

'No. A hot tub model.'

'Hot tub model?' Holly slammed her hands on the table and stood up. 'I didn't realise you were putting girls in the tubs! That's so sleazy.'

'Everyone does it.' Tom shut his eyes.

Holly shook her head. 'I doubt that very much. How dare you spend my savings on girls.'

'She's a model, not a prozzy.' The chair scraped as Tom stood up to face her.

'How old is she? Eighteen?'

'Nearly twenty and we're together.' Tom's Adam's apple moved up and down.

Holly clutched the table. 'I can't believe you're ruining everything we have for someone you've been seeing for what? Two weeks?'

Tom raked his hand through his hair.

'Oh.' Holly sat down and clutched her forehead, feeling she was an idiot for not seeing it. 'How long?'

'Two months. I wanted to tell you but –'

Holly placed both hands on the table in front of her. 'You said you needed time to think.'

Tom raised his eyes to the ceiling.

'So much for us starting a family.' Holly's voice became louder. 'How could you?'

'Oh, come on. Things haven't been great for a while. Have they?' Tom paced the room.

'Not surprising is it? If you've been at it with little Miss Hot Tub. No wonder you've gone cold on me these past few months.'

'Don't blame it all on me.' Tom swung around to face her. 'You don't need me. Don't pretend you do, just to make me feel bad.'

'I don't believe this. What's happened to you?'

Tom shook his head. 'Maybe we jumped in too soon. Didn't get to know each other. You're not the same person that you were when you were seventeen.'

'Of course, I'm not. We all have to grow up at some point. Clearly you've regressed.' Holly sighed. Where was the guy that cracked jokes every five minutes? Who made her feel really beautiful? 'It was you who proposed to me, remember? I hardly forced you into it. You wanted the quick wedding. Said … you said I was …' Holly stopped as her throat tightened.

'I made a mistake.'

Holly clenched her fists by her side. 'Who are you, Tom? I don't even recognise you.' She shook her head. 'You never complained about our relationship. How many times did you call me your soul mate? Your everything?'

Tom stopped pacing and stared at her. 'Look, it's over. All over. Grace needs me.'

'Spare me the details.' Holly's legs shook under the table.

Tom's mobile phone rang and he pulled it out of his pocket. 'Hi, babe, I won't be long I –'

Lowering his arm, he scowled at the screen. 'Battery's dead. Can I borrow a charger?'

'No, you can't.' Holly's heart pounded. *Is this really happening?* The kitchen appeared to turn red before her eyes. Rising, she pointed to the door. 'Get your stuff. And go.' Holly's hand shook at the end of her extended arm.

Tom left the room. Slumping back to the table, Holly folded her arms, placing her head onto them as she sobbed silently, feeling a cold chill fill her veins.

STILL AT THE KITCHEN TABLE, Holly heard Tom's car engine as he drove off. She was unaware of the time but it was now dark. Standing up she pulled a bottle of red from the wine rack and took it upstairs. Opening the door to her bedroom she saw the wardrobe, half empty, where Tom had removed his clothes. She slammed its doors shut, before lying on her bed fully clothed. A picture flashed in her mind of when they'd arrived home from their wedding party. Tom had whispered in her ear, 'Welcome home, Mrs. Stone.' Even though she had not changed her name; Loveland women never did for it was the name of the nursery. It had been a small ceremony at a hotel in Wells with a champagne toast, then back to the Eversley Arms for drinks and a buffet. Tom had said he did not want to save for a big ceremony – 'Let's do it now. I know you're the one.' And she had believed him, trusted him.

Breathing in the pleasant scent of her freshly-laundered bed linen, she planned to scrub the cottage through from one end to the other, to get rid of every trace of Tom. Sitting up, she unscrewed the wine, pouring some into the glass at her bedside, usually reserved for water. The cold liquid, nowhere near room temperature, tasted unpleasantly bitter. Pulling a face, she refilled the glass. Holly ached to call Jaz, to hear a friendly voice but she had left her mobile, along with the painting, in the van. She had missed the competition deadline.

Downing the last of the wine she placed the empty glass on the bedside table and fell into a restless sleep, with the empty bottle at her side.

Holly dreamed she was in a cave with Tom and Grace. Laughing at her, they pointed, throwing back their heads, holding their sides. Searing siren noise rang in her ears like the soundtrack of a horror movie as she was sucked forward towards a furnace. Feeling the heat of the flames lashing at her, the Devil appeared, his red-tipped, spindly fingers beckoned her. Lost souls wailed; grey, naked bodies covered the floors, writhing as if in pain. A sickening smell of burning flesh filled her nostrils. Then came violins playing a two-beat march in the distance. She turned towards a light, her legs felt heavy as she dragged them along – her mind raced towards the brightness – willing herself to get closer. There was an explosion.

Holly woke in a sweat, her clothes felt soggy against her skin. Finding it hard to drag herself out of the dream, the smell of burning remained in her nostrils and her ears filled with the noise of sirens. Her eyes took time to adjust, her head still muzzy from wine. Then she saw it – smoke snaking into the room from under her bedroom door.

Holly launched off the bed, hearing the wine bottle fall then roll across the floor. She spluttered as rising smoke gushed up her nose and into her mouth. Rubbing her stinging eyes, she moved her head from side to side trying to focus on something, to get her bearings. The room seemed to be spinning. She reached out and felt for the wardrobe and steadied herself – shocked at how quickly the smoke filled the room. Thinking she was going to vomit, she bent over spluttering as charcoal air puffed into the back of her throat.

Moving forward, she gingerly touched the door handle and screamed as metal burnt her fingertips. The fire was too close. Shutting her eyes, she realised the need for calm – now was not the time to take deep breaths. Knowing the only way out was through the window, she took small steps towards the curtains then stopped, wondering whether there would be a backdraft. Sliding across the floor she made for the bed, her legs shook. Her head was dizzy from the lack of oxygen. Ripping the eiderdown off her bed, she dragged it to the door plugging the gap where the smoke plumed. Sitting down on the soft material, she looked towards her escape route. *I haven't much time,* she thought as she pulled herself up to standing.She staggered over to the window and lifted the latch as blue lights flashed in the customer car park. Gulping in fresh air, she sat on the windowsill swinging her legs over so they dangled off the ledge. She observed the ground below. A ladder rose up and she heard taps on the metal from the fireman's boots as he raced up and grabbed her hand. Another explosion ripped through the nursery. Holly wobbled as she clutched onto the rungs of the ladder.

With teeth chattering and body vibrating, she scanned her studio, nursery and home. Fire flickered in the windows and flames shot up through the roof. A flutter of ferocious orange and yellow embers danced like birds to a deafening tune as they pecked away at her life, her history, her world.

'Come on, we need to be quick,' the fireman shouted.

As she descended the ladder, the heat came in waves, mixed with a whipping wind, which fed the furnace as mist from water-jets basted her cheeks.

'Is anyone else inside?' called the fireman supporting her on the ladder.

Without taking her eyes off the burning buildings she shouted above the din. 'No. I live alone.' Holly breathed in sharply then wailed until her lungs were empty.

HOLLY SAT in the ambulance with an oxygen mask on her face, wrapped in a foil blanket, feeling like left-over food from a barbecue. The paramedic held her hand, speaking to her gently. She found it calming, even though she could not make out what he was saying.

'Holly isn't it?' A woman's high-pitched voice cut through the blur.

Before her, she saw a police officer had entered the ambulance with a pen poised over her notebook. Removing the oxygen mask Holly opened her mouth but no words came out. Hot tears stung her cheeks. Nodding, she wiped her face with the back of her hand.

'My name is P.C. Erin Bartlett. Do you know how the fire started?'

Holly shook her head. 'No. I was asleep.' She felt cold,

even with the foil blanket. Cold inside, right inside her bones, staring at the flames flickering in the distance.

'Do you remember anything? It seems to have started in the middle building.'

'That's my – my art studio.' Holly held back a sob. Losing all her artwork was like losing her gift. And the dream of the arts hub – gone. *Hold it together. I'm alive, still alive,* she told herself.

'Were there any lit candles? A deep fat fryer? Tumble dryer left on?'

Holly shook her head.

'Any other electrical equipment which could have gone up?' Erin bit the end of her pen.

'The light bulb blew today – it's happened three times this week. I guess it's an electrical fault,' she said, wishing she had called the electrician out. In her imagination, Holly watched her art work floating up amongst the smoke, individual pieces passing her eyes as if on a gameshow conveyor belt. *It's all my fault,* she thought. There had been thirty-three paintings. Each one consisting of hours of thought, hours of planning and hours of painting; some took more than a year to perfect. *Gone. Gone forever,* she thought as she took a sharp breath and winced. 'There's a heater, but it definitely wasn't on today.' Holly rubbed her chest.

'Have you been drinking?'

'A little – I had a bad day.'

Erin scribbled in her notebook. 'You're lucky.'

'Do you have to question her now?' The paramedic took Holly's hand again and urged her to put the oxygen mask back over her face. 'She's in shock and needs to rest.'

To Holly, the oxygen seemed cool, like taking a refreshing long drink. Shutting her eyes, she prayed that when she opened them it would all have been a bad dream.

But as she raised her head and stared front, the smoke continued to billow out of her cottage.

Erin cocked her head to one side. 'The Fire Service will assess the position but the most important thing is that you're safe. Thankfully, your neighbour raised the alarm.'

'Neighbour?'

'Yes. There he is,' she said pointing to a figure approaching. 'Mr Booth from the farm.'

Holly saw Erin smile as Mitch walked towards the ambulance against the backdrop of flames, thinking it looked like something out of an action movie.

As Mitch reached them, he opened his mouth, closed it, then opened it again. 'Your front door was locked and I couldn't ram it open. I could see the light on upstairs and guessed you were in bed.'

Holly held his gaze but could not manage a smile.

'I told Holly how lucky she is, that you were there.' Erin glanced down at Holly. 'What with the alcohol she's been drinking.'

Holly frowned and removed her mask, 'I only had –'

'I've just been to check on your animals.' Mitch pointed in the direction of the petting zoo.

Holly put a hand to her mouth and struggled to stand up. 'I must see them.'

The paramedic scooted forward and Holly felt his hand on her shoulder. 'Stay calm, Holly. Breathe slowly. Please sit down and put the mask back on.' Holly sat down with a thud, her legs wobbling. The paramedic glanced from Erin to Mitch. 'Can we calm things down here? She's taken in quite a bit of smoke. You can see her shivering, she's suffering from shock.'

Holly's teeth chattered as she pulled the foil blanket tightly around her.

Mitch nodded at the paramedic. 'Sorry, I understand.' He turned to Holly. 'The animals are fine; the fire hasn't reached them and the air seems clear. The wind's blowing in the opposite direction. But they're restless. The goat's bleating.' Mitch gestured towards the nursery carpark entrance. 'There's a crowd forming. I'll tell them to go home.'

'Good idea,' the paramedic said.

Mitch walked off in the direction of the gate.

Erin clicked her radio. 'I'll call out the RSPCA, Holly, to check on the animals and put your mind at rest.'

Holly coughed and replaced the oxygen mask. She did not want to continue crying in public and was glad Mitch had walked away.

Once Erin had finished her call, she smiled at Holly. 'I'll leave you now but I'll be in touch if necessary when we've received the fire report.'

Noticing the way Erin gazed in Mitch's direction as he returned, Jaz's words came back to Holly 'He's every woman's type.'

'Goodbye then, Holly. And Mr Booth.' Erin smiled as Mitch returned and then walked away.

Mitch moved into the ambulance closer to Holly. 'I got rid of the crowd. It's all reality TV and social media these days. Some kid had his mobile phone out, recording.'

Holly removed her mask. 'Thanks. And thanks for raising the alarm.' She stopped herself from saying, but couldn't help thinking, *now run along back home and leave me alone.*

'I still can't believe it.' Mitch shook his head and his dark hair flopped forward. 'If there's anything I can do?' He peered at her.

Holly shook her head as she stared into his ice-blue eyes, unable to think of anything to say.

'Is there anyone I can call for you?'

The paramedic appeared again, placing his hand on Holly's shoulder. 'Yes, Holly, who's your next of kin?'

Holly felt dizzy. 'I don't have any. Apart from an aunt up north, in Oldham.'

'Any friends?' Mitch asked.

'My best friend's in Exeter overnight. There are my staff – but I don't want to bother them.' Only Val lived in the village and she did not want to drag her out of bed.

'So, you don't have anyone to accompany you to the hospital, then?' the paramedic said.

'No, I'm not going to the hospital.' Holly felt the palpitations start. Holly had not been to the hospital since she had identified her parents' bodies.

Mitch raised his hand. 'I can come with you.'

Holly spoke quickly. 'Oh no. Not necessary.'

'Well if you could move up further inside the ambulance. I can take you in,' the paramedic said.

'No. No, please. I'm fine. Please, I can't go.'

Holly turned to Mitch, he raised his eyebrows. 'I've got a spare room.'

'No.' Holly certainly did not want to stay at Booth Farm.

The paramedic shook his head. 'We can't leave you here, on your own. You need to have other people around you for at least twenty-four hours, in case you have any issues. I need to take you to the hospital.'

'She can definitely stay at mine.' Mitch nodded.

Holly hated asking others for help – least of all a Booth. But hospitals reminded her of death. Of her parents' deaths. She was pretty sure that, while Mitch might be happy for her to join him for a sleepover, his uncle would be far from impressed. *And his wife might not be too chuffed either,* she thought. 'I don't think that would be a good idea.'

Mitch pointed in the direction of his farm. 'You can stay in the guest room. It's got an en-suite and it's recently decorated. You'll have your privacy. There's a herdsman coming for a trial at the weekend so the room's already prepared for his visit.'

'I couldn't,' Holly said. 'I don't think your uncle would like that.'

'Sid's sick – really sick. He rarely gets up without assistance these days and has a carer in the next room with an alarm fitted to rouse her if he starts moving about. He won't know you're there.'

A fireman approached the ambulance. 'The flames are out but it may continue to smoke for a while. The damage is extensive I'm afraid.' He rubbed his hands. 'We're getting off now but one engine will remain until the temperature of the site reduces to an acceptable level. We'll review the situation when it's light and let you have our report for your insurance company and the police. They need to eliminate arson.'

'Arson?' Holly shuddered. 'You don't think it's that, do you?'

The fireman shook his head. 'No signs at present, it's just procedure.'

The fire engines rumbled out of the nursery carpark. A bleeping noise came from the front of the ambulance and the paramedic moved towards it then returned. 'We've had another call come in. We need to get you to the hospital right now.'

Holly thought she was going to be sick, imagining the bleeping machines and nasty sickly smells.

Mitch held out his hand to her. 'Come on, come to mine.

It'll only be for a few hours. You can get some sleep. Honestly, it's no bother and it's the easiest option.'

'I've got to wait for the RSPCA.' She folded her arms. 'The police called them out.'

Mitch glanced over his shoulder and then back at Holly. 'I think they can take a look without us.'

'I want to know my animals are safe.' Holly could hear her voice rising in pitch. She realised she sounded neurotic but was beyond caring.

Mitch put up his hands as if she was pointing a gun at him. 'Okay, we'll wait together.'

Holly did not want to hold up the ambulance. Someone might be at death's door. She stood up. Instead of taking Mitch's outstretched hand, she held onto a rail in the ambulance as she got out, taking her foil blanket with her.

The paramedic jumped out, then slammed the back door shut. 'Good luck, Holly.' He turned to Mitch. 'I'd keep her awake for another hour at least to make sure there are no respiratory issues. Then she needs rest.' He turned back to Holly. 'A proper-lie in for you tomorrow. I know it's hard, you've a lot to take in and some tough times ahead. But your health is number one. You won't be able to handle anything without your strength. So rest up. Yes?'

Holly nodded.

The paramedic gazed at the burned ruins. 'And I suggest you get to your GP as soon as you feel able.' He turned to Mitch. 'Any problems tonight – any at all, go straight to Accident and Emergency.'

Holly took one step forward, the gravel beneath her feet felt rough and sharp through her socks as she took small steps. Feeling woozy, she was unsure whether it was from the wine or smoke. Mitch came to her side and guided her by the elbow. Holly wanted to tell him that she did not need his help, but decided against it. After all, she did owe him. Her body felt like it was tightening, as if the blood in her veins was solidifying and slowly turning to stone. An icy cold emanated from inside as she watched her breath in the cooling air.

The ambulance rattled away, lights flashing, on to another poor lost soul. *It could be worse,* Holly thought. *I could have been scarred for life or burned to death.* She swallowed hard. Apart from a lone fire engine, she was left with Mitch.

He broke the silence. 'You shouldn't walk far without shoes. You need to be inside.' He scanned the car park. 'I don't want to leave you here, while I get the truck.' Holly watched his face as he rubbed his jaw. 'I could carry you there. Piggy-back style?'

Shutting her eyes she gave an inward groan. *Please, no.* Delving into a pocket in her cargos she pulled out her keys. 'My van – it's parked over there.' She pointed towards the van and clicked the key fob. The side-lights flashed as it unlocked.

Mitch took the keys from her. 'You stay here, I'll bring it over.'

Holly watched as he strode away. A fox cried out in the distance and she shivered, listening to the distant squabble of her hens and the odd bleat from Charlie the goat. She wanted to rush over to calm them but lacked the energy. The van's engine came to life, cutting through the night-time chorus. Mitch slowly drove up to her and she stepped forward. Jumping out, he opened the passenger door before helping her. Once inside, she pushed her folio and mobile phone, still on the passenger seat, into the middle of the three-seater van and sat down.

'You okay there?' Mitch asked as soon as he got into the driver's seat.

Holly nodded, her mouth felt dry and tasted sour. A mix of smoke and wine. Leaning forward, she pulled a tub of gum from the cup holder and popped some into her mouth. Offering them to Mitch, he took one and smiled.

Mint danced in her mouth as she crunched on the coating of the gum. Whilst refreshing, it irritated her throat. Mitch stared straight ahead. The silence would have been awkward if she had cared. Peering out of the side window, Holly observed a few orange coals glinting like beached stars. She wanted no-one's pity and that was what she could see in Mitch's eyes when he looked at her.

Holly tapped her folio, which was positioned between them. 'At least I have one painting left.'

'You still paint?'

'I'm an artist.' The words echoed in her head. *Am I an artist? Still an artist, with no work to show for it?* She coughed away a sob. Art had always saved her. It had been the thing she turned to in times of trouble. 'Apparently the fire started in my studio.' Holly stroked the folio. 'Now this is my last remaining piece of work.' They sat in silence for a while until the headlights of a small van lit up the car park.

'I'll take them over.' Mitch jumped out of the van as the RSPCA officer parked up. Holly watched Mitch lead the yawning officer towards the animals until they were out of sight. She drifted off to sleep.

HOLLY JOLTED awake as Mitch slammed the van door and started the engine.

'Sorry to startle you but you need to stay awake for at least another half hour. Paramedic's orders.'

Holly straightened herself up. She felt warm, too warm, so shrugged off the foil blanket. Picking out a discarded receipt from her glove compartment, she removed the chewing gum from her mouth.

'Good news though. All the animals are safe and have settled down. They'll probably need extra attention tomorrow. I can see to them if you like?'

'No, no that's fine.' The last thing Holly wanted was Mitch interfering with her life. 'I'll have staff coming in and it'll give them something to do – what with the nursery ...' Holly's voice trailed off and she stared into the darkness of the night as Mitch began the short drive to the farmhouse. She had never been to Booth Farm. As a child, she used to find it odd at school when they learned in assembly to 'love thy neighbour,' when she did not speak to hers, having only seen Sidney Booth up close a few times. From what she could gather, the bad feeling was due to an historic land dispute. The Loveland's had bought the higher ground from Sidney Booth's grandfather and the sale was later disputed on the grounds of old Henry being ill at the time and not of sound mind. But she knew there was more to it than that, something to do with her granny.

Someone at school had once told her that Old Man Booth had loved Granny Ivy but when she had told her mother, she had gone crazy. 'Don't listen to village gossip. Ever!' After that, she had refrained from asking her mother for any further details. Her mum had always got upset when she had talked about Granny Ivy, because Granny Ivy had died giving birth to her.

As they drove down the nursery drive the van swung around a corner, passing the gate covering an entrance between the nursery and the farm.

Mitch coughed. 'I haven't managed to open that gate.

That's why I popped over earlier. There doesn't seem to be a key for the lock, I had to jump it to get up to your place tonight.'

'I've never seen it open.' Holly exhaled and winced at the sharpness of her chest. 'And I don't have a key. As you are well aware, our families have not been on good terms for some years.' Holly's comment dangled in the air. Even though there had been a rift between the Lovelands and Booths, the Lovelands had always had the upper hand. She wondered whether Mitch was enjoying the tables being turned. Moving about in her seat, she felt oddly disrespectful to her ancestors for accepting generosity from the family who had painted the Lovelands as being ruthless. A reputation she had had to live with too – even though she was far from tough on the inside.

Holly wondered whether Mitch's wife would be waiting at the door, she had not noticed him call anyone. She rubbed her forehead. *Make conversation, be nice,* she told herself. 'Where did you meet your wife? In the farming community?'

Mitch paused for a few seconds and Holly looked across at him.

'Erm ... Essex. The Booth family have the Somerset farm and two in Essex. We've a strong history in the farming community, as you know, and yes that's how I met Vanessa.' He paused for a few seconds and Holly heard him take a deep breath as if he was going to speak, but he remained silent.

They soon entered the driveway to Booth Farm and yellow lights flashed on as they approached the house. Mitch parked and cut the engine. Getting out, he walked around to help Holly. When she got out, she was pleased for the smooth paved path, much easier to walk on in her socks.

Stuffing her phone into her pocket, she grabbed her folio and followed Mitch to the old red brick house, through the front door and into a porch with a coat stand. Mitch opened the inner door which lead to a dark corridor with dado rail and dingy striped wallpaper. He beckoned her to follow him and soon opened a door and motioned for her to go in.

'You'll be the first person to stay in here since it was decorated.'

Holly walked into the room and was met by an aroma of paint mixed with lavender. Mitch turned on the light which filled the modern space with a homely glow. It was a real contrast to the corridor.

Holly glanced down at her dirty clothes. 'I hope I don't make a mess.'

'There's a towelling robe in the en-suite you can wear. I'll sort some clothes for you.'

'There's no need.'

'Get yourself cleaned up and you'll feel much better. There's a kettle, tea and coffee on the table and fresh milk in the mini fridge. Here's my mobile number.' He fished a business card out of his pocket with *Booth Farms, Mitchell Booth, Director* and his mobile number on it. 'The paramedic said I shouldn't leave you alone but I'm sure you want your privacy. If you have any breathing difficulties or dizziness, call me immediately.'

'I'm fine.'

'Okay, but call me if that changes. I'll pop a charger down for your phone.'

'Thanks.' Holly bit her lip.

'You need to rest. It's getting on for two a.m.'

Holly felt drained, her feelings of animosity towards Mitch began to ebb. She had been angry. Angry at the situation, angry at the world, there was no need to take it out on him. After all, she may have died if he hadn't dialled 999. He would probably be great for the village and great for the farm.

'Maybe it's time for a change,' she said. 'I don't know what I'll be doing now. What with the nursery and studio gone, I might move on.'

Mitch put his hands up. 'This is no time to make life decisions. Things will seem different in the morning.'

Holly felt her lip quiver. 'If you want to buy my land and extend the farm ...'

'I'm always up for expansion, Holly. But look, let's not talk now. You need rest.'

Then he was gone, and she was alone. Really alone.

CHAPTER 4

*H*olly opened her eyes. Her head thumped and she groaned. Her throat felt as if she had gargled with facial scrub. Oddly, the feeling of dread and nausea which had been with her for the past few weeks had lifted. A picture of Tom's face flashed into her mind. Rolling over in the bed, she attempted to force the image away. For nearly two years he had been the first person in her thoughts when she woke up, the first person she told news to and the last person she spoke to at night. Now he was gone. *At least things can't get any worse,* she thought. Val often said, 'You're the best person to have in a crisis.' Maybe that was true because she felt nothing, not sadness, not joy, just a smooth cool nothingness.

She looked around the bedroom, taking in the newness of it all. The walls a pale grey, the paintwork white. The bed was comfy and whilst Holly preferred blankets and sheets, she liked the simplicity of the white duvet. The room was far from boutique style but radiated a homely, fresh feel. Pushing the duvet off, she sat up and hugged her knees. She shut her eyes and visualised herself painting.

Maybe this is the first day of the rest of my life, she told herself.

Opening her eyes, she hesitated, staring at the curtains through which the sun glinted. Considering the direction of the sun, she realised she must be positioned to see the nursery. But she was not ready to look out of the window and up the hill to her property. She remained still, cocooned in the safe environment.

Holly glanced at the bedroom chair over which she had thrown her dirty clothes, they were gone and in their place was a bulging supermarket bag-for-life. Reaching for the towelling robe beside her, she got out of bed. Her whole body seemed to creak. *This must be what it feels like to be eighty,* she thought, picturing Val who always groaned every time she got out of a chair. The bag was full of clothes. Lifting them out individually she found a pair of jeans, two T shirts and a blue hooded sweatshirt with a white logo on it. There was also a plastic pack of four bikini style pants, a pack of socks, a pull-on sports type bra and a pair of trainers which were luckily her correct size. Over the back of the chair hung a green Parka coat with a grey-fur-edged hood. Stuck on the bag was a handwritten note:

Hope these fit. Call when you are ready. I have a proposition for you. Mitch.

Holly assumed Mitch's proposition was about him buying her land. *Typical of me and my big mouth,* she thought. Remembering her offer to Mitch in the early hours, she bit her lip. Her parents would not have been pleased about her offering the Loveland acres up for a knock-down price, least of all to a Booth. Although she still wondered whether a change of scenery might be for the best. Maybe she could pursue a job in an art gallery or get a teaching qualification – rent an art studio, start afresh, away from

Eversley, away from Tom. She decided to grab a quick shower and get dressed in case any of the Booths came in to check on her.

On her way to the en-suite she noticed her mobile phone plugged in on charge. She hesitated, wondering whether to check her messages but continued to the shower – not wanting to see the missed calls or messages, or catch any videos posted on social media with #Lovelands #fire, going viral. She wanted to live in this safe bubble for a little while longer, pretending everything was fine and that she was on a weekend break somewhere, a million miles away.

Covering herself in pine-scented body gel and washing her hair in an all-in-one shampoo, she felt alert. They were male products, she loved the freshness of the zesty, woody fragrance. Once dry, she put on the new clothes. *Hmm, snug,* she thought as she checked her reflection in the mirror. Not ill-fitting, but tighter than her usual attire of polo shirts and cargo trousers. Turning to the side, she flushed red. The clothes really were figure-hugging and the bra, maybe a size too small, was pushing her boobs up and creating a cleavage which the V-necked T-shirt could not hide. *I'll definitely be wearing the hoodie,* she thought. Locating a hair dryer in the bedside cabinet, she rough dried her locks. Without a brush, her natural blonde curls blew around.

Holly pulled on the hoodie and zipped it up. Taking a few deep breaths, she stared at the curtains. *Here goes.* Pulling them wide open, the blackened buildings loomed up like a haunted house perched on the hill. Her eyes smarted with hot tears and she could not help the sobs. With her heart pounding she covered her mouth, as if to stop herself screaming.

A fire service van was parked up next to the wreckage. She presumed they were carrying out their inspection.

Shaking her head, she knew she couldn't leave the nursery. Couldn't leave everything her relatives had built – like it had been thrown in the bin. Discarded. And then there were her staff. *Oh no, the staff,* she thought.

Holly squinted in an attempt to see who was up there, realising she should have texted. She picked out Val's canary scarf. Quickly making the bed, she grabbed the undies she had slept in and stuffed them in the supermarket bag. Pulling the phone away from the charging cable she looked at the screen, there were many missed calls. She texted Joe, her head groundsman.

Sorry – should have warned you ... stayed at Booth Farm. Don't think there is much we can do today. Let everyone know they can go home and I'll text an update later.

Holly put her phone down, watching her hand tremble. A reply came through from Joe.

Thank God you are safe. Shall we come down to you? No one is going anywhere – here for you.

Holly shook her head and texted him back

Coming up now. Can you check on animals? x

As well as the text, she had three missed calls from Val and the remaining calls, fifteen of them were from Tom. A knot tightened in her stomach. He had probably heard the news, she assumed. She would have to call him at some point, she needed her savings back. Not knowing how long it would be until the insurance was sorted, she would need to find somewhere to live. Checking her phone for her broker's number she decided to call him from the van. *Best get that out of the way,* Holly thought. She would face Tom tomorrow.

As Holly headed towards the door she saw her folio propped against the wall. Opening it she removed the painting. The fields she had painted, were the fields of Booth

Farm and the house in the distance, was the house she was in. It felt odd, like she had painted her future. She shivered – the painting felt eerie to her now. She did not want to take it with her. Placing the watercolour on the bed, she turned over the note Mitch had left with the clothes and took a pen from the dresser and wrote:

Thanks for calling the emergency services and for letting me stay. And for the clothes, I will pay you back. Please accept this painting as a thank you. Holly.

OUTSIDE, the farm appeared quiet. Holly hesitated and glanced back at the house. *Should I phone Mitch?* she thought, then shook her head as she walked towards her van, guessing he would attempt to convince her to stay in bed and rest. Holly unlocked the van and opened the passenger door, placing the bag of remaining clothes, her new coat and the empty folio inside. Walking around to the driver's door, she hoisted her aching body onto the seat. She started the engine then called her insurance broker's number, waiting for the hands-free to kick in. Taking a deep breath, she drove away from the farmhouse onto the main village road. As she turned into the narrow lane which led to Lovelands, she left a message on her broker's answer machine. Reaching the nursery drive, the blackened buildings seemed to shrug in disbelief. Val stood in the car park with a hanky in her hand. Joe had a comforting arm around her shoulders. Although a man of sixty, Joe was young enough to be Val's son. They walked towards the van as Holly parked up. Joe opened the door for her and Holly was hit again with the smell of smoke.

Val pushed in front with her arms outstretched. 'Oh

love, I've been beside myself, I really have.' Her voice faltered, her cheeks were crimson.

Joe gently moved Val aside, holding out a hand to help Holly down. 'You're a sight for sore eyes. We've been phoning around the hospitals searching for you. And Jaz isn't answering her phone.'

'She's in Exeter.' Holly took Joe's hand, jumped down and gave him a hug. 'Does she know?'

Joe shook his head. 'Not from me, I only left a message to ask her to call.'

Val moved forward and hugged Holly. 'Love, I'm so glad you're safe,' she said dabbing her eyes. 'It probably looks worse than it is.'

Holly took in her cottage, studio and the main nursery building. A mixture of sooted stone and charred wood.

'Oh love – how did it happen?' Val asked.

Holly shrugged her shoulders. 'They think it started in the studio.' She pointed to the fire brigade on site. 'It might have been an electrical fault. The lights have been blowing for days. It's my fault – I should have had the electrics updated a long time ago.' Holly saw Julie approach from the petting zoo. 'The animals – how are they?'

Julie with eyes wide open replied, 'They're fine. Anne's making a fuss of them, doling out extra food.' Julie reached Holly and put a hand on her shoulder. 'I'm sorry this has happened to you.'

Julie and Anne were sisters in their late forties and had worked at the nursery since they were teenagers. Both had been on the staff, on and off, for nearly thirty years.

Joe patted Holly on the back. 'You know, there's no rush to decide what to do. We'll support you and understand if this is the end of the road for you here.'

Val wagged her finger at him. 'Oh, Joe, don't you be talking like that. With all that defeatism.'

Joe repositioned his nursery-issue cap. 'Well, our Holly might want a new start. Get back to London. Don't forget, she's an artist.'

'True and a good one at that but ...' Val's eyes streamed with tears.

Holly stepped back, her hair blowing in her face. She swept it behind her ears. 'I must confess – last night I offered the land to Mitch Booth.'

Val took a sharp intake of breath and put her hand to her mouth.

Holly pulled Val's hand down and smiled at her. 'But this morning ...' She turned towards the ruins. 'I realised I can't leave it like this. I'd always feel a failure. I'm going to rebuild it.'

'Have you told Tom?' Joe furrowed his forehead.

'No, but he must have heard as I've had fifteen missed calls from him. But I can't face him today. He wants a divorce.'

Val shook her head. 'The wrong'un. You know we're all here for you.'

'Yes, anything you need.' Joe coughed and lowered his eyes.

It seemed to Holly, as if everyone knew about Tom's indiscretion. *Village news travels fast,* she thought.

'I know you've lost your parents and all, but us, we're your family.' Val wiped her eyes with her hanky.

Holly rubbed Val's arm.

They turned at the sound of a dog barking. Striding into the carpark was Mitch, with Trixy tugging on a short lead. Holly felt a burning sensation in her stomach and blushed.

Val raised her eyebrows and put a hand to her chest. 'Oh, the young Booth. So much like Sidney when he was young.'

Mitch waved as he approached. 'I checked in on you but you'd gone.'

Holly walked towards him.

He rubbed the back of his neck. 'I shouldn't have left you without supervision. After all, I was in charge of your care. I should have asked Sid's carer, Magda, to sit with you. Sorry. You're probably distraught.'

Trixy jumped up at Holly but Mitch was able to restrain her with the leather lead before her paws came into contact.

Val and Joe kept their distance and Holly could hear their hushed voices behind her.

'No, I should apologise for leaving without a word. I saw the staff here and rushed up. Thanks for letting me stay the night.' Holly glanced down at her feet. 'And for the clothes and trainers.'

'Thanks for the painting, it's great work – and of the farm too.'

'It's the view from my favourite bench.' Holly pointed to the bench, perched on the edge of the hill before the land gradually fell away under a green blanket of grass. 'I love watching the sunset from there.'

Mitch smiled and nodded. 'I can't accept it, though. Not since you told me it's your last remaining piece of work.'

'No honestly, it's not my usual style. I don't paint land-scapes. It was for a specific competition.'

'Really?'

Holly paused. It seemed surreal to be discussing a painting when behind her, her life was in shreds but some-thing about talking to Mitch, made the world seem a little normal. As he smiled at her she felt transported back to her childhood, filling her with a comforting warm glow. She blinked, then carried on. 'The competition was for the Wells Arts Festival. The theme being, *The Beauty of Somerset*. The deadline was yesterday. I missed it.'

'Oh?'

'Yes, I ... I ran into some – trouble.'

'Maybe under the circumstances they'll extend the deadline?' Mitch pulled Trixy back as she strained to get to Holly.

'Deadlines are deadlines up at the town hall and now it really doesn't seem important.' Holly looked behind her at the blackened buildings. 'I want you and your wife to have it. It's perfect as a thank you.'

Mitch blinked hard. 'Erm ... Well I'll accept it, but my wife is –'

Mitch must have left some slack in the lead because Trixy jumped up, attaching herself to Holly's new hoodie.

'Woah,' Holly said as she grabbed the little dog.

'Here we go again. At least her paws are dry.' Mitch retrieved the wriggling Trixy tucking her under his arm. 'I also came up because I have a proposal for you.'

Holly was reminded of their conversation the previous evening and blushed. 'Sorry. I know last night I said I wanted to sell the land – I was just a bit emotional. But I'm not sure what I want.'

'No.' Mitch shook his head. 'I'm not after buying your land.' He pointed behind him. 'What I'm proposing is – Sid's caravan. The old caravan that I used to stay in, when we visited. Sid wants it scrapped but it's still sturdy. I thought you could live in it while your place is being rebuilt.'

Holly swallowed. 'Oh, no, no. That's fine I don't think Sidney would like that.'

'He won't notice. I'll bring it up here once I've sorted the gate.'

'But you've already been so kind. I really couldn't.' Holly stared into his eyes, thinking how clear they were, *get a grip,* she told herself.

'I was going to pay to get rid of it. Honestly, you're doing me a favour.'

Holly noticed the warmth creep up her back. Mitch's hair flopped in the wind and she felt hot and flushed. She did not want to feel beholden. And finding him so attractive was making her uncomfortable. Telling herself it was just a ridiculous childhood crush, she attempted to clear her thoughts and undid the zipper of her hoodie to let the cool air in.

Mitch broke the silence. 'The clothes fit well.'

Holly glanced at her cleavage and zipped the hoodie back up, her face burning.

A flash of blue caught her eye as Tom's Mazda swept in. Her heart pounded hard in her chest and she was aware of the pain in her rasping throat as it tightened.

'Trouble's here,' Val called from behind. All three staff soon appeared at her side, Trixy barked. Val nudged Holly. 'I'll be telling him to get lost, or worse.'

Tom was soon out of the car, walking towards the small crowd, his gaze fixed solely on Holly.

Stopping in front of her, he ran a hand through his hair. 'I've been trying to get hold of you. Are you OK? I heard what happened.'

She took a deep breath. 'There's no need for you to be here.'

Tom stared at the buildings. 'Flipping heck.'

'You best steer well clear, Tom Stone.' Val put a hand on Holly's back.

Tom turned, scowling at Mitch, they were at eye level. 'And you are?'

'Mitchell Booth.' Mitch did not stretch out his hand, Holly noted.

Tom gave Mitch a stare and narrowed his eyes.

Holly took Tom by the arm, walking him back towards his car. She spoke in a hushed steady voice. 'What I want from you are my savings back.' Holly pointed to her cottage. 'As you can see, I need the money.'

Tom rubbed his chin. 'I haven't got it right now.'

'Well get it. Speak to the bank and take out a business loan. That's what you should have done in the first place.'

'You seemed happy enough to lend it to me at the time.' Tom put his hands in his jean's pockets. 'You said it was the sensible thing to do, to avoid interest payments.'

Holly shook her head and bit her lip. 'I didn't realise you were going to use it to buy a mistress.'

'Lay off, will you? The tubs haven't worked out. I've had to sell the stock.'

Stepping back, Holly put her hands on her hips. 'What? You said they were selling fast.'

'I well and truly messed up. I went for the wrong market – the luxury end. It's the economy tubs that are selling. It's the latest craze for the lower classes, not the uppers. The other traders were killing it in cheap tub sales. It was too late by the time I noticed.'

Holly gritted her teeth and took a deep breath, aware of her sore lungs.

Tom nodded at the buildings. 'You're insured, right?'

'Of course I'm insured, but I've got plans.'

'For what?'

'Nothing.'

'Not that hare-brained art gallery thing?'

'It doesn't concern you. And to be honest, if I was

seeking business advice I wouldn't be looking in your direction.'

'Alright, you've made your point.'

'Get the money.' Holly turned and began to walk away.

'I've got a claim on this place you know.' She heard Tom say from over her shoulder.

Holly swung around. Her hair flapping wildly in the breeze. 'What are you on? It's been in my family for generations.'

'We're married.' Tom kicked a pebble.

'You're joking. You've added nothing to this place. Nothing at all. All you've been is a drain.'

Tom swept his arm across the horizon. 'I've been speaking to a few people. By rights, half this land is mine.'

Holly felt her jaw tremble. 'Get real, Tom. We've not even been married a year.' Holly turned away and shouted over her shoulder. 'Just repay me.' Her voice became louder and her throat burned. Her mind flashed back to the paramedic – *Get some rest make sure you see your GP.*

'We'll talk about it later.' Tom opened his car door.

Holly swung around, marching back to him. 'No, we won't and I don't care who you've been chatting to down the pub. You're getting nothing from me.'

'Look at the place, Holly. It's trashed. I feel bad about what's happened but this is a chance for a new start for both of us. This place has got to be worth a few hundred grand, even with the burned buildings. Sell up. You can get back to London. Start afresh.' He leaned on his car door. 'It'll be good for you to get out of Eversley.'

Holly clenched her teeth, heat rising up her neck. Realising that Tom wanted to remain in the area, with his new girlfriend, while pushing her out of Eversley.

Joe appeared at her side. 'Give it a rest, Tom. Can't you see what she's going through?'

'So what? 'Cos I'm a bloke and she's a woman?' Tom pointed at Holly. 'Plenty of wives walk away with money. Mate, your views are outdated.'

Holly could hear Trixy growl in the distance.

'It's all right, Joe.' Holly put her hand on Joe's arm, feeling how tense it was. Knowing Joe would definitely come off worse in a fight with Tom, she left Joe's side and approached Tom.

'Please, Tom. Now is not the time.' She tried to keep her voice steady but could hear it wavering.

'Look, I feel sorry for you, babe. I'm only saying how it is. I've not got the money to give you. If I did I would, but Grace ...'

'What? She likes her designer clothes?' Holly said.

Tom raked his hand through his hair and shifted his feet. 'She's pregnant.'

Holly felt her shoulders droop. Her lip trembled. 'Leave.' She swallowed. 'Just go and don't think of coming back here again. Ever.' She turned, nearly banging into Mitch.

Mitch steadied her with one hand and guided her behind him. 'Do as she says.' It sounded to Holly as if he must have his teeth clenched, as he spoke with a deep growl. Mitch took one pace towards Tom.

Tom opened his car door wider and got in, shouting out of the open window 'I'll call you, Holly.' Then drove off, leaving a cloud of dust in his wake.

Val reached Holly with Trixy at her side. 'Who the hell does he think he is? Jumped up excuse of a toe-rag.'

Trixy yapped and Mitch took the lead from Val.

Holly hated the thought of leaving her land, or renting a room in the village. She wanted to be on site, to keep an eye on it, to protect it. She turned to Mitch. 'Yes please, I'd like to borrow your old caravan. If you don't mind.'

'Of course you can and I'm not lending it to you – you can have it.' His eyes stared deep into hers. 'As I said, it would have cost us to get rid of it. I'll bring it over later.' He pointed at where Tom's car had disappeared. 'Although you might not want to live alone with your ex sniffing around.'

'I've lived here alone before and I'm not going to be bullied by anyone.'

Val laughed. 'That's the Loveland spirit.'

Holly felt more determined than ever to rebuild the nursery into an arts hub. 'If Tom thinks I'm going to give up and bail out – he's got another think coming.'

Mitch frowned. 'Are you okay for somewhere to stay tonight?'

'Yes, yes. I'll stay with my friend, Jaz.'

He stuck out his hand. 'It's a deal then.' Taking his hand, she felt the familiar roughness of his skin against hers which again sent shivers over her body. *That's all I need, fancying a married man,* she thought. Mitch smiled fleetingly and whisked up a yapping Trixy and strode in the direction of the farm with a nod of his head.

Holly joined Joe, Val, Julie and Anne who had returned from seeing to the animals. Hugging Val, the warmth of her embrace reminded her of her mum and she felt her chest shudder even though she kept the tears from her eyes.

'Tom's got someone pregnant.'

'I heard that bit. Is it that young girl I seen him with in Wells?'

Holly nodded.

'I'm sorry, lass. I can't believe how he's turned out,' Joe said.

Holly cried softly as Julie stroked her back from behind.

They turned at the sound of a car. The red Audi swung in and Jaz got out.

Jaz pulled off her sunglasses and stared at the scene. Her jaw dropped and she turned towards Holly open-mouthed, but no words came out.

CHAPTER 5

*H*olly ran over events with Jaz, who stood, mouth agape, sticking in the odd 'O-M-G, I don't believe it,' and swore every time Tom's name was mentioned. Once Jaz was up to date, Holly left her talking with Val, Julie and Anne.

Alone, she checked on the animals. Charlie the goat bleated as she arrived. Holly scratched his head, listening to the chickens squabbling but that was nothing new – indeed it was comforting. The 'small fluffs' as Anne called the rabbits and guinea pigs, were acting as if nothing had happened. Spending time with the animals calmed her nerves.

The sound of voices caught her attention. She saw her insurance broker, Gary approaching with a man she did not recognise. Standing up, she washed her hands at the petting zoo sink then opened the gate and approached them.

Gary, a man in his late fifties with greying cropped hair, shook her hand. 'I'm sorry to hear your news. This is Dave, the loss adjuster.'

Dave nodded. 'I know it's hard, but the sooner we get this done, the better.'

Gary eyed the buildings and gave a low whistle. 'The fire officer spoke to us as he left. He asked us to avoid the areas they have taped off.'

Joe arrived at her side. 'Do you want me to come with you?'

'No, no, that's fine.' She knew she would be better going around alone. Joe's care and affection would tip her into tears. She had to be strong.

'I'll get to work on the gardens then,' he said rolling up his sleeves. 'Lucky it didn't spread to the old barn. I'll make it tight and clear it for storage.'

Val ambled over, followed by Jaz.

'Val you get off – it's not your work day today anyway.' Holly turned to Jaz. 'Can you give Val a lift home?'

'Sure. Then I'm coming back for you. You'll need that drink tonight after all. I know I do.'

Holly smiled. As different as they were, she appreciated Jaz now as much as she did when they were younger, when she was her protector from the school bullies.

Holly re-joined the men. Dave passed her a hard hat which she put on her head as they walked around the periphery of the charred remains, which still reeked of smoke. Holly stared at the buildings taped off like a murder scene. As they moved around, Holly explained what had been lost as Dave made notes on a plan of the site and Gary snapped photos with his mobile phone. She felt numb, as if this was a parallel universe she had dropped into. The nursery resembled a war zone, with tables overturned from the force of water jets. The cash till, usually placed on top of a counter, lay on the floor. What used to be her life was now a huge black and grey mess dripping with water. When they reached the cottage, Holly kept her distance – not wanting to see it up close. The furniture, trinkets and ornaments that generations of Lovelands had collected had been snuffed out. Memories flashed through her mind. Born there, grew up there, played there, worked there. Turning her head, she stared at the vegetable patch – *was it really only yesterday I was turning it over?* she thought, feeling separated from that Holly – the old Holly. Everything had changed.

An hour later in the car park, Gary shook her hand promising to be in touch once the report came in from the Fire Service. Walking over to Jaz's car, Holly's legs shook. Jaz was in the driving seat, on her mobile phone, but ended the call as Holly approached.

'I've spoken to work and booked a couple of days off.'

'Are you sure? Won't your figures go down this month?' Holly knew how hard Jaz's boss was, insisting she worked every hour possible to reach the ever-increasing sales targets.

'We exceeded the targets this year and won big at the awards evening.'

Holly put her hand up to her mouth. 'Sorry Jaz, I forgot to ask how it went last night.'

'Seriously?' Jaz grabbed her steering wheel. 'Look at the place. You can be forgiven.'

'So how did it go?'

'Get in and I'll tell you.'

Holly walked around the car, opened the passenger door and sat on the cream leather seats.

Jaz started the engine letting it tick over as they spoke. 'Our team won best branch and I was awarded Sales Executive of the Year.'

'Oh my goodness – that's amazing. Did you get a trophy?'

'Better than that. I got a five-grand bonus. But ...'

'What?'

Jaz turned to face her. 'Basically, the CEO wants me to go train the troops and travel around the country. But I don't want to do that now – not with you like this. I want to help you get the place back together.'

'You can't hold back your career for me. Everyone knows you're on a quest to make a million.'

'You're more important to me than money.'

'I'm fine and I'd feel too guilty keeping you here. What sort of position is it?'

'The CEO says he wants me to work underneath him.'

'I bet he does – you be careful.'

'He's married – you know I'd never go there with a married man. Not after what Stacey went through with her men.'

Jaz never referred to her mother as 'Mum' always as Stacey. Stacey had been in many failed relationships. One guy had had countless affairs and Jaz blamed that for her mother's alcoholism. Holly watched as Jaz checked her reflection in the rear-view mirror, reapplying her lipstick and smoothing down her hair, thinking how different she was to the purple-haired teenager her parents had given a job to in the nursery café. Jaz had been brilliant at up-selling Val's homemade cakes. Later, she had moved in with Holly and her parents and become more of a sister than a friend.

Jaz glanced sideways at Holly's outfit. 'We need to go shopping for clothes.' She frowned. 'Whose clothes, are they?'

'Mine, the Booths bought them to tide me over. They're supermarket, not your taste, I know.'

'Definitely not my brand hun but they suit you – being tight. Seriously we need to update your look.'

'A new wardrobe is the furthest thing from my mind,' Holly sighed.

'Insurance covers clothes you know.' Jaz put the car into gear and revved the engine. 'That's decided then, we're off to the designer outlet.'

Holly smiled at the way Jaz seemed to turn a disaster into an opportunity. She was going to be great at her new job. Jaz was going places. Hitting the big time. Holly felt a pang of sadness. She stared in the wing mirror at her burnt ruins disappearing from view, as the car rounded the bend, she hoped that she would make something of her own dreams.

Travelling along the lane they passed the boundary gate between Booth Farm and Lovelands. Mitch and a large man were lifting the old barrier off its hinges.

'Wow,' Jaz said. 'I've never seen that open before. He's definitely into you.'

'Don't be silly. He needs to open it to get the caravan through. And he's married remember?'

'So you say.'

Holly had an odd feeling – like butterflies in her stomach. The sooner she met Vanessa Booth, the better. Then she could view Mitch as her married neighbour rather than her hot neighbour. *Very hot neighbour,* she repeated in her head.

HOLLY SAT on the cream leather sofa in Jaz's apartment in Wells, surrounded by bags of new clothes. She wasn't entirely sure about them but Jaz had been set on being her personal shopper for the day. Focusing on simple things had freed her mind from the enormous issues that were otherwise buzzing around her head. Jaz had popped out to get a bottle of wine so Holly was alone, observing her friend's trendy apartment, considering how different it was from the house Jaz grew up in, situated on the Eversley Burrows Estate, just outside the village. Jaz had definitely come a long way from nothing. *Unlike me,* Holly thought. *I had everything and now I've lost it.*

Holly focussed on the laptop which Jaz had set up on the coffee table so that she could check the nursery email account. Realising it was another thing she had lost. All of her computer equipment, her printer, the list was endless. Shutting her eyes she breathed in deeply. Her chest felt as if it was easing and the black sneezes had stopped. Leaning forward she logged into her website. Joe had texted earlier to say he would put a 'closed for refurbishment' sign at the nursery gates and Holly wanted to update her website with the same. Her inbox had plenty of emails from customers but she left them unopened. She could not face them. She needed to relax even if it was only for one day.

She updated the nursery website with a banner advising of the temporary closure, and wondered whether it was indeed temporary, or whether she would have to close permanently. She rested her head on the back of the sofa. Her body felt heavy and she dozed off.

HOLLY WOKE two hours later to find Jaz standing before her wearing a tight red dress.

'You're dolled up – where are we off to? A movie premier?'

'No. Just the pub on the market square.'

'I thought the place was more like a café full of tourists and families.'

'You obviously haven't been there for ages, hun. There's a new licensee. It's gone wine-bar-boutique.'

'Sounds interesting but I'm not sure I should go out, not with the smoke inhalation.' Holly puffed out a sigh.

'Hun, it'll do you good to get out, even if it's just for an hour. We won't stay long.'

'I'm a wreck.' Holly rubbed her forehead.

'Nonsense, you're always beautiful. I'll run the shower.'

An hour later, Holly wore a pretty floral number and gazed at her reflection in Jaz's full-length bedroom mirror. It was not something she was used to wearing, but she had to admit, it did suit her figure. The heels were a bit tricky to walk in but Jazz was right, they did make the outfit. She looked confident even if it was a different story on the inside.

Stepping into Jaz's lounge with her hair loose around her shoulders, she put a hand on her hip. 'It's a bit glam for the pub.'

'Rubbish, you can never be too glam.'

'This is all mad. Totally mad. I should be in bed.'

'Maybe true. But Dr Jaz says let your hair down.'

THEY STEPPED out of Jaz's apartment block which was in a low-rise development, a stone's throw from the Cathedral and market square. Holly pulled a thin blue pashmina close to her body tripping along in the heels, hoping she wouldn't twist her ankles on the cobbles.

Jaz caught her arm. 'They're not even high, hun. We should have practiced.'

As they walked into the pub, Holly noticed several guys turn their heads in their direction.

'Just like the old days,' Jaz said. 'Always a good move to be best friends with the hottest girl in town.'

Holly shook her head. 'I'm not hot.'

Jaz laughed. 'You so are.'

Holly scanned the room. 'This is awful, Jaz. They're all staring.'

'Of course they're gawping, you're a stunner.' Jaz put her arm on Holly's back. 'Relax, you clearly haven't been out for ages. Enjoy yourself. Have a bit of fun.'

Holly noticed a man smiling at her from the bar.

'He seems familiar,' Jaz said.

He had neat fair hair and Holly vaguely recognised him. 'I can't place him.'

'Maybe he's someone off TV?' Jaz said.

'When do you ever watch TV? You're always at work,' Holly said with a laugh. 'He's probably someone from school.'

'Trust me, I knew a lot of the boys from school and he's not one of them.' Jaz smiled at the man.

He waved.

Two suited men approached and chatted to Jaz, she flashed a big smile at the guys then turned to Holly. 'These guys are two of my work colleagues. They're getting a bottle of bubbly to celebrate my award.'

The man at the bar saluted Holly before turning back to his drink. *I definitely recognise him,* she thought.

Holly and Jaz sat at a table and were soon joined by Jaz's colleagues. Holly stifled a yawn, her throat felt sore and she wished she had stayed at home. She pondered on the word home. She of course was now homeless.

Jaz belly-laughed, pushing one of the guys on the shoulder. One of the men walked around and sat beside Holly.

She tried to show interest as he threw quick-fire questions at her.

'What do you do? Where do you live? Any kids?'

She gave brief answers: 'This and that, Eversley and No.' She wanted to escape. 'I just have to pay a visit.'

Holly made her way across the room towards the toilets, her ankles wobbling in her shoes as she trotted across the stone floor.

She took a lot longer than was necessary in the ladies, deciding to make her excuses when she returned to the table. As she passed the bar, the guy she thought she recognised walked up to her.

'Holly, it must be like ten years and you've not changed a bit.' He looked her up and down.

Holly scratched her head and bit her lip.

He laughed. 'It's me – Ethan, from college.'

Holly wondered which college. The one locally? Or in London?

'I've changed my appearance, I guess,' he said smiling. He wore a tight white T-shirt under an open blue shirt teamed with a pair of Levi's. He was very well presented and appeared to know it.

Holly peered into his hazel eyes which had a black fleck on the left. 'Ethan, oh my goodness! I'd never have recognised you.' They'd studied at sixth form college together.

'I've lost a lot of weight. And the spots – all cleared up.' He laughed. 'You however haven't changed a bit. Although your mate seems less scary.' He nodded over to Jaz who was laughing loudly in between the two men.

Holly smiled watching Jaz. 'Yes, she ditched the gothic look years ago.'

'So tell me, what's the prettiest girl at college doing now then?'

Holly nodded towards Jaz. 'She sells flash cars.'

'Not Jaz, I meant you.' Ethan smiled showing his dazzling teeth. 'I thought you'd gone to London.'

'I came back a couple of years ago. It's a long story and I've already been talking about me, me, and me, to those guys over there.' Holly nodded at the table to Jaz and her friends. 'Tell me what you've been up to.'

'I went to Lancaster Uni, studied architecture, got into the gym and the weight fell off. I've been back in Somerset for three years now. I built my own house over at Shepton Mallet. I've tried to fuse nature with art. You'll have to come over and see it sometime.' He reached into his back pocket and handed Holly his business card. 'You'd better get back to your date.'

Holly shook her head and sighed. 'He's not my date. I'm actually tired. As I said, it's a long story but I'm going to get off now.'

She glanced down at his card which said, *Moss Architecture.* 'It'd be great to catch up.' *I'll probably be needing his services,* she thought, as she leant forward and gave him a kiss on the cheek. 'Great to see you again.'

Ethan nodded. 'Ditto.'

Holly returned to Jaz. 'I think I'd like to go back to yours now. I feel so rough.'

'No worries, hun. You do look proper peaky.'

'Oh, no, so soon?' one of Jaz's colleagues said.

Jaz smiled. 'Sorry, Sean, but we only popped out for a quickie.'

'Wey hey,' he said.

Jaz shook her head. 'Don't get too drunk – you'll never have a chance of keeping the showroom in the top rankings if you have a hangover tomorrow.'

· · ·

ONCE OUTSIDE, Jaz linked arms with Holly. 'Who was the guy at the bar then? Don't think I didn't notice you chatting him up and giving him a sneaky kiss.'

'I wasn't chatting him up.' Holly laughed. 'It was Ethan from college.'

'Not flabby, spotty Ethan?'

'Don't be unkind. But yes.'

'No way. What a change. So you got his number then?'

'I don't want to start another relationship.'

'So that means you did get his number?'

'Yes. He's an architect. I'm going to need his services.'

'Yeah right, you minx.'

Holly giggled, they both knew Holly was no minx and that she had never dated around. As they neared Jaz's apartment, Holly wished she could tap into some of her usual strength. Tom was gone, Jaz would be travelling the country. It would be up to her and her alone to sort out her destroyed world.

CHAPTER 6

*H*olly's stomach lurched as Jaz drove towards the village. Eversley comprised of a large green, surrounded by five cul-de-sacs of houses, which had gradually sprung up over the years. The buildings around the green were made from quarried stone. Low walls lined the roads sprouting aubretia, which grew in crevasses bursting with purple blooms for much of the spring and summer months. There was a post office-come-corner shop, an antiques auction house, which brought in the 'grockles' as Joe called them – otherwise known as tourists, and The Eversley Arms – the only pub in the village, with its benches sprawling onto the village green.

Jaz parked in the small pub car park. They planned on having lunch before Holly went to check out her new home – the caravan. She did not want to do that on an empty stomach. Mitch had texted her earlier to let her know that her new home was in situ, and the key was in the lock.

As they approached the pub entrance, Julian the landlord ushered them in. 'Sorry to hear about your troubles, Holly.'

'Thanks, Julian. It's a bit of a weird time for me. But as they say – the only way is up.'

'Good for you.' Julian pointed to a table in the window. 'You can have the best seat in the house.'

'Thanks,' Holly said, smiling.

Julian had that big brother feel about him which Holly found comforting.

They walked through the dimly-lit pub with its small windows partly covered on the outside by a fast-growing wisteria. Holly gazed at her feet as she walked. She hated being the centre of attention and she was aware of all eyes on her. Her mum had always called The Eversley Arms a *hot bed of gossip*. But Holly had made more of an effort to be sociable since she had returned from London to Eversley. Networking was great for business.

Sitting in the window seat, Holly appreciated how pretty the village green was on a sunny day. She hoped that the sun would make her burned out home appear less terrifying when she went back there.

Julian handed them a menu each and smiled at Jaz. 'That colour suits you. You really cheer this place up.'

Jaz's face coloured up, clashing with her yellow top.

He returned to the bar to serve a waiting customer.

Holly raised her eyebrows. 'What's the blushing all about?'

'I was so not blushing. More like red with embarrass-ment.' Jaz pouted.

'Why don't you put Julian out of his misery? He's adored you for years.'

'He's too old.'

'He's only four years older than us. Hardly ancient.'

'And he's got a kid.'

'Noah's lovely and it's not like he lives here all the time.

Julian's an every-other-weekend dad. You'd get to do all the fun stuff.'

'I don't want to get involved with broken families.' Jaz stared out of the window.

Holly stretched her hand across to Jaz knowing how sensitive she was when it came to her childhood. 'Julian and Sophie have an amicable relationship. It's quite normal these days.'

Jaz raised her eyebrows. 'Right. So you get Ethan, the buff architect, and I get the slobby barman.'

'He's not slobby. He's big because he plays rugby and it's all muscle. And he's not *a barman,* as you put it – he owns the place. And so what if he was a barman? He's hard-working and good-looking. And that thick sandy hair of his and the beard. He looks like a viking.'

'Maybe I'm not into that look. Shh,' Jaz said as Julian returned to the table.

He placed beer mats in front of them. 'What are you drinking?'

'Sparkling water for me,' Holly said, smiling.

'Make that two,' Jaz said quietly.

'Heavy night was it?'

Jaz stared up to the ceiling and groaned.

Holly kicked her under the table. 'Jaz is driving and I've got work to do this afternoon. A lot of work.' Holly glanced out of the window.

'If you need any help or tradesmen, I'll put word out.'

'Thanks, Julian.' Holly watched him walk back to the bar. 'See, a lovely man.'

'Be my guest.' Jaz stared at her phone as if checking for messages.

Holly smiled at her friend, it was plain to see there was a chemistry between Jaz and Julian, but Jaz always brushed it off for some unknown reason. Julian soon returned with their drinks and took their meal orders, all the time beaming at Jaz.

After a plate of thick, salty ham, eggs and chips, Holly took a deep breath and glanced at the door. 'It's time to face my new reality.'

HOLLY'S HEARTBEAT pounded as Jaz drove the short five hundred meters from the pub to the nursery. Cruising along the drive, they saw Joe's *closed for refurbishment* sign. Jaz drew into the carpark and stopped alongside Holly's transit. Holly's solar plexus burned. Into view came the caravan, placed behind her favourite bench. Joe was hooking up an orange gas bottle.

'Come on then, hun. It's a shame that sexy Mitch isn't here to carry you over the threshold.'

Holly shook her head. 'How many more times? He's married.'

'You've got that so wrong, hun. That man is single and you best get in there quick.'

Holly tapped her friend's arm playfully. 'Jaz, you're the one that's wrong.' But she was glad Jaz was distracting her with their usual banter, and felt the atmosphere lighten.

They walked beside a wide trail of tyre tracks cut into the grass towards the caravan.

Joe turned to face them as they approached. 'You've got gas there for cooking and heating. I've got Larry coming in to sort out an electric hook up but tonight you'll have to live by lamplight.'

Holly had seen it from a distance of course, but the light-green caravan was longer and wider than she had imagined. 'Thanks Joe.'

'Shame himself's not here – he's gone off to some sort of farmers' meeting. Says he'll be back tomorrow evening.'

Jaz grabbed Holly's hand. 'Come on then. Let's look inside.'

The door opened with a squeak.

'I'll WD40 that for you,' Joe said.

Inside, the caravan was colourless. Beige furnishings, beige carpet, beige cupboards. *Definitely in need of re-upholstering,* Holly thought as she surveyed the split seats with yellowed foam poking out.

Joe squeezed Holly's shoulder. 'I'm sure you can make it a home. If you give them cupboards a lick of paint it'll freshen the place up no end. Val says she's got spare bedding you can have.'

'No. That's fine, I'll buy new.' If Holly was going to make it her own, she wanted the contents to be items she had chosen.

Jaz clapped her hands. 'Another shopping trip.'

Holly glanced out of the window which was situated above the sink. Looming up like a black ghost were the nursery buildings. She moved forward and closed the dusty curtains.

Joe led them to a small shower room with a toilet. Poking her head around the corner Jaz hopped from side to side. 'As soon as I see a loo. I have to use it.'

'Well, it's good to go,' Joe said with a laugh. 'Lucky we have water piped through, with this being a nursery.'

They left Jaz to christen the toilet. Joe pointed to a vase of roses and a bowl of fruit placed on the half circle dining table between the kitchen and the lounge area.

'They're from Julie and Anne. They wanted to brighten the place up and make it homely.'

Holly was not usually a fan of cut flowers but was struck

by the colours. Various shades of green foliage were set against the pink blooms of roses. Turning, she looked out of another window on the opposite side of the caravan which framed the landscape. The same view as her *Beauty of Somerset* composition. She smiled. 'Don't worry, I'll make it my own.'

'It was tricky to get up here, mind. Made an awful mess of that there grass. A bit of seed'll sort it out though.' Joe rubbed his hands. 'The Booth lad says he'll not intrude, not with the stress you're under. Though of course he's had his own share of troubles.'

Holly was about to ask Joe what Mitch's troubles were, but Jaz entered the room shaking excess water from her hands.

'Soap and towels are the first thing to add to the shopping list.' she said. 'Not forgetting loo roll. Are we taking my car or your van, hun?'

'Not sure your boot will be big enough for bedding and pillows. We'll take the van.'

Joe put his cap on. 'I'll be getting meself off now. If you need anything – just holler.'

They called out their goodbyes as Joe left.

'Are you sure about this, Holls?' Jaz asked, gazing around the room. 'You could stay at my place. I won't even be there.'

'I'm fine. It feels like our old Wendy house. Do you remember? We slept out in it one night?'

'Of course I do. I've never eaten so many sweets in my life as we did that night.' She moved forward and gave Holly a squeeze. 'I love you so much, hun. You know that, right?'

Holly felt her eyes sting as she nodded her head. 'Don't, Jaz, else you'll have me in tears again.' She pulled away. 'Have you got a pen and paper in your bag? Let's make that shopping list.'

❀

FIVE HOURS LATER, Jaz popped a bottle of Prosecco. The cork shot across the caravan and bubbles spilled onto the rug Holly had bought.

'Hey, I know it was cheap but go easy,' Holly laughed.

While she had managed to get a few items left over from the spring sales, there were limited funds in Holly's account. She did not want to eat into the money she had set aside for staff pay. Sipping her drink, Holly wondered what the following week would bring. Gary had told her he would keep her updated on the insurance claim but said he expected it would be some time before it was processed but that he would rush through an emergency payment for immediate needs.

Sitting on the sofas, they drank the fizz and ate their way through a large box of chocolates which Jaz had insisted they both needed. Holly surveyed their afternoon's work. They had popped by Val's on the way back from the retail park so that Holly could borrow her sewing machine, having bought swathes of material for re-upholstering the seating area and chairs. Her chosen colour scheme for the caravan was green and cerise, inspired by the vase of roses given to her by Julie and Anne.

Val had said, 'Well, it's definitely not bland is it? Gypsy Rose,' when she had shown her the colours. Holly had smiled at the sound of her mother's name, Rose. All the Loveland women who had been at the nursery were named after plants or flowers. Firstly, there was Iris, then Ivy, then Rose and herself Holly, born at Christmas.

Looking at the sewing machine, which took up a large part of the small dining table, Holly smiled. A creative project would keep her mind focussed on something positive.

Jaz sighed. 'I'm sure Mum would've loved the colour scheme.' Jaz had referred to Rose as Mum ever since she had moved in with Holly and her parents.

Holly nodded, sipping her fizz. 'I'll have to stop this drinking malarkey. That's three nights in a row.'

'You're allowed under the circumstances. I'd have another glass myself but I'm driving. Now, hun, are you sure you're okay with me going away?'

'Yes, of course. I'm proud of you. When you've made your million, you can take me on a world tour to celebrate.'

'Well that's my goal. I don't want to depend on some bloke or have his snotty kids.' Jaz stood up. 'I need to get off now. Unless you want me to stay the night?'

'No, not when you're travelling north tomorrow. You need a good night's sleep.'

'I'll be gone for two weeks this time.' Jaz hugged Holly. 'Text me every day. I'll call you whenever I can.'

Holly waved a goodbye, as Jaz headed towards her car, and until it growled away from the nursery. Holly was alone. She could hear the cries of birds roosting in the line of tall trees which ran along a section of the Booth farm boundary. After closing the caravan door, Holly padded to the small shower room in her new slippers. She cleaned her teeth but the shower would not work until the electrics were in. After splashing her face with cold water, she glanced at the cabinet mirror, which was dotted with rust coloured splodges. She was surprised at how awake she looked in her reflection. She wondered whether it was adrenaline from the stress she had endured.

In the bedroom she found the bed inviting. Jaz had

convinced her to go for a duvet, rather than the sheets and blankets she preferred to sleep beneath. It would only be for a short while, she hoped having no idea how long a renovation would take. She had brightened the room with a floral throw and pink scatter cushions. Changing into her PJs, Holly climbed into bed. She hugged herself, realising that all of her soft toys had perished in the fire, including her childhood teddy which had sat on the chair beside her bed at the cottage. She felt the tears run down her face. Without anyone around to be brave in front of, the sobs came in waves. Wiping her eyes on the back of her hand she rolled over, needing to change her thoughts, not wanting to drift downwards into murky regrets and other negative emotions. She needed to eliminate the internal chant of - *I should've got the electrics checked*. Hopefully Gary would call on Monday to put her mind at rest on the insurance front. Shutting her eyes, a picture of Mitch's face appeared. *Oh*, she thought, *I must introduce myself to his wife.*

CHAPTER 7

*H*olly headed across her land towards the old barn. She unbolted the heavy door and pulled it wide open to let the light in. It creaked in a lonely cry which echoed around the yard. No staff were around since Holly had put weekend working on hold. The barn was full of stock which Joe had salvaged from the fire but at the front were pots that Julie and Anne had filled with an array of colourful plants. Holly smiled, the splashes of blue, yellow and red lifted her mood. Picking out a blue fired pot filled with a multitude of coloured pansies she looked towards the farm. *This one will be an ideal gift for Vanessa,* she thought. Heaving the pot up, she set it down outside the barn and locked up.

Holly trudged towards the farm with the pot clutched in her arms, pausing as she reached the gap between the two properties where the gate had been removed. Stopping to catch her breath, she balanced the pot on the wall, wondering whether the gate would be replaced or left open as a sign that relations between the Booths and Lovelands had improved. Holly held the pot in her aching arms and carried on. However, when she saw movement, she stopped. About twenty metres in front of her was a woman facing away, hunched over something. Holly paused, *maybe that's Vanessa?* Taking a deep breath she moved forward with what she felt was a breezy smile on her face. Now much closer, she could see the woman was bent over a wheelchair.

Holly whispered under her breath. 'Oh no. Sidney.' She was not prepared for any confrontation. They had not noticed her, therefore Holly decided to retreat and return later. But it was clear that the wheelchair was stuck in the ground. *I can't just leave them,* she thought. If they were to mend the rift between their families, she should be reaching out to Sidney Booth.

Holly swallowed hard, took a deep breath, stood tall and walked towards the wheelchair with the pot in her arms and an even broader smile. As she approached the woman turned.

'You must be Vanessa, I'm Holly.'

The young woman frowned. 'Vanessa? No, I am Magda.' She spoke in an accent which Holly placed as Eastern European. 'Would you help me?'

'Yes, of course.' Holly placed the pot on the floor. 'I was popping over to see Vanessa.'

Sidney spluttered from the chair. Holly bit her lip. She should have introduced herself. He may think she had ignored him because he was in a wheelchair.

'She's gone.' Sidney's voice crackled as he spoke. He strained to turn his head.

Holly remained where she was, attempting to summon up the courage to face him.

'What business have you here?' he croaked.

Magda placed a hand on his shoulder. 'This nice lady is helping me get the chair off the grass. I did say this was not a good idea. Mitchell said to me not to go off the paths. He will not be pleased if he comes home and finds us stuck in the ground.'

Although Sidney was clearly abrupt, Holly felt a measure of compassion, noticing how frail he was – even from behind. He had been such a broad man, a large character storming across the land in his long wax jackets. But the man before her was not much more than skin and bone.

Holly pulled at the chair with Magda easing it free. 'Mr Booth, I was just bringing a pot for Vanessa. But as you say she's away with Mitch. I'll help Magda get you on the move and then I'll be gone.'

'Not away, girl,' he said with a cough. 'Passed. Gone. Dead.'

Holly opened her eyes wide. 'Dead?'

'Terrible accident. Crushed by a tractor. Ages ago. Coming up to two years.' Sidney spluttered.

Magda walked around to face him. Taking a tissue from her pocket she cleaned his mouth. Holly remembered how Mitch had reacted when she mentioned his wife. *But why didn't he say?* she asked herself.

Sidney stopped choking after taking water from a bottle held by Magda. 'Come here and let me see you. Who are you anyway?'

Holly inched around until she was in Sidney's line of vision.

Peering up at her his pale eyes stared and his pupils widened. He grabbed the arm of the chair. 'Ivy.' His voice a mere whisper. He lowered his head and his chest rose, then fell.

'It's Holly. Ivy was my ...'

'Don't patronise me, girl. I know who she was. You Lovelands are thieves and liars. Take, take, take.'

Holly took a deep breath. 'Mr Booth, I was hoping that maybe we could get to know one another.' Holly did not know why she said that but she could not think of anything else on the spot and wanted to remain positive. Her palms began to sweat.

'Get off my land,' he said as he coughed uncontrollably.

Magda put a hand on Sidney's shoulder. 'Stay calm. We need to get back to the house.' Magda's face flushed red.

Holly looked to Magda. 'I'll help you to the path.' She observed dark clouds approaching. 'I know you had a falling out with my family, Mr Booth, but there's just me now – they're all gone.'

'You're all the same.'

'Please let me help Magda get you inside, before the heavens open.'

'Full of self-importance, the lot of you,' Sidney grumbled as Holly helped Magda down the slope until the chair ran smoothly over the fine gravel path.

'Thank you. Don't forget the flowers.' Magda pointed to the pot placed in the grass.

'I'll leave it here. You can have it, Magda.'

'Are you sure?'

'Of course.'

'That is kind. It is beautiful.'

It began to rain.

'Hurry, girl,' Sidney growled.

Magda lowered her voice. 'He's a sweet man most of the time. I love caring for him.'

Holly placed a hand on Magda's shoulder. 'You'd better get in and I'll fly off as I think this gentle rain is going to get much worse.'

Holly ran back up the hill, going over the times in her head that Vanessa had been mentioned. They'd been brief, she had assumed Mitch was not fond of discussing his family. *A widower and Vanessa crushed by a tractor?* Holly shuddered. No wonder Joe said Mitch had his own troubles.

She had not managed to avoid the downpour and felt the rain seep through her clothes over the last fifty metre stretch.

HOLLY WOKE on Monday morning shortly after nine, to the ringtone of her mobile phone. Keeping her eyes closed she patted in different places on the duvet until she found it. She squinted at the screen and saw it was her broker.

'Hello Gary?'

'Hi, Holly. Hope you're keeping well. I need to pop over and see you. Where are you staying?'

'In a static caravan on my land. Is everything okay?'

'I have the fire service report. I'm afraid they've deemed there's a possibility of arson. There'll be a further investigation.'

Holly's heart raced. 'Why arson?'

'They found accelerants on the premises. They need to know what chemicals you had in there.'

'In the art studio?'

'Yes, that's definitely where it started.'

'I had oil paints and spirits to clean the brushes.' *Take deep breaths it's easily explained,* she told herself.

'Yes of course, that's probably it. Also they mentioned wax? Did you have any candles in there?'

'No candles in the studio – just some for show in the rest of the house. I did have a glue stick. You melt the glue and it drips on the ...'

'There's no need to go into details right now. Have a

think and make notes of everything in the studio and I'll be over Wednesday about noon?'

Holly checked the calendar on her phone then put it back to her ear. 'Yes, that's fine. If they think it's arson does that mean they won't pay out?' Holly felt herself shake. No insurance pay-out and she would have to sell.

'They tend to go on the offensive. But even if it was arson it wouldn't be a problem unless they thought the occupants had caused it.'

'That's ridiculous as if I'd do that. I was alone in the house.'

'Yes, we have that on record, although the insurance company have asked about your husband. He's on the electoral role?'

Holly wanted nothing to do with Tom unless he wished to talk about returning her seventy-five thousand. 'As I said the other day, he left two weeks ago.' *It's not a lie,* Holly thought. Tom would probably convince them to pay the insurance money direct to his bank account or claim half, if he was involved.

'I'll let them know he's no longer residing at the property.'

'Thank you.' Holly's hand shook as she ended the call. Laying back on the bed she stared at the ceiling. Feeling nauseous, she wondered whether she should have mentioned that Tom was there that day. Was that withholding information? Could she get into trouble? Tom was not present at the time of the fire – he had left hours before. As much as Tom had surprised her during their split, she knew he would not have tried to burn the house down with her in it. No, if he wanted to kill her for her money, he would have pushed her down the stairs, faked a suicide, created some sort of accident, not burned down the buildings reducing the value of the property. Holly shuddered, realising she hardly knew Tom any more. Although, she knew in her gut that he was no killer.

Heaving herself out of bed, the caravan shook with every step as she padded to the lounge. Having spent the weekend upholstering the caravan, it was much brighter. She had covered the seating with a leaf green material draped with pink throws. At college Holly had studied textiles alongside Art and always enjoyed working with fabric. It was totally transformed from generic caravan to a bright space, smelling of the paint she had used to cover the units to give it a sense of newness. Peeping through the new curtains, she saw Joe, Julie and Anne, mugs in hand chatting in front of the wreckage. There were enough funds to tide their wages over for two weeks. It would break her heart if she had to lay her staff off.

Holly lifted her phone, flicking through her contacts until she reached Jaz. She hesitated. Distracting Jaz from her new job with her woes would be wrong. Scrolling on she saw Ethan's name, having already plugged his number in from the business card he had given her. Hovering over the call button she pressed it. Holly left the phone to ring twice but had second thoughts and hung up, placing the phone on the table. The ringtone split the silence. *Ethan calling* came on the display.

Oh no, Holly thought and blushed as she answered it. 'Hi Ethan.'

'Who's this? I got a missed call.'

'It's Holly.'

'I'm so pleased you called. I've been thinking of you. I heard about the fire, I tried calling the nursery number but there was no answer and the mailbox was full.'

'That's something else I need to sort out.'

'You never mentioned the fire when we met.'

'I wanted a stress-free evening. My head was all over the place.'

'I can understand that – you must be gutted. What's next?'

'I'm going to rebuild it. The nursery is the only thing I've left of my family.'

'Awful about your artwork as well.'

'How did you know about that?'

'It's on the Gazette's website.'

'Really? Maybe I should put a statement out that I'm rebuilding.'

'I'll take you into their offices today if you like? You can tell them your plans.'

Holly paused, she did not feel ready for that.

'Sorry,' Ethan said. 'That's probably too soon. I can't imagine how I'd feel if I lost all my work. And I'm not half as good, as you.'

'Rubbish, your compositions were brilliant. As far as the rebuild is concerned, I already had plans to convert the old barn. I'm considering rebuilding it as a community creative space attached to the nursery.'

'Now this sounds interesting. Something positive could come of this. I might be able to help you out.'

'I must confess, I was going to pick your brains about the plans.'

'Great – I'll pick you up at noon. We can have lunch then come to mine. I'll set it up on my design programme.'

CHAPTER 8

*E*than was due within the next half an hour. Holly pulled on jeans, a white camisole and a peach canvas jacket that Jaz had picked out; telling her it set off the blue in her eyes. Holly with her artist's head on guessed it was true, juxtaposing colours did work well together. Picking up her mobile from the dining table, her mind flashed back to her visit to Booth Farm the previous day. It had been nagging at her in the background, throughout the morning. She considered texting Mitch. But did not know what to say. 'Sorry I thought your wife was still alive,' did not seem appropriate. It was him, after all, who had mentioned Vanessa and not clarified the position. She felt torn between being respectful of his clear wish to remain silent and her inner need to give her condolences. She heard her mother's voice in her head full of wisdom. *If you can't think of the right thing to say, don't say anything at all.*

There was a rap at the door. *Ethan's early?* Holly thought as she opened it, but found Mitch at the foot of the metal steps with Trixy on a lead. The little dog yapped, choking on her collar to get to Holly.

'Hi! Come in,' she said, overwhelmed with a rush of warmth, feeling the need to say something.

'She's got mucky feet,' Mitch said pointing at Trixy. 'And I'm well aware that I'm continuing to break the no-dogs rule.'

Holly laughed. 'That rule has been relaxed. Anyway, she's not a big dog, much smaller than Charlie the goat. He'd never be afraid of her. Carry her in. I'll get a towel.'

Holly wondered whether Mitch was aware that she had seen Sidney.

'I don't recognise the place,' he said looking around the room with a wide grin on his face.

Holly smiled as she entered the small second bedroom and called out. 'I thought I'd brighten it up a bit.' She frowned at her fluffy fresh towels stacked in a small pile on the single bed, she realised having every-thing new was nice but sometimes you needed old things set by for times like this. At least the towels were cheap.

As she returned to the lounge area she found Mitch wiping Trixy's feet with a disposable cloth. 'You had a couple of these on the side. I hope you don't mind?'

'No, that's fine.'

'They're only small feet. All done. They can dry on my lap.'

Trixy wagged her tail and barked at Holly.

Holly placed the towel on the side. 'I'll come and sit next to you.'

'Probably best,' Mitch said with a smile as he surveyed the modest space. 'You've a great touch. I can't believe this is still the same old caravan.'

Holly felt herself flush. 'I thought you'd think this was too bright?'

'I love it. Maybe I should get you to decorate the farm-house. If I stay, that is.'

Holly's arm brushed against Mitch's and she felt tingles covering her skin. Trixy clambered onto her lap, her paws now dry. She made herself comfortable then sat down putting her head on her paws and shut her eyes.

'I seem to be very popular with Trixy.'

'Well animals can tell, can't they? If someone's nice.'

A silence fell. Holly's arm pressed against Mitch's but she could not move because Trixy was now snoring and she didn't want to wake her. *Shall I mention Vanessa?* she thought, feeling the heat rising from her chest. The topic loomed in the air but she did not want to be the one to bring it up.

'Tea? Coffee?' she said, desperate to break the silence.

Mitch smiled. 'I'll have tea. But I'll make it.' As he rose, his head nearly reached the ceiling of the caravan. He had his back to her. 'I'm sorry, by the way. For not explaining about Vanessa. I said she'd chosen Trixy, I should have said that Trixy was my late wife's dog.' He turned back to her, still holding the kettle under the tap. 'I didn't want to mention it when I took you to the farm that night. You were resisting my offer of help and I thought if you realised ...'

Holly bit her lip and looked down at Trixy. *He's got a point,* she thought. She may have refused his help.

'Then the next time I saw you I was about to explain when your husband showed up.'

Holly raised her head. 'Ex-husband,' she said realising it came out too loud – and too quick.

Mitch turned back to the kettle as water splashed all over him. 'Oh, no. Sorry.'

'It's just a bit of water.' Holly sucked in her lips to stop herself laughing. She did not know if he was about to open up about his marriage or whether he had finished. 'It must have been awful for you, it's hard when we lose people we love. I get upset over my parents. It still feels raw and that was two years ago now.'

Mitch clicked the kettle on and turned around. 'It's been a tough year or so. There was an inquiry. The police were involved – the local rag had me down as a killer.'

'Oh, my goodness. How awful.'

Mitch rubbed his jaw. 'They eventually found a manu-facturing fault with the tractor's brake.'

'How dreadful.'

'It was.'

Mitch turned back to the sink and a silence hung in the air.

'I can't imagine how that must have been for you and I think I've got problems.'

Mitch turned around. 'I'm getting my life back now. I've had enough sympathy to last a lifetime. And I'm sorry about Sid's behaviour too. He's getting a bit cantankerous. I'm sure I'll be a right old grumpy git when I reach eighty-four. If I'm lucky to get that old, that is.'

'We both know he's never been a fan of my family. I over-stepped the mark and walked into it, trying to make friends. I shouldn't have upset him like that, when he's sick.'

Mitch walked over to the window and opened the curtains to a slither. 'I noticed on the way up, that your staff are in the barn. What are they up to?'

Holly stroked Trixy's head. 'We're filling all available pots with plants. There are loads stacked to the rear of the building. We have indoor planters and outdoor which escaped the fire. We're thinking of selling them at Wells market.'

'Why at the market? You could sell them here?'

'I don't think health and safety would allow that. The buildings are subject to a public safety order.'

'There's plenty of land here though. You can cordon it off.' Mitch pulled the curtains open and pointed. 'Put up a shed over there for the cash till.'

'Who's going to come out here? Just to buy a pot?'

'Trust me, lots of people love to look at disasters.'

'Charming,' Holly said with a laugh.

'Not you. You're not a disaster.' Mitch turned and smiled at her.

Holly felt her cheeks heat up. She lowered her eyes to Trixy. 'She seems happy. I wish I could feel that relaxed right now.' Turning back to Mitch she stared into his familiar eyes as he leaned against the sink with his arms crossed.

'You're doing great, Holly. Anyway, are you tea or coffee?'

'Tea, please.'

Mitch brought over two floral cups of tea and sat beside her. Holly told him about the insurance problems and he listened in silence as she off-loaded. After a while, she realised she was rambling. She also noticed that Mitch was not taking his eyes off her which made her feel nervous.

Mitch placed his empty cup on the table. 'I was after a favour. I'm taking Sid to Essex for a big family event in a couple of weeks. Would you mind Trixy for me? Magda will be coming with us.'

Holly paused.

Mitch stared at her with his eyebrows raised as if searching for a reaction. He rubbed the back of his neck. 'I know you're busy. And have your zoo up here. I shouldn't have asked.'

'Of course I can look after her.' Holly realised she'd paused for far too long. It was his eyes, she found it difficult to think when she gazed into them. Trixy woke up and licked Holly's hand. 'Trixy will be a nice distraction for me.'

'There's one other thing I wanted to ask.'

'Yes?'

'Last week you said you didn't remember me.'

Holly blushed and bit her lip. She would have moved if Trixy had not been so happy on her lap. *Stay cool, stay cool,* she told herself.

'We used to chat over the wall for hours, I can't believe you don't recall.'

Holly coughed and glanced downwards. 'Maybe there is a distant memory.'

Mitch laughed. 'I'm not likely to forget my first kiss.'

Holly grinned, feeling transported back fifteen years. *It was his first kiss too?* she thought. And of course she remembered it. They'd agreed to meet at seven in the evening after dinner when his Uncle Sid would be with the cows. And her parents would be settling down to watch a soap. It was the last day of Mitch's holiday, the last time she had seen him in Eversley until recently. The sweetness came back to her of that warm night. She breathed in deeply.

'I knew you remembered.' Mitch smiled.

'So why did you stop visiting?' Moving her hair from her face, she could feel her heartbeat quicken.

'I started college and worked in my holidays. Grew up, I suppose. Lazy summers in Somerset were gone. I've been over to visit Sid as an adult, but I never saw you here.'

'I moved to London. I only came back two years ago when Mum and Dad died.'

Trixy jumped up at Holly and she held her away from her. 'Whoa don't get me dirty I'm off out soon.' Holly saw a flicker of something in Mitch's eyes. Did his expression change? Was it disappointment? She could not tell. As if on cue there was a rap at the door. Holly stood up, handing Trixy to Mitch so she could open it.

'Wow, you look gorgeous – as ever,' Ethan said, grinning up at her.

Holly heard Mitch behind her, clipping Trixy's lead on. 'I'll be off then,' he said

Holly stepped to one side as he passed. 'Thanks for popping over.'

Ethan's eyes widened as he eyed Mitch. 'Alright?' he said.

Mitch nodded at him and put his boots on as Trixy jumped about. She sniffed at Ethan's feet and growled. Mitch nodded at Holly and walked away with Trixy pulling on the lead, attempting to return to Holly.

'Who's my competition?' Ethan asked Holly from the bottom step.

Holly gave a short, nervous laugh. 'He's my neighbour. He popped over to ask me to babysit his dog.'

'Oh really?'

'There's nothing going on, I can assure you.' Holly's voice reached a higher pitch than usual and it echoed in her head as if she was trying to convince herself, rather than Ethan. Deep down she knew Mitch was more than her type but he was a Booth and she knew that spelled trouble – it always had done. *Anyway, it must be lust,* she told herself. Not the gentle love she had felt for previous boyfriends or the carefree love she had originally felt with Tom. No, this was something quite animal – an urge. Not something she needed in her life.

CHAPTER 9

*M*itch pulled at Trixy's lead but she stuck her paws into the ground. Eventually his attempts worked and she allowed him to guide her down the path. However, she stopped to sniff at something in the bushes. Due to her size, Mitch was forever worried he would strangle her if he pulled the lead with his full strength.

'Come on, Trix.' He tried to lift her up but only managed to raise her back half and her front paws remained on the ground with her head in the bush. Hearing Holly's voice travel over the shrubs he remained quiet.

'There's nothing going on. I can assure you.'

Mitch shook his head and yanked Trixy who yelped. Picking her up he stuffed her under his arm attempting to settle her down so he could comfortably walk away without her wriggling free. Looking over the hedge to the caravan he shook his head. He had been sure there was a spark between himself and Holly. If she was making excuses to that guy, maybe they had a thing going on? Although it did seem a bit soon after the husband. And there was him holding back, wanting to be respectful with her having recently split from her ex. Mitch heard voices approaching and ducked slightly to mask himself from view as Holly walked past towards a black sporty Maserati, which had a thin stripe of the Italian flag colours running up and over from boot to bonnet.

Mitch shook his head. 'Flash git,' he muttered.

This was not how he wanted things to pan out. He had planned to ask Holly to have dinner with him and to see if things progressed. He had not had any female friends since Vanessa died, not that he had been short of offers. But this was the first time he actually felt like getting to know someone. His stomach lurched at the memory of Vanessa. The sickly feeling of guilt that never left him. The haunting memory of finding her covered in blood between tractor and barn door. *If only I'd been there in time to save her,* was a mantra he repeated so often that at times he thought he would go insane.

Seeing Holly again, all of his carefree boyhood innocence flooded back to him. With Holly he felt like a bloke again with bloke thoughts. *Anyway, I'm nothing like him*, he thought watching Ethan with his belted jeans, tucked-in shirt and shiny shoes get into his car. *If that's her type, I've no chance,* he thought as he rubbed his chin, which was already sprouting stubble, he was only ever clean shaven for a few hours of the day. *Then there's her husband, another bad penny.* Mitch shook his head. *I'm best off out of it.* As if reading his thoughts. Trixy licked his chin as the Maserati rumbled by, kicking up gravel as Ethan accelerated away.

Mitch strode back to the farm along the stony lane. It was a much shorter trip since he had pulled the gate out, not having to walk via the village road. He knew there'd been bad feelings between his family and Holly's for years and had no interest in continuing that rubbish. It would die with his uncle as far as he was concerned. Even if Sid would never forgive them, to Mitch all was fair in business, love and war.

The Mendips rose before him at the far boundary of the farm, like a protective barrier between this world and the hell of a life he had endured over the past two years in Essex. Surveying the farm, he considered how different it was from Booth Essex, which was on flatter land.

Reaching his destination, he opened the back door of the farmhouse and stepped onto the stone flanked floors. There were no plush furnishings in this section of the house which was purely functional and held the kitchen, a utility area and meeting room where he addressed the staff. Sidney's dog had been relocated to the Essex farm. Bruce, the working dog was too aggressive. He could have maimed Trixy – or worse. Security was no issue as Trixy yapped if anything came within sniffing distance of the house. Watching her slurp water out of a metal bowl, he went to the cupboard and fetched a handful of dog biscuits, which he set out for her.

Mitch leaned against the worktop visualising Holly. Her athletic body, her hair that fluttered around her face, making her appear fragile. Halting his thoughts, he turned on the tap, filling a long glass with water and drank it down in one, pushing thoughts of Holly from his mind. Although in business, he realised, Holly would definitely make a great associate. She had bags of energy and determination. He admired her resilience. They'd be good for each other, in a business sense.

'Nothing more,' he said to Trixy as she stared up at him, licking her lips.

Mitch crossed over to the private side of the farmhouse with Trixy in tow. Removing his boots, he walked over the threshold into the living room. It was full of his uncle's life-time clutter, with a huge red paisley rug covering much of the wooden floor. High-backed chairs and sofas were placed around the room. At the end was a plant-filled conservatory where Sid appeared to be sleeping in a chair. Magda sat opposite him reading a book.

Mitch glanced at the sideboard where he had propped Holly's painting. He was unsure about where to hang it. *It's a shame about that competition,* he thought. Studying the picture, it seemed as if the farmhouse was situated in the centre of a beautiful, colour-filled paradise.

'What a waste – a real talent,' he said to himself. 'Let's see what we can do,' Trixy jumped up at his legs. 'You're not coming though.'

After letting Magda know he was off out and asking her to mind Trixy, Mitch picked up the painting and left the farmhouse.

Mitch strode along Wells High Street, meandering here and there to avoid bustling shoppers and sightseers. Whilst there were some young families with prams, most of the visitors were the retired, mooching around, as tourists do. The shops were a mixture of those built from red brick and those in Bath stone. He had been to the Town Hall before, so knew where it was – straight ahead to the Cathedral then hang a right at the pub. He had changed into a pair of jeans and a blue jumper. His Barbour jacket was open as the day was warm. He approached the reception desk with Holly's bubble-wrapped painting under his arm.

A smartly dressed woman smiled at him. 'Can I help?'

'Yes, I'd like to speak to someone about the *Beauty of Somerset* competition.' Mitch held up the package.

She cocked her head to one side. 'I'm sorry but the deadline has passed. There'll be another competition next year though.'

'I'd still like to speak to someone about it.' Mitch smiled.

'Well, um, yes. I'll see what I can do. Can I have your name, please?'

After Mitch gave his name, the receptionist had a low-voiced telephone conversation then glanced up. 'Ian Sykes is coming down to see you. Please take a seat.'

Mitch wandered over to the waiting area but did not sit down.

A short, balding man approached. He was wearing grey suit trousers, an off-white shirt and a red tie. He held out his right hand. 'Pleased to meet you, Mr. Booth.'

Mitch shook his hand.

'Come this way.' Ian gestured towards a door.

The door opened into a short corridor leading to a small meeting room. Light streamed in through a huge window.

'I won't keep you long.' Mitch unwrapped the picture. 'My neighbour painted this for your competition and has had a personal tragedy. Her house and business were burnt to the ground.'

'Lovelands?'

'Yes, that's right, Holly.' Mitch continued to unwrap the picture. 'I did say to her to bring it down. But as you can imagine she's got other priorities.'

Ian rubbed his head. 'The competition is closed. The deadline was five days ago. We've never allowed a late submission before.'

'As I said, she's lost all of her worldly possessions. Everything. A lifetime of artwork and this,' Mitch said lifting the painting now free of bubble wrap, 'is her only remaining piece of work which would have been submitted before the deadline, had she not encountered an emergency.'

Ian studied the painting, 'Didn't the fire occur after the deadline? Therefore, it's not really relevant.'

Mitch stared at Ian furrowing his brow. 'She had other domestic issues.'

'Deadlines are deadlines. As difficult a time as I imagine she's experiencing, we all have our problems.'

'But we haven't all lost our home, livelihood and business. I would have thought that the Council might wish to be seen as promoting local business people. Especially a sole trader with a business that's etched on Eversley's history?'

Mitch noticed Ian frown, hoping he had struck a nerve.

'We're always keen to promote locals. Indeed we have a meeting here in a few weeks on that very subject. We're forming a committee with business people from Wells and the surrounding villages.' Ian stared him in the eye.

Mitch took a deep breath, unsure whether he would be staying in Eversley long-term. And a committee was the last thing he wanted to get sucked into, with endless time-wasting meetings.

'I assume you're related to the Booths of Booth farm?'

'Yes,' Mitch said, placing the painting on the table.

'Someone like yourself, a farmer, would be a valuable asset to the team.'

Mitch rubbed the back of his neck. 'Assuming you could help me out here, I'll sign up.'

'Excellent. I think I'm correct in believing that the artwork judges are meeting this evening, to go over the entries.'

'So, you'll accept it?'

'Assuming you will be joining the committee, then yes.'

'Thanks, that's great.' Mitch pointed to the painting. 'And it's unbelievable how the colours ...'

Ian put one hand up in a stop sign motion. 'I'm not a judge – no need to sell it to me any further. Wait here and I'll get an entry form for the competition, and a registration pack for the committee.'

MITCH WALKED around the periphery of the market square. Today was not market day and the square was being used as a car park. He liked the feel of the place. He had to admit, Somerset was growing on him, even though he missed the farm back home. It was only natural for Mitch to be the one to take over the Eversley business. His sister had not stayed in the industry, having chosen a career as an accountant in the City of London; neither did she have the relationship with Sid, having spent her summers show-jumping. His Dad's brother managed the second Essex farm and his children were much younger and unable to take on the responsibility.

Mitch passed a café and feeling his stomach rumble went in and approached the counter.

'Can I help you, my love?' a woman asked, she was wearing a white catering hat covering the top of her curly brown hair.

Mitch gazed at the spread of pastries and cakes. 'Yes, thanks. A pasty and a coffee.'

'Eat in or take out?'

Mitch scanned the room dotted with tables and chairs, it was quiet.

'If you eat in you get refillable coffee.'

'Eat in.'

'I'll take for it now and bring it over.'

After paying, Mitch walked to a table. His pasty soon arrived and he ate it slowly. He had never been that keen on pasties in Essex but they tasted so much better in the West Country. The vegetables tangy, the meat soft and the pastry flaky with a gooey bit where the gravy had soaked in. He missed other people's cooking. Not that he was a bad cook but he tended to prepare food that served a purpose as fuel, rather than anything he would call tasty. He missed Vanessa's cooking, she had been creative in that department and used to pick up recipes on their travels across Europe. He reached for his coffee and took a gulp. He needed to move on. Holly came to mind, although he felt a pang of guilt, acknowledging that what he felt for her was different. Different to his marriage. A feeling he had not had for a long time, not since he was a teenager.

'Would you like another refill?' the bakery assistant asked.

Mitch blinked then checked his phone, he was surprised to see it was nearly one o'clock. He needed to get back to the farm as he feared Trixy would be chewing up everything in sight. He left a tip in the jar on the counter on his way out. He stopped in his tracks as he entered the square, recognising the black Maserati which swung in front of pub opposite. He watched as Ethan exited the car and walked around to help Holly out. Once out of the car, Holly glanced over her shoulder. Mitch stared back then turned and strode away. *I should have smiled,* he thought. *Why does what she does bother me*? He knew the answer, but refused to acknowledge it.

CHAPTER 10

*H*olly watched Mitch on the other side of the market square. She felt Ethan's arm on the small of her back, and resisted the urge to shrug him off as he guided her to the pub.

Once inside they sat at a table by a picture-lined wall and Holly checked out the menu. She had been relieved when Ethan pulled into a parking spot in the market place. The idea of going for a leisurely country drive on a sunny spring day had appealed to her. However, the reality had been a journey full of winding country roads which Ethan had taken at speed, and her stomach was still churning from being lurched from here to there. She ordered a beef pie and chips. Jaz had told her the pies were amazing. Ethan ordered a superfood salad.

'I'm keeping down my meat intake and have cut out sugar,' Ethan said as he sipped his sparkling water.

'You've lost enough weight, Ethan.'

'It's not for weight loss, it's for health. I start every day with a green drink with added spirulina.'

Holly smiled, as she sipping her wine.

'Have you tried it?'

'No. What is it?'

'It's a supplement, high in valuable nutrients.'

'I just eat my greens. I've never bothered with extra vitamins.'

'Sugar can cause cancers and strokes. You know if you swapped sugar for certain sweeteners, that could help. Are you aware that in Denmark ...'

Holly nodded as Ethan told her the difference between good and bad sweeteners and the merits of Stevia. He went on to cover the effect of flossing on longevity of life as she gazed at the dessert menu, wondering whether to go for the Eton Mess or chocolate fudge cake.

'Do you agree?' Ethan said as Holly became aware of him addressing her.

'Absolutely. Healthy options. Best choice.'

'Great, we'll go to the health food store right after this and get you sorted.' Ethan patted her hand.

Holly decided to pay attention to what Ethan said in future, not knowing exactly what she had agreed to.

Holly's phone rang, *Jaz Calling.*

'It's Jaz. Do you mind if I quickly take this?' she said, smiling at Ethan.

'Sure. I'll get us some more drinks.' Ethan stood up and went to the bar.

Holly answered the phone. 'Hi, Jaz, did you arrive safely?'

'Yeah, it's an amazing hotel. I can see the Mersey from my window. Where are you?'

'I'm in Wells with Ethan, having a pub lunch.'

'Really? So, you and him?'

'He's going to help me with the hub drawings.'

'Okay.' Jaz spoke in a slow voice.

'Why do you say it like that?'

'I never really liked him. Found him a bit anal.'

'Jaz. Surely you're not going to go all green-eyed on me?' Holly laughed.

'To be fair, hun, this is the first time I've spoken to you since the fire where you actually sound like yourself again. I guess Ethan must be doing you good.'

Holly had experienced an exciting feeling since the morning, but she knew it was nothing to do with Ethan. 'I've got something to tell you about Mitch.'

'Now there's a man I like to think about.'

'He's not married.'

Holly heard Jaz laugh down the phone. 'I told you that. I've no idea why you thought he was.'

'It's quite sad though.'

Jaz stopped laughing. 'She's not dead, is she?'

'Yes, he's a widower.'

'Sorry for laughing. I didn't realise.'

Ethan walked over smiling and passed Holly a sparkling mineral water.

'I have to go now, sweet.'

'Call me later,' Jaz said.

'Definitely.' Holly made a kiss sound down the phone placing her mobile on the table. It rang again. 'I'm so sorry about this.' Holly looked down at the mobile, flashing, *unknown number*. 'I'll have to take it, in case it's the insurance.' She answered the call. 'Hello?'

'Is that Holly Loveland?'

'Yes.'

'Erin Bartlett here. I'm the police officer you met at the fire? I've been passed a report about possible arson.'

Holly rubbed her forehead.

'What's up?' Ethan whispered.

'Police,' she mouthed back.

'Where are you at the moment?' Erin asked.

I don't want to tell her I'm in the pub, Holly thought. *She already thinks I'm a lush.* 'I'm in Wells, picking up supplies.'

A guy on the next table shouted at the barman. 'Mate – I'll have a pint of Speckled.'

'Right.' Erin sounded curt. 'Can I arrange to come out and see you later? I need details of any accelerants on the property and a list of everyone present that day.'

'I've already explained to my broker. I had many accelerants on site. I'm an artist. Paints. Cleaning spirit. I'm sure nothing untoward happened. As I said, the electrics have been on the blink.'

'I have to follow correct procedures. Where are you staying? Are you available at four?'

Holly arranged to meet Erin at the caravan. She switched her phone to silent and placed it on the table and let out a sigh as she rested her head in her hands.

'Hey, what's up?' Ethan moved a hand across and touched her arm.

'Everyone's making a fuss about accelerants and the police are coming to the caravan at four.' Holly took a gulp of mineral water, the bubbles made her nose sting. 'So we won't be able to go over my plans today.' She shook her head. 'It's not arson. It's ridiculous. You and I both know – artists have chemicals. The lights have been blowing for a couple of weeks, I've told them – it was the electrics.'

'Are the police accusing you?'

'No, not at all. But it's bad enough losing all my stuff, without this.'

'Who's your broker?'

'Gary Cox of Glenworth.'

Ethan nodded. 'Don't worry, Holly. I'm sure it'll be fine.'

Holly smiled at Ethan. He did not set her heart racing but he definitely had a calming influence. Life was such a whirlwind and calm was good. She listened as Ethan reminisced about college as they ate their lunch. It was as if the clock had been turned back to a time when she was carefree and had family around. Back to when her mum and dad were alive.

Holly's mobile vibrated where she had placed it on the table. Taking a deep breath, she glanced at it. *Tom Calling.* Lifting her phone, she showed Ethan the display. 'That one can go to voicemail.' She replaced it on the table where it vibrated for a few more seconds.

Holly tried to enjoy the chocolate fudge cake when it arrived but her stomach lurched as she wondered. Wondered what Tom wanted. Wondered whether she was going to be accused of arson. Wondered whether she would ever raise the money to rebuild her life. And then there was Mitch. *Why is that man forever coming into my thoughts?* she asked herself. She knew he had his own demons to deal with.

'Are you okay?' Ethan touched her hand. 'You're frowning.'

'Oh, yes. You know what it's like when your life's in tatters. Little things get blown out of proportion.'

Ethan patted her hand 'It's not a little thing, Holly. You're allowed to be concerned. Don't worry, I can give you any support you need to get through this.' He smiled.

Holly gazed at him, thinking that he was really attractive with soft highlights in his hair. Although she realised it was probably salon streaked.

'Now, let me get you down to the health shop. I can set you up with the best supplements.'

Holly nodded and smiled. *Be open-minded. Maybe a bit of a detox would be a good thing?* she thought as she eyed the half-eaten fudge cake on her plate and contemplated scoffing it down in one.

ONCE INSIDE THE HEALTH STORE, Ethan seemed to be in his element and really knowledgeable on the subject of supplements. The young assistant behind the counter, looked up a couple of times from his phone and appeared to be taking notes. Holly could not concentrate. All she was thinking about was the fast-approaching police visit, but not wanting to spoil Ethan's fun she oohed and ahhed in all the right places, trying not to gag when he asked her to sniff a jar of fermented vegetation.

Once outside she took in long deep breaths of fresh air, swinging the paper carrier containing her new supplement regime. As they walked in the direction of the car, an older guy in a tweed jacket smiled at them.

'Ethan, my boy, is that you?'

'Graham, hi.' Ethan stretched out his hand, stopping to talk.

'Glad I've caught you. I have a quick question.'

From the discussion, Holly guessed Graham was a client. Zoning out, she stood smiling sweetly. Remembering Tom's call, she pulled her phone from her pocket and walked a few paces leaning against a wall. Maybe his silence over the past few days was positive, and he had come to his senses? Her phone indicated he had left her a message so she called her voicemail.

'You have one new message and no saved messages. First

new message received today at one twenty-one.' Then came Tom's voice. 'I need to know what's happening. Are you selling up? Give me a call.'

Holly shook her head. 'My life isn't any of your business,' she said under her breath. Her blood felt cool in her veins. She was still shocked at how much Tom had changed. It hurt that she had given him so much and he did not seem to realise it. Whenever he came to mind, she saw pictures in her head of Grace. A pretty, tummy-bulging, pregnant Grace. Sighing, she returned her phone to her jacket pocket.

Holly woke from her thoughts as Ethan approached her.

'Sorry about that,' he said. 'I'm halfway through a job with him. Great guy and I'm hoping for some further work.'

Later, when they drew up in the nursery car park, Ethan glanced at her. 'Do you want me to stay until the police arrive?' He did not cut the engine therefore Holly presumed he was merely being polite.

She shook her head. 'I'll be fine. But thanks anyway and I'll let you know what happens,' she said. She still had over an hour until Erin was due, but she needed to prepare.

'Don't worry, I'm sure it'll be fine.' Ethan leaned over and pecked her on the cheek.

No shiver, no spark, she thought as she smiled at him and got out of the car. His Maserati crunched the gravel as he pulled away.

Letting herself into the caravan, Holly felt it certainly had a homely atmosphere to it. She felt safe here. She could see her things – even if they were new things. At least she had some possessions. She put the bag of supplements into her cupboard. Ethan had generously paid for them, although she knew he had wasted his money. She was unlikely to be using them. Picking up a notebook from the table Holly read through the list she had collated earlier for

Gary, detailing all the items in the studio on the day of the fire.

As the time approached four, she heard the sound of a vehicle outside and observed the police car entering the car park. Erin Bartlett stepped out, her dark hair was tied back in a pony tail. She stopped and put her hat on. Holly opened the door before she knocked.

Erin climbed the steps into the caravan. 'I need to run over the events of the day of the fire. I also need to make a note of anyone who was present that day. It is not formal at this stage, I'll call you into the station, if I need to question you further.'

Holly's mouth felt dry. She hoped she would not be dragged in for an interrogation. Her face coloured up. *Why am I acting guilty?* she thought as she moved a stray curl from her hot forehead.

Erin sat on Holly's soft seating and opened her note-book. 'How did the day of the fire start?'

Holly sat at the table. 'I had breakfast early. Then I logged some artwork in my studio.'

'Why were you logging your artwork? For insurance purposes?'

Holly closed her eyes, took a deep breath then reopened them. 'No, I recorded them for prospective competitions.'

'Okay.' Erin scribbled in her notebook. 'So then what?'

'I spent a couple of hours digging over my vegetable patch.'

'Did you see anyone?'

'We were busy. I saw quite a few customers from a distance. I couldn't possibly identify everyone here that day.'

'I assume you provide card facilities? Would your customers have paid by card?'

'Well, yes, most people do use contactless these days.'

The last thing Holly wanted was for the police to hassle her customers.

'Do you have any CCTV? An alarm system?'

'No. If I did it would have been burned in the fire.'

Erin stared at her, flared her nostrils then poised her pen over her notebook. 'Okay. So you were digging. Were you doing this on your own?'

'Yes. The staff were here, taking care of the business for me.'

'I'll need a list of everyone on your payroll. Did anyone visit you personally that day?'

A picture of Mitch flashed into her mind.

'In particular, was there anyone you saw during the day that came to the scene when the fire was in progress? Arsonists like to watch the place burn. Or anyone who visited the site the following day? Viewing the burned buildings?'

Holly thought of Mitch, but remained silent.

'Holly?' Erin had a frown on her face.

'Oh sorry, I was just thinking. My staff obviously turned up for work the next day. And my best friend.'

'Name? Contact details?'

'Jasmine Swift. She's out of town at the moment with work in Liverpool.'

'So.' Erin scribbled in her book. 'She's left the area?'

'It was an electrical fault.' *How many more times do I have to say this?* she thought.

'And Jasmine's contact number is?' Erin asked, ignoring Holly's comment.

Holly shook her head as she gave Jaz's mobile number.

'Please give me the names of the others present.'

'Mitchell Booth, my neighbour.'

Erin smiled. 'Oh yes, it might be helpful to go through

events with him.' She paused as she made a note in her book. 'Anyone else, come to your house that day?'

Holly hesitated, she didn't want to bring him into it, but felt she had no choice. 'Tom Stone, my ex.'

Erin raised her eyebrows. 'Are you on good terms with Mr Stone?'

Here we go, Holly thought as she groaned. She regretted mentioning him. She feared he would be on the case, complicating everything. She did not want him muscling in on the claims process.

Erin's walkie-talkie buzzed and bleeped. Answering it, she spoke into the receiver attached to her chest. There was a burst of fuzzy feedback mixed with a voice that Holly could not hear properly.

Erin put her pen and notebook into her pocket and took in a deep breath. She stood up 'Thank you for your time. The fire service has now ruled out suspicious circumstances. I'll not keep you any longer.' Nodding at Holly, she left.

Holly felt stunned. She sat in silence for over a minute until her mobile vibrated in her damp hand. *Gary Cox Calling.*

'Hi, Gary.' She felt breathless.

'Holly, good news, I've still got to finalise the claim but I'm confident the insurance company will pay out.'

'Thank goodness. Thanks, so much for your help.'

'The thanks goes to that young man of yours, Ethan. He was at the fire station this afternoon. Has mates in the service, apparently.'

Holly ended the call. 'Yes!' She felt tears pricking her eyes. Ethan was definitely a great guy to have around. It was an alien feeling to her, accepting other people's help after having been used to doing everything for herself for so long and being the one who helped others. She would have to treat Ethan to a meal to say thank you.

Standing up, she gazed at the closed curtain above the sink which masked the blackened nursery buildings. Now she could dream. Dream about her rebuild and plan her future. Dream of the things she wanted to achieve. Pulling open the curtains, she took a sharp intake of breath. Tom was walking up the path to the burned property with a suited guy in tow.

CHAPTER 11

*H*olly stared at Tom as he stood on her land. She put her hand to her mouth, her heart thudding at speed. The man accompanying Tom carried a clipboard. *What is he playing at?* She thought as she took deep breaths. Standing up, she smoothed her hair back. *Stay calm, be the better person,* she told herself.

She remembered what her Mum used to say when she had been bullied in primary school. *Hold your head up high, love. Don't let them know you're scared.*

Feeling a surge of strength, she moved towards the door. 'This is my land, my family's land,' she said to herself.

Holly stomped around the periphery of the caravan towards the two men. Tom turned as she neared him. His eyes widened and he ran a hand through his hair.

'I've caught him off guard. Good,' she mumbled.

'I didn't realise you were here,' he said as she reached him.

'Of course, I'm here. Where did you think I'd be? I live here.'

Tom pointed to the caravan. 'In that?'

'Yes, in that. Now cut the small talk. What's going on?' Holly heard her voice becoming louder, her hands were clenched in fists at her side.

Tom put his hands up. 'Let's stay civilised here.'

'If this isn't a good time.' The man in the suit pressed his clipboard close to his chest.

Holly looked him up and down. He had a tight, snappy blue suit, a crisp white shirt, a cerise tie and highly polished shoes with a beard so neat, it looked sprayed on. 'And you are?'

The man stuck out his hand. 'Jack from Bliss and Dunt.'

She had heard the name of the estate agency before; they were based in Wells. Holly left his hand hanging. 'I think there's been a misunderstanding, Jack.' She placed her hands on her hips. 'This property is not for sale and I'm the sole proprietor so if you would care to leave, as swiftly as possible, that would be perfect.'

Holly's teeth clenched together as she told herself to breathe. She attempted a smile but from the reaction shown on the estate agent's face, she guessed she was just baring her teeth. Jack mumbled something to Tom, then hurried down the path.

Tom raked his hand through his hair. 'Well done. Why are you stopping things from progressing? It's mad. We both need to get on with our lives.'

'What are you on about? I'm not selling. I'm rebuilding.'

'It'll cost a frigging fortune. The insurance won't cover it and the cottage'll never be the same.' He pointed to the remains of her family home. 'Will it?'

Holly followed Tom's gaze over to the wreckage. Every day she avoided looking at the cottage. But gazing at it now, the stark black pile jumped out at her. A tear stung her eye. 'You've no idea what I've planned for the rebuild.'

Tom laughed. 'Of course I have. You've been banging on about that gallery idea since we got married. It isn't viable. You can't afford to run a not-for-profit.'

Holly felt her body tremble in a deep, all-consuming rumble. Leaning forward, she moved her arms to push Tom away. He stepped to one side. Not wanting to hold on to him to steady herself, she fell in what felt like slow motion until the crisp dried mud stung the palms of her hands as her body slammed to the ground.

Momentarily stunned, she lay blinking. Tom's arm came into her vision. She slapped his hand away, scrambling to her knees.

Tom spoke in a patronising voice. 'I know it's hard. And I've let you down. You're bound to be upset. But I never thought you'd resort to violence.'

Holly rose to her feet. Her knees were sore and her hands were grazed and covered in dirt. 'Get off my property and keep away from me.' She pushed her hair out of her face smearing dusty mud onto her cheeks.

'I'm going to have to report this. You need to learn how to have a sensible discussion as we will have to agree a settlement.'

'You only ever took from me, Tom. You're getting nothing.'

He stepped backwards. 'We'll talk later.'

Holly moved towards him. 'No. I'm done with you. If you want to speak to me about repayment of the money I loaned you, then fine, I'll talk. Other than that? Leave and don't ever come back.'

Tom walked away. 'You've given me no choice.'

Holly shook as she watched him get into his car and drive off.

'I paid for that car too,' she screamed after him. The

tears tumbled down her cheeks, as soon as he was out of sight.

❦

HOLLY WOKE the following morning in the main part of the caravan. Her body ached and head hurt as she viewed the empty bottle of fizz, a home-warming gift from Joe that had been in the fridge. Hearing voices from outside, she remembered the staff were coming in to finish off the pots. Peeping through the curtain, she groaned at the sight of the cottage, bringing back memories of Tom the previous day. She glanced at the grazes on her palms, which looked less angry, but were still sore.

Half an hour later, Holly walked over to her staff, feeling much better, having showered and dressed in fresh jeans and a floral T-shirt. She had donned a pair of sunglasses, it was a lovely sunny day and a couple of painkillers dulled her throbbing head.

Joe waved as she approached him. Smiling, he thumbed over his shoulder. 'Do you want to come and see what we've done?'

'Of course.'

As Holly followed Joe, she brought him up to date on the insurance and told him that Tom had been sniffing around. As they approached the planting area, she could see Julie and Anne watering pots. Holly was impressed at the colourful spread. Val had not been in for work as she avoided the heavy jobs, which were not appropriate at eighty-two. *I must get over and see her*, she thought.

Holly clapped her hands together. 'Wow, they look amazing, guys!'

There were at least thirty pots filled with pinks, blues,

yellows and lilacs. She felt guilty. She should have joined in more and worked with the team. Picking up a trowel, she fetched one of the empty pots, realising it was time to get her act into gear.

After an hour of potting, Holly began to feel more like her old self. Her mobile dinged with a text from Ethan. She had messaged him the night before to thank him for his help with the insurance, although she avoided telling him about Tom's visit. She did not want to sound like the forever victim. They had rearranged her design session for the coming afternoon.

Pick you up at three – I'll bring you back here and use my software to help draft your plans xx

Holly's heart dropped slightly, even though she felt excited about her plans. She looked down the hill to the farmhouse, wondering where Mitch was. *This isn't helping,* she thought. She had to focus. The Mitch crush – was a distraction. She fetched a fresh tray of plants. *Just keep on track,* she told herself.

HOLLY PUT a hand on the dash of Ethan's car as he swerved at speed down a road which felt so small, it was as if she was on a toboggan run. If a car came in the opposite direction it would have been impossible for it to pass.

I wish I'd driven myself over, she thought. Even if it would have been a tight squeeze for her van, at least she would be driving slower. Her stomach churned and just as she thought she would be sick, the road opened out into a clearing and a house came into view. It was a sleek building backed by trees. The house reminded Holly of two huge shoe boxes – one stacked at an angle on top of the other, clad in wood. It seemed out of place, yet also sympathetic to the surroundings. As they got closer, the wood shone and huge floor-to-ceiling windows reflected the sun. Ethan parked up and walked around to help Holly out of the car. She felt uneasy with his over-gentlemanly nature but appreciated it, as she struggled to get out of the car's bucket seats. Her Ford Transit might not be pretty but it was a lot more practical.

'I love your place.' Holly pointed at his home. 'I assume you designed it yourself?'

Ethan nodded and smiled. 'I'm glad you like it.' He gazed into her eyes.

'So beautiful,' she said, quickly turning away to focus on the surroundings.

Holly noticed as Ethan gave her a tour of his house that, whilst it was indeed beautiful in a contemporary way, the inside was rather empty. As if no-one lived there. The floors were hard, with stone downstairs and wood upstairs. It was open-plan, with few dividing walls. The dining table was long and boardroom-like. The windows were massive, with huge white curtains which billowed in the wind like tall ghosts as Ethan opened them. The only area that appeared lived-in was his bedroom. The bed was slightly ruffled, a huge TV was affixed to the wall with a games console attached. Free-weights were piled in the corner and a towel lay discarded on the floor. *This is where he lives then?* she thought.

What she could not fault though was the view. It took her breath away as she gazed out to the sweeping landscape of hills, trees and farming land with Glastonbury Tor in the distance. Ethan approach from behind.

She turned. 'It's breath-taking.'

'You're breath-taking too, stood in the window like that.'

Ethan smiled at her. 'I fancied you like mad at college. You know that, right?'

Holly gave a nervous laugh. 'Er ... no?'

'But then all the lads wanted to get with you.' Ethan stepped back.

Holly breathed out.

'Sorry, I didn't mean to crowd you.'

Holly felt her face colour up. 'No worries. It's just a bit soon. You know – since Tom?'

'Of course.' Ethan clasped his hands. 'Let's get downstairs, then. I'll show you the plans I've started.'

She followed him towards his office area, feeling a trickle of sweat travel down her spine.

THEY BEGAN work on the plans. Holly explained that she wanted to rebuild the nursery buildings, making use of the remaining stone walls that were still there, albeit in a blackened state. But she wanted the art barn to be a modern space. The plans Ethan had prepared were impressive and he had clearly put many hours of work into them but they were a lot starker than Holly's vision. She spent time explaining her ideas, as Ethan adjusted the computer drawings to more of what she had in mind. This included a relaxation area, a zen garden and clearly-defined spaces. Holly relaxed into it and Ethan reminded her much more of the old Ethan – the one she had worked with in college. As the sun dipped below the horizon, it created an orange hue over the house. They sat back, looking at the computer screen.

'That's amazing. Thanks so much.' Holly smiled, feeling a warm sensation inside.

'A lot different to my original design. You've obviously been thinking about this for months.'

'A couple of years, actually. It's what kept me going after Mum and Dad passed. They gave me the gift of life and the nursery. I want to give back to others. To make myself feel good, I guess. Because since my parents died ...' Holly felt a lump form in her throat.

Ethan put a hand on hers.

Holly took a drink from a glass of water. 'You've really brought it to life with this programme. Thanks. I'm impressed and truly grateful.'

Ethan rose, stepped back from the computer desk and stretched. 'You know this is going to cost more than the insurance pay-out?'

Holly took a deep breath. 'Yes. I was saving up for it. But, as I said, I stupidly lent the money to Tom.'

'There's always the bank.'

'True. I need a business plan. But I feel they'll want an income stream before they lend me anything. That's why I'm setting up temporary retail sheds, away from the damage, to get the nursery back up and running.'

'You sound fired up, I'm sure you're going to pull it off. Let's celebrate new beginnings.' Ethan beckoned her to follow him. Holly walked behind him, towards the kitchen area, wanting to slip into the conversation that she was ready to go home.

Ethan pulled a bottle of bubbly from the huge Ameri-can-style fridge. 'Do you want to stay over?'

Holly bit her lip.

Ethan smiled. 'It'll be like the old days, at my Mum's house. You'll be in the spare room, of course.'

A poem came into Holly's mind, from her childhood. One about a spider trying to tempt a fly into its parlour. But she had not seen Ethan drink any alcohol, with him being on water most of the time, due to driving. Clearly, he wanted a relaxing glass of fizz or two.

'I could rustle us up a pasta dish?' Ethan reached into the fridge and took out various ingredients. 'Peppers, onions ...' Naming them, as he placed them on the worktop as if presenting a cookery show.

What's wrong with me? Holly thought. She knew Ethan was a great guy. He had spent a lot of time on her, got her out of a pickle with the insurance and it was not as if they would be sharing a bed.

'I know your situation and I'm not going to force myself on you. We'll have a chilled evening.'

She did not fancy being driven home in his car, at great speed, along dark country lanes. Ethan popped the cork and poured the bubbly liquid into champagne flutes.

Holly took a glass. 'Okay, but I'm quite tired, I won't be able to drink too many of these.' She took a sip.

Ethan smiled. 'Don't worry, it's non-alcoholic.'

HOLLY SMILED as her caravan came into view. It was slowly feeling like her place, which was a good thing since she imagined she would be living in it for some time to come. Ethan killed the engine and jumped out and sped around to her side of the car. Determined to avoid his help, she hoisted herself out of the seat but he reached her in lightning speed and grabbed her hand, pulling her up with such force that she found herself slap against his chest. With their similar heights, they were at eye level.

'It was great to spend time with you again. I had an amazing evening,' Ethan said, gazing into her eyes.

'Sorry if I wasn't that much fun,' Holly said. 'Falling asleep like that, after dinner.'

'Holly, you're always perfect company.' Ethan leaned forward pressing his lips to hers. Holly would have turned her head if she was able to, however he held her in a vice-like embrace. She pecked him back, attempting to make it friendly. He leaned forward again, as if going in for something a tad more passionate, but she wriggled free before it developed.

Ethan laughed. Taking her hand, he rubbed it. 'I know. Take it slow.'

'There's no need to see me in. Thanks again, Ethan, for the plans.' She retrieved her hand.

'Don't forget the print-outs.' Ethan reached into the car, fishing out a folder. 'I've emailed you the originals, for when you replace your computer. Remember, I'm happy to lend you a laptop.'

'Thanks. But there's no need for that. I'm hoping to hear from the insurance company soon.'

Ethan drove off the nursery property with a toot. As soon as Holly entered the caravan, she plopped herself on the soft seating. Reaching for her mobile phone she scrolled to Jaz's number. Jaz had called and Holly had let it go to voicemail, sending her a text to say she was at Ethan's.

Jaz answered immediately. 'Hi, hun.'

'How are you getting on with your new job?' Holly asked.

'Fine. What I want to know is, how are you?'

'Ethan and I worked on the plans for the arts hub yesterday. It was amazing, they really came to life. You should see them.'

'Yeah, yeah. He showed you his sketches. Did he kiss you?'

'Jaz, please.'

'You never did? You didn't stay the night? Did you?'

Holly paused.

'You mucky mare,' Jaz said.

'For goodness' sake. I'm not about to jump into bed with anyone at this moment in my life. We had a nice evening, that's all. I stayed in the spare room. Nothing else to tell.'

'Okay. But did he try it on?'

Holly flashed back to the awkward kiss with Ethan.

'Hello? Liverpool to Holly?'

'Just a peck.'

'I knew it. And?'

'And nothing.'

'Come on, tell me. Hot? Passionate? Sloppy? Sexy? Details, please.'

Holly thought of the kiss. There had been no fireworks. But not all kisses were like that, were they? Fireworks never went off whenever she had kissed Tom, either. It'd been comforting at a time when she was lonely.

'You still there? You keep going quiet.'

'I'm not in the right frame of mind for a relationship, Jaz. Ethan's great, but –'

There was a knock at the caravan door.

'Sorry, Jaz, someone's here. I'll call tonight. What's the best time?'

'Seven.'

Holly ended the call, placing the phone on the table. She walked to the caravan window. It was Mitch.

CHAPTER 12

*M*itch saw Holly's face at the caravan window. He smiled, wishing he had not just seen her from a distance in what looked like a kiss with that flash bloke. The caravan door opened and Trixy went wild.

Holly laughed. 'It's nice to be so popular.'

He turned his head to the sound of a vehicle drawing up. It was a post office van. 'Here, you take Trixy and I'll fetch your post.' As he passed the dog lead to Holly his arm brushed against her soft skin. He swallowed and then walked towards the car park as a woman got out, dressed in the usual red and grey uniform.

'Hi there, one signed for and two regulars.' She handed over a black chunky tablet and he scribbled on it with his finger. Taking the letters, he walked back to the caravan. Holly stood in the doorway watching and smiling. *I wish she wouldn't smile like that,* he thought as his body reacted.

Holly stretched out her hand and took the envelopes from him. Removing his boots, he followed her in.

'I'll just make us a drink and get water for this little rascal.' Holly scratched Trixy's head.

Holly poured water for Trixy into a dessert bowl as the little dog's tail wagged at speed. Mitch wondered what had happened between Holly and Maserati man. Had they spent the night together? Holly appeared a lot less stressed. In fact, she seemed to glow as she smiled at him. *Maybe she's really hitting it off with that guy,* he thought.

'I've got something to show you,' she said flicking on the kettle.

He watched her open a folder and pass him various sheets of paper. 'These are the plans for the nursery rebuild, to include an arts hub. I'm so excited.'

Mitch studied the designs in his hands. 'They're really detailed.'

'Ethan created them with professional software.' She pushed her hair away from her face. 'He's my architect and ... friend from college. You met him the other day, remember?'

Mitch looked at the plans. 'They're extremely profes-sional.' *He's not just a pretty face then,* he thought. 'I'm glad things are moving along for you.'

Holly poured out the hot drinks and passed him a mug, placing hers on the worktop. 'I'd better open these,' she said, picking up the first envelope.

Mitch turned his head to see Trixy, making herself comfortable on Holly's soft seating. 'No, Trixy. Down.'

'That's fine,' Holly said. 'She's on the throw, it'll be going in the wash at some point.' Holly opened the letter. Her face broke into a broad smile and she waved it above her head. 'Written confirmation of my insurance claim. The business interruption insurance will kick in now, so I'll get a monthly payment for staff wages and living expenses. They've asked for a list of the items I'm replacing immediately, so I can get an interim payment.'

'Great news. So they stopped the enquiries into accelerants then?'

'Ethan knew someone at the fire brigade, who pulled
some strings.'

Typical, he thought.

Holly picked up the next envelope. Mitch watched her
face as, the colour left her cheeks.

'Are you okay?' Mitch leaned forward.

Holly shook her head, passing the letter to Mitch. The
paper was thick and embossed. He read the first line.

*We act on behalf of your husband Thomas Stone and set out
below, proposals for the financial separation.* He lifted his gaze
back to Holly.

'He wants half of everything I own. Even a share of the
van. He's got a nerve.'

'You need to find a decent solicitor to act for you. How
long were you married?'

'A year this month.'

'If you need any help ...' Mitch watched Holly shaking
her head and fought off the urge to take her in his arms.

She frowned at the last envelope. 'This one is recorded
delivery. More bad news knowing my luck.' She turned the
envelope over. 'It's from the Council, probably a parking
fine.' Tearing it open, her eyes opened wide as the page fluttered in her hand.

'Not more bad news?'

Holly moved the letter closer to her eyes, as if she was
trying to focus on it. 'It's from Wells Council, congratulating
me on making the short list for the *Beauty of Somerset*
competition.'

Mitch grinned, 'I knew you could do it.'

'How? I never entered.' She peered up at him, her eyes
narrowing. Then she grinned. 'You entered it?'

'I thought it would help.' Mitch swallowed.

'But how did they accept it? After the deadline?'

'It was touch and go. I've had to volunteer to sit on a rural business committee.'

Holly laughed. 'I've managed to avoid those for years.' She approached him, he stood up and she wrapped her arms around him. Mitch felt a jolt through his body as she pressed against him. He could smell the scent of her shampoo, feel the smooth skin of her arms and softness of her against his chest. Under different circumstances he would now be lifting her chin and going in for a kiss, but he was not clear about her relationship with Ethan. But neither did he want to let go, so he remained there with his arms around her. Hoping she was oblivious to how deep his heart was thudding or how much he was attracted to her. Trixy yapped, jumping up at their legs, but they ignored her.

THE FOLLOWING DAY, Mitch sat on a low brick wall outside the farmhouse eating a slice of toast with butter and marmalade. He had been up at dawn to oversee the workers and had popped back for a bite to eat. There had been a few issues up at the sheds and also on the land with the crops. He knew he had been neglecting his duties by letting things tick over. But he did not want to undermine the new herdsman or existing staff, deciding to let the dust settle before he implemented any changes.

However, the time to move matters up a gear had arrived. The staff were now indicating a willingness for change. Government grants could also be cut as part of the ever-changing economic climate, all of which needed contingency plans. It was time to step things up a gear. He had big plans.

Looking up the hill towards the nursery, Mitch thought of the proposition he had in mind for Holly. He decided to approach her later that day. As he returned to work, Vanessa flashed into his mind. Again, the familiar sickly feeling of guilt ebbed into his chest. Did he deserve success after what had happened to her?

THAT AFTERNOON MITCH walked through the gap in the wall between the Loveland and Booth properties. He left Trixy at home. She had been sleeping next to Sidney and he did not want to disturb either of them. Magda had been in the conservatory reading, so was around if Trixy was a nuisance.

He stopped dead when he saw Ethan's Maserati parked in the corner of the nursery car park.

The caravan door swung open. Ethan stepped out followed by Holly. He watched as Ethan leaned towards her. Mitch moved away, but Holly called out to him.

'Mitch, hi.'

He turned around and she beckoned him over beaming. Ethan nodded at Mitch, as he passed.

'I had a call this morning from the Council about the awards night,' Holly said as he reached the caravan door. 'I'd like you to come with me as my guest. It's a full presentation with a meal, drinks and a talk from the Arts Council.'

'Don't you think you should take your – friend?' Mitch nodded towards Ethan as he drove away, with a hoot of his horn.

Holly bit her lip. 'Ethan? No, it wouldn't seem right. Not with you having entered me.'

Mitch's eyes widened and he saw Holly blush as the last line echoed in his mind.

'The painting. Entered the painting,' Holly said quickly

'Sure,' he said trying not to laugh. 'I'd love to. I've nothing in my social diary, so I'm sure I'll be free. *Do I sound like a saddo? he* thought. 'I came up to ask you about something.' Mitch rubbed the back of his neck.

'Come in.' Holly's voice sounded a higher pitch than usual. 'No Trixy today?'

Mitch followed her into the caravan then stared at her as she stood against the table. He felt an overwhelming urge to hold her close again. To tell her that over the past week he had felt like a different person. To tell her that he actually wanted to get up in the mornings. To tell her that he always took Trixy for a walk near her property in case he might bump into her. Then he remembered Ethan. A silence fell between them.

Holly clapped her hands together. 'I've just got to make a couple of calls, then we can talk. Take a seat or feel free to help yourself to anything in the fridge.'

Mitch listened to Holly chat on the phone as she discussed her rebuild with a contractor. Mitch checked out the contents of her fridge, to make it appear as if he was not listening. Chocolate, ham, some salad items and a huge block of cheese. Even if he was tempted he would not raid her fridge. He turned and watched her as she paced the caravan as she spoke. He was desperate for things to be okay for her, and longed to hold her again.

He made tea and by the time it was ready Holly had ended her calls. Mitch carried the mugs outside and Holly followed, clutching a pen and a few sheets of paper. They sat on the bench and Mitch held the hot drinks.

'This is what I do,' Holly said, waving the paper. 'When

things get tough, I write everything down that needs to be done. It doesn't seem so big when you can fit it all on one page. Or two. Or maybe three.' She laughed, as she took the cup of tea he passed her.

When Holly laughed, it did something to Mitch inside and he fought down the images flashing through his mind. *Get a grip, man, you're supposed to be doing business here,* he told himself as he shook away the thoughts. He looked away and over at the view of the fields. The scene which reminded him of Holly's landscape.

'When the Council return the painting, can I keep it?'

'Of course you can,' she said. 'I've already given it to you once.' Holly laughed and he could feel her body brush against his arm.

After a short silence he turned to her. 'Now I've settled at the farm. I'm going to implement changes. Parts of the business model I introduced in Essex increased the income stream.'

'Sounds interesting.'

'I intend to open new lines of business. After I left agricultural college, I shook things up back home. The whole organic thing was big back then, but organic farming is a nightmare.'

'I used to buy organic,' Holly said. 'But now, I just buy locally produced food. Most of that tastes really good anyway.'

'Exactly. *Local tasty food* is slapped across our branding.'

Holly smiled at him.

He was momentarily put off his thoughts. He leaned down and picked up his tea, taking a gulp. 'I was thinking of trialling a farm shop,' he said resting his mug on the arm of the bench. 'If that's a success, I'll introduce a small box scheme.' The food delivery service he introduced in Booth

Essex had earned him respect both within the family and the community. Indeed, it had led to him becoming a director of the family business. His mother had taken over the day to day running of the box scheme in recent months.

'A farmers' market is a great idea. We have to trudge to Wells for our fresh supplies. Those in the village without cars have to get the bus for non-supermarket veg.'

'The thing is, Booth Farm isn't as accessible as your land. And there are all sorts of hoops to jump through to add retail to our land. So I was thinking ...'

'You're after my property?' Holly put her tea down on the floor and it tipped over, running into the grass. Sitting up, she folded her arms.

'No. Trust me, this Booth is not after buying Loveland property.'

'So that's what you understand the arguments were all about?' Holly placed her hands on her lap. Her eyes taking on a childlike expression. 'Is the property dispute the reason Sid hates me?'

Mitch paused. He knew there was more to it than that. But decided to steer clear of family gossip. 'I don't think he actually hates you. But yes, I guess so. But I don't want to buy your land, I only want to rent a spot.'

Holly bit her lip.

He realised he needed to sell the idea to her. 'I see it as a mutually beneficial project. I don't expect you to make any decisions now, not with everything you have going on. It's just something to mull over.' The last thing he wanted was for her to make a decision and then change her mind later down the line. Although, being honest with himself, he had questioned his motives, since he spent a lot of his days wracking his brain for any excuse to spend time with her.

'I'm not sure I want to give up control of any of my property, even if it is a short-term tenancy.'

Watching Holly scowl, Mitch was reminded of her from his childhood days, when they used to chat over the boundary wall. He couldn't help it, he wanted to get to know her more. To spend time with her – to get close to her. 'Could we come to some sort of business partnership agreement? You hold the market on your land. I supply my produce and source in goods from neighbouring farms. We split the profits?'

Holly's face widened into a huge grin. 'Oh my goodness. Yes, that sounds amazing.' Holly stood up. 'As well as the area we've cleared to sell the stock, we're setting up a café shed, for teas and coffees.' She gestured around her land. 'This would fit perfectly.' She put her hands to her cheeks, which flushed pink.

Mitch watched an animated Holly, sketch on her paper.

Two hours later, not only had Holly completed her list of things to do but they had a plan to move the farmers' market forward, including the layout and location. They ate together outside the caravan, sitting at a table and chairs that Mitch had help Holly carry over from the old barn. Holly made him a Ploughman's, with thick ham and tasty cheese from nearby Cheddar.

'Your list of things to do is huge.' Mitch took a sip from a bottle of beer. 'If there's anything I can do?'

'The most pressing things, I have to do alone, I'm afraid. Like sort out a divorce solicitor.'

'Do you not have a family solicitor?'

'Yes, but I'm not sure divorce is his thing. There's a solicitor's office above a shop owned by a friend of mine. Apparently, she's a hot-shot when it comes to divorce.'

'It's not five yet, maybe you should call her?'

Holly put down her knife and fork and wiped her hands on a sheet of kitchen paper. 'You're right, I do need to book that now. Hang on.'

Mitch watched her walk up the short steps into the caravan. He chased a pickled onion around his plate with his fork, then gave up. Picking it up, he popped it into his mouth.

'That's sorted then. Two o'clock Monday morning.' Holly stood in the doorway.

'That was quick.'

'I just caught her before she left. Her name is Jill Dawkins. That's one job done off the list.' Holly walked down the short steps and picked up the plates.

Mitch smiled. *If only every teatime could be like this,* he thought as he glanced at the time on his phone, knowing he should get back. Trixy was probably playing Magda havoc, while she would be getting Sid's supper ready.

'Thanks so much for tea. I'm feeling positive about the farmers' market,' Mitch said as he stood up. 'And with your insurance being agreed And now a hot-shot solicitor helping you out – I'm sure you'll be back on your feet in no time. I'll have to be off now, but good luck tomorrow. If you need anything – just call.'

Holly smiled. She hesitated and then gave him the lightest peck on the cheek. He felt a rush inside, but resisted the urge to pull her close. It was much more than the farmers' market exciting him. As he reached his farmland, he looked back over his shoulder, feeling a sadness. Why did Holly have to find someone else so soon, before he could get to know her again?

CHAPTER 13

*H*olly passed the shop 'Something Special', her insides churning as she remembered seeing Tom standing outside with Grace. It seemed like a lifetime away. Luckily, Nina was not visible. She was probably helping someone with a dress fitting. Nina often joked about downstairs doing the weddings and upstairs sorting out the mess when things turned sour. Holly wondered how many other customers from the bridal store had walked up these stairs.

Opening the glass-filled door etched with *Dawkins & Co, Solicitors,* she felt as if she was stepping back in time as she entered the reception. It was furnished with an array of polished antique furniture, including a huge desk where a young guy sat, reading a celebrity gossip magazine. The sort of thing she only read in the dentist's waiting room.

He raised his eyes and smiled. 'Hi, is it Holly Loveland?'

'Yes, I'm a bit early.'

'Early is great. I'm Oliver,' he said, standing up and pulling a file from a cabinet. He took out a sheet of paper, handing it to Holly. 'Can you fill this in, please? All the usual particulars. Jill's free, so as soon as you're done, I'll take you in.'

Holly sat on a large leather Chesterfield and filled in the form. Name, address, date of birth, status? She paused. *Separated, I guess?* she thought as she heard the tick tock of a huge grandfather clock, standing to the side of the door like a sentry post.

'Have you worked here long?' she asked Oliver.

He tapped away at his keyboard. 'I came here last summer for a job between college and university. I never left.'

Holly handed him the completed form. 'You must like it then?'

'Yes, Jill's my aunt. We're on a better wavelength than I am with my parents.' He smiled. 'Well let's take you in, shall we?'

Oliver opened the door for her. Jill stood up from her desk with her hand outstretched. She was mid-forties, her dark hair, streaked with grey, was cut in a stylish crop. She wore a blue pinstripe shirt and navy tailored trousers.

Holly took her hand. 'Pleased to meet you.'

Jill's grip was quite firm. 'Likewise. Do have a seat.'

Holly heard the door close behind her and passed over the letter she had received from Tom's solicitor. 'I received this two days ago.'

Jill donned a pair of metal-framed glasses and read the letter. At times she raised her shaped eyebrows, then pursed her lips. Placing the letter on the table she brought her hands together as if praying. 'Really and truly, they're trying it on. Ballsy lot. Well known for this sort of approach.' Jill leaned back in her chair. 'They go on the offensive, hoping for a settlement, but rarely go to court. I'm not fond of their methods and that goes in your favour.' Jill peered over her glasses at Holly. 'I will not let them ride rough-shod over one of my clients.' Jill picked the letter up again. 'I propose we stick to our guns. Tell them to jolly well get lost and see what happens.'

'Right. So, he isn't entitled?'

'Well, you can argue anything in law. But given the short marriage, the adultery, and that this is your business and only means of support, it's unlikely. We'll fight it. Send him off with the bare minimum.'

'Okay.'

'The way his solicitor works is to run you down until you cave in to at least a small offer. But this bunch of cowboys don't really have the expertise to back up their arguments at a full hearing.'

'I don't think I owe him anything. In fact, he borrowed a large sum of money from me to start up his own business and is refusing to give it back.'

'Is that so? I'll draft a letter, telling them point-blank we do not accept that he has a claim against you. I warn you, the response won't be pretty. They'll hit you hard and bring in all sorts of accusations. But we'll deal with that at the time. The big question is. Do you want me to act on your behalf?'

Holly nodded.

'Excellent. I'll get Oliver to put a date in the diary and we'll meet again in order to gain a full run-down of the relationship.'

'Thanks. I definitely want you to deal with this for me.'

Jill smiled. 'Super. I'll ask them to correspond with me direct in future. That way, you won't be bothered by anything at home. It's a tough time, considering the distress you must feel after the fire. But it will pass.' She pushed a document forward. 'Now here's my letter of engagement. Read it through carefully and I'll ask Oliver to bring us coffee.'

Holly read through the document smarting at the hourly rate, but she liked Jill. She made the whole messy situation sound like just another day at the office. Holly drank her coffee and signed the form. Jill asked her not to discuss the position directly with Tom. That would be easy – she never wanted to speak to him again.

Once outside, Holly walked in the direction of the bakery, ducking her head to avoid Nina's gaze as she passed the front of the bridal boutique. Hearing rapping on the window, she turned her head and Nina beckoned her in but Holly shook her head and mouthed *I can't*. Nina made a heart shape with her fingers before placing her hands to her chest. Holly forced a smile and walked away. She could not face the pity. Whilst Nina was not her favourite person on the planet, she knew she was being sincere. She also knew that, in Nina's world, no woman's life was complete unless she had a man in it, even though Nina herself was single. Whilst Nina always seemed to be surrounded by men, Holly had never known her to have a serious relationship. She always said she was waiting for 'Mr Right'.

At the bakery, Holly picked up three slices of lemon drizzle cake. She was off to Val's with her laundry.

'Come here, young'un.' Val opened her arms wide at her front door. 'I feel so much better to see you. I hate being cooped up in here, without me job to go to.'

'I'm working on that, Val.'

'Well come in. Let's get that wash on. You've got at least a couple of loads there.'

Holly bent down and picked up her dirty clothes and bedding, which she had stuffed into two black bin liners. Once inside, calm trickled over her like a warm shower. She used to stay with Val and Len as a child when her parents were away or out for the evening. Val lived at the end of a 1930's cul-de-sac sprouting from the village green. Her family had been in the house since it was built and Val had been born there. Unlike the other cul-de-sacs, *The Laurels* was untouched by incomers.

'Are you after tea or coffee?' Val called as she went to the kitchen.

'Coffee.' Holly followed with her bags.

'That's good news, I knows if you're drinking coffee, you're in a good mood – tea's for when you're sad.'

'I wouldn't say good mood. Maybe a determined mood.' Holly dumped the black bags on the floor. 'I'm having issues with Tom.'

Val shook her head and muttered as Holly told her about her meeting with Jill. As soon as the first load was in the machine, they moved to the sitting room to drink their coffee accompanied by the delicious lemon drizzle. The extra slice was left for Len who was out at a bowls match. Holly filled Val in on the rest of her week, and spent a lot more time talking about Mitch and the farmers' market.

Val sat in her chair animated. 'You know what, love? It'd be great if there was a joint Loveland-Booth thing after all that nonsense that's been going on for years.'

'What was it all about, exactly?'

Val paused. 'Only a load of old silliness. Arguments over land and what have you. Anyway, we don't need to bother with all that. What's happened to Sidney Booth, anyway? I heard he was poorly.'

'Yes, really poorly. He's practically skin and bone these days, poor man. Mitch has taken over the management of the farm, so the family can decide whether it's viable to keep it when Sidney passes. That's why he's exploring additional income streams. Because as things stand, the farm isn't making a profit. But back to Sidney – he's wholly dependent on his carer now. Her name's Magda, I met her the other day.' Holly paused. 'And I spoke to Sidney but he was quite rude. Magda said he's usually rather sweet. Wouldn't it be good if he could come to the farmers' market?'

Val snorted. 'I don't think that one will be coming anywhere near your place – ever.'

Holly opened her mouth to press her for more details, but Val looked towards the door. 'The first wash's nearly done.' She started to get out of her chair as the thundering from the kitchen ended and the machine made a large clicking noise. She was nearly to standing when she swayed and plopped back down into the chair again.

'Are you okay?' Holly stood up.

'Just a bit dizzy, love. Usual aches and pains. I'm old. Nothing out of the ordinary.'

'Maybe you need to see the doctor?'

'Nonsense, I'm eighty-two, love. It's old age.'

'You stay put. I'll sort it.' Holly noticed Val wincing. *I really need to get her to the surgery,* she thought.

Holly removed the clothes from the machine and transferred them to Val's tumble dryer. She much preferred her clothes to dry in the wind, but rain was forecast and there was no way it would dry in time.

Back in the lounge, Holly told Val about Mitch losing his wife in an accident. But Val had already heard about it.

'Jaz was right when she said I'd never make a Miss Marple,' Holly said. 'I always seemed to be the last to know about the local news.'

Val filled her in on some village gossip about the antiques auction house but Holly zoned out, eventually drifting off to sleep on the sofa.

Waking later, Holly found her clothes and bedlinen had been cleaned, dried and folded into neat piles. After a quick chat with Len, who was wolfing down his cake, she thanked Val for her help with the washing and headed home.

IT WAS the weekend and Jaz was back in town. Holly rapped on her apartment door which swung open and Jaz pulled her in for a hug.

'Whoa, let me in first,' Holly laughed.

'I'm so pleased to be back. It's nice helping the guys and all, but I don't want to be away forever. I really don't.'

Jaz took Holly by the hand and dragged her inside. Upon Jaz's white breakfast bar was a huge glass of white wine.

Holly raised her eyebrows. 'It's only ten.'

'I know. Not good is it? I don't know what to do. I love the job title, *National Training Manager*, but I don't like living out of a suitcase, even if it is a Louis Vuitton.' She took a sip of her wine. 'I want my old life back, battling for sales with my boys.'

'Just tell them. They won't sack you, you're their shining star.'

'I don't want to let them down, hun.'

'You're not letting anyone down. You know what you do best. And so do they.'

Jaz took another sip of wine and ran a hand over her

kitchen worktop. 'Sean told me sales were down at our showroom this week. Paul's going ballistic at the lads.'

'So, he'll jump at the chance of getting you back.'

Jaz shrugged her shoulders and took another gulp of wine. 'I'm supposed to be in Belfast next week.'

'Why so far?'

'That's where they need extra sales.'

'Can't they do it via video call?'

'That's not their style. But enough of me. What's been going on with you?'

Holly told Jaz what had happened with Tom and the solicitor.

'That's settled then. You need me here, chick. To help get your new life sorted and protect you from that snake. I'm staying put. I'll call the CEO on Monday.'

'No Jaz, that's precisely why I didn't tell you on the phone. I don't want to affect your decisions. Your career is important. You want to make that million, remember? And I've started to get things in motion now at the nursery.'

'Take me to Eversley. You can show me these plans. I can have a sleepover in your caravan and I'll worry about my life later.'

THEY WERE SOON SITTING at their favourite table situated by a large window in the Eversley Arms, drinking cider.

'Just like old times, except the cider isn't warm,' Holly laughed.

'Yeah, it tastes much better these days. Lovely over ice.' Jaz sipped hers. 'Especially this blackcurrant and pear.'

'A bit like that snake-bite and black you used to knock back.'

Julian strolled over. 'Nice to see you both in here. I've got a special on steaks today, if you want one?'

'We're eating later.' Jaz sipped her drink.

'I've only got salad back at the caravan,' Holly said. 'So I might take you up on the offer. I'm sure Jaz will, too.' She winked at Jaz. 'Once she's warmed up.'

'You won't be disappointed. We've a few sauces to choose from.' Julian smiled and went to the next table to pick up an empty glass before he returned to the bar.

'Stop winking at me,' Jaz hissed. 'Anyway, you told me about the farmers' market on the way over, but do you still have a crush on Mitch?'

'Keep your voice down.' Holly frowned and looked about her to see if anyone was listening. The slightest sniff of anything interesting, and it'd be twisted and churned and recycled until the village would be reporting that she split with Tom because she was having an affair with Mitch.

Jaz leaned forward. 'So, are you going to make a move or what?'

'No. He hasn't indicated he's interested. He probably needs time. Anyway, Ethan seems to be carrying on like we're an item. I need to see what's happening there.'

'Hun, I go away for a couple of weeks and come back to find you in a full-on love triangle.'

'No, it's not. Ethan's just got the wrong idea and Mitch isn't interested. He's very brotherly-like.'

'I doubt that, chick.'

'I think you need to concentrate on your own love life, Jaz. It's alright going from pillar to post, but one day you'll want to settle down. You haven't had a serious boyfriend for years.' Holly glanced at the bar then back at Jaz. 'Why don't you give Julian a shot?'

'I don't know why you're forever trying to fix me up with him.'

'Because it's plain to see you have a thing for him.'

Julian walked over with a small plate. He flushed as he smiled at Jaz. 'I wondered if you wanted to sample the steak?' he said holding out the plate, upon which there were chunks of sirloin on cocktail sticks.

'We'd love to,' Holly said, taking a sample and chewing it, passing the other to Jaz. It was delicious. She nodded her head. 'Yes, please. We'll have two medium-rare, with all the trimmings.' Holly smiled at Jaz. 'My treat.'

Once Julian was out of earshot Jaz sat up straight. 'So, onto a more interesting subject. I assume you need a plus one for the awards night?' She ran a hand though her choppy bob. 'I'll need to book myself into hair and make-up.'

'Well,' Holly blushed.

Jaz leaned forward. 'If you take me, it'll be so much more fun than if Ethan goes.'

'I've asked Mitch.'

'Mitch?' Jaz sat back. 'Brother-like, my backside.'

'Well he did enter the painting into the competition.'

'So, I really am bottom of the pile then?'

'I thought you'd be away – working.'

'True. I probably will be.' Jaz's face broke into a grin. 'So Mitch then?' she said wiggling her eyebrows.

Holly laughed. She was so pleased Jaz was back. Banter with Jaz was certainly a distraction. And whilst she'd never ask Jaz to, she secretly wished she would come back to the Somerset showroom.

'So, what are you going to wear?'

'Seeing as my occasion dresses went up in smoke, I'll have to buy something new.'

'I tell you what – I've a fab dress you can wear. It's been hung in my wardrobe for ages as it's way too long and I've not got around to taking it up. It'll be perfect for your date.'

'It's not a date. It's a networking opportunity.'

As Jaz laughed, Julian brought over their steaks.

They enjoyed their food in silence and Holly thought about the awards night. *Does Mitch think it's a date?*

CHAPTER 14

*A*rriving at the Town Hall, Holly paid the taxi driver and stepped out of the car, wearing the full-length dress. The chill of the evening hit her bare arms as she had not worn a jacket. The only two coats she possessed were the green parka and peach canvas jacket. And her blue pashmina did not go with the red satin dress either. Holly passed an A-frame with *The Beauty of Somerset Awards* written on it, followed by an arrow pointing to the entrance. Once inside, she spotted Mitch before he saw her. Her eyes were drawn to him immediately and a shiver ran up her back. He appeared different in his dinner jacket. Even though she knew with certainty it was him, she still peered through her professionally made-up eyes to make sure. He was closely-shaven and his hair was neat. Whilst she found his slightly dishevelled look incredibly sexy, she also appreciated the groomed Mitch. Her palms became damp. His eyes caught hers and he stared momentarily, before a smile spread slowly across his face.

He was soon at her side. 'Wow, you'd fit in at the Oscars.'

Oh, no, I've overdone it, Holly thought as she blushed. 'It's my friend's dress. I told her it was a bit OTT.'

'Not at all. Red suits you. And your hair …'

Holly touched the nape of her bare neck. 'Jaz also booked me in at the hairdresser. She said that I needed an *up-do.*'

Mitch smiled. 'You really are, *The Beauty of Somerset.*'

Holly's blush travelled down her chest.

Mitch held out his arm. 'Let's join the crowd.'

Walking into the function room, Holly noticed a few people stare at them and heard a woman whisper, 'who are they?'

Nina approached, wearing a knee-length cerise, body-hugging, satin dress with a huge bow on the left shoulder. It showed off her enviable curves and tanned legs. Holly had expected Nina to be there with her councillor hat on.

'Holly,' Nina said leaning in for an air kiss. 'Lovely to see you and this is?' She flashed a smile at Mitch.

'This is Mitch, my er …' Holly glanced at him.

'Neighbour,' Mitch said, smiling at Nina.

'Okay. Not a couple then?' Nina's smile grew, showing her whiter than white teeth.

'No.' Holly pulled her arm away from Mitch. Why did he have to point out he was just her neighbour? He could have said friend, at least. For a moment she had imagined they were on a date. Holly forced a smile. *Networking, remember the networking,* she thought. 'I gave Mitch the landscape painting as a thank you for saving me from the fire. And he entered it into the competition.'

Nina looked from Holly, then back to Mitch. 'Amazing.'

'So, as a thank you, I invited him to accompany me this evening.'

Nina widened her eyes. 'Oh. How sweet. And you're the one that rescued Holly from the flames?'

Holly shook her head and was about to explain but Nina hooked an arm into Mitch's. 'Let's get the hero a drink,' she said as she led him away.

Holly sighed. Thrusting her shoulders back she followed them towards the drinks table. She noticed Mitch turn his head but she glanced downwards to avoid his gaze. Holly was glad that she had chosen to wear flat shoes with the dress. Her long legs meant she looked elegant with or without heels. Arriving at the table, upon which the pre-dinner drinks were being served, she took a flute of champagne. Noticing Mitch trying to catch her eye, she avoided his gaze and surveyed the room but could clearly hear Nina chatting away and Mitch laughing loudly, every now and again. *I'm here to make contacts, this isn't a date,* Holly told herself. *Why didn't I just bring Ethan?* If Nina was all over Ethan, she would not have been bothered in the slightest.

A man approached. He was, she guessed, what Jaz would call a *silver fox*.

'Hello there, are you here alone?' he said.

'No, I'm with my neighbour.' Holly pointed to Mitch who was laughing as Nina poked at his chest.

'Ah, Councillor Smith is keeping him entertained.' He smiled. 'And you are?'

'Holly Loveland.'

'Oh yes, indeed. The landscape artist. I'm Councillor David Bunning. I love your work.'

'Thank you.'

'We've an interesting evening ahead. Before the meal there's a tour around the exhibition room, where everyone can view the artwork. It's all really very good. There's a plethora of local talent. We've sculptures, paintings, tapestries and more.'

'I can't wait to see it.'

'You won't be disappointed. Then we'll return to the function room for the meal and presentation of the awards. And of course, Trudy Wall from the Arts Council will be speaking.'

Holly nodded. 'I'm looking forward to that.'

'Oh? Do you have a project in mind?'

'Yes. A large project.'

'I'd love to hear about it. We're on the hunt for decent Arts Council applications to support. Between you and me.' David tapped the side of his nose. 'You should get any request in PDQ. There's a limited budget.'

Holly smiled. 'I've plans on paper with drawings.'

'What's your idea?'

'To build an arts hub out in Eversley village.'

'I've not been to Eversley yet. Although I've been here in Somerset for a few years now.'

'It's one of the smaller villages.'

'Yes, I've heard of it, but not visited.'

'I own a garden nursery there, so already have a profitable business on site. Or should I say, I did have. We recently had a fire.'

'Crikey, that was your nursery?'

'Yes, but the insurance has been approved. Whilst it's been heart-breaking, losing so much, I've now got something to throw myself into.'

'It's refreshing to hear someone so incredibly positive. I'm sure Trudy will love you. I'll introduce you.'

David led Holly to the Arts Council rep. Ten minutes later, Holly felt elated. It was great to discuss her plans with someone passionate about art. Whilst it was brief, Trudy said she would welcome her application, especially if it was supported by the local councillors.

As Trudy moved on, Holly turned to David. 'Thanks for the introduction. It's starting to feel more than just a dream.'

'No, thank you for being full of energy. We must catch up and you can tell me more. Here.' David fished into the inside pocket of his dinner jacket and handed her a business card. 'Call early next week.'

'Thank you.' Holly smiled as she placed the card into the clutch bag that Jaz had lent her.

Hearing a bell ring, Holly turned her head towards the sound and saw the town crier had entered.

'Oyez. Oyez. Oyez. Welcome one and all to the fair city of Wells on behalf of the Mayor and Aldermen. You are invited to view the delights of The Beauty of Somerset Exhibition, which is now officially open.'

Holly moved towards the exhibition and Mitch soon appeared at her side.

Mitch puffed, as if out of breath. 'Nina's a bit full-on.' He rubbed the back of his neck.

Holly nodded but remained silent biting her lip.

As soon as they entered the exhibition room, Holly saw her painting and took a deep intake of breath. She beamed. It was in the centre of the room, underneath a spotlight. Mitch took her hand in his and squeezed it. 'I'm proud of you, Holly Loveland.'

Lifting her eyes and seeing Mitch gazing at her, she felt a warmth wash over her body like a soft tropical rain.

He turned to study the painting. 'It's breath-taking. It's you all over, making the every-day bright. Even with what's going on in your life, you're standing here, radiant and calm.'

Holly felt a lump in her throat and tears threatened her

eyes. She did not want to make a fool of herself. Putting on a show was hard at times and she felt so many emotions just under the surface, ready to bubble over if she were to let her guard down. Blinking away one solitary tear she took a deep breath. Mitch squeezed her hand again, then led her towards the other exhibits.

After viewing the artwork, they took their seats in the function room which was filled with large round tables set out for the meal. Holly was happy to note that their seats were nowhere near Nina. Two more artists and a councillor sat at their table accompanied by one guest each. When Holly mentioned the hub to the artists, both took a real interest and they exchanged contact details. The food was delicious and Holly felt relaxed, as if she were at a friend's wedding. The wine and conversation flowed and it felt natural to be with Mitch.

The town crier rang his bell again and gave David Bunning a comical introduction, before he stood up and addressed the room.

'It's my pleasure to be able to hand out the awards in absence of Mayor Greening, who could not be here this evening.' Behind him was a collection of trophies and plaques.

After a few awards had been given, David pulled out the next gold envelope. 'And the winner of best painting goes to.' He retrieved the announcement card. 'Holly Loveland.'

Holly felt tears threaten.

Mitch rubbed her arm. 'Well done.'

She stood and smiled down at him, feeling a rush of adrenaline which chased the tears away. Those on her table stood and clapped as she went up to collect the silver cup.

David passed her the microphone.

'I'd like to thank the judges. I'm thrilled that you like the artwork I created. I'd also like to thank my friend and neighbour, Mitchell Booth, for submitting my entry. The painting is actually of his farm and as we know, farming is an integral part of our local economy. So, let's hear it for Somerset farmers.' Nodding at Mitch, she held up the trophy as those present applauded.

Mitch gave her a kiss on the cheek as she returned to her seat, which sent a few shivers down her body. After a talk by the Arts Council Representative, a small band played and Holly was pleased that Nina was monopolised by an eager admirer. *Maybe I misread her signals,* Holly thought. She had known Nina for years and she had always been sociable. Holly danced to upbeat tunes with a couple of the other artists, while Mitch chatted away to the others on their table. She caught him glancing at her now and again and smiled.

'And now we are going to slow it down,' the band leader said as the instruments played the soft tones of a ballad.

Mitch appeared at her side. 'Dance?'

'Sure,' she said. The wine had been flowing and she felt a little more confident.

Mitch held out his hands. Holly's palms felt hot, not wishing him to feel anything sweaty, she placed her hands on his shoulders. Smiling into her eyes he put his hands around her waist and they swayed to the music. As the love song developed, she laid her head on Mitch's chest and he squeezed her tight. There was no denying it, she wanted him. She felt it inside – deep inside.

IN THE MARKET SQUARE, Mitch opened the taxi door for Holly. Closing it after she was seated, he walked around the car to the other side, noticing Nina a few feet away, propped up against a building chatting to David Bunning. He was surprised how his hackles had gone up earlier as he had watched David chatting to Holly. Nina turned and waved at Mitch and blew him a kiss. He had discovered through chatting with her, that she was chairing the rural business committee he had been roped into when submitting the painting. He nodded at Nina and got into the back of the taxi next to Holly.

Holly leaned forward. 'Eversley, please. Lovelands Nursery.'

Mitch looked sideways.

Holly smiled. 'Thanks so much for tonight and for the caravan. It's really becoming a home for me.'

'I'm glad you like it.'

Holly looked back to him. 'So am I. Which is lucky, because I think I'll be there for an awfully long time.'

'How far are you down your to-do list?'

'I'm still deciding on a builder. I could use the contractor recommended by the insurance company but they're from out of town. I do like to support local people.' Holly turned away from him. 'Ethan recommended someone to me.'

Great, he thought. He had forgotten all about Ethan. Forgotten that she was with another guy. He could feel the warmth of Holly next to him and was aware of her every movement. He had to lose this longing he had for her, otherwise it was going to ruin their friendship and their future business plans. A joint business venture would be great for them both and the village. It would bring more trade to the area. Neither did he like the idea of stealing a girl off another guy – even if that other guy was a flash git.

The taxi swerved around a bend and Holly placed a hand on Mitch's leg, he assumed this was to steady herself but he reacted to it immediately. He swallowed hard.

Holly smiled. 'How's your Uncle?'

'Brighter this week. I even pushed him down to the cows. It's surprising how lucid he becomes, as soon as he sees the herd. The farm has been everything to him.'

'Does he know about your plans for the farmers' market?'

'I haven't mentioned it. I don't talk much about the future. Not with him being ill. It seems cruel as he hasn't got long.' He knew that was not the only reason he had not told Sid. Mitch knew he'd go mad. The very mention of the name Loveland and Sidney went into his shell – not talking for days. It had been that way for as long as he could remember.

When Holly made no comment, he glanced sideways, noticing she had her eyes shut. She looked serenely peaceful as she clutched her winners' cup to her body. The rest of the journey was made in silence until they drew up at the caravan.

Holly had already opened her eyes. 'Do you want to come in for a drink?'

Mitch nodded, even though he knew he would have to take the long walk home via the lane, because his shoes were not made for the grassy slopes. He paid the driver and followed her into the caravan.

Mitch was amazed every time he came in at how homely and beautiful Holly had made it. He had imagined it going to the breakers. Maybe Holly could turn the caravan into a holiday let when she was back in her cottage.

'I'll just get out of this dress.' Holly went off in the direction of the bedroom.

Picking up Holly's trophy from where she had left it on the table, he could see that they had already etched her name onto it. She soon returned, wearing a T-shirt and shorts. He rubbed his face thinking how cute she looked and attempted to eliminate the X-rated thoughts going through his mind. He loosened his tie.

'That's better,' Holly said. 'I enjoyed dressing up but it was nice to get it off.'

'I wish I could get my clothes off.' Mitch noticed Holly blush. 'Oh no, I didn't mean right now.'

Holly laughed. 'Do you want tea, coffee, Prosecco?'

'Coffee will be best. I've been up since five.'

Holly soon handed him a steaming mug. 'The Arts Council talk was interesting, wasn't it? I've made a few artist contacts as well; they were eager to get involved with the hub. I'm thinking of printing some large-scale plans to display at the first farmers' market. Is that okay?'

'Of course, it is. It's a great idea.'

'I'll send invitations to local artists and councillors. More customers for the market too. Maybe something positive will come from all this mess.'

'You'd have got there anyway, Holly, I'm sure. But the fire, it's brought it closer.'

'I'm going to meet David Bunning next week. I had a chat with him about the hub when you were with er ...'

'Nina.'

'Yes, Nina.'

'I thought you knew her?'

'Yes, I do. We went to the same college. She was in my textiles class. I think she originally wanted to be a clothes designer, but she went on to do a business degree at Bath.'

'It's good to have friends in high places.'

'Yes, she's very successful. A real catch.'

A real catch? Mitch repeated in his head. It sounded as if Holly was suggesting he went out with Nina. 'Hopefully you'll get support from both councillors then.'

'I mentioned the idea of a gallery few times to Nina, at breakfast business meetings I used to attend with Tom.'

Mitch noticed Holly's voice change at the mention of Tom's name. 'Have you heard any more from him?'

Mitch listened as she told him about the latest letter Tom's solicitor had sent. *What a total waste of space,* he thought, wishing that the guy would self-combust. 'Sounds like your solicitor has got it covered. I'm sure it'll be fine. But you can do without this stress, eh?'

Holly nodded.

'At least you have Ethan.' *Why did I say that?* Mitch rubbed the back of his neck. Would Holly think he was fishing for details of her relationship? Mitch watched Holly nod her head slowly a few times – she was clearly going mushy at the very thought of this Ethan. This was the best time for him to make an exit. 'Right. I'd best be off then. Early start tomorrow. I'm going off to see a pig farmer in the morning to discuss the market. Once I secure firm commitments, we'll have to get together and plan it out.'

'Yes, of course.' Holly beamed. 'Thanks, Mitch, for your hard work.' She reached over and brushed her lips across his cheek.

He stiffened, battling the urge to grab her for a long lingering kiss, and stepped back. 'See you.' He turned and left.

See you? How lame, Mitch thought as he marched back to the farm. Forgetting to take the long way round, his shoes, slipped here and there, on the wet grass. He knew for sure he wanted to be more than Holly's business associate. More than her friend. More than her neighbour. He wanted her – full stop.

CHAPTER 15

*A*s Holly sat in the Well's café, she regretted her choice of table as the sun shone through the window pane making her feel uncomfortably warm. Scanning the café for an alternative table, she bit her lip. *There must be a coach party or two in town*, she thought. With it being market day the square was full of visitors mulling around. She removed her jacket and pulled at the neck of her T-shirt. Sipping her piping hot coffee, she wished she had chosen a cool drink. She had chosen coffee in the hope that the caffeine would kick in. She had been up most of the night sketching, in a frenzy. She had felt inspired. Inspired by the heat which had coursed through her body after spending the evening with Mitch. It had begun as a little flame at the start of the evening and turned into a raging fire. She had replayed the previous evening over and over again in her mind. The evening she'd had with Mitch had been perfect, although he had left the caravan abruptly. *Did I scare him off?* she thought as she looked in the direction of the café door. Nina had texted her first thing saying she wanted to meet Holly, to discuss some ideas she had for the hub.

Holly pushed away a curl which had fallen in front of her eyes, noticing the blooms falling over the side of hanging baskets which came into view when the wind blew. She noticed a couple in the corner gaze into each other's eyes and share a tender kiss. She recognised something in them, something she felt inside herself. Ethan came to mind, she knew that was an entirely different relationship – certainly not the sort of thing the couple in the corner had. Ethan had been pushing her for a date and she knew it would go nowhere with him. She needed to tell him straight. And even though you should not mix business with pleasure she felt she needed to let Mitch know how she felt about him.

'There you are.' Nina woke her from her thoughts, dumping her designer bag on the table.

'Hi.' Holly smiled.

Nina waved at the waitress. 'Skinny latte, please.'

Holly wondered if there was such a thing as a truly skinny latte. She opened her mouth then closed it, deciding Nina would not appreciate the comment.

Nina applied her lipstick. 'You look tired, darling. Was last night too much for you? What with the strain you must be under at the moment?'

'No. It was a great evening. I've been up half the night.'

Nina snapped her compact mirror shut. 'Oh. I see. Did your neighbour keep you busy?'

'No, no.' Holly blushed. 'My mind was buzzing with ideas.'

Nina smiled and leaned over the table. 'He's rather gorgeous, isn't he? And single?'

'Yes.' Holly crossed her arms. 'So, the hub? You said you wanted to discuss it?'

'What ideas do you have?'

Holly sighed. Nina had clearly said that she wanted to meet to talk about her own ideas, not Holly's. Holly took a deep breath. 'Well, one of my ideas was to hold breakfast meetings with local craft workers and artists, to gauge their interest in renting art space at the hub. It would be at reasonable rates, as the hub itself would be a not-for-profit venture.'

'That's a great idea. I can let you have some dates and free room hire for the meetings at the Town Hall. I can promote it through the local news and on the website.' Nina's latte arrived and she took a sip. 'That's sorted, then.'

Well that was brief, Holly thought as she drank some of her own coffee.

Nina leaned forward again. 'Mitch. He's divine.'

Holly bit her lip. *So that's what this is all about,* she thought. Nina wanted to talk about Mitch.

'You know me and my luck with men. Mother tells me I'm too picky. But Mitch – wow – we hit it off. Like we had a real connection.' Nina smiled. 'Do you know what I mean?'

Yes, she did know what Nina meant. Exactly what she meant. Jaz's comment came back to her, yet again: *That man is every woman's type.* Maybe the connection she felt with Mitch was nothing surprising, nothing special. *Maybe he's just a hot guy,* she told herself. But she still wanted to find out if he felt the same. 'He's a nice man.' Was all she could say.

'So, tell me more.'

Holly gave a brief outline of Mitch, careful not to say anything that was not common knowledge, although she still felt uneasy as Nina had the knack of twisting every word into some sort of fantasy story. She mentioned he was a widower, but nothing about the accident and police investigation. Nina seemed to become more excited the more she said and Holly felt her body droop in equal measure.

'So, let me have his number and I'd better get back to the shop.' Nina retrieved her phone from her bag. 'Mother's minding things, but I don't like to leave her for too long. Otherwise she rearranges my shelves.'

Holly fumbled with her phone on her lap and turned the power off. After a couple of seconds she lifted it up showing it to Nina. 'Oh. Sorry. I've run out of charge.'

Nina frowned. 'Well, text it to me later.' She smiled as she rose. 'Lovely to catch up.'

Holly bit her lip as she watched Nina breeze out of the café.

MITCH WOUND down the window of his pick-up as he drove home. It was surprisingly warm. The DJ on the radio station said they were experiencing an early heatwave and it would be the hottest June since records began. He'd had a great chat with the pig farmer called Ed, who was straight talking and easy-going, reminding Mitch of the farmers back home. It was usual that as soon as the Somerset farmers heard his accent, which most perceived as cockney, they mistrusted him. They saw him as an incomer, here to take their business and land, even though his family had owned the farm in Somerset for over one hundred years.

Trixy woke. She had been cooped up in the pick-up truck while he was in his meeting and now yapped as he reached Lovelands. It was as if she knew where she was. He guessed he should call in with Trixy as Holly had agreed to sit her. The trip to Essex with Sid was looming up. He realised it would be the last visit Sidney could make to Essex with his health in steady decline and the consultant had warned Mitch that Sid was unlikely to see Christmas.

Driving into the car park, Mitch spotted Holly, her hair glistening in the sun. She had tied it back in a ponytail and she looked graceful. She stood with three men, one he recognised as pretty-boy Ethan and the other two he assumed were builders, based on what they were wearing. Holly appeared to be talking confidently – pointing to printed plans and then gesturing around. *She looks like she can handle herself,* he thought. Although, he remembered, there had been moments over these past two weeks when Holly had gazed into his eyes and had seemed helpless and vulnerable. Those were the times he felt acutely attracted to her, wanting to make everything better in her world. Trixy yapped and he realised he was staring. Holly waved at him. He nodded and put the truck into reverse to drive away as she was clearly busy, but she beckoned him over.

He jumped out of the truck with Trixy tugging on her lead. Bending down, he attempted to pick her up but dropped the lead and she scampered over to Holly. Mitch followed and joined the group. Ethan gave him a short nod with a bullish flare of his nostrils. Mitch smiled inwardly, imagining Ethan scuffing the floor with his shined shoes. Not the right footgear he noted, for surveying a building site.

Mitch smiled at Holly. 'I won't interrupt, she's been cooped up in the truck while I was in a meeting. I dropped by to let you know we have our first farmer on board and I thought you might like to see Trixy before you have her to stay. But I can see you're busy.'

Holly bent down and stroked Trixy. 'Oh yes, it's this Monday.' Holly stood up with Trixy in her arms. Trixy was all over her. 'Do you want me to take her now and get her used to the caravan? I'll pop her back down in a couple of hours.'

'Are you sure? I can see you're busy.'

'Oh, we've nearly finished here.' Holly turned to the men. 'Guys, this is Mitch Booth, the neighbour I was telling you about.' She swung back around and gave Mitch a big smile.

The workman nodded their heads.

'If you don't mind, that'd be great,' Mitch said, not sure whether Holly was trying to get shot of him; the expression on Ethan's face certainly said, *jog on*. But Mitch was pleased she would be coming down to visit him. 'I'll see you later then.' Mitch waved and left. He glanced over his shoulder after a few strides, but Trixy was far from pining for him as she snuggled up to Holly.

Returning to Booth Farm, Mitch felt positive, knowing that he would see Holly again in a couple of hours. As he walked in the back door his mobile rang, he hesitated not recognising the number, then answered the call. 'Mitch Booth.'

'Hi, Mitch. Nina here. We met last night?'

'Yes. Yes we did.' *I don't remember giving her my number,* he thought.

'I met Holly today and she said you were lonely and might be in need of some female company.' Nina's voice seemed to purr at him. 'I'm at a loose end this evening and wondered if you wanted to meet up?'

Mitch knew he was free. He never went out in the evening, other than for Trixy's walk. He shook his head, feeling like a tyre with a slow puncture. *Holly's obviously not interested if she's fixing me up with her mate,* he thought.

'I thought I'd come on over to your place. Cook you a

meal? It'll be nice to get to know one another before the first Rural Business Committee meeting.' Nina's voice had a cheeky sound to it. Mitch's first instinct was to say no. But if he did – would she let up? He had been in this situation before. He decided it was probably best to let her come over and make it quite clear during the evening that he was not interested. Nip it in the bud.

'I've a few Nina specials I can rustle up for you,' she went on.

Mitch inwardly groaned. Nothing he couldn't handle though, after the line of women he had rejected in Essex. He was sure they meant well and he was used to letting them down gently.

After Nina had checked he had no food allergies, she said she would drive herself over.

Mitch filled the kettle with too much force splashing water everywhere. *Calm down,* he told himself. He knew he was grumpy because Holly was clearly not interested in him, pairing him off with Nina. Maybe he was an idiot to think that Holly would get involved with him. She was the one being sensible, given their planned business arrangement. Still, he wanted no-one to fix him up with a girlfriend and he decided to put her straight when she returned with Trixy. But he would have to calm down first. If he was rude, it might give his feelings away.

He shook his head 'How did I misread those signals?' he said to himself.

Mitch cleaned the kitchen. The scrubbing helped chase away any anger. After all, Holly was probably trying to be kind. He knew she would never do anything to upset anyone. He was just sore because he wanted her to want him.

Later, having had a shave and dressed in a short-sleeved

polo shirt and a fresh pair of jeans, he checked his phone for the time, wondering how long Holly would keep Trixy. She had said a couple of hours but it had been three. Nina was due in three-quarters of an hour. *I'd better call Holly.* He heard the doorbell. *There she is,* he thought. Although wondered why she had not used the back door. Opening the front door, he found Nina wearing the flimsiest dress he had ever seen, with a sheer black cardigan over the top. *Oh, no.*

Nina fanned herself with her hand. 'It's so, hot. Sorry, I'm a few minutes early. We did say six, didn't we?'

No, half past, he thought as he looked at the carriage clock sat on the porch table which said five forty-five.

'I've got all sorts of goodies in the car.'

'I'll help you get it in.'

'The shopping bags are in the boot.' Nina led the way to her car, a white SUV.

Mitch lifted the boot. 'I get less than this to last a week.'

Nina giggled. 'I couldn't make my mind up what to cook. So I thought I'd do us finger food.' She lowered her eyes and smiled. 'Something to nibble on.'

Mitch realised he would need to tell her he was not interested, as soon as possible.

Once in the kitchen, Nina began to unpack the items. 'I'll start the prep, shall I? At least it's nice and cool in your house.' Nina picked up a box of pre-prepared blinis. 'I couldn't find anything to wear.' She removed her cardigan. 'I found this.' She pulled at the straps of her dress. 'It was roasting in my little apartment, the sun streams in like a greenhouse in there.'

'Er ... nice.' Mitch rubbed the back of his neck. He was sure she'd told him she owned a dress shop, so found it hard to believe that she would she have nothing to wear.

'You'd never guess, but it's actually a little nightdress. I think it doubles up nicely as daywear, don't you?'

Mitch saw the outline of a nipple. *I need to tell her I'm not interested – now.* He took a deep breath but before he could speak, Nina launched into conversation.

'I met Holly today for coffee in town. We discussed holding a few breakfast meetings to help with her art project.'

'Great idea.'

'Yes, it is. And she told me all about you.'

'Really?' he said, wondering what exactly Holly had been saying about him.

'Yes. Out here, caring for your invalid uncle and in need of female company. So I thought I'd come and cheer you up.'

I sound like a right saddo, he thought. Mitch shook his head. Was that how Holly saw him? She felt sorry for him? A lost cause?

Nina turned around, leaning up against the worktop. She picked up a bottle of red wine she had placed there. 'Shall we open this? I brought it home after a trip to France.'

In the distance, Mitch heard Trixy barking and realised that Holly was arriving. He told himself to remain calm and discuss it with her later. After all, Holly probably had his best interests at heart. But he would be making it known to her quite clearly – no match making. He could see her hair glint as she passed the window and there was a rap at the door.

'Expecting someone?' Nina raised her eyebrows and smiled.

'Hellooooo,' Holly called in a bright voice.

Nina reached the door and pulled it open. Mitch

watched Holly's face as her mouth opened and her eyes blinked rapidly.

'Come in. We're opening a bottle of wine.' Nina stepped aside to let her in. 'Oh, not sure about your dog though.' Nina pointed to Trixy. 'I'm not really a canine fan.'

'She's not mine,' Holly said, the brightness now lost from her voice as she shoved the lead past Nina into Mitch's hand. 'I won't interrupt.' She turned and marched away.

'What's up with her?' Nina asked as she swung back to Mitch.

Trixy growled.

Mitch put his hand to his forehead. 'Don't ask me.'

olly ran up the grassy slope. Everything had felt so right last night with Mitch. So natural, so real. Once through the boundary wall and onto her own land, she slowed her pace. She pulled at the neck of her T-shirt which stuck to her skin in the balmy evening. *Maybe I got the wrong message?* she thought. Maybe she had been seeing what she wanted to see, not the reality of the situation. After all, they had not kissed, they had not talked about anything relationship-wise.

Back at the caravan, Holly plonked herself on the soft seating. Picking up her mobile phone she decided to call Jaz. Her friend was now back for good and had returned to a management job at her old showroom. Her boss had taken the national training job instead, taking his wife with him. Scrolling through her phone, she picked Jaz's number. Hopefully, she was finished for the day.

'Hi ya,' Jaz answered in a loud voice. Holly heard background noise of people talking and laughing.

'Where are you?'

'I'm in the Eversley Arms. Come on over.'

'I'll just have a quick shower and change. Order me a very large glass of something.'

HOLLY MARCHED across Eversley Village green. The early evening sun painted everything pink. If only her life could be tinted that way. It was a busy evening at the pub, with people sitting outside on the grass drinking and laughing. *Where have my carefree days gone?* she thought.

Holly heard Jaz's voice as soon as she walked in the door. Jaz was propped up at the bar, laughing with Julian. He had his elbow on the top with his bearded chin cupped in his hand, staring deep into Jaz's eyes while his staff worked around him.

Holly approached with her eyebrows raised. 'What's going on here?'

Jaz put a hand on Holly's arm. 'Julian came into the showroom today – after a car.'

Julian smiled broadly. 'Jaz got me a great deal.'

Holly shook her head. 'You do know she's a cutthroat saleswoman?'

'She told me I got a manager's special.' Julian winked at Jaz and then went to serve a guy who was hollering at him.

Holly spoke to Jaz in a hushed voice. 'So? I thought you weren't into Julian?'

'He's so cool, he's got a kind of laid-back vibe. I'm not sure how I never noticed,' she giggled. 'It's always the quiet ones, eh?'

'I've always thought you two would get along if you only gave him five minutes to chat to you.'

'We chatted for longer than that. He's gonna take me out once he gets the car – to some posh restaurant in Devon with a celebrity chef.'

'I can't keep up with you. You go from one extreme to the other.'

'Anyway, you can talk. I've only got one bloke in my sights – you've got two, missy.' Jaz winked. 'I want to know all the details of what happened last night.'

Holly shook her head.

Jaz placed a hand on her arm. 'Hun, what's up?'

'Last night was amazing. But...'

'What?'

'I went down the farm earlier to have a chat with Mitch and guess who was there?'

Jaz opened her mouth. 'Who?'

'Only Nina blinking Smith.'

'No way. How did she meet him?'

'At the awards event.'

'What last night? When he was out with you?'

'Yes.' Holly plonked herself on a bar stool and put her head in her hands. 'We had such a great time yesterday evening. It made me realise – me and Ethan, it's never going to be anything more than friends. No spark. Nothing romantic at all.'

'There's a spark with Mitch then?'

Holly nodded. 'A big one.'

Jaz touched her arm. 'Sounds like you've got it bad. Did you and Mitch have a kiss or something?'

'No, just a dance. But I was so relaxed and happy, even though I've got all this rubbish going on. We chatted about anything and everything and he listened as if he genuinely believed in me.'

'We all believe in you, hun.'

'He doesn't pooh-pooh everything like Tom does. Or should I say did.'

'Tom's a prized plonker – we all know that.'

'I feel such an idiot, I practically ran down the hill to the farm. I was going to ask him over for dinner and see if he ...'

'Made a move on you?'

Holly hesitated. 'Well, yes. And then Nina was standing there in lingerie.'

'You are joking me?'

'No. A nightdress. Unbelievable.'

'She's a fast mover that one. What did Mitch say?'

'Nothing, he just stood there with his mouth open.'

'I'm not surprised, hun. You caught him out.'

'Hardly. He was expecting me. I was taking Trixy back after having her for the afternoon.'

'Maybe he thought you weren't interested, chick. Some blokes need you to practically jump their bones to get the message.'

'I think he's getting the message from Nina.'

Julian walked over. 'What's up?' He glanced at Holly then to Jaz. When neither replied he said, 'You two look like you need a stiff one. It's on the house, what can I get you?'

Holly smiled into his kindly face. 'Something strong.'

Julian turned away, grabbing a cocktail shaker and added measures to it from various bottles.

'So, it's definitely a no-no with Ethan?' Jaz asked.

'He's too overbearing and way too preened. Did you know he even shaves his ...'

'Balls,' Jaz said, looking over Holly's shoulder.

'Probably.' Holly laughed until she noticed the serious expression on Jaz's face.

'Keep calm.' Jaz put a hand on her arm. Not tenderly, firmly – as if to restrain her.

Then Holly turned and saw them – Tom and Grace standing in the doorway, hand in hand as if they had been beamed in from Stepford.

Julian turned around. 'Two Passionfruit Martinis.' He placed two shot glasses of Prosecco and two full cocktail glasses with half a passion fruit floating in each, on the bar.

'I'm getting out of here.' Holly stood up.

Julian's face dropped as he saw Tom and Grace. He called out to them. 'Maybe you two would like to take a seat outside? I'll come and take your order. Will you be eating?' Julian swiftly went to the door, picking up a couple of menus before he ushered them outside.

Holly plonked herself on the stool, downing the cocktail and chaser.

'Good move,' Jaz said, picking up the shot glass.

'Lord forgive me.' Holly stood up.

Jaz put out her hand. 'No. He's not worth it.'

Holly turned and stormed out of the pub, passing Julian on his way back inside. She watched Tom guide Grace onto a bench seat at a wooden table. Holly stopped and crossed her arms. 'So, this is why you want my money is it? So, you can wine and dine your mistress?'

'Don't make a scene.' Tom ran a hand through his hair.

'A scene? Why not? Because you don't want everyone to know that you're trying to take away what little I have left?' Holly pointed to her chest with her thumb. 'My land. Which has been in my family forever.' Holly pointed to Tom. 'You lived off me for nearly two years and now you're parading your new little girl-friend around my home village?' Holly pointed to Grace.

'Excuse me,' Grace said. 'It wasn't my fault. Your relationship was over long before Tommy met me.'

'So that's what he told you is it?' Holly put her hands on her hips.

'Yes. And to be honest.' Grace's eyes scanned Holly, up and down. 'You're exactly as Tommy described you.'

Holly held up her hands. 'Oh, p-lease.' She felt a rage like never before, welling up inside. She knew she had to get away. She could hear Jaz behind her.

'Leave it, Tom,' Jaz said, as he took a step towards Holly.

'She's the one on the attack, showing herself up.' Tom pointed to the people watching. Various tables of customers quickly returned to their pints, restarting conversations.

Jaz turned to Grace. 'You'll find out soon enough kiddo – what this snaky creep is really like.'

Holly trembled. *Walk away. Walk away,* an inner voice repeated in her head – so she did.

Holly imagined everyone watching as she stomped across the green. She heard Jaz behind her panting and calling her name. Turning, she waited for Jaz to catch up, watching as she sunk a stiletto heel into the grass with every step. Jaz turned back to the pub waving her mobile phone at Julian, who stood in the doorway.

When she reached Holly, she held her hand. 'I hate seeing you like this, hun. It's not you. Me? Yeah, I'm really gobby, but not you. Not Holly Loveland.'

'I'm going crazy, Jaz. I can't do this. I can't think straight.' Holly felt her eyes stream and her nose run. She had neither hankie nor tissue with her. She wiped her face on the back of her hand. 'I can't do relationships. I can't fight a divorce. I can't do the rebuild, or the market. I can't do any of it.' She looked up to the red sun as it clipped the hills. 'I'll just sell up and leave. I want this all to go away.' She felt Jaz's arms around her. 'And the solicitor told me I mustn't speak to Tom. Now I've made everything a whole lot worse. He's probably collecting witness statements.'

They walked the path back to the caravan, arm in arm and in silence.

Once inside, Jaz made tea.

Holly sat on the soft seating, playing with a sheet of Kitchen paper she had used to wipe her eyes. Her head thumped in time with her heartbeat. 'I've got to take time out somehow. But, how? With all this going on?'

'This place, hun, with the fire. It's in your face the whole time.' Jaz put a hand on Holly's arm. 'Maybe you should consider selling. But don't give a penny to Tom. We could go away. Make a new life, in a new town. Whatever you want to do. Thelma and Louise – I'll be there.'

Holly sipped her tea. 'No, I'm not running away. I'm not letting him win. He can't push me out of my home. But I can't deal with Ethan and I can't deal with Mitch. I know they want to help and they're both nice guys.' She gestured in the direction of the farm. 'Mitch is entitled to have a girl-friend after what he's been through. I've never told him I like him in that way, so I can't blame him. I've just got to sort this mess on my own, without distractions.' She reached for her mobile.

'What are you gonna do, hun? Don't you think you ought to sleep on it?'

Holly shook her head and rang Ethan's number.

'Hi, babe. Wanna meet up?' he said as he answered.

She bit her lip. 'No, Ethan. I've called to say I've got so much going on. I need to clarify; we should keep things as friends only.'

'I'm happy to take things slow. You can have as much time as you need.'

'What I need is space. I can't have a relationship. It wouldn't be fair on you. You're a great mate, always were. I don't want to spoil everything.' Her voice broke.

'Hey. Holly, don't get upset. Do you want me to come over? Just friends?' Ethan's voice was soft.

'No, no, that's fine. I'm getting an early night.'

'Take care, babe. If you need any extra help on the designs, let me know.'

Holly could hear the disappointment in his voice. She coughed to clear her throat, not wanting to cry again. 'I'll pay you for your time.'

'No way. Anyhow – you take care and maybe we'll pick up where we left off sometime?'

'Thanks, Ethan.' Holly ended the call and stood up. 'I feel so awful,' she said to Jaz.

'Don't worry, hun. You're doing the right thing. No point leading him on.'

'I don't know what's happened to me. I feel like I'm going crazy. I don't want to be this person anymore.'

'Don't be harsh on yourself.'

'From now on, the old Holly is back. I'm determined to make this work. To rebuild the nursery and start the hub. I'll fight Tom with my last breath to protect my land.' Looking out of the window over the scene with the farmhouse in the distance she wished things with Mitch could have been different. But, she was sure that for a Loveland and Booth, some things were not meant to be.

CHAPTER 17

*H*olly reached the entrance to Dawkins & Co. She had noticed when passing Nina's shop that it was not yet open. *Maybe she stayed over with Mitch?* she thought before telling herself not to dwell on what Nina and Mitch were getting up to. After all, it was none of her business. She was better off and much stronger alone. With that thought, she pushed the solicitor's door open with a little extra force than she had intended.

Oliver was on the phone and gave her a startled expression. 'Morning.' He breathed out before returning to his call. 'Go for the leather one. Fabric's so passé. Have to go now. Bye.' He put the phone down. 'Jill told me to send you straight in. Coffee, isn't it?' Oliver peered at Holly, over his thick-rimmed glasses. 'Or would tea be better?'

'It's definitely a tea day.'

'I'll add some biscuits then.'

Holly smiled at Oliver and knocked on Jill's door before entering.

Jill glanced up as Holly walked in. 'Great, you're early. Sit down and we'll get started.'

Taking off her peach jacket, she placed it over the back of the chair and sat down.

After pleasantries, Jill picked up her pen. 'I need to get an understanding of your marriage. How you met. Anything you discussed about the future. And when things went wrong.' She looked down to her pad.

'We met when I was at college. Tom had a job at one of the local holiday sites.'

'So, years ago?'

'Yes. But we went our separate ways after two years. He got offered a job on an oil rig in the North Sea and I went to art college in London.'

'You kept in touch?'

'We did for a year or so and met up a few times. But as long-distance relationships often do, it fizzled out.'

'When did you start a relationship again?'

Holly's eyes misted over. 'My mum and dad had a car accident and died a couple of years back.' She swallowed. It was still difficult to talk about her parents. 'I came back to Eversley to run the nursery, being their sole heir.'

'That must have been hard. What were you doing in London?'

'I painted and also managed a gallery in Soho. It was great, as I was allowed to show my own work, when space permitted. I sold a few of my pieces, too.'

'The nursery must mean a lot to you, to give up a career in London?'

'Yes, but I've been making plans to build an educational arts hub on site, to include a gallery-come-café.'

'I see.' Jill scribbled on her note pad. 'I take it, that this would be good for the local community?'

'Absolutely, it will be a not-for-profit venture.'

'Great. This is positive stuff. So, when did you and Tom get back together?'

'A month or so after I returned to the village. He'd lost his job and was in Eversley visiting mates.'

'Where was he living?'

'He was staying at the pub. The Eversley Arms – working a few hours in the bar.'

'I see.' Jill looked down to the desk, and all Holly could hear was the sound of her pen scratching her pad.

'So, he lost his job on the oil rig. Do you know why?'

'Absence. He was angry and tried to sue for unfair dismissal.'

'On what grounds?'

'He said they were making him work long hours, which led to a series of illnesses.'

'So, the grounds for dismissal was too much absence?'

'Yes, and he lost his appeal.'

'How was it in the beginning? I take it you must have hit it off quite well when you rekindled your relationship, considering you got married after what – a year?'

'Yes. We used to laugh and joke all the time. We were inseparable, as if we'd never been apart. Maybe naively, I assumed because of that, it was the real thing. It honestly seemed perfect.'

'And the proposal?'

'We were out for a walk and he said, "Why wait to start the rest of our lives together when we're so certain?"' Holly felt a lump in her throat. She wished Oliver would hurry with the tea, as her mouth felt dry.

'And how did he make money once he came to Eversley? Did he remain at the pub?'

'No. He moved in with me. He got on great with the staff

and customers – he can be a real chatterbox. He helped my groundsman out and sometimes in the shop.'

'Okay, this could be tricky if he was working the business. On what basis did he work?'

'Basis?'

'How did he get paid?'

'I gave him a payslip and a salary. All above board.'

Jill smiled. 'Super, that's great.'

She turned over a fresh page in her pad. 'Now to the breakdown of the relationship. When did things go wrong?'

'Quite soon after the wedding. He'd set up a hot tub business. He was working long hours. I helped where I could.' Holly took a deep breath; she felt an idiot saying it. 'And I took money out of my savings so that he could buy stock.'

'Can you remember exactly what items?'

'Hot tubs, mainly, to show at exhibitions.'

'And the value?'

'Fifty thousand initially – then a further twenty-five.'

Jill shook her head and Holly watched her write *75K* on her pad and underline it three times.

Holly spoke rapidly. 'Setting up a business is always a bit expensive. I studied his plans, they all seemed in order.'

'Are you a shareholder in his company?'

'No.'

'And where are these hot tubs?'

'He hired a lorry on a long-term contract. He picked them up in the lorry from the supplier and then toured the country with them, selling at home exhibitions and country shows. He didn't bring them back home. He's since told me that he sold all his stock and has no money left.'

'So, you didn't see the lorry or the hot tubs?'

Holly shifted in her seat and felt hot. 'Well no. But he

sent me photos of them. He was definitely at the shows. Indeed that's where he met his new girlfriend.'

'You say things started to go bad when he began the business? How exactly?'

'He became bad-tempered and short with me. He wasn't as affectionate as he used to be and began criticising me, putting me down, rolling his eyes whenever I spoke, tutting, that sort of thing.'

Jill glanced up. 'I see this a lot these days – men intimidated by their wives. Trying to belittle them to make themselves feel better when they are themselves failing.'

Holly thought that made sense. It would fit with Tom's, *You don't need me,* tirade. Initially, he was probably pleased that he had somewhere to live and work. 'I guess when we met all those years ago, he was older. The one with the job, the car and the money and I was the college kid living with my parents.'

'What happened immediately before you split up?'

'I mentioned us starting a family. He said he needed time out to think, he wasn't sure he was ready.' Holly took a deep breath. 'Then after two weeks I found out he'd been having an affair for months with a girl called Grace. Who incidentally is pregnant.'

Jill raised her eyebrows. 'And Grace's full name is?'

'I don't know.'

'And where does she live?'

'I don't know that either. But I don't think it's far and I assume he's living with her as he's been over to Eversley a couple of times.'

'Oh yes, your village green confrontation.'

Holly shifted in her seat. 'You got my email then?'

'Yes. What's done is done.' Jill set her pen down, placing her palms on the desk. 'Looking at what you've presented to me, I think we've got a case to send him packing with nothing, especially as he owes you this money. I'm not sure if I'll be able to recover that for you – especially if he has apparently spent it.'

'I feel so stupid to have been sucked in.'

'You married him in good faith. Sounds to me like he put himself out there with this business, it failed, and this young woman is some sort of ego massage. And now he's going to be a father. This is a man about to have a rude awakening – mark my words.'

'What's the next step with the divorce?'

'He's using the grounds of unreasonable behaviour. We have to defend that and put in a counter attack of adultery. He'll probably argue that you drove him into the arms of another woman – same old clap-trap.'

Oliver walked in. 'Sorry I'm late with the teas.'

Jill waved her notes at him. 'Can you type these up and we'll go over it this afternoon, after I've seen Mrs Brown.'

Oliver left the room with Jill's notes in his hands.

Jill poured the tea. 'I'm sure Tom's solicitor is bluffing about court. I'll keep fobbing them off and gather as much information as possible to use in your defence and the counter-claim.'

Holly bit her lip.

'Now don't worry. This is what I do. You concentrate on getting your life back in order.'

After making small talk over tea about her plans for the rebuild, Holly bade Jill farewell.

Back in the small reception she watched Oliver staring at his computer.

'He's a right slippery character if you ask me, darling.' Oliver tapped at his keyboard. 'Well rid I say.'

❦

Back at her caravan, Holly chatted to Jaz on the phone. She smiled as Jaz told her she was whipping her staff into shape. In the back of her mind Holly had worried that Jaz had come back because of the fire. Hearing her happy at the showroom eased her sense of guilt.

Finishing her story, Jaz paused. 'What are you up to today?'

'Mitch is bringing Trixy over.'

'You're still minding her then?'

'Yes, he texted me, saying he could put Trixy in the kennels if it was too much. I messaged back and said it was fine, and made an excuse about having a bad day when I dropped her off.'

'I think you're being overly nice, considering he mugged you off for Nina.'

'We've got to keep on good terms for the farmer's market. I'm thinking business and not clouding my thoughts with emotions.'

'Well if you can handle it – fair play.'

'I'm a bit nervous about seeing him, though.'

''Cos you fancy the pants off him?'

'No. Because I showed myself up.' Holly flushed red at the memory. 'I must have looked a right idiot, storming off like that when we're just business associates.

'I think you were more than that, hun. What about the smooch at the award's night?'

'It wasn't a smooch. It was a dance.'

'Flippin' 'eck, love, if I was pressed up to that body on the dance floor after a month's drought, I'd be gagging for it.'

Holly laughed. 'No doubt you've been keeping Julian busy?'

'Don't try and change the subject.'

Holly heard the familiar yaps of Trixy. 'He's here already. I best go.'

'Tits and teeth, hun.'

'What?'

'Smile and stick your chest out. Let him see what he's missing.'

Holly laughed. 'You're so bad.'

'Yes, and that's why you need me, chick.'

Holly ended the call, took a deep breath and opened the door before Mitch knocked. She smiled brightly, deciding to stick to the teeth bit. 'Hi.' Trixy jumped up at her and she picked the little dog up ruffling the hair on her head. Trixy brought a warmth to her heart that she welcomed.

Mitch had Trixy's soft bed under one arm and a full heavy-duty shopping bag hanging off the other. 'I'll bring this lot up – it's heavy.'

Stepping aside, Holly gave him space to pass.

'Thanks.' Mitch put the bag down, gesturing at its canine-related contents. 'There's food, bowls, a ball and a spare lead.' Mitch scanned the caravan. 'And where do you want the bed?'

Holly shrugged her shoulders, noticing that Mitch, whilst cordial and polite, was not being his usual jovial self. He had not smiled at all, which was good. She knew how her body reacted when he grinned at her. 'Leave it by the sofa for now.'

'Thank you for agreeing to do this, I really appreciate it. She eats dried food first thing, then wet food at lunch and in the evening.'

Holly thought that Mitch seemed to be avoiding eye contact. *Maybe he feels bad?* she thought. He had certainly been in chattier moods. She had the whole speech ready, about misunderstandings and keeping things simple, that they would make great business partners but would keep it business only. But with him acting so polite and not at all personal, she found it difficult to broach the subject.

Noticing a silence had fallen, she lifted her lips in a smile. 'Would you like a drink?'

'No thanks. I'm setting off to pick up the hire car for the trip.'

'Okay. Have a great time with your family.' Holly saw something shift in his expression.

Mitch gazed at her as if searching for something. 'Thanks, Holly.'

Holly felt a warm glow. 'Don't worry about me – I have my guard dog.' She pointed at Trixy, who had got into the dog bed and fallen asleep.

They both laughed and she felt the mist between them lift.

'Well, I'd better be off.' Mitch stepped forward and she thought he was going to embrace her, then he quickly stepped back and left.

'See you in a week,' she called after him.

Watching as he strode away, she wondered what was going on in his mind.

CHAPTER 18

*H*olly walked towards her burned buildings with George, the contractor she had appointed. It was time to get things moving.

'Heel, heel,' Holly called to Trixy as she tugged at her lead. 'I'm training her,' she said to George then pointed to the ruins. 'As I explained before, I need the dangerous areas to be cleared and cordoned off.'

George nodded. 'Of course.'

'And if you could make the house as safe, as possible, Joe, my groundsman, has offered to sort through it, to rescue any personal items remaining intact, before it's totally cleared.' She doubted there would be anything salvageable, but Joe insisted on going through it for her. 'Once the area is prepared, I'll be putting the rest of my land to good use.'

'You're planning to reopen before the building work is done?'

'Yes, it's not to cover loss of earnings, as such – the insurance pays out for that, but I want to keep my customer base. Otherwise, people will forget about Lovelands, and go off to the big chains.'

George nodded. 'I've notice a few of them open up. They're very popular.'

'Yes, there are a lot of garden centres in Somerset. That's why I'd like to keep this place beautiful, rather than a big metal unit. As mentioned, I want to expand on the buildings when we rebuild.' Holly pointed to the old barn. 'That will be linked up to the rest of the nursery buildings, with an extension, to become an all-weather attraction. We're likely to be busier on rainy school holidays with the indoor activities, which are always popular.'

'I can see you're passionate about this. Once I've had a chance to go through the plans, I'll let you have a quote as soon as possible and discuss materials and their costs.'

'I have a suggested schedule of works I can send you. And I'm leaving the cottage until next year – at least.' She stared at her charred family home as Trixy slackened the lead and sat down. Holly wondered whether it would be years before she got back in there; she only had enough funds to rebuild the entire property exactly as it was, no money for the extra works required for the hub so something would have to be left and that would be her home. She had to focus on the parts of the property which would be making money.

Back in her caravan after George left, Holly felt positive. He had a real can-do attitude, which she found reassuring. Buoyed up, she pulled open her box of papers and took out David Bunning's business card, noticing that his business was in motorhomes. He had said he would drum up support for her and knowing the local council meeting was looming up, she wanted to contact him. Nina had texted the dates of all the upcoming business breakfasts, and with David on side, that would be two votes. But she would have to drum up a lot more support than that and hoped David could help her out. She rang his number and it was answered immediately.

'Bunning.'

'Hi, David, it's Holly Loveland. Can you talk?'

'Yes, of course.'

'I wondered if we could meet? To go over the funding application?'

'Sure, I'm having a spot of lunch with my daughter. I can meet you back at the Town Hall, in half an hour?'

'That would be great, but I'm looking after a friend's dog.' She did not want to leave Trixy to chew up her new furnishings.

'I'm in the pub next to the Town Hall. In the beer garden. We can have a chat here if you like. Half one suit?'

Holly glanced at her watch. That was in twenty-five minutes. 'Yes, that's great.'

Lifting Trixy into the van, Holly watched as the little dog made herself comfortable on the passenger seat. *Maybe I should have borrowed a pet cage,* she thought. She went back into the caravan, returning with Trixy's bed, which she laid on the van floor in front of the passenger seat. Trixy ignored this and remained on the seat, her tongue flapping as if in anticipation of an adventure. Giving up on pet safety, Holly climbed into the driver's seat and set off.

They walked up the High Street in stops and starts, Holly repeating, 'Heel, heel,' as Trixy tugged on the lead in front of her. She reached the pub and walked around to the rear beer garden, which was more of a patio, filled with colourful flower pots. She saw David stand up and beckon her. He was with a blonde woman she presumed was his daughter. The woman turned and Holly's face fell. *Grace.*

Grace raised her eyebrows and gave Holly a smug smile.

Oh no, really? Holly thought.

David walked forward. 'This is my daughter, Grace. Grace this is Holly a local artist.'

'Yes. We've met,' Grace said with a sweet smile.

'Have you?' David turned to his daughter.

Grace kissed him on the cheek. 'Oh, yes. Thanks for lunch, Daddy. I'll speak to you – later.'

'Bye, poppet.'

Holly nodded at Grace, forcing a smile as she watched her walk away.

'How do you know my daughter?' David pulled out a seat for Holly to sit down.

'Oh, I don't know her as such, we met briefly. I know her er – Tom.'

'Pretty dog you have there.' David sat down. 'You know Tom, then? Great guy – shame about his hot tub business. We met him on the road, when I was showing my motorhomes.'

So at least that was the truth – he did have a hot tub business, Holly thought. She was surprised that she felt relieved, not wanting to be seen as a total mug.

'I was a bit worried about Grace, getting involved with a guy with a failed business. But I've given him a job at the showroom and he's doing great, a natural salesman, has the gift of the gab.

Don't I know it, she thought.

'He's hoping to buy into the business, which will be great if things work out. I'm going to want to take a back seat in a year or so. It's ideal.'

'Really?'

'Yes, he's got a bit put by. I like that in a man, no-one

saves these days. It's all fast cars, smart TV's and gym memberships.'

'That's a surprise.' Holly's hands shook and her face coloured up. *Maybe Tom's ripping David off?* she thought. Wondering whether she should warn him.

'He's got quite a sizeable sum stashed away already. Sensible idea to sell up before he lost the lot.'

Holly felt the anger rise inside and her face flushed. Trixy barked so she bent down to pacify her, hoping to mask her reaction.

'He's going to put part of it down on a home for the pair of them. I've told them not to rush into marriage, you can make awful mistakes. Fools rush in.'

Holly gave a nervous laugh, realising she was that fool. She wanted to know more about the money Tom appeared to have. 'Lucky him being able to save enough for a deposit. Property is so expensive these days.'

'I've checked his bank account. He showed me, he's got eighty thousand.'

Holly opened her mouth to speak, then shut it as her heart raced.

'And apparently, he's got a share in land which is up for sale. Says he hopes that it'll go through within the next month or so. Not sure of the details, but it's over your way somewhere.'

'Interesting,' Holly said through gritted teeth.

'How exactly do you know Tom then?'

Luckily, Trixy jumped up, barking.

'I won't be able to stay long, she's restless.' Holly took a deep breath, looked up and moved some hair which had fallen over her face. 'Will I need to do a presentation at the next Council meeting?'

'Oh no. No need for that, your application has already

been circulated and it's very clear. I can assure you, young lady, I'll argue your case. I think it's far superior to the others awaiting consideration. Indeed, the most professional I've seen for a while. I don't see anything getting in the way of Council support. It's ambitious, I'll give you that – but exciting. It's bound to bring more employment, more people in and ultimately, more money to the area. Well done.'

Holly smiled but guessed that as soon as David spoke to Grace, AKA *Poppet*, Holly would no longer be receiving his support.

Their discussion turned to the state of the high street and its future as a concept in a changing society. Ten minutes later, she bade David farewell and headed straight to Dawkins and Co. There was no way she would allow Tom to buy a new house, or invest in a business, with her money.

CHAPTER 19

*M*itch sat at Sidney's bedside. listening to him wheezing. He was hooked up to oxygen which the local hospital had set up for them. Sidney had not travelled well and had been in bed for most of the time they'd been in Essex. Magda had been brilliant and nursed Sid all week, but Mitch had sent her off to catch up with her relatives. She would be staying with them overnight. It was not a long journey into London from the farm as Braintree was within the commuter belt.

Sid stirred and opened his watery eyes, which were near translucent, the rims, red.

'I'm here, Sid.' Mitch placed his hand on top of his great-uncle's and squeezed it. He knew how much he meant to Sid, and that he had always seen him as more than a great-nephew. He was his heir, although the farm was included in Booth Farms Limited, it was the thought that counted and Sid had left him his possessions in his will.

Sid groaned.

'You've been asleep for some days. Travelling wasn't good for you was it?'

Sid moved his head slowly to the side. 'Home.'

'Yes, we'll get home as soon as the doc says you're strong enough to travel. I'll get a larger hire car this time, and we'll stagger the journey if you like. With more stops.'

'Don't want to die here.'

'Don't talk like that.' Mitch rubbed Sid's hand. 'The doctor said you're improving. We have to stay put until you can breathe without the oxygen. They reckon that'll be about three to four days.'

'Good lad.' Sid closed his eyes and appeared to be sleeping again.

Mitch breathed out a long sigh. He hoped Sid would regain his strength, he would hate for him to die here and not have his final wish of passing away at home in Eversley. He had gone to great lengths to find Magda, someone who was prepared to live in, so they could avoid placing Sid in a care home. He heard the door open and his sister, Shona, walked in.

Mitch turned, speaking in a whisper. 'He woke up for a short while. Hopefully he's on the mend.'

Shona placed her hand on Mitch's shoulder. 'Did he speak?'

Mitch nodded his head. 'Let's go to the kitchen.'

Picking up the portable baby monitor from the bedside, Mitch switched it on as he followed Shona out of the bedroom. The monitor was a godsend, he had borrowed it from his cousin. It meant they could keep an eye on Sid from the rest of the house.

The Essex farmhouse was much different from the one in Eversley, it was a sprawling single-storey property, built in the sixties when his grandfather moved over from Somerset. It was split into two living areas, one where his mother and father lived and the part he used to live in with Vanessa. He passed the partition door leading to his ex-marital home but did not go in. He could not face it – not yet. He was staying in his parents' area.

Once in the kitchen, he prepared coffee. 'Sid was asking to go home.'

'I feel mortified about dragging him over here for my engagement. Especially as he was too ill to come to the party.' Shona shook her head as she opened the fridge to retrieve the milk. 'In fact, I feel totally selfish.'

'He wanted to come.'

'Maybe he wanted to say goodbye to us. We should have all come to Eversley instead. That would have been a lot more considerate.'

'He probably wouldn't have liked that. He might have felt he'd have to get the place ready for you all,' Mitch said as he topped the cups with milk and passed the bottle back to Shona.

'I've not been down for years; it would have been nice.'

'Come in a few weeks' time. You could stay in the village if you want to bring Steve. They're doing bed and breakfast at The Eversley Arms now.'

Shona took a sip of coffee and sat down at the kitchen table. 'Have you been in touch with Holly yet?'

'No.'

'You'll have to tell her you're delayed.'

'I'll text her,' he said, looking out of the window at his parents' wide landscaped garden.

'Text? She's looking after your dog.'

Mitch took a sip of coffee without comment.

'You're just sore because she fixed you up with her mate, when you fancy her.'

'I don't like being set up. Anyway, I'm still confused over that matter.'

'You need to speak to her, then. Find out what it was all about.'

'I don't like people interfering with my life.' He nodded towards Shona.

She laughed. 'I'm not interfering. I'm just saying, if you like her, then you need to tell her. Good looks can only carry you so far, big bro.'

'You seem to think you're an expert on my private life.'

'I'm just basing my thoughts on what you told me at my party.'

'That was a strong brew. I should have known to steer clear of Steve's homemade poison.' Mitch laughed.

'Being in here is making me peckish – shall we make lunch?'

Before he could answer, Mitch's phone buzzed in his back pocket, he fished it out, *Nina Calling*. He puffed out and hesitated but realised if he ignored it she would only call back. 'I'll help after I've dealt with this call.' He stepped outside his parent's property through French windows. 'Hi, Nina.'

'Mitch, how's it going?'

'Not that great. My uncle is ill. Unfortunately, I'm stuck here until he's well enough to travel.'

'Oh, I see. It's the first Rural Business Meeting the day after tomorrow.'

'I doubt I'll be back by then,' he said, thinking that every cloud has a silver lining.

'I understand you wanted to talk about the farmers' market. I was getting excited to hear all about it.'

Mitch noted the disappointment in her voice. 'You could ask Holly, with her being my business partner.' Although Mitch imagined the request to Holly would be better coming from him. 'I'll call her and ask, then get back to you. Is that okay?'

'Yes, of course it is.' Her voice softened. 'When do you think you'll be back in Eversley?'

'Hopefully within a week.'

'Maybe we can catch up then?'

It had felt awkward back in Eversley when he had told Nina he wasn't interested in a relationship. He thought he had made it clear and hoped he would not have to be blunt with her. 'I've got a few busy weeks ahead. Make sure you pop over to the farmers' market, if I don't see you before.'

'Okay, I'll wait to hear from you then.'

Mitch ended the call and put his phone away. He took a small stroll around the garden, which was mostly laid to lawn with a few flower beds. It was flat, unlike the Booth land in Somerset, with its tufty, grassy slopes. This garden was prettier, with a wide range of flowers but way too twee for him. He guessed his mother would love the nursery. *She'd probably bring a van load of plants back with her*, he thought. Mitch breathed out a long, slow breath, realising he would have to phone Holly. He had been thinking of her constantly. So why was he putting it off?

'Mitch,' Shona called. 'I thought you were going to help with lunch?'

I'll wait until this afternoon, he thought.

CHAPTER 20

*H*olly cleaned the pens in the petting zoo as Trixy sat patiently watching her from the gate. She did not even bark when Holly set out Charlie's food as the goat bleated. She rubbed Charlie's back, realising that she had not spent as much time as usual with the animals since Trixy had been with her. Although Anne, who usually focussed on the retail side, had taken on full responsibility for the petting zoo, while Holly was managing the reopening. Holly had enjoyed training Trixy and was surprised at what she had achieved in a week.

Her mobile phone rang. After quickly washing her hands at the outdoor sink, she answered it. It was Mitch.

'Hi, Mitch. How's it going?'

'I'm fine. But Sid's unwell.'

'Oh no, I'm sorry to hear that.'

'I can't really leave him here, in case it's the end.'

'I fully understand. It must be hard for you.'

'The doctor is hopeful he'll be able to travel, in about three days' time. I'd rather not risk it before then.'

'Don't worry about Trixy, she's fine. I love having her with me.' Trixy yapped at the sound of her name. Holly realised it must be a difficult time for Mitch, especially in Essex, with the memories of his wife.

'And there was something else.'

'Yes?'

'Nina called me. I was supposed to be attending the Rural Business Committee meeting on Thursday. But I'm not going to be able to make it. They were interested in hearing about the farmers' market.'

'Do you want me to go?'

'If you don't mind? I feel really bad dumping it on you like this.'

Holly realised she could not say no. After all, Mitch was only on the committee because the Council agreed to accept her painting as a late entry. 'That's fine. Leave it with me.'

After a quick exchange about the weather, Holly hung up. She was used to committee meetings and realised it would be a good opportunity to talk, not only about the farmers' market, but also about the hub. Not seeing Mitch for a few days longer was also a bonus because she was feeling a lot more herself, without the silly schoolgirl-type crush clouding her thoughts. She had convinced herself that it must have been the stress of the fire. She looked over at Trixy who sniffed at the ground. After spending so much time training her, she was starting to feel as if the dog was her own.

Surveying her land, she could see things taking shape fast. George was great at getting things done. *At least something's going well,* she thought. They were going to open the following week for the sale of current stock and to promote the farmers' market. The initial works were near completion and she and her staff would soon be able to set up the retail sheds. It was only two weeks until they planned the trial market. She hoped Mitch would be back by then.

Holly's mobile phone rang again. It was Jill.

'Hi. Any update?' Holly crossed her fingers.

'Yes. Not good, I'm afraid. Tom's refused mediation. He says he'll see us in court.'

'I thought you said ...'

'I'm pretty certain it's a scare tactic. He's trying to wear you down.'

'Well, it's working. What about the counter-claim for the money he owes me?'

'You'll have better chance of success if we wait. We'll surprise him, kick him when he's down.'

'What if he spends it? Or does a disappearing act?'

'It's possible, but I doubt he'll move on. Not when he thinks he's on to a winner. Delay is a good thing.' It was alright for Jill saying delay was good, but Holly had plans. She had an Arts Council application in the pipeline and workers on site. What if she was forced to sell the land? Her stomach burned with the pain of nervous indigestion, the way it always did when she thought of the divorce.

'I'll call you next week, unless there are any major developments.' Jill sounded matter of fact; Holly wished she could be just as calm about it.

After thanking Jill, Holly dragged her thoughts away from Tom. She had not seen him since the outburst at the Eversley Arms – she hoped that meant David Bunning was working him like a dog. She guessed he was travelling the country shows, which were well under way. She wondered whether Tom and Grace were modelling the motorhomes as a happy couple.

Holly left the petting area and Trixy fell in line, trotting at Holly's side. Holly was surprised to find she had a natural gift for dog training, especially as she had never owned one before. *Interesting, the tips you can pick up on YouTube,* she thought. She toyed with the theory that Trixy loved her so much she would do anything for her. She had taught Trixy how to walk to heel, to sit and stay, and even to put out a paw for a treat.

Holly stared up into the cloudless June sky and felt the warmth of the sun on the back of her head. She was pleased to see the fence around the ruins was near completion, it was made of thick chipboard and masked the view of the burned buildings. It also served a purpose to stop any debris blowing over to the area she intended to trade from. Holly had asked for strategically placed Perspex windows, to allow nosey customers and villagers a view of what was going on, with some placed lower down for the children to peer through. While Mitch had pointed out that people love to see a disaster, she thought it might also attract sympathy and encourage visitors to spend big. She had seen a few people so far nosing at the ruins and had to ask them to leave due to health and safety reasons. She had told them to come back for the nursery opening.

Trixy stopped to sniff something and Holly called her to heel. Holly's stomach rumbled as she headed for the caravan, so she decided to make a quick sandwich before preparing for her staff meeting. As she approached, she spotted Val ambling along the drive and Holly frowned, watching her stop to rub her hip.

Running over with Trixy scampering beside her, she took Val's arm. 'Lean on me, you should have called for me to collect you.'

'Nonsense. I need the exercise.'

'But you're limping.'

'Ruddy hip. Len keeps telling me to get to the doctor but I hate them places.'

'You might be doing yourself an injury. Book yourself in for a health check, please?'

'Ruddy people poking at me. No thanks.'

Holly stopped. 'I'm taking you myself. Next week, no excuses. I'll make an appointment.'

Val grumbled but Holly noticed her wincing. She felt terrible. She had not seen Val as much as usual, only once a week with her washing. *I must make more of an effort,* she told herself as she squeezed Val's arm.

Once they reached the caravan, Holly helped Val up the steps.

'Alright, love, I'm no invalid. Not yet anyways.' Although it was clear to Holly, that Val would not have been able to get up the steps without her assistance.

'I'll make you some tea.' Holly filled the kettle.

'I've bread pudding in me bag.' Val rummaged in her shopping bag, pulling out a large foil wrapped slab. 'I should get back to proper baking. Something a bit more adventurous than adding fruit and spice to soggy bread. But I can't stand and mix like I used to.' Val plonked the pudding on the table. 'How's you been, lovey?'

'Fine. Clear-headed, considering the aggro going on with Tom.'

'You know I never approved of his ways. But to stoop so low. Your mum and dad would have gone mad.'

'I know. But the solicitor's fending him off. I told you, didn't I? He's still got my money in his bank account?' Holly set out five cups, she expected the rest of the staff to arrive shortly.

'Yes, you did, love, and it's taken all me energy not to send one of the boys over to that Bunnings place, to thrash it out of him.'

Holly laughed. 'No, Val, that wouldn't be appropriate. And I've already told you and Jaz, even though the solicitor told me not to repeat it to anyone, so you mustn't tell the gossips.'

'You know me. I listens, but I don't spread.'

Holly ate a sandwich. She had also made one for Val, but Val only picked at hers. There was a rap at the door and in filed Joe, Julie and Anne. Trixy jumped up, but one word from Holly and she soon settled back down in her bed.

Joe pointed to the little dog. 'You've certainly got a way with her. Nothing like the yappy, jumping scrap she was a couple of weeks ago.'

'I know,' Holly said. 'I'll be upset when she goes home.' Life had been much sweeter with Trixy in the caravan.

Once tea had been made and Holly had dished out the bread pudding, she made a start on the staff meeting. 'Thanks so much for your help with sorting out the stock, you've been so patient.'

Julie smiled. 'We're only doing our jobs. Don't forget you pay us to do this.'

'Well, you've not exactly been working to your usual job descriptions.'

'We don't have job descriptions,' Anne said.

Holly laughed. 'True.'

'This is real cosy,' Julie said smiling. 'I loves it in here, I do.'

'Don't get too comfortable,' Joe said. 'There's work to be done.'

Holly laughed. 'So, the boundary fence is up and Joe and myself will put up two large huts. The new stock is being kept in the old barn for now. That will be transformed into the art barn, once the main nursery building has been finished.'

'What's going in them huts?' Val asked.

Holly smiled and turned to her. 'One will be the snack shack, where hot drinks and cakes will be on offer. I've bought a couple of massive urns which we'll fill.'

'I can bake some cakes, if I get Len to help me with getting them in and out of me oven.'

'Just focus on being comfortable.' Holly wagged a finger at Val.

'Well I can come sell other cakes, if I don't manage to make any.' Val sipped the last dregs of her tea.

Holly raised her eyebrows. 'Well, we'll see what the doc says about your hip first.'

Val pulled a face.

'I can come over to your place and make the cakes with you. I can be your apprentice.' Anne smiled at Val.

Val opened her mouth to speak, but Holly got in first. 'Great idea, Anne.'

Val's brow furrowed but she nodded in agreement.

Holly pointed out of the window. 'The second hut is where customers will pay for nursery purchases, such as plants, ornaments and the pots we've filled. And I'll have a display in there, about the hub and the farmer's market.'

'Sounds like you've got everything organised, as per usual,' Julie said.

Holly nodded. 'I hope it's going to run smoothly. So Anne, can you cover the snack shack? And Julie cover the sales hut? Then I'll do general selling and answering questions. My usual role.'

The women nodded.

'Then Joe can keep the stock flowing to and from the old barn.'

'Sounds like a plan.' Joe picked up the last crumbs of his bread pudding and popped them into his mouth.

Holly lifted a leaflet. 'I designed this.'

Julie held out her hand. 'Let's see?'

Holly handed them all a copy. 'I've had one thousand printed and I'm going to do a drop around the village this afternoon and the Eversley Burrows estate tomorrow. I've left a load at the school to be sent home in the kids' bags and I've paid for an additional batch to be printed and inserted in the Gazette. As you know, that covers a ten-mile radius.' Holly sat back in her seat. 'Hopefully, word will reach our regulars. If you think you can distribute any, then let me know and I'll get you a batch.'

'Len could take some to his bowls club,' Val said.

'That's a great idea,' Anne added.

'And I've updated our website, adding links to social media, which I've set up nursery pages for.' Holly had avoided social media up until this point, but realised it was an essential marketing tool. She needed to get word out that Lovelands would soon be back in business, and would need to promote the hub and the farmers' market. 'It's all been a bit time-consuming, but it's given me something to do at night.' There followed a silence. Holly felt as if they were suddenly focussing their minds on her personal life.

Julie broke the silence. 'Heard anything from Mitch? Ouch!'

Holly guess Anne had kicked Julie under the table.

'What about the play area and animals?' Anne asked quickly.

'That's passed the health and safety checks.' Joe pointed

in the direction of the petting area. 'As you can see, I've given it a good lick of paint and wood preserver.'

'We have the latest crop of rabbits, we can sell some of those and deliver them once they're ready to leave their mother,' Anne said.

'Fab,' Holly said. 'I've been in touch with the coach tour companies. They're a bit hesitant, what with the place being in ruins. But a couple of the owners will be popping by to suss it out. I said I'd give a talk about Lovelands' history and explain what the future plans were. They said they may put us back on their route. Apparently, their customers are not keen on the big chain nurseries they've been stopping at, they said it was like going to the supermarket.' Holly smiled; these were all positive steps forward. She picked up the pile of leaflets 'When we reopen on Monday, I'll have different leaflets printed showing details of the farmers' market.'

'Will Mitch be back for Monday?' Joe asked.

Holly could see Val staring at her, but she kept her voice steady, even if she could feel her skin turn pink. 'I've had a quick call from him, saying that Sidney's not strong enough to travel.' Holly brushed the hair out of her eyes. 'Which is why I want us to smooth out any issues on the nursery side before he gets back.'

'He's coming back, then?' Val said, her eyebrows lifted.

'Of course he is. He's just been detained due to Sidney's ill health.' Holly noticed the way her stomach flipped. She realised she would be extremely disappointed if Mitch failed to return.

Val snorted. 'Sidney's probably sick 'cos his nephew's going into business with a Loveland.'

Holly decided to quiz Val on the full details of the family feud. There was clearly more to it than an ancient land dispute. She would quiz her in the car. Val, usually tight-lipped, seemed to be in the mood for talking.

Holly clapped her hands. 'Let's get to work.'

LATER, when Holly drove Val home, she wasn't able to ask her about the Loveland-Booth feud, because Val dosed off in the van. It would have to wait.

CHAPTER 21

*A*fter a long day preparing for the imminent opening of the nursery, Holly drank fridge-cooled water and fanned herself with a nursery leaflet. The caravan's metal shell had heated up throughout the day and even though it was evening, she still felt like she was being baked in an oven. As Holly got ready for bed, she wondered whether anyone would show up for the reopening the following day. She hoped so, the Rural Business Committee meeting she had attended at the Town Hall late last week had gone well. Nina had been unable to attend, which Holly was relieved about. The rest of the committee were encouraging about the farmers' market. She had also spoken at great length about the arts hub and was pleased by how interested the committee members were, which included two more councillors. That would be four votes, assuming David Bunning would still support her after what she assumed Grace might have told him about her.

Holly's thoughts were interrupted by her phone which dinged with a text. Walking to her table she picked the phone up to see it was from Mitch.

Hi, we're back. Will come over first thing in morning. Would pick Trixy up now but was a long journey, got caught in holiday traffic. Looking forward to seeing you x

Holly swallowed. *A kiss?* she thought. The feeling began in her stomach and spread over her body with heat rising up from her chest, making her face flush. *Remember, he's got a thing for Nina,* she told herself as she padded through to the bedroom.

Later, Holly tossed and turned, unable to sleep. The caravan felt too warm and the sheets stuck to her. Checking her phone, she saw it was just after midnight. She got up and opened the caravan door to let in some air. Squinting, she thought she saw something over at the farm. A figure was moving in the distance, in front of the farmhouse. She wondered whether it was a dog. But the figure appeared to be much larger than a dog but not big enough to be an escaped cow – yet it was on all fours. Shuddering, Holly worried about her animals. There were often rumours in the village about big cats roaming farmland and killing off livestock. Hugging herself, the cool air met her moist skin and she decided to go back inside. As she leaned out to grab the door handle, she saw the figure rise on two legs.

'Oh! It's a person,' she said.

They took two steps, then slipped to the ground. She saw a flash of a face in the moonlight. She stopped still. What if it was Mitch? Was he hurt? Holly grabbed her mobile. Having no time to change out of her pyjama shorts and vest, she fetched her hoodie and grabbed her work boots and quickly pulled them on. Shutting the caravan door behind her, she jogged towards the farm.

In daylight the journey took only five minutes but in the dark, with only the moonlight to guide her, she felt as if she had been jogging for ages. She rang Mitch's mobile but it went unanswered and diverted to voicemail. Not wanting to go too fast, for fear of slipping, she kept her eyes focussed on the figure which remained motionless on the floor. She hoped Mitch, if it was Mitch, was okay. Maybe he had been drinking trying to relax after the long journey home. She turned on her phone's torch app, to help navigate the last hundred metres.

As she got closer, she stopped. It was a body but not Mitch's. This body had white hair and wore crumpled pyjamas. *Sidney.* He remained motionless. Holly crept forward slowly. Reaching him, she touched his shoulder. 'Sidney, can you hear me?' She rang Mitch's number again but he still did not answer,

A groan came from the elderly man.

'Are you hurt? Can you tell me where you feel pain?'

Sidney opened his eyes and spoke in a rasp. 'Oh Ivy. It's time.'

Holly sat on her hunches and stroked his back, she called 999. 'Ambulance, I have an elderly man collapsed.' She gave them the address and told them to be quick. As she ended the call, her phone lit up. It was Mitch.

'Holly? Did you mean to call me?' He sounded groggy.

'Yes, it's Sidney — he's outside your house. He's collapsed.'

'What?'

'Yes, about ten meters from your back door.' She heard a window open above.

Mitch leaned out. 'I'll be right down.'

Sidney groaned. 'Getting old, so old. You never got old. My Ivy.'

Holly stroked Sidney's hand. 'Mitch is coming.'

'He's a good boy, such a good boy. He could have been our boy. Such a waste.'

The door flung open and Mitch appeared, his hair dishevelled, his face full of stubble. Holly's back tingled. *Not now,* she thought. *Not at a time like thi*s. She looked back to Sidney. His eyes were full of tears.

Mitch bent down, carefully easing Sidney into the recovery position. A trickle of dark blood seeped from a gash in his head, moving through his pale white hair.

Mitch stood up. 'I can't believe he got himself out here. It must have been an adrenaline rush or something. I'll get the truck. We need to get him to hospital as soon as possible.'

'I've called an ambulance.'

'They could be ages, it'll be quicker if I drive.'

They fell silent as Sidney's breathing rasped even more, wheezing with a whine. 'So silly, wasted moments,' he spluttered as blood came out of the corner of his mouth.

Mitch crouched down, stroking Sid's head. 'Hang on, Sid. Help is coming.' His eyes glistened.

Holly knew they would be unable to move Sid and willed the ambulance to arrive.

Sid opened his eyes. 'Don't you waste time like I did, son. She was my world. If only I'd been here, things would have been different ...'

Mitch rubbed Sidney's arm. 'Rest, Sid, save your breath. They'll be here soon.'

Sid turned his head in Holly's direction. 'I thought you were my Ivy, coming to collect me.'

Holly smiled. 'Val always says I'm the image of my grandmother.'

'I'm sorry, my dear, it's not your fault.' He took a deep wheezy breath. 'The Lovelands and the Booths never got on, not even before she and I ...' Sidney began to splutter and blood trickled down his face.

Mitch pulled his T-shirt off and used it to wipe Sidney's cheek. Holly averted her gaze, scared she would stare at his muscular torso.

Mitch touched Sid's shoulder. 'Well, me and Holly, we get on. Holly has no problem with us.'

'Your grandfather, Bill ... he was a good sort ...' Sidney's voice trailed away, his breaths began to come faster, his body and chest pulsated with every wheeze until the last one.

Mitch took Sidney's limp wrist, feeling for a pulse. 'Sid, Sid, wake up.' He looked up at Holly with a shake of his head.

Holly felt tears stream down her face. She had not seen grief this close up before – other than in the mirror.

Mitch gently placed Sid's head down on the floor, resting it on his bloodied T-shirt, then rose to standing. He turned his back to Holly, his shoulders hunched. Holly had an overwhelming urge to hold him, to comfort him and she moved forward, then back again, unsure how he would react. She gazed at the lifeless, yet peaceful, elderly man, nothing like the broad figure she used to watch stomping across his land. She had seen the dead before, having been required to identify her parents. That had been awful – their bodies were broken. She shuddered and blinked away the image. This was different, Sid seemed at rest. She turned away, staring again at Mitch, aching to hold him but not wanting to intrude on his private moment of grief, but neither did she want to ignore it.

'Shall I call someone?'

Mitch coughed. 'It's okay, let's wait for the ambulance.' He shook his head. 'It's all my fault. I should have stayed with him. I let Magda go home for the night, seeing as she's been with us in Essex for over two weeks. For some reason, Sid seemed stronger than he's been in months.'

'He must have been, to get himself out here.' Holly said.

'I seem to have a habit of letting people down.'

Holly realised Mitch was referring to his wife. 'Nonsense this is not your fault. You've been caring for him, you've made his last weeks much brighter. Without you, he might have faded away in a nursing home.'

Stepping forward, she felt now was the time to comfort him, but they both turned at the sound of the ambulance arriving. The lights were flashing but no sirens were needed on this quiet night. Holly left Mitch and approached the vehicle as the paramedics jumped out.

'How is he?'

'I'm afraid he's gone. He's been poorly for some time. It seems he came out for a walk and fell. I saw him from my caravan.' She pointed to her home. 'But Sid had hit his head and he passed a few minutes ago.' Holly shook her head and felt her voice breaking up.

'I'll check to confirm the death and speak to the next of kin.

Holly nodded her head and led them to Mitch and Sidney.

The paramedic had a quiet word with Mitch, which she could not hear and then bent down and held Sidney's wrist. Checking his watch, he wrote on a piece of paper. 'I'll call out the doctor and the local undertaker.'

Mitch nodded.

The paramedic turned to Holly. 'Could you take Mitch into the house. Get him something warm to wear and a drink.'

Mitch remained silent and let Holly lead him back into the house. She took a hoodie, which hung from a hook inside the back door and handed it to him.

Once inside the kitchen, Mitch sat at the table, zipping

up the top. 'The brandy's in the bottom cupboard.' Mitch pointed to a kitchen unit.

Holly poured the thick liquid into two mugs and passed one to Mitch.

Mitch took a gulp. 'Vanessa was too young to die. I should have told her not to get the tractor. I was in a rush. It was my job. If I hadn't been on the phone, if I'd checked the time, I would have realised how long she'd been gone. An hour, an hour I left her.' He put his face in his arms.

Holly bit her lip and tasted the tears as they fell down her cheeks. 'You can't keep blaming yourself.'

Mitch looked up. 'She bled to death. If I'd discovered her quickly enough, she'd still be alive. How's that not my fault?'

'I can't say anything to make you feel better. But I know that you clearly loved her and it wasn't your doing.'

'I'm sorry.' He sat up and rubbed the back of his neck. 'I didn't mean to be morbid and self-absorbed.'

'It's a shock when people die, even when it's expected.'

Mitch nodded. 'I've not spoken about it – about Vanessa – apart from to the police. Not a word since she died.'

Holly reached a hand across the table and touched his fingers. Mitch held her gaze and she felt a warmth travel over her body. Her arms ached, she wanted to embrace him, to be with him. Bringing her hand back, she broke contact, knowing this was not the right time.

Holly jumped as there was a loud rap on the door. 'I'll get it.' She stood up to let the paramedics in.

HOLLY FELT SURPRISINGLY awake for the reopening of the nursery, considering how little sleep she'd had. Looking out of the caravan window, she admired the information boards in the distance that she had set up to promote the farmers' market. They had decided to call it, West Country Farmers' Market, not wanting to use either the Loveland or Booth names. Mitch had suggested they called it 'West Country' rather than 'Somerset' as he had two contacts in North Devon who were keen to bring stock over.

Holly looked down towards the farmhouse, wondering how Mitch was. She had texted him first thing to offer her help over the coming days, which she knew would be full of paperwork and arrangements, but she hadn't heard anything from him yet. Staring at the inside of the caravan door she straightened her uniform.

'Let's get this nursery open,' she said to a yapping Trixy

There was a steady stream of customers from the village. Holly guessed that Jaz had bullied everyone she saw into coming, considering she had been spending a lot of her time in the Eversley Arms. There were villagers who came through the gates that she had never seen before at the nursery. Holly had been over to the Eversley Arms for a few evening meals, and had got to know more of the locals. Holly had been feeling much more connected to the village, realising that over the years the Lovelands had always been perceived as being somewhat aloof, with her family histori-cally keeping themselves to themselves, as had the Booths. She wanted to feel a part of the village now, hoping that the planned arts hub would bring everyone together.

Holly had considered offering a free cup of tea to entice people in, but Jaz had told her to have more confidence. And she was right, as there were many people forming a queue at the snack shack. There were few free spaces at the tables and chairs which Holly had set out. She still had 'for sale' notices on the garden furniture, hoping that customers would enjoy using it and order a set. Her staff buzzed around; Val was not there due to her hip hurting, but she had baked many cakes with Anne's help.

Kids of all ages were using the play area. Some gawped through the fence at her burned-down house. The younger ones were calling to their parents, 'Mummy come see.' *Mitch was right,* she thought. As soon as she pictured Mitch in her mind, she saw him walk up the path, Trixy yapped wildly. Holly ran towards him with Trixy at her heels. She was surprised to see him after the shock he had the previous evening. Once he reached her, he avoided her gaze. Trixy jumped up at him, he picked her up and the dog licked his face.

Mitch smiled, but Holly thought his tired eyes had lost their shine. 'Someone's pleased to see me?' He ruffled Trixy's fur.

'Yes,' was all Holly could manage. *Don't be awkward*, she told herself.

'You look great.' Mitch stared at Holly's uniform then lowered his gaze.

Holly smoothed down her cerise, figure-hugging polo top, sporting the new nursery logo which she had teamed with khaki shorts.

'There are a fair few people here. I won't disturb you while you're busy.' Mitch tucked Trixy under his arm. 'I'll catch up with you on Monday about the farmers' market. It's rushing up.' Mitch's voice sounded flat.

Holly hated seeing Mitch this low.

'Do you have Trixy's lead? I'll get her from under your feet.'

'Oh, yes. Yes, of course.' She walked back to the caravan,

feeling glum. Opening the door, she picked up Trixy's lead and bed, then turned – Mitch had followed her in and was standing close.

'Thanks, Holly,' he said staring deep into her eyes.

Holly smiled. 'See you soon.' She watched as Mitch put the lead on Trixy then stuffed the soft bed under his arm. He turned and left, with Trixy jumping up at him. Holly felt the urge to run after them both but instead took a deep breath and returned to work.

'WELL THAT WAS A SUCCESS.' Holly said, sitting outside the caravan on an iron table and chair set with Joe. He wore his green polo with a pink logo. An inverse of Holly's top as he had been far from keen on the cerise. Holly had joked that meant he had to wear pink trousers, but let him get away with green shorts as well, realising she had got carried away with her 'Gypsy Rose' theme.

Joe finished the last dregs of his bottled beer. 'How much did we take?'

'Just over six thousand, can you believe it?'

'My, that's some cups of tea.'

Holly laughed. 'With the hot weather, people wanted the tables, chairs and sun umbrellas. I've put in a massive order on-line, so you'll be out on deliveries next week, I'm so pleased. You know my greatest fear was that I'd have to let you all go.'

'Well, it's early days.'

'True, and we can't expect this every weekend. But let's hope the weather stays put.'

That evening, the caravan seemed eerily quiet in contrast to her busy day. Holly pulled the duvet over her aching body. 'Trixy,' she called waiting for the bundle of white fluff to bounce up onto her bed. She sighed, remembering Trixy had gone home. Too tired for the loneliness to keep her awake, she drifted off to sleep imagining she could hear Trixy bark and whine.

CHAPTER 22

*A*few days passed and Holly washed up her breakfast things, as she looked out of the caravan window and saw a thick front of grey cloud moving in. The sun, still shining, gave the clouds an almost purple hue. Holly bit her lip, it was the day of the meeting with three of the farmers that Mitch had convinced to join the market. A downpour would not show the land in its best light considering it was far from pretty following the fire and much of the ground was muddy due to the heavy machinery moving around the site. The sun always brightened it up.

She cleaned every surface of her small living area and set out glasses for water and cups for hot drinks. Glancing up to the caravan's ceiling, she heard the pitter patter of rain on the metal roof. The noise grew louder sounding like an avalanche of stones falling. Mitch arrived with the men in tow. Holly flung open the door and they removed their boots before entering.

'Do you think we should go to mine?' Mitch shouted over the din.

'Let's wait. It may pass. I'll make drinks.' Holly said, over-mouthing her words. She took their orders and coats and brought in the tub she had left outside for their boots, placing it in her spare room away from the rain.

Without speaking, they listened to the downpour as they drank tea and ate biscuits. After what seemed to Holly like forever, it dissipated.

'That was some cloud burst. Maybe a week's worth of rain,' the youngest farmer said. He had a shock of red hair.

'About time,' said another. 'Been too dry this year.'

Mitch took a sip of tea. 'Right. I'll do the introductions.'

Holly made a note of their names on her pad. She was glad as they all seemed enthusiastic about the market.

'The bigger units are going up this week,' she said. 'The electrics are already in place for the fridges and freezers.' She was pleased this was a joint venture, as Mitch had helped out with the cost of the white goods. 'I'm going to prepare a leaflet for each of your farms, with background information and photos.' Holly picked up a pile of A4 sheets of paper and handed them out. 'I've prepared a short questionnaire for each of you. Just for some details, so I know what to include in the blurb.' She picked up a colourful A5 leaflet. 'This is one I mocked up for Booth Farm, so you'll get an idea of what I'm thinking.'

'Has this gone to print?' Mitch asked as he took a leaflet.

'Oh no, I wouldn't do that without your approval. I just prepared this as an example.'

Mitch smiled as he read the leaflet. 'It's great. Do you mind if I take it? I'd like to add some info about Sid and what he did for the farm.'

'That would be lovely.' She nodded at the men. 'And if you could all email me a small photo of yourselves people love to see a pictures of food producers.'

'Next you'll be asking us to do a calendar,' Ed, the red-haired farmer said.

The men fell about laughing. Other than Mitch and Ed, they were middle-aged and greying.

Holly liked the way the atmosphere had relaxed and turned to Mitch. 'Maybe if you have a picture of Sid?'

'I can probably fish one out. I'll find one of him, in his younger days.'

'When's the funeral?' Ed asked.

'Next week – up at the Church.' Mitch nodded towards Eversley Village.

'Where my family are?' Holly asked.

'Yes.' Mitch coughed.

Holly became aware of an awkward silence and the caravan began to feel warm now that the sun had come out. 'Well, the rain's stopped. I'll show you the site.'

The men followed her out. Even though there were puddles on the ground, the sun had brightened the place up.

Holly spoke about her plans for her arts hub project. 'With an increased footfall at the nursery and arts hub, the farmers' market will of course benefit from this. In fact, we've already started to attract customers back, even with the nursery in this state.'

As if on cue, two families entered the nursery grounds.

Holly nodded at them and they all stepped back to let the customers pass.

'The rates we've offered to you for the rental of units on this site are extremely competitive and would remain at the same rate for three years.'

'We appreciate it's a bit of a punt, guys,' Mitch said.

Holly nodded. 'But your loyalty will be rewarded for getting in at the ground floor.'

The meeting ended with three very firm handshakes. Holly felt butterflies in her stomach. *It's really going to happen,* she thought. *The market, the rebuild, the hub.*

WITH JOE'S HELP, Holly put the final touches to her new art studio. It was in the second bedroom of the caravan. With things starting to move along, she wanted to focus on her vision. It was more than reopening the nursery, it was also about her art. Holly knew she had to focus on rebuilding her portfolio. With no work to display it would be some months, maybe a year, until the hub opened. If it opened. What if Tom refused to back off? Forced her to sell? With no land, she would have no nursery, no arts hub and no home. Holly pushed the negative thoughts out of her mind. But they were always lurking there in the background — the disaster waiting to scupper her plans.

'Perfect,' Holly said, stepping back looking at her new workspace. 'I told you there was enough room for an easel. And the cupboard is the ideal size for my palate to perch on.' Holly was excited at the sight of the paints she had bought from her favourite art shop in Bristol.

Joe scratched his head. 'Make sure you keep the window open, love. For ventilation. And no matches.'

Holly put her hands on her hips. 'I never started the fire, Joe.' She shook her head. 'I still maintain it must have been something to do with the electrics. Too much of a co-inci-dence, the fire starting after the light bulb blew.'

Joe raised his eyebrows. 'So you keep saying.'

Holly knew Joe was teasing her, but she did wonder at times whether people thought the fire was her fault. She guessed she would never know exactly what happened.

Holly waved Joe goodbye. Picking up her new computer

tablet, she opened her cloud storage to view the paintings she had logged before the fire. *Where to begin?* she thought. It was her aim to reproduce the paintings. Whilst it had taken years to create the collection, much of the time had gone into conceiving the ideas. Flicking through the images she came to a multi-coloured dragon in acrylic. It was her first competition piece from when she was a teen. A carefree time she wanted to tap into.

She set up her materials, then took a deep breath, staring at the canvas. Dipping her brush into the paint, she made the first stroke.

TWO DAYS LATER, Holly was still working on her dragon. She had left her staff to cover the nursery. Since the reopening there had been a steady flow of visitors, especially on sunny days. Some brought picnic blankets and sat on the grassy slopes of the top field as their children played, enjoying the cakes and refreshments bought on site. As well as the snack shack doing a roaring trade, the pots and hanging baskets had proved popular. They had sold so many, Holly wondered whether there were any houses left in the village without a Lovelands' filled pot or hanging basket.

Holly stopped painting as she heard a rap at the caravan's open door, followed by Trixy barking.

'Come in.' She turned to see Mitch lifting a white plastic bag with the logo of Eversley's local store on it.

'I've brought lunch.' He smiled at Holly's acrylic splattered apron. 'You've been painting?'

'Yes,' she said to her uninvited but most welcome guest.

'Do I get to see your work in progress?'

'Okay, but don't feel pressure to say you like it if it's not your thing. It's very different to the landscape.'

'I'm sure it's great.'

Holly was surprised at how much she was able to achieve. 'I've been trying to recreate my collection. This is the first one, but it's taken on a freer vibe compared with the original.'

She stepped to one side as Mitch squeezed into the small room beside her.

'It's tight in here,' he said. 'I'm surprised you don't pass out with the fumes.'

'It's not ideal, but it's a space. It's called *Dragon's Mouth*.'

'I can tell it's yours,' Mitch said.

'The dragon's mouth is wider than before.' Holly pointed at the canvas. 'And I've added flecks of blue to its eyes.'

'I love the way the blue juxtaposes the red fiery scales of the body.'

Holly laughed. 'You sound like an art critic.'

'My artistic knowledge is pretty limited. But I know I love your work.'

Holly blushed, feeling hot in the enclosed space, aware of his body in close proximity to hers. 'I painted the original when I was seventeen. I tend to stretch the spectrum a lot more these days.' Holly felt a tear in her eye. 'One of the reasons I want to set up the hub is so that people who might not have painted before can step back and get a buzz from looking at their own creations.'

'I'm sure the hub will come off.' Mitch smiled at her as she turned and faced him. His eyes travelled down to her lips. She swallowed hard. Holly heard Jaz's voice calling her in the distance. She was unsure whether she was relieved or annoyed at the interruption, convinced that Mitch had been about to kiss her. He stepped back to allow Holly out of the room.

Walking to the window, she saw her petite friend

approaching the caravan holding hands with Julian who seemed like a giant at her side. 'Well, well.' She shook her head. 'Who'd have thought?'

Jaz appeared at the door, with her face flushed.

Julian grinned.

Holly raised her eyebrows. 'Hi, you two. You seem to be spending a lot of time together.'

'Yes, we are,' Julian said and put his arm around Jaz's shoulders. 'We've been in each other's erm –'

'Pockets.' Jaz giggled and dug Julian in the ribs as he planted a kiss on her nose. Jaz looked over Holly's shoulder. 'Hi, Mitch.' Then winked at Holly.

'I came up to see Holly about the farmers' market and I brought lunch.' Mitch pointed to the carrier bag he had left on the table. 'I've more than enough if you want to join us, although it's only a crusty loaf, cheese and ham.'

'Suits me.' Jaz climbed up the caravan steps followed by Julian.

Holly opened her kitchen cupboard. 'I'll get us some plates out.' She also fetched a knife, butter and a couple of jars of pickle.

Julian put out his hand to Mitch. 'Sorry to hear about your uncle.'

Mitch shook his hand. 'Thanks, mate. I'll have to come into the pub sometime.' Mitch turned to Jaz. 'Holly's told me lots about you.'

'Oh dear,' Jaz laughed and led Julian to the small dining table and they sat down.

Mitch emptied the items from the bag on the table. 'Where's Trixy gone? I haven't seen here since I arrived. She hasn't run off has she?'

Holly bit her lip, realising that she was probably asleep on her bed.

At the sound of her name Trixy trotted into the living area and sniffed around Holly's ankles, then returned to the bedroom.

'Julian's had an amazing idea.' Jaz placed her hand on his chest.

'It was your idea, Jazzy,' Julian said.

'Rubbish. He's being overly modest.' Jaz squeezed Julian's leg. 'It was his idea.'

Holly sat at the table, as Mitch cut the bread into thick slices. 'So, what's the big idea?' she asked.

'Well, I was saying to Julian how I miss the fairs – you know, the ones we used to have on the village green?'

Holly nodded. 'Until 2009, when the rains came and it wrecked the grass and they had to re-seed it.'

Julian laughed. 'It was like Glastonbury. A right mudbath.'

Holly smiled. 'I loved the stalls – the competitions, the animals, the music. I looked forward to it every year.'

Mitch nodded. 'I went to one, only the once. Sid would never have gone, but I was up here with Mum. I loved it. We took one of Sid's calves to show in the baby animal competition.'

'Hey, I remember a calf being there once,' Jaz said, as she sliced cheese.

'Yes, it got loose,' Mitch said.

Holly laughed. 'No-one will forget that.'

Holly watched Mitch smiling, thinking that he got better-looking every day. She averted her eyes, focussing them on Jaz. 'So, you want to start up the village fair again?' She turned to Julian. 'Do you have possession of the green as your tables are on there?'

Julian shook his head. 'No, I arrange for the grass to be

cut for the entire green, and the committee let me off rent. I can't use it for any other purpose.'

Jaz glanced at Julian and then back at Holly. 'We were going to ask you.'

'Me? I'm not on the village committee.'

'No. To have it here, at the nursery – you've all those acres with not much happening.' Jaz pointed out of the window.

'Here?' Holly asked.

Jaz nodded. 'Yeah, on the high ground and you could do egg rolling or something down the hill.'

'Egg rolling? It's not Easter,' Holly said.

'Or cheese rolling,' Julian said, then popped a piece into his mouth.

Mitch turned to Holly. 'Well it is feasible. You've certainly got enough flat land up here for the stalls. And if we do it the same day as the farmers' market, it could be great publicity. If we could convince one of the cider farmers to come over, they often put up their own marquee.'

'Is it one thing too many? What with the nursery, the hub, the market?' Holly bit her lip.

Jaz clapped her hands. 'No, they all go together. It's a great idea. You could show some of your work, too. Put up the hub drawings.'

'I've only got one painting so far.'

'You've got the competition painting,' Mitch said.

'I guess I could invite the Mayor to open the fair. That way she'll get to see the plans and hopefully support the Arts Council application.'

Mitch finished his mouthful. 'And invite the rest of the councillors. You need as many on side as possible.'

Holly could feel the excitement welling up inside.

Jaz clapped her hands together, sending her sandwich

flying across the table. 'It's a yes then. Yay!' She slapped a high five with Julian, then retrieved the bread and cheese, putting her sandwich back together.

'When's the farmers' market then?' Julian asked.

Mitch smiled. 'Two weeks Saturday.'

Julian buttered another slice of bread. 'I can put a notice up in the pub and get word out.'

Jaz touched Holly's hand. 'We'll co-ordinate all the stall requests from the pub, and borrow tables from the Village Hall. You've enough to do here. The deadline will work well, people won't have time to think about it – they'll just say yes.'

'Might be tricky getting a cider farmer in,' Mitch said.

'Leave that with me. Worst case scenario, we'll hire a marquee ourselves, and I'll place an order from my usual brewery,' Julian said.

Holly's mind was spinning. *Is this possible?* she thought.

'Show them what you've been painting.' Mitch pointed to the mini-studio.

'You can't all fit in there, I'll bring it out.' Holly went to retrieve her painting, resting it against the door. There were gasps and compliments. 'It's all very well me painting. I guess I could do three more over the next couple of weeks, but I've nowhere to keep them. The sheds aren't dry enough and the old barn has a few leaks.'

Mitch put his hand up. 'Bring them to my place – I'm having a clear out anyway, now that Sid's gone.'

Holly saw the sadness return to Mitch's eyes. 'If you're sure? Although it still needs to fully dry before I can move it. I'll pop it by tomorrow.'

They finished the bread, ham and cheese and chatted some more about memories of the annual fairs of their childhood.

Mitch stood up. 'I'd better get Trixy. I have a few jobs this afternoon. Where is she?' Mitch looked around the space for her.

Holly stood up and went into the bedroom, Trixy was on the bed asleep.

Mitch appeared behind her. 'I see. This is why she won't sleep at mine anymore.'

'Trixy, time to go home.' Holly watched as the little dog woke up and bounded across the bed, jumping into her arms and licking Holly's face before burying her fluffy head under her chin.

Mitch shook his head. 'I've only seen her do that to one other person.' He gave a little smile.

Holly felt a lump in her throat, realising he must be referring to Vanessa.

'She's been pining for you, and keeping me awake at night. I've been shattered. I've had to let her into my room.'

Holly bit her lip. 'Sorry, I guess I may have spoiled her a little bit while you were away. Although I've trained her to behave in public, I wasn't so strict behind closed doors. Do you want to leave her with me tonight? So you can get some sleep?'

'I don't want to impose. You already put up with her for two weeks.'

Holly laughed. 'I said I'd do whatever I could to help you out at the moment. If it helps you get some sleep, then that's how I'll help.'

Trixy yapped.

Holly laughed. 'See, she wants a sleep-over.'

Jaz appeared behind Mitch. 'What's this about a sleep-over?'

Holly felt her face heat up. 'Trixy is staying here tonight.'

Jaz winked. 'Well me and Ju Ju have to get back to the

pub. He left Simon, the barman in charge. He's training him up in management, to take the pressure off.'

Mitch smiled at Holly. 'I'll be off too, then. If you need help bringing the painting down tomorrow, let me know.'

Holly shut the door as soon as she was alone. Even though she knew any relationship with Mitch was not a great idea and mixing business with pleasure should be avoided, she could not help feeling excited about taking the picture down to him the following day. Especially after the near kiss they had experienced earlier. She smiled to herself as Trixy jumped up at her legs.

CHAPTER 23

*A*fter breakfast the following day, Holly covered her dragon painting in bubble wrap for transportation to Booth Farm. It was a fine day, but she did not want to run the risk of the painting becoming wet in any unexpected downpour. Trixy stayed at Holly's heel as she carried the painting to her van then the little dog jumped up to the passenger seat, settling herself as Holly drove the short distance to the farm.

Once they arrived at Booth Farm, Holly gave Trixy a treat for behaving herself. Trixy trotted ahead as they walked around the back of the house to the kitchen entrance. When Holly reached the door, it swung open and Mitch stood before her with a broad smile. He wore jeans and a black T-shirt. Holly took a deep breath, then slowly released the air from her lungs.

Mitch stepped to one side and motioned her to come in. 'Where is it, then?' he asked.

'Oh yes, the painting. It's in the van.'

'I'll fetch it – is it locked?'

Holly shook her head.

Mitch nodded towards the inside of his house. 'I'm clearing out the rooms – I've got stuff everywhere and it's a bit of a hazard. It might be safer if you stay in the kitchen.'

'I'll make us coffee.'

Mitch's phone rang and he pulled it out of his back pocket. 'I've got to take this. I'll bring the painting in afterwards.' He walked outside, pressing his phone to his ear.

Holly filled the kettle at the sink and clicked it on. Listening to the sound of the water boiling, she realised Trixy had become unusually quiet. She scanned the kitchen to find her gone.

Holly heard yapping from further inside the house. 'Trixy,' she called.

With visions of the dog overturning piles of precariously stacked items she followed the sound of her bark. Standing at the kitchen door, Holly peered around the corner, the small corridor was empty of clutter. Seeing a door open with light shining out and the distant sound of the pitter patter of Trixy's paws from that direction, she decided to retrieve her. She took a deep breath and walked along the corridor passing the guest room she had stayed in on the night of the fire, towards the open door. Once inside, she found the room was dimly-lit but at the far end was a conservatory, full of plants – she could smell them from where she stood.

'Wow,' she said aloud. 'I wasn't expecting this.'

There was a wide and full, floor-to-ceiling bookcase with a ladder on a runner. The wooden floor was covered in part by an old paisley rug. Her gaze stopped when it reached the fireplace. Above it was a painting of a woman wearing a long flowing floral dress — the hair was the same as her own and the eyes, hers also. Holly put her hand to her throat and gasped, blood whooshed through her ears, her mouth agape. *Why has he got a painting of me?* she thought. Trixy jumped up at her. Scooping her up, Holly walked towards the portrait. It appeared not to have been painted recently, indeed it was aged. She puffed air out and shook her head, as she realised it was Granny Ivy. *But why is it here?* she thought.

Holly hurried back to the kitchen with Trixy in her arms, as Mitch opened the back door and walked in with her dragon painting in his hands. Trixy jumped to the floor and ran over to him.

Mitch placed the painting up against the wall and frowned. 'You okay?'

Holly's face burned red. 'Yes. I couldn't find the coffee?'

He pointed to a large tin on the worktop with *coffee* written on it. 'Didn't look too far then?' he chuckled.

Holly shook a little as she spooned the instant coffee into mugs then filled them with boiling water. Why would Sid be given the painting unless they were close? It would mean her Mum might not have told her the whole truth when she said that the relationship between Sid and Ivy had been a one-sided infatuation.

Mitch picked up one of the mugs of coffee. 'You're quiet. Are you okay?'

Holly took a sip of coffee and felt her hand shake. The painting she had seen of Ivy was so large, it was as if she had seen her Granny's ghost staring at her. 'So, when's the funeral?'

'Next Wednesday.'

'And he's being laid to rest in the church grounds?' Holly sipped her hot drink.

'Yes. I ...' Mitch coughed. 'Maybe we should talk about our families.'

'In what respect?'

'About Sid and Ivy.'

Holly bit her lip. While she wanted to find out the details, she still felt a bit shaky having just seen Ivy's portrait, and preferred to hear it from Val. 'It's all water under the bridge. Did you know my Granny Ivy was the last to be buried up at the church?' Holly took a deep breath. 'She died giving birth to my Mum.'

Mitch nodded.

'They ran out of space. So my grandad and parents were cremated and the ashes scattered over the family plot.' Holly took a sip of her coffee. 'So Sid's being cremated is he?'

'No, a burial.' Mitch rubbed the back of his neck.

Holly frowned.

'He reserved a plot years ago. Before it filled up.'

'Really?'

Mitch coughed.

'Sorry, didn't mean to sound critical. I'd like to come.' *Why did I say that?* she thought. She hated funerals.

'No.'

Holly frowned at Mitch. 'Oh, are Lovelands not welcome?'

Mitch cleared his throat. 'My family would welcome you, but Sid indicated he wanted the service to be family only and as I said, maybe we should talk about Sid and your grandmother, Ivy.'

Holly sipped her coffee. 'Another time.'

'Okay, but all I am doing is respecting his wishes. Come here for the wake afterwards – it'll be at two o'clock.'

'Do you need any help with the food?'

'No, my parents and sister will be here and they'll no doubt be wanting to busy themselves with the preparations.'

'If there's any help you need whatsoever, just let me know.' Holly wanted to change the subject. She studied Mitch, and realised that whilst she felt a connection, there was so much she did not know about him. What was his favourite colour? What was his favourite football team? Maybe he was a rugby kind of guy?

Holly put her cup down and folded her hands on the table. 'What football team do you support?'

Mitch laughed. 'That's a bit random.'

Holly blushed.

'Are you after a date for a football match?' Mitch smiled.

Holly swallowed. 'No, I just wondered what you were into.'

'What I'm into?' Mitch sipped his coffee, smiling at her over the cup, his eyes not leaving her face.

She felt hot and instantly regretted what sounded like a chat up line. 'Sports-wise.'

'Well, I love ice hockey.'

'Ice hockey? Is that big in Essex?'

Mitch laughed and sat back in his chair. 'No. I went on an agricultural field trip with college and we spent some time in Canada. I watched a few games and was hooked, even had a go myself and I wasn't that bad either. It's not something I could do back home in Braintree, but I've continued to follow it.'

'Interesting.'

'Is it?' Mitch grinned. 'What are you into Holly? Sports or otherwise?'

'The only sport I've played in recent years is darts, up at the Eversley Arms.'

'Really? That surprises me.'

'Only against Jaz. I'm not on the team.' Holly drained her cup, scalding her throat. 'Well, I'd better get back to my little studio.'

Mitch raised his eyebrows; did she detect disappointment?

'Don't forget there's also the competition piece, which I should be getting back soon.'

'I'll let you know when I've finished the next one.' Trixy was immediately at her heel and they both trotted out of the house and she was half-way back to the nursery in the van, before she realised that she was supposed to be dropping Trixy off.

'Oh well, one more sleep over,' she said to the dog.

Back at the caravan, Holly filled a bowl with food for Trixy. She still had a supply in her cupboard. She sent a text to Mitch, apologising. He replied, suggesting she return Trixy the next time they met – adding that he looked forward to it. Was that looking forward to having Trixy back? Or looking forward to seeing her? Holly's thoughts were interrupted as her mobile rang – it was an unknown caller. She hesitated, then answered.

'Yes?'

'Hi, it's me.'

Oh no, not Tom, she thought.

'It's Tom,' he said when she remained silent.

'Yes, I know who it is. What do you want?'

'I want us to come to an agreement. It's not going to be nice you know, going to court.'

'My solicitor has advised me not to discuss the situation with you.'

'Of course she has, Holly. She's fleecing you with over the top fees. I've heard she's a right rip-off.'

'The fees don't bother me, seeing as I'm suing you for the costs. You're the one that should drop it.'

'You won't win. They know that. Your woman's always on the phone begging my man not to go to court. She's not up to the job, Holly. You'd be much better off settling. I still care about you, you know. I don't want to see you hurt. Can't we sort this out and move on?'

Holly took a deep breath and counted to ten, remaining silent.

'Okay then – have it your way.'

Holly felt as if her blood was boiling. 'You're wasting your time, Tom.'

'I'm only thinking of you. Things get out of hand with solicitors, why don't we meet up, you and me alone and try and sort this thing out?'

'As I said – I was advised not to discuss it with you.'

'Don't get too deep into those plans of yours.' Tom hung up.

Holly bit her lip, she hated that Tom might be asking around and snooping on her. But he was right, she felt uncomfortable investing in the business with this separation hanging over her head. The farmers' market and fair were to take place in under two weeks, everything was happening at once. She sat at her small dining table and put her head in her hands. Holly had too much to contend with. Her mobile phone rang and she jumped. It was Jill.

'I'm afraid Tom's solicitor hasn't backed off,' Jill said after the usual pleasantries.

'Yes, I know, Tom said.'

'Oh, he's been on to you, has he?'

'Yes, telling me I'll get torn to shreds if it goes to court.'

'That's good.'

'How's that good?'

'If they were confident – they wouldn't bother to wind you up.'

'I've got so much going on, I don't think I can do this. Maybe I should go to the bank and see if I can raise some money to settle with him.'

'I told you from the outset, they're a bunch of cowboys. Hang tight. Trust me, it won't go to court.'

Holly placed her phone on the table after ending the call. Trixy jumped onto her lap and she stroked her, finding it comforting. She watched Joe through the window as he worked on one of the new large sheds. She could see Anne in the snack shack, serving a queue of people. Julie was handing over change to a customer who was paying for a pot. Holly realised she would have to stand her ground with Tom. But dread filled her veins. She asked herself, *Am I going to lose everything?*

CHAPTER 24

olly stood outside, watching the development of the land. The landscape of the nursery was gradually changing as sheds for the farmers to sell their goods from were built. Luckily planning permission had been rushed through. Holly had hired a carpenter to assist Joe with the erection of the larger sheds. The contractor was making headway in clearing the nursery ruins of the materials to be discarded and ensuring the remaining stone walls were safe, although it seemed to be happening a lot slower than Holly would wish. She had not seen Mitch for a few days. He had been making arrangements for Sid's funeral and was tied up with quarantining a sick cow. So Holly was surprised to see a text come through from him.

Are you free today? I need help searching through Sid's papers and have something you may like to have. I could do with the company x.

Holly's heart gave a quick flip. Flushing hot, she stared at the phone. *Stop reading stuff into it,* she told herself. *He might just be after his dog back.* Holly sent a quick text to let him know she was on her way. Walking back to the caravan, Trixy trotted in front of her. She realised she had become part of her life now and Holly wished she could stay.

'Come on, girl. We'd better get you back.'

Holly arrived at the farmhouse with Trixy at heel. After greeting her, Mitch gestured for Holly to follow him and led her through the house as his little dog jumped up against his legs. Holly could see they were heading for the lounge and her heart pounded against her chest.

'I've made space for you to store your paintings in Sidney's lounge.'

'Oh, really?' She followed him into the room.

'It's quite dark this end, so the sun won't damage them.' Mitch pointed up the room. 'There's a conservatory, full of Sid's plants. They keep the sun from this end.'

'They're amazing.' Holly said, looking at a tall rubber plant with shiny leaves.

Mitch rubbed the back of his neck. 'I was going to ask you about that. I'm never going to be able to manage them. Magda used to look after them but she's already got a new job.'

Holly smiled. 'I can keep an eye on them if you like?'

'Or sell them at your place, if it's too much? But I'll see if there are any my mum wants to take back with her after the funeral.'

Holly thought she was doing a good job, acting as if it was the first time she had ever seen the room. 'It's like visiting an old stately home.'

'Not quite stately, but certainly like stepping back in time.'

'Well, I think it's beautiful.'

Trixy ran over to a worn chair, sniffed the seat, then jumped onto it, laying her head on her paws.

'It's as if she knows he's gone,' Mitch said as he walked over and ruffled the fur on Trixy's head.

Holly studied the fireplace. It had a grey and red marble surround, and a jet-black hearth. She avoided looking up at the painting, but soon found herself staring at it.

Mitch shifted his weight and cleared his throat.

Holly turned to him.

'She's so much like you. In fact, it could be you.'

Holly looked back to the fireplace and stared at the portrait.

'Can you see the likeness? It's your grandmother.'

Holly nodded and swallowed.

'She's beautiful,' he said in a low voice.

Holly felt the heat rise up to her face.

Mitch walked up behind her and put his hand on her shoulder. 'And I wondered if, when you've rebuilt your cottage, you might like it. Seeing as you've lost all your ancestors' furniture and family photographs.'

Holly's eyes filled with tears. 'Are you sure?' She walked towards the painting and put her hand to her throat.

'Sorry, Holly. I've caught you off guard. I should have warned you. I forget you've no blood family left. I'm insensitive.'

'No, it's a lovely gesture and I'd love to accept it. So how did Sid come by this?'

'He painted it.'

'He was an artist?'

'Yes, I have a few of his pieces but he stopped painting when ...' There was a pause of silence before Mitch continued. 'He taught me a lot about art.'

'Oh, I see. That's how you know so much about it when you don't paint. It's very detailed, he had a true talent.'

'I'm guessing she must have posed for it.'

Holly turned to Mitch. 'So, he didn't just admire her from afar then?'

'I understood they were very much together – well, until she met your grandfather, that is.'

Holly bit her lip, to stop herself from blurting something out she might regret.

Mitch stroked the back of his great uncle's chair. 'He was a broken man – never the same, according to my grandad.'

Holly took a deep breath. She felt herself shaking. 'Lots of people have failed relationships.' Holly crossed her arms. 'I've had a few.'

Mitch raised his eyebrows. 'A few?'

'When I say a few, I mean two.'

Mitch smiled.

Holly realised he was teasing her but continued. 'My grandfather was an amazing man. So kind and respectful. He brought my mum up on his own, you know.' She felt a lump appear in her throat. 'Sid's not the only one who remained single for the rest of his life.'

'Hey.' Mitch walked over and put a hand on her arm. 'I fully respect that – I know what it's like to lose a wife. I can't imagine how it would be to also be left with a child.' He pointed at Trixy. 'I've only had her to deal with and I've not done a great job there, have I?'

Holly glanced down at the dog, asleep on the armchair, whilst telling herself to calm down. She felt her heartbeat slow a little.

'Trixy doesn't even want to live with me anymore.' Seemingly hearing her name, Trixy woke up, jumped down from the chair and ran over to Mitch wagging her tail.

'Sorry. I've kept her for far too long. It was selfish of me. You're grieving and I'm hogging your dog.'

Mitch received a text and checked his phone. 'I've got to

run down to the sheds.' He gestured around the room. 'I've got to find Sid's birth certificate. Could you do me a massive favour and start searching for it? I'll only be about twenty minutes. Then we can carry on together. And I do need to talk to you about the whole Sid and Ivy thing properly. There's something you need to know.'

'Right,' Holly said. 'I'll get down to it.'

Mitch gestured to the bureau. 'It'll probably be in there. I won't be long.'

'Do you think he'd mind me going through his stuff?' Holly felt a shiver go down her back.

'He moved on – you saw it. You heard him.'

'Okay. I'll start it off.'

'Are you sure this is okay? I know you're busy.'

'Yes. Get down to the sheds.'

'I'll take Trixy with me – see if she still likes me.'

Holly felt a chill in the air as Mitch and Trixy left. She stared up at the picture of Ivy wearing a floral dress, standing in a meadow of wild flowers, reds, yellows and blues. *It does look like she posed for it,* she thought. Why did she feel so defensive about it? She realised she would have to shake it off. After all, they were now business partners.

Holly walked over to the bureau. It was made of dark wood. Running her hands over it, she opened the drawers. They were packed to the brim with papers. She leafed through, grabbed a pile and took it to a table further down the room, closer to the conservatory where it was brighter. This pile included a bundle of bank statements dated in the 1970's. Shaking her head, she decided to put the papers into different piles according to type; important, financial and miscellaneous.

Half an hour later the piles had grown. It was difficult to judge whether something was important or not without reading it. Opening the third drawer, she saw a pack of letters tied with string. Untying the bow, only two envelopes were open, they appeared personal. She checked to see if Mitch was around. Silence. *Well he did ask me to help, didn't he?* she thought. *It's not snooping, as such.* She pulled the letter out of the already opened envelope and turned it over in her hands. The paper shook as soon as she saw the signature'

Forever in my heart, Ivy.

Holly put her hand to her mouth. Taking the pile of letters over to Sid's chair, she sat down, and began to read.

Dear Sid,

I hated seeing you upset today. I wanted to explain but I could not find the words. Father intercepted the letters you sent me from France. I found them under my parents' bed some weeks after I married. I opened the first letter, Sid, to make sure they were from you. I want you to know that I love you with all my heart. When I did not hear from you, I thought you had moved on. I had no knowledge of your accident. It was a year of no word from you.

Bill is kindly and we get on well. He comforted me. I've not read the remaining letters, I left them sealed, so you would know that I never received them. I want to prove to you that I did not know you were waiting for me. I was led to believe you had gone on National Service and decided to stay. If I'd known you'd become ill, I would have come to you. I'd never have moved on if I'd known you still loved me. You will always be my true love. But now I am married and expecting a child it would not be right.

I should have trusted your love. My regret will be eternal, as will be my love for you.

Please forgive me, my darling Sid.

Forever in my heart. Ivy.

Holly heard a door bang in the distance and slipped the

letter back into its envelope, and scooted back to the bureaux and deposited them at the very back of the unit.

'Have you found it yet?' Mitch asked.

Holly shook her head.

'Are you okay? I can always apply for a copy of the birth certificate.'

'No, no. Let's get on with it.' Holly's hands were clammy and shaking. She was finding it hard to cope with the fact, that her great-grandfather had been deceitful and her family had lied to her.

It only took another five minutes of hunting to find the birth certificate.

Mitch waved it above his head. 'Yes.'

At this point Holly's mobile rang. It was George – there were a couple of questions he had, so she bade Mitch farewell and went back to the nursery, her mind was so full she didn't even register that Trixy was following her home.

IT WAS A LONG AFTERNOON, looking at alternative materials, boundary walls and water pipes. But whilst Holly had lots to concentrate on, an image of Ivy's letter to Sid kept popping into her mind. Later, back at the caravan, she called Jaz.

'It's all ancient history, chick.'

'I'd always been told by Mum that Sid had some sort of obsession with Granny Ivy, not that she'd reciprocated. Like he was a stalker. I feel lost, my whole family lied to me.'

'Hey, you don't know that. Granted your great-grandad knew and Ivy but your own Grandad and Mum may have been none the wiser.'

'And I'll never find out.'

'Does it matter, hun? You've got so much else to worry about.'

'Yes, it does matter. All I have left of my family are my memories of them; their history. They are a part of me, of who I am. I'd like the facts to be correct.'

'What I heard was that your gran and Sid were an item. He went away and when he got back, Ivy had run off with your grandad, got pregnant and had to get married.'

'Where did you hear that?'

'It's common knowledge, hun.'

'Great – and you never mentioned this before?'

'You've always shut me up when I tried to.'

Holly realised that was true. 'For good reason. Village gossip is usually a load of rubbish.'

'Are you sure you're not making too much of this, hun?'

'I've already explained.'

'I know – your family's reputation and what have you. But you've got Tom on your back, a business to rebuild, a market to prepare for and a fair. With so much going on, do you think this is maybe becoming a bit of a fixation?'

'You think I'm going mad or something?'

'Maybe you're focusing on this because you can't face the here and now.'

Holly took a deep breath. The Loveland-Booth feud had always been there, as if it were tangible.

Trixy barked.

'You haven't still got his dog, have you?'

'Yes, she followed me up and I'm just so used to having her, I didn't twig until I got back. I've had to text another apology.'

It was the day of Sidney's funeral, Holly sat in the caravan staring at her watch, the wake was not for another hour, she decided to pop over and see Val afterwards, to ask her for a warts and all accounts of Sidney and Ivy's relationship. Val always had a sensible and calming influence on her and Jaz's comments had touched a nerve. If she was making a fuss about nothing, Val would be the one to bring her back down to earth. And Val would know the truth, she had been Granny Ivy's best friend.

It was twelve fifteen. Holly opened the caravan door and descended the metal steps. She wore a black dress of Jaz's and a black jacket. The dress was a little shorter than she would have liked because Holly was a lot taller than Jaz. But she could not buy too many new clothes as she had limited storage space in the caravan. The church steeple was in sight. On the spur of the moment, she decided to watch the burial from the back field. She could keep her distance, and give the family their respect. *They won't know I'm there*, she thought and planned to double back to the farm for the wake.

Holly walked along the village road and then up a path to an area of waste land behind the church. There was a break in the hedge which Trixy was forever squeezing through; Holly had followed her in there on a number of occasions. Thinking of Trixy she heard her yaps carried on the wind. Joe was minding her today.

Close enough to the cemetery, Holly heard the murmurs of the reverend and moved closer. *Hmm, Sid's being buried quite close to my family area, by the looks of it,* she thought as she observed the small gathering. There was Mitch, a tall woman with dark hair she presumed was his sister, holding hands with a guy who she guessed was her fiancé. A couple in their fifties who she realised must be Mitch's parents. Finally, there was blonde Magda – dabbing her eyes with a tissue. As the party began to disperse Holly checked her phone for the time. She would have to be quick or else they would spot her. They moved faster than Holly expected and she missed her opportunity to escape unnoticed. She leaned back into the bushes as the family stepped onto the road. Then darted in the opposite direction, taking the full perimeter of the church, waiting for everyone to leave. Putting her head down, she smoothed her clothes, her heart beating as fast as it did as a child when she and Jaz used to steal plums from the trees in the old reverend's garden.

Walking into the churchyard, she stopped still and steadied herself, holding onto a tree. The freshly dug grave was slap bang next to her Granny's – so close it could be considered a joint plot.

'What on earth?'

'Holly.' She heard the reverend's voice behind her.

'Why?' she said, pointing to the grave. 'Why has he been buried on the path next to my grandmother?'

'It's not a path – it's been reserved since before my time. For Mr Booth.'

'But my grandad could have been buried there.'

'Maybe you should discuss it with the family?'

'This is madness – they've hijacked my family plot.' Holly felt her voice crack into a sob.

'Maybe you'd like to come inside?' He pointed to the church door.

Holly shook her head and ran out of the churchyard. 'No wonder they didn't want me at the funeral.'

She ran as fast as she could towards Val's, tears streaming down her face. Mad at the Booths for stealing her family's space.

CHAPTER 25

*H*olly ran across the village green towards The Laurels cul-de-sac. She wanted to know the truth. How could Sid be buried with Ivy? What would everyone in the village say, when they saw? They would be gossiping about her family all over again. How would she be able to tell what was truth and what was gossip? It was time for Val to explain why she was lied to.

Rounding the corner to Val's, she stopped short. Outside the house was an ambulance. Fear gripped her chest. Rushing over, she found Len crying as the paramedics brought Val out on a stretcher.

'What's happened?' Holly asked.

'Are you family?' the paramedic asked.

'No, I'm –'

'I'll have to ask you to step aside.' The man quickly helped Len into the ambulance and it sped off, with the sirens sounding, leaving Holly standing in the street.

She turned to the growing crowd of concerned neighbours. 'Do you know where they've taken them?'

A lady in a green cardigan shook her head. 'I don't know,

love. They change their minds. One week it's Weston, and the next it's Musgrove.'

A young woman holding a baby spoke. 'I'd try Weston. My dad was taken there by ambulance last week.'

Holly shouted her thanks and ran back to the caravan. She texted Joe and asked him to drop Trixy down to the farmhouse.

Arriving at Weston General, Holly recognised the paramedic she had spoken to, jumping into an ambulance at the A&E entrance. Parking up, she sat in her van, clutching her steering wheel, peeking up at the three-story hospital. She stared at the accident and emergency entrance. *I can't do this,* she thought. She twisted the ignition again, hearing the van's engine, then killed it. 'You have to – it's Val,' she said to herself.

Taking deep breaths, Holly got out of the van. Her palms were damp and her heart raced. Once inside, she felt dizzy as the distinctive hospital aroma hit her. She steadied herself by holding on to the back of a chair. She felt as if the walls were drawing in around her. Len's voice reached her ears and she saw him sitting in the waiting area. Adrenaline coursed through her, as if she had been slapped in the face. *Get a grip, they need you,* she thought.

Len's eyes were red. 'She collapsed, love, and I heard a crack. I'm gonna lose her I know it.' He lifted a handkerchief to his face.

'We don't know that. What have they said?'

'They're doing tests. I thought I'd stay out here in case you came. There's another waiting area further inside.'

'I'll get us some water first.' Holly's hands shook as she filled two flimsy cups with water, from a cooler. Passing one to Len, she sat by his side. 'Drink this and then we'll go through.'

Holly wanted to take the time to calm herself. She needed to be strong for Val and Len.

'She's been in pain for weeks with that hip,' Len said.

'What did the doctor say last week at the appointment I booked?'

'She didn't go. Said not to make a fuss.'

'I knew I should have taken her myself. It's all my fault. I've let things distract me.'

'Of course it's not your fault, love.' He patted her hand. 'You've got the whole world on your shoulders.'

A male doctor approached them. 'I'm Mr Heath, the surgeon. Do you want to come through?'

Holly helped Len to his feet.

The doctor turned to her. 'And you are?'

'Our granddaughter,' Len said before Holly could answer.

Holly squeezed Len's arm as they followed the surgeon out of the waiting area, along a corridor and into a private office.

'I'm afraid Valerie has broken her hip and from the x-rays it was in a pretty sorry state. Has she been complaining of pain?'

Holly nodded. 'She said she didn't want to make a fuss.'

'Well, the poor lady must have been in agony. She may have simply passed out, due to the pain. But we've carried out routine tests to see if anything else flags up. Assuming all her vitals are in order, we'll need to operate immediately to replace the hip.'

Len nodded.

'Of course, general anaesthetics come with risks.' The doctor looked at Len. 'Do you understand what I'm saying?'

Len turned to Holly and they both nodded.

Holly swallowed. 'Yes, we understand.'

'Do you know when she last ate or drank?'

Len's voice wobbled. 'She's not eaten today. Felt too ill and only took a few sips of her tea this morning.'

'I'll ask the staff to prepare for the operation. There are a few questions we'll need answering, so I will leave you with my colleague to take the details.'

Mr Heath left the room and they were joined by a nurse who went through a questionnaire on Val's medical history and any symptoms she may have had recently. They answered as best they could. Holly found it difficult to concentrate. If only she had taken her to the doctor. Made sure she had gone – Val would not have had the fall and would not be having an operation in such a weak state.

The nurse lowered his clipboard. 'It'll be a long wait if you stay, although we do have a small café. If you return to this waiting area, we'll update you at the desk on how things are progressing.'

Len went to visit Val before the operation. Holly sat in the waiting room, feeling her emotions rise. She had decided it was better that Len went alone. She was afraid of showing her feelings, she didn't want to distress Val further.

Len returned from Val with a different nurse. 'They'll be some time,' she said. 'You may want to go back home and pick up some things for Valerie? Nightclothes, toiletries and any of her usual medication?'

'I'll do that.' Holly stood up.

'I'm not going anywhere,' Len said. 'You've got a key haven't you, love?'

She nodded. 'I'll be at least an hour, but I'll be as quick as I can.'

. . .

HOLLY ENTERED THE CUL-DE-SAC, and two neighbours approached the van as she parked it on Val and Len's drive.

'Any news?' asked a middle-aged woman with a round face.

'She's broken her hip. They're doing an emergency op on it now.'

'Poor Val. But never you worry – she's strong as an ox, that one.'

'I'm sure, she'll pull through,' said the other neighbour wrapping her cardigan around herself.

Holly went into the house, leaving the neighbours to chat amongst themselves. She could smell Val's favourite perfume as soon as she went in, imagining her at the kitchen sink chattering away. Up in the bedroom, she fetched the small overnight case which Val kept under the bed. She opened a drawer and took out a couple of nighties and underwear. Opening the wardrobe, she chose a smock style summer dress for when Val came out. Holly gulped back the tears. *Please God, let her be okay.* Picking out one of Val's cardigans, she lifted it to her face breathing in its freshly laundered scent then placed it in the little case which had just enough room left for Val's shoes and toiletries.

After picking up the necessary items from the bathroom, Holly carried the case downstairs. As the stairs creaked underneath her weight, she thought of the pain Val must have been in, climbing those stairs with her hip the way it was. *I should have been thinking about what's most important,* she thought. *Not obsessing over an ancient family feud.* Right now, even the hub felt self-indulgent. *What's the point in achieving anything, if there's no-one to share it with?* A lump formed in her throat. Val had always been in her life, always been there for her. And now she felt she'd let her down.

Pouring herself a glass of water in the kitchen, Holly gazed into the little garden. In her mind, she could see Val throwing crumbs out for the birds. Wiping her eyes, she blew her nose on a sheet of kitchen paper and stuffed a couple more sheets into her back pocket. Picking up the case, she headed outside.

'Send her our love,' the neighbour called out as she climbed into the van and set off for Weston.

HOLLY HAD BEEN SITTING in the waiting room with Len, for what felt like hours. Finally, Mr Heath came to see them.

He smiled. 'It was a success. No bone damage, other than the hip we replaced. Valerie is conscious.'

Holly stood up. 'Can we see her?'

'Yes, follow me.'

The surgeon led them to the recovery room, Holly and Len were both teary-eyed when they saw her. Holly forgot all about her fear of hospitals. All that mattered in that moment, was that Val was okay.

'You silly old sod,' Val said, as Len gave her a big kiss.

Holly left Val and Len to have some time alone and went to the café where she forced herself to eat a sandwich. Scrolling through the contact list on her phone she called Val's sons, Ben and Nate, then Jaz and Joe, and updated them. Checking her mobile phone, she saw an hour had passed, so returned to the ward.

Val was propped up in bed, turning her nose up at a plate of food put before her. 'Just look at the colour of them runner beans, they're grey! And it's stone blinking cold.'

'Well it won't be as good as your cooking, lovey,' Len said smiling at her.

Holly grinned. 'You seem well.'

'They says I have to get up and walk tomorrow – need the bed, I presume.'

Holly laughed. 'It's to get the hip working. Don't worry, they're looking after you here.'

Val patted Holly's hand. 'Len, love. Get yourself off and have some food. Let me sit here with Holly for a while. She's had a bit of a shock.'

Len nodded and left the ward, checking his wallet.

'So, young lady. Why were you coming over to see me? Len said you were all dressed in black. I'm guessing you went to the funeral?'

'Yes.'

'And you saw where Sidney was buried?'

'You knew?'

'If you mean that he was going to be buried next to your granny, then yes, I did know. I haven't seen you since he died. I was meaning to tell you but this blinking hip, the pain, I couldn't think of anything else.'

'I got myself all worked up realising my family had lied to me. Saying Sydney was some kind of stalker.'

Val pushed the plate of food away and leaned back into her pillow. 'I should have explained before. But your Mum hated gossip. Thing is, I don't think she had any idea about your great-grandad hiding Sid's letters, because as you know, Ivy died in childbirth. And if she had heard it, she would have seen it as idle gossip. There was already tension between the families because of the land dispute.'

Holly turned as the nurse came over to the bed. 'Right, Valerie. You've had more than enough excitement for one day. You need your rest.'

'But ...' Val protested.

'Take this painkiller. It's time for lights out. The other

patients here are all post-op as well and everyone needs some sleep.'

Holly rubbed Val's arm. 'I'll come by tomorrow then?'

'Yes, love – and I'll tell you everything I know about Ivy. Warts and all.'

*M*itch walked up to the farmhouse from the sheds. He had been up since five and was on his way back for a late breakfast, which his mother was preparing. He felt hungover after drinking too much wine at the wake, after the reverend had discretely mentioned that Holly had been distressed when she had discovered the location of Sid's grave. Mitch blamed himself as he had not managed to discuss the matter with Holly beforehand, although he had tried.

When they'd first met, he thought there was a definite attraction between them. There certainly was from his point of view but she seemed to be in a relationship with that flash Ethan. But then she seemed angry when Nina had invited herself over. After that, he thought maybe Holly was interested – he had even been about to move in with a kiss at one point. And now this had thrown a spanner in the works. Would they ever have a chance to get to know one another without something getting in the way? *Probably not,* he thought. Of course, he should have warned her about the burial. But at every attempt he made to discuss family, Holly had a habit of shutting him down. Although, he had to admit, part of him had not pressed the issue, worried Holly would have put a stop to it. Sid would never have forgiven him if he had not fulfilled his wish of being buried beside Ivy.

Ascending the sloping land with his dog yapping by his side, Mitch realised he missed his walks with Trixy, although he felt guilty taking her back as Holly's face lit up whenever Trixy was around her. He felt, in some way, that it was him making her smile – the one putting the light there. He looked up at the sound of an engine and saw Holly driving her van. She caught his eye and he put his hand up, but she shook her head and drove off.

Mitch stared after the van as it rounded the corner. *Is there another crisis?* Is that why she didn't stop? Or was she shaking her head to say she never wanted to speak to him again? What he really needed was to have a heart to heart with her. To go somewhere quiet, have a proper talk. Get it all out without the distractions. He had nothing to lose. Taking his mobile phone out of his pocket, Mitch located Holly's number and sat down on a large rock, to compose a text as Trixy sniffed around the grass.

Saw you drive by – hope everything is okay. I have a meeting in Ilfracombe tomorrow morning with a fishmonger interested in the farmers' market. Can you come? We can chat on way x

Standing up, he took a deep breath. *The ball's in her court now,* he thought.

HOLLY HAD PICKED up Len so they could be at the hospital for ten. Len chattered away about his bowls club and the weather on the journey. After parking up, they walked to the ward as fast as Len could manage.

Holly went up to the ward desk. 'We're here for Valerie Bloom.'

'Ah yes. She's just been taken down for a scan.'

Holly frowned. 'Why? I thought the operation went well.'

'It did, but they need to check that she had the fall due to the hip and no other complication.'

Len wrung his hands. Holly saw the fear in his eyes as they were ushered to the waiting area. Holly took her mobile phone out of her pocket. She had heard a text come through earlier when she was driving. Seeing it was from Mitch, she opened it.

Saw you drive by – hope everything is okay. I have a meeting in Ilfracombe tomorrow morning with a fish monger interested in the farmers' market. Can you come? We can chat on way x

She texted back:

Val in hospital. Had hip op and they are doing tests. Not sure what's going on.

She sat back in the chair anticipating another long wait.

After forty minutes the nurse approached them. 'She's back on the ward now if you want to see her, but she's quite tired.'

They followed the nurse to Val's bed. A multitude of leads ran from Val to various bedside machines, which were bleeping. Val appeared frail but managed a smile when she saw them approach.

'Holly,' she whispered. She looked tired.

Holly sat on the edge of the bed, leaving Len to sit in the visitors' chair. She took her hand. 'Are you okay?'

'Awful night, can't get any sleep with all the noise and

some poor beggar was moaning half the night. But I'm still here,' she said giving a weak smile.

Holly was struck by how serene Val seemed – compared to her usual brusque self.

A buzzer sounded on the equipment and Val shut her eyes.

'Val, are you okay?' Holly said, as a nurse approached.

The nurse put a hand on Holly's shoulder. 'It's an alarm to tell me to check the blood pressure. Valerie's tired. You'll have to let her sleep.' She looked across to Len. 'She needs a proper rest so she can gain enough energy to get up on that hip. I'll see if we can move her into a single room. I know you've come quite a distance but I suggest you both go home and then come back later this evening for visiting time.'

On the way home, Len received texts from his sons who were travelling to Somerset from their respective homes in London and Manchester to see their Mum with the grand-kids in tow. On the way back to Eversley, they decided it was better for Holly to get some rest.

It was approaching twelve o'clock when Holly arrived back at the caravan. Joe greeted her as she got out.

'How is she, love?' he said with a grave expression.

'Tired. I probably won't be able to see her now for a day or so because the boys are coming over and she won't want to be crowded. I sent her your love.'

Holly remembered the text she had received from Mitch. As soon as she pictured him, she felt a warmth. It would be good to clear the air. Val's accident had made her realise, she needed to focus on the present day rather than the past. She texted Mitch back.

Val is still in hospital. But I'm free tomorrow, as her boys are visiting. Although I'd like to be back for evening visiting time.

A text pinged back almost immediately.

Pick you up at 7:00 a.m.

Holly noticed the sudden flutter of excitement which appeared in her stomach. She told herself that she was only going along to smooth things over. They had business to do. But deep down she knew she longed to spend time with him – alone.

CHAPTER 27

*D*awn broke over Eversley with a crisp blue sky on the first official day of summer. Hearing Mitch's truck drive up, Holly stepped outside. She wore a pair of jeans and a yellow top with a white hoodie wrapped around her waist. On her back she carried a ruck sack with a pack-a-mac – in case the weather turned, plus a vest and shorts in case the day got hotter. Good old British weather, she could never tell how it would turn out.

Mitch jumped down from his pick-up and opened the door for Holly where an excited Trixy yapped. 'Your carriage awaits.'

Holly laughed, feeling instantly relaxed, as if nothing negative had happened between them.

'How's Val?'

'Len says she's doing fine and the nurse got her up for a walk on her new hip yesterday evening. Although she had to use a frame, which she hated.' Holly clipped on her seatbelt. 'Val's so independent. She hates being in there, but they have to keep her hooked up to the monitors, for observation.'

Mitch put the pick-up into gear and drove out of the carpark. 'I'm pleased she's making progress. It's best to enjoy life while you can, eh? We all get old.' Mitch drove out onto the main village road.

Holly nodded. 'And die.'

'Listen to us being positive.'

Holly laughed and so did Mitch. She watched his eyes crease up at the edges and he flopped his dark hair back then turned on the radio, flicking channels until he found some lively music. He was, Holly thought, the best-looking guy on the planet.

Holly dragged her eyes away. 'I'll be over to The Laurels for a few days when Val's out. Len will need help to support her, and if I know Val, she'll never let the carers in.'

Trixy settled on Holly's lap as she stroked her head. 'So, where are we going again?'

'I've a fishmonger I wanted to see – about the farmers' market. Then I thought if we have time, we could swing into Croyde Bay where I have a sheep farmer contact. It's for wool not meat. She sells goods made by locals. A nice addition to the market, I thought.'

'Yes, that would be great as it crosses over to the arts hub theme. I haven't been to Croyde for years. I used to go there for holidays with Mum and Dad.'

'We spent a lot of time there too. We could take Trixy for a walk along the cliffs.'

'And jump off.'

Mitch laughed. 'It's not that bad is it?'

'Things have been better.'

'True, but we've got lots to feel great about.' He smiled at her.

Holly sat back, watching the passing countryside. Glancing across at Mitch, she grinned as he whistled out of tune, to a song on the radio. She needed to take a leaf out of his book and stop taking herself so seriously. Sitting up, she decided to have a positive day.

HOLLY STRETCHED her arms and Trixy sat up, as Mitch drove into the small carpark in Ilfracombe. After paying the parking fee, they walked down the hill towards the main stretch beside the sea and cliffs.

'I won't be that long,' Mitch said. 'Less than an hour unless you want to come with me? Although it might be awkward with Trixy.'

Trixy leapt up at Mitch, barking.

Holly clipped the lead onto Trixy's collar. 'It would have been nice to introduce myself, but maybe I should take her for a walk.'

'Okay I'll meet you in half an hour or so, at The Rocks café.' Mitch pointed towards the front. 'It has seating outside.'

There was a strong breeze blowing into the harbour, so Holly pulled on her hoodie. Boats bobbed up and down with their flags billowing in the wind. The sound of clanging sails accompanied the cries of chattering seagulls. It felt good to get away from the nursery and all her difficulties. The threat of the court case with Tom was forever there, even if Jill was convinced that it would never come to that. *I must phone her,* she thought. Holly had been reducing the number of times she called Jill for an update, knowing she had her head in the sand, ignoring it in the hope that it would all go away. Part of her wished she could fast forward her life and get to the bit when the divorce was settled.

Holly took in a deep breath, tasting the salty coastal air on her tongue. Trixy pulled at the lead. It was quiet with few people around, so she unclipped it and crouched down, wagging her finger at the little dog. 'You'll have to walk at heel.'

Holly stood up, and was pleased that Trixy obeyed her as they passed the end of the harbour. Holly wondered how her application to the Council for support with the Arts Council application was progressing. David Bunning had been quiet on that front. Holly assumed the funding application was not going to be supported by him, guessing that Grace had told 'Daddy' all about Holly being Tom's crazy ex-wife who shouts in public. She hoped the other councillors would help. She knew the Arts Council process would be trickier without their backing. She pushed it all out of her mind – *I just want one day where I don't have to think about any of this,* Holly thought. She wanted to blow away the cobwebs of hassle which clogged up her mind. All that mattered at that moment was Val getting back on her feet, and for Holly to enjoy the here and now.

The half hour was soon up and Holly walked towards the café to find Mitch already sitting outside with his long legs stretched out in front of him. He wore sunglasses and was so still, Holly wondered whether he was asleep.

Trixy barked and Mitch raised his head towards Holly as she approached. 'I've ordered you a cappuccino and a pain au chocolate.'

'Thanks,' Holly said. 'How did it go?'

'Great. They already have a delivery scheme which covers Somerset. He's going to bring his van to the first market and decide if he'll make it a regular thing.'

Holly felt her stomach rumble as the pastry was placed on the table, not realising how hungry she was until she saw it there ready to be devoured. Trixy jumped onto Mitch's lap.

'Hello, girl. I love you too,' he said as she tried to lick his face.

'Can I have a bottle of water, please?' Holly asked the waitress then pulled out Trixy's bowl.

'What? She's on mineral water now?' Mitch chuckled and scratched Trixy's head. 'You are the most spoiled dog in Booth history.'

Having filled Trixy's bowl and given her a dog biscuit, Holly enjoyed her own treat, eating slowly as she savoured the flaky pastry with bitter chocolate filling. 'Thanks for asking me to come along. I feel calm for the first time in months. It's great to get away and view life from a distance.'

'I knew you were upset about the grave. I thought we could clear the air. I tried to mention it beforehand but –'

Holly's chest tightened momentarily. 'I don't want to talk about that now, Mitch. I did. But with Val so sick, and being here now, away from the stress, I feel it's just small stuff. It doesn't matter what happened in the past. Let's just have a nice day, eh?' She took a sip of her coffee. 'Without all the ...'

'Crap?'

'Precisely.' Holly smiled at him and he smiled back.

When they finished their drinks, Mitch left cash under the condiments, waving at the waitress as they departed.

It was a short drive to Croyde Bay. Holly stared out of the truck window as they drove through the little village with shops advertising ice cream, fudge and pasties.

'We used to come down to Devon after visiting Sid and see Rita, the sheep farmer. She's an old family friend,' Mitch said.

'I remember the sand dunes and surf school.' Holly

brought a picture to her mind of summers with her parents on the beach and felt a fleeting moment of sadness.

'Are you okay with us popping in to see Rita? Or would you rather not?'

'That's fine with me.'

'She's very friendly. I'm sure you'll love her.' Mitch drove the truck through black iron gates into the sweeping drive of a large house. He parked up and a lady in her mid-fifties walked out.

'Mitch,' she said and gave him a huge hug. 'Great to see you.'

Mitch turned to Holly. 'This is Rita. My mum's best friend.' Then he turned to Rita. 'This is Holly my er ...'

'Neighbour,' Holly said stretching out her hand and gave a small smile to Mitch.

Rita shook Holly's hand then pulled her in for a hug. 'And you brought your dog?' Rita smiled at Mitch.

'Actually, she's more like Holly's dog now. Trixy prefers her to me.'

Rita laughed and bent down to ruffle Trixy's coat. 'Well come in and have tea.'

Rita poured the tea out, as they sat at her large kitchen table. 'Can you surf, Holly?'

'Yes, but I've not done so for years.'

'Let's do that today,' Mitch said.

Holly laughed. 'I don't have anything with me.'

Rita smiled. 'My Izzy's in Borneo. She's plenty of spare swim costumes and a wetsuit.' Rita turned to Mitch. 'And you can hire one, love.' Rita stood up. 'I'll look after that ball of fluff while you go. Dogs aren't allowed on the beach, I'm afraid.'

Holly opened her mouth.

Mitch put his hand up as if to halt her protest. 'It'll be

fun.' He grinned and Holly felt a surge of warmth cover her body.

They took lunch on Rita's decking area, which had a stunning view over green fields, dotted with black woolly sheep. Below that was the beach with rock pools in the foreground a huge expanse of sand, which met a glistening sea, with white waves charging in. The beach was backed by sand dunes, where long grasses sprouted up in tufts.

Rita chatted endlessly, reminiscing about Mitch's holidays as a child and telling embarrassing stories about him. Holly laughed at the stories and her body relaxed, like a slow melting ice-cream. She ate a sandwich made with doorstep slices of fresh seeded bloomer, delicious ham and fresh-from-the-garden tomatoes. After they'd eaten homemade fruitcake, she wondered whether she would have a pot belly poking out of the wetsuit, it certainly was not an energising lunch. She felt more like having an afternoon nap than riding the waves.

Rita stood up. 'Come on then, missy. I'll show you the bathing costumes and sort out the wetsuit.'

Holly was surprised at how brief the bikinis were. Most were triangle patches held together with string, reminding her more of bunting than something fit to cover her body parts. She found one in a sporty style, although once Holly put it on, it showed a bit more bum cheek and side boob than she would have liked. She pulled the wet suit up as Rita came in to help.

'It's a bit tight.' Holly stood panting as she pulled it over her hips.

'It's supposed to fit like a glove, love. It's perfect for you. Now don't zip it up fully until you get down there, else you'll be sweating buckets, it's jolly hot out there today.'

Holly walked down the stairs feeling stiff. Mitch grinned

with an almost boyish expression. In fact, she noticed, he seemed so much younger today.

MITCH AND HOLLY walked through the village to the surf shop. They hired a wet suit for Mitch and two surf boards. Heading down the beach towards the sea, Holly held the front of each surfboard under her arms and Mitch carried them at the rear. Holly felt a flutter of nerves. *Is this such a great idea?* she thought. She had not been surfing since she had been to Newquay with Tom when she was eighteen, just before she had left for London.

When they reached the beach, The tide was quite a way out and it took some time to reach the water. The wind blasted inland, therefore Mitch spoke loudly.

'How strong a surfer are you?'

'I'd say novice,' she said, turning her head as far as she could.

'I'll give you a refresher lesson then,' he called.

They walked the last stretch through warm shallow puddles towards the surf, stopping short of the waves and placed the boards on the beach. They zipped up the back-fastening wetsuits for each other.

Mitch turned around grinning. 'Now for a quick lesson.'

Holly watched him lay on the beached board, miming paddling, then he rose up into a standing position.

'Now you try,' Mitch said.

Holly moved about on the board pretending to paddle through the waves. She stood up leaning from side to side, imagining she was on the surf. It came straight back to her and she felt free with the wind in her loosely-tied-back hair, the sun warming her face.

Mitch smiled. 'A natural.'

'I'm not on the water yet,' Holly said laughing.

The sea felt cold but she soon became accustomed to it. They took their respective boards and strapped the rope attached to them around their ankles. They passed the breaking waves and were soon bobbing up and down on the water.

Mitch kept close to her and pointed to the waves, shouting above the noise of the surf. 'Choosing the right wave will become an instinct in the end.'

Finally, after a few failed attempts, Holly managed to get up to standing position and travelled in on a slow, shallow wave. She was soon back in her stride feeling the stress being teased and tossed out of her body.

After an hour of catching waves, they sat down on the boards, placed on the beach, looking out to sea. Holly could taste the salt from the sea water on her lips.

'Thanks, Mitch, that was amazing. It was just like being a kid again.' Holly laid back and shut her eyes. She felt warm. She felt free.

After a half hour of lying down, she heard Mitch's voice.

'Let's get back then. You ready?'

Holly heaved herself up and they got into position again with one board under each arm and walked back along the beach to the hire shop.

AT THE FRONT door of the house, Rita handed them fresh towels. 'You can use the holiday let if you like. The last guests left this morning and the next lot aren't due until Sunday. So you can get changed in there.' She pointed to a small holiday lodge situated on a plot of land adjoining her property. 'In fact, you can stay over if you like.'

Holly blushed.

'I'd love to, but Holly has a friend in hospital,' Mitch said.

Holly bit her lip.

Mitch turned to her. 'Why don't you phone to see how Val is?'

Holly nodded. 'You have a shower.'

Holly waited on the doorstep not wanting to walk sand through the house, while Rita fetched her phone. Taking her mobile from Rita, she walked into the gardens surrounding the lodge, trembling with a flutter of excitement. Having had such a great day, a longing washed over her like a warm, smooth heat. *You only live once,* she thought. Sidney had said not to waste your life, Val had said just as much. She switched on her phone.

There were a couple of messages. The first was from Jaz, who wanted to visit Val in the hospital that evening, and asked if Holly was prepared to give up her slot. The other was from Len saying Val was doing well, but as the weekend was coming up there would be no consultant to sign off her discharge. She would be in there until at least Monday.

Holly called Len and said she was thinking of staying in Croyde.

'Don't rush back, love,' he said. 'Jaz is going in today and they says they don't want too many visitors and our boys are here of course and three of the grandkids and a couple of great grandkids. Even if you were here, I doubt they'd let you in until tomorrow, earliest.'

Holly still felt a pang of guilt but as it was unlikely she would be able to visit Val within the next twenty-four hours, it seemed silly to rush back. She called Jaz.

'Where are you?' came Jaz's voice. 'Len said you'd gone off for the day on business with Mitch. Hope you two aren't fighting.' Holly had already told Jaz about the funeral.

'Er, no. He went to see a fishmonger.' Trixy bounded over to her yapping.

'And?'

'And we are having a really nice time together. We've been chatting away about everything and anything.'

'About Sid and Ivy?'

'Well, no. Everything apart from feuds, death and divorce.'

'You sound loved up, hun.'

'Today, it's been as if we're a couple.'

'At last, you two are going to get together.'

'And he wants to stay over – in Croyde, for the night.'

Jaz screamed. 'Go for it, you lucky mare.'

Holly laughed. 'It's so different, away from Eversley.'

'Everything's under control here, chick. You have a nice evening. You deserve it. Anyway, I've got a customer appointment in a sec, so I'd best go. I'll give Val your love. Call you later.'

Holly walked towards the lodge and entered with Trixy in tow.

She stopped to admire the view over the bay, then jumped as she heard Mitch's voice behind her. She turned to find him standing bare-chested with a white towel wrapped around his waist. Her face instantly coloured up.

He smiled. 'How's Val?'

'She won't be out until Monday soonest and she's maxed out on visitors, as her sons are down and Jaz hasn't seen her yet.' Holly bit her lip.

'You don't need to rush back then?'

Holly looked around and blushed. 'I er ...'

Mitch thumbed behind him. 'There's a separate bedroom. I can take the couch. It's all decent and above board,' he said grinning.

Holly did not get the impression he wanted them to be in separate beds and her body definitely was having other thoughts.

'It would be great to relax here, rather than get stuck in the mad Friday traffic,' Mitch said.

Trixy yapped and jumped up at him, grabbing the towel between her teeth. He held onto it as she wrestled with it, pulling her head from side to side.

'Woah,' Mitch said.

Holly laughed. 'I'd love to stay. I'll leave you to sort yourself out.' She walked past him to the shower room, giggling as Trixy continued to fight with him.

RITA RAPPED on the window of the holiday let. It was, Holly thought, like a massive beach hut. A wooden structure with a sitting area and sofa bed, a separate bedroom and a shower room. There were tea and coffee-making facilities but no kitchen area, Rita provided a bed and breakfast service.

Rita waved at her with three dresses over her arm. She opened the glass sliding door. 'I sorted these out from my Izzy's wardrobe and I have some smalls there too. I'm washing the clothes you came in. I was doing a load anyway.'

Holly stood wearing a towelling robe, eying Rita as she took the clothes, wondering whether she was on a mission to pretty her up. Looking down at the smalls, she noticed they were very small indeed.

'I'm pleased you're staying; I haven't seen Mitch this relaxed, for ages.' She pointed to the dresses. 'I'm thinking the blue and white dress, but brought the other two in case you preferred them.'

Holly thanked Rita and went to the bedroom to try them on as Mitch came out.

'I'll let you get sorted,' he said.

Trying the outfits, Holly concluded that Rita was right, the blue and white dress did suit her the most. It was tight around the chest, so she did not need to wear a bra with it, which was good as Izzy's smalls were way too small. The straps were adjustable. The dress was loose over her hips and brushed the top of her knees, her own sandals went perfectly.

Mitch's eyes seemed to open wide when she walked into the main room. 'That really suits you, Holly.' He stepped towards her.

Holly flushed hot and her skin tingled, feeling as if she and Mitch were in a bubble. Holly and Mitch, not a Loveland and a Booth. Stepping towards him, she felt as if she had been nudged from behind. He looked down into her eyes and then at her mouth. The kiss started as a gentle brushing of the lips but soon became urgent. She felt his arm come around her waist as she moved closer to him, inching her hands up and underneath his shirt, feeling the strength of his strong back. As the kiss developed, she wanted him, really wanted him.

Mitch pulled away, smiling at her. 'I've wanted to kiss you like that for weeks.'

'I think we'd better go out for that meal,' she whispered.

Mitch laughed and stepped back. Taking her hand he led her out of the lodge. Holly smiled as they stepped outside, realising there was no rush, they had all night.

CHAPTER 28

*A*fter the short walk into Croyde village, Holly sat at a table in the pub garden while Mitch went to the bar.

Mitch returned with their drinks. 'How do you get the inspiration for your art?' he asked.

'It's only my interpretation of events, of nature, of experiences.' Holly picked up the cool wine glass from the table, running her hand over the condensation forming on the outside. Lifting the glass to her lips, she took a sip before placing the glass back on the table. 'In fact, I've seen quite a lot today that inspires me.'

'Me too,' Mitch laughed.

Holly grinned at him and picked up a menu. 'I think we should order food, don't you?'

Mitch nodded. 'I'm starving.'

After a minute Holly looked up from the menu. 'What are you having?'

'When in Rome. I'm having beer-battered cod and chips.'

'Good choice. I'll have the same.'

Mitch ordered the food at the bar and returned. Sitting for a while in silence, they watched a small skiffle band, consisting of a guitarist, drummer, fiddlers and a vocalist,

After they'd eaten, Holly smiled as she watched Mitch tap his foot, slightly off-beat to the fast-paced folk music.

Mitch turned to Holly, when the performers broke off. 'I thought we could get a bottle of red from the bar to take back and watch the sun set?'

'Sounds good.' Holly said.

Fifteen minutes later, Mitch reached out for her hand, a bottle of wine in the other. As they walked out of the pub, Holly felt as if they'd been dating all along, in some parallel existence.

As they neared the lodge, Holly's heartbeat quickened. Mitch said he would see if he could find a bottle opener, glasses and some cheese from Rita. Holly approached the garden table, situated in front of the lodge. She arranged two chairs facing out to sea so they could watch the sun set. There were still a few surfers on the waves and distant voices drifted from the lane. Mitch appeared behind her and placed a plate of cheese and crackers on the table and reached for the bottle. He opened it and filled their glasses. They watched the orange sun turn pink as it lowered towards the horizon. Holly felt the fiery tension between them and wondered if maybe he would be a gentleman and sleep on the couch. *I hope not*, she thought.

Mitch picked up a cracker and placed a small piece of cheese on it, before passing it to her.

'Mmm,' she said, nodding as the tangy cheese met her taste buds.

Mitch leaned back and smiled at her. 'I feel different today. A totally different person. You seem different too.'

'You know what? I think I am a different person. I'm

sorry for the way I've been acting of late. I've not been myself.' She rubbed her hand on her leg then turned to face him. 'I don't think you've been getting to know the real me.'

Mitch outstretched his hand. 'I like the Eversley Holly and the Croyde Holly. But I've realised that life is much better when we're both on the same side.'

Holly placed her hand in his and moved ever so slightly forward, he pulled her towards him until she was sitting on his lap.

Her hands went to his face, slightly rough with stubble and moved forward, finding his lips with hers. Her body felt alive and on fire. Slipping her hand under his shirt, she stroked his chest.

'Shall we go inside?' he asked.

She stood up and smoothed her hair with her hand.

'Are you sure?' His voice seemed lower than usual, his eyes searching.

She saw a flash of something. *Guilt? Vulnerability?* She realised she was likely to be his first since Vanessa. 'As long as you are.'

Mitch stood up and held her close, breathing into her ear. 'One hundred percent.'

They pulled apart and exchanged a smile as they walked together towards the lodge. Once inside, Mitch closed the glass doors behind them.

Mitch moved a tendril of hair from Holly's face. 'You're beautiful, Holly Loveland.' He smiled then kissed her urgently. Holly's mind flashed back to her very first kiss with Mitch when they were teenagers. It had held the same excitement. She had never wanted someone this much. Not felt such an ache, deep inside and could feel that he wanted her, just as much.

Mitch moaned deeply, kissing her ear, his warm breath

tickled her as he spoke. Picking her up, he carried her into the bedroom. He stopped by the bed and placed her on her feet, slowly pushing down the straps of her dress.

'So gorgeous, Holly.'

'Only when I'm with you.'

Later, as they lay entwined. Holly felt as if she had breathed out for the first time in years.

MITCH LAY on the bed as the morning sun streamed through the window. Standing up, he lifted the latch and a breeze blew the long voile curtains into the room. He watched Holly as she slept peacefully, wishing it could always be like this, wishing he could keep her there in that room forever. He eased back into the bed gradually, taking care not to wake her, as he gently pushed a strand of hair off her face, remembering how she had been the night before. Passionate with a level of intensity he had not experienced before. He drifted off to sleep, consumed by the peace of his surroundings.

Waking later to the smell of coffee, Mitch squinted as Holly came into view. She wore a robe and Trixy passed her, jumped on the bed and licked his face.

'That's not the wake-up kiss I was dreaming of.'

Holly laughed and made no effort to get Trixy off. 'Rita dropped her in. I thought we could go in search of breakfast.'

'That's a great idea.' Mitch heaved himself out of bed.

'I'll have a shower first,' she said.

Mitch stared at Holly, thinking how naturally beautiful she looked. He could feel the familiar urge. He took the coffee cup out of her hand and placed it on the bedside table. Then pulled her onto the bed. 'I need to do something first.'

Holly giggled as he kissed her and Trixy yapped.

'Hang on.' Mitch quickly put Trixy out of the bedroom. Holly grinned at him and they were soon entwined.

AFTER HIS SHOWER, Mitch called to Holly.

'I'm just off to see Rita, I won't be long.'

Trixy followed as he left the lodge, walking up the grassy slope to Rita's house. He found Rita in the kitchen.

She held a pot of filtered coffee. 'Want some?'

'Yes please.'

Trixy sat under the table and settled down.

Rita handed Mitch the steaming cup. 'How long have you been seeing each other?'

'It's complicated.' Mitch leaned back against the worktop.

'Isn't it always?'

'We're neighbours and friends and business associates and she's a Loveland. We're setting up the farmers' market I told you about, together.'

'That would be a very good resolution. I have the launch date in my diary, I'm looking forward to finding out more. This could be good for business, if you two got together.'

'If we're not cursed, that is. It's not been a great history.'

'Surely you're not superstitious?' Rita said as she filled a bowl with water for Trixy.

Mitch placed his coffee cup on the kitchen table. 'No, but it's not been easy. This is the first time we've spent together, as two normal people.'

'Normal doesn't exist, my love.'

'Life certainly hasn't been normal for Holly. The nursery,

including the cottage she lived in, burned down, and her ex is suing her for half of the remaining land.'

'Wow.'

'So this,' Mitch said, gesturing out of the window towards the lodge, 'is a bit of escapism. We've not talked about us. I don't know if there is an us.'

'But you hope there is?'

Mitch nodded as he sat down at the table.

Rita walked over and took the chair opposite him. 'I've never seen you like this with anyone, not even Vanessa.'

They sat in silence for a while until Rita broke it.

'You've got to stop blaming yourself, Mitch. It wasn't your fault. I think you should see what happens with Holly. Really, I do. Especially now the old man has gone. There's no-one to upset.' Rita stood up as a slice of bread pinged from the toaster. 'Where are her parents? Did they retire?'

'They died two years ago – road accident.'

Rita turned back to face him. 'The poor girl. So much to deal with.'

'I know. But she never wants help. I have to dress everything up like she's doing me a big favour.'

Rita laughed. 'Give her space, that's my advice. When all these troubles are done, she'll come to you – I'm sure of it.'

Mitch stood up and gave Rita a hug. 'Now where do you suggest I take her for breakfast?'

'I'd cook you some here but I'm off out after this slice of toast. I'm collecting supplies for the new intake before the tourists flood the supermarket. There's Bella's café, on the path to the coastal walk. You can take the dog there, too.'

Mitch nodded. 'Great idea. Come on, Trixy.'

By the time Mitch returned to the lodge, Holly was dressed and ready for the day. He pulled her close. 'You smell nice. We'd better go before I get you messy again.'

. . .

THEY WALKED along the road to the café, Mitch squeezed Holly's hand. 'I don't want this to have been a one-off.'

'Me neither,' Holly said. 'I wish every day could be as simple as this.'

'I don't want to put any pressure on you.'

'Nor me on you. We've both got our baggage.'

'I feel as if I don't want to go back.' Mitch stopped and pulled Holly to him, kissing her, holding her tight.

Reaching the café, they sat down. It was situated half-way up the cliff with a view of the bay before them. A long stretch of wide beach was visible with waves tumbling in – already dotted with surfers and further along, families with body boards. In the foreground there were children and adults climbing over the rock pools, with buckets and nets in bright greens, pinks and blues.

Holly finished checking the menu. 'I'll get this – my treat. What are you after?'

'Bacon buttie and a mug of tea,' Mitch said. He watched her walk into the café. Trixy stood up, so he grabbed her lead and pulled her close to him. 'Stay,' he said as she squirmed. He wondered why Holly was able to control his dog with one word and he failed.

Holly returned, smiling at him. She definitely suited shorts. He loved her outdoors look. A picture of Nina flashed into his mind.

'Nothing happened with Nina you know,' he said.

Holly raised her eyebrows. 'Where did that come from?'

'Not sure,' Mitch laughed. 'That day at the house, she left after tea. But I wasn't sure why you gave her my number and told her I was a lonely loser.'

Holly laughed. 'I said nothing of the sort. And I didn't

give her your number. She must have got it from someone else and nothing happened with Ethan either. I called it off.'

Their conversation was interrupted. 'Two bacon sandwiches and a sausage on the side?' the waiter said as he placed the tray on the table.

'Are you having a bacon sandwich and a sausage?' Mitch raised his eyebrows. 'Got an appetite?'

'No.' Holly grinned. 'The sausage is for Trixy.'

Mitch laughed. 'No wonder she does everything you say.'

Holly picked the sausage off the plate and Trixy sat up, her head upright, her tongue flapping in and out as if tasting the air like a snake. Then she raised a paw.

'There you go, girl.' Holly gave her the sausage which lasted all of three seconds.

Trixy licked her lips and sniffed for some more.

'That's it, girl. Now lay down.'

Trixy did as she was told.

'Well it works,' Mitch said. 'But she'll be wobbling home at this rate.'

'It's just a treat.'

He bit into his sandwich, which tasted great – salty bacon mixed with soft buttery bread. He felt relaxed, more relaxed than he had for years. It was easy being with Holly, comfortable yet still exciting.

Mitch finished his tea. 'Let's work this off then.'

HOLLY STOOD on the cliff feeling as if she was on the top of the world. With the wind blowing her hair from her face she felt totally free. Black-fleeced sheep grazed on the grass; Mitch had pointed them out as Rita's flock. Mitch had Trixy stuffed under his arm after she had yapped at a sheep and went so frantic, Holly feared the dog would fall off the edge of the cliff. Trixy was definitely not a farm dog.

Mitch put his free hand in hers. Holly wanted the day to last forever but knew they had to get back.

After five minutes of silence she turned to Mitch. 'I hate to say it, but we'd better get back to Eversley.' She pushed her hair which blew across her eyes, away from her face. 'Val will hopefully be out of hospital Monday and I wanted to get over to her house and prepare for her return. I'll be staying there for a few days, but I'll pop over and see you, if you like.'

'Of course, I'd like. I'd like that very much.' Mitch put Trixy down to the ground, hooking her lead over his wrist and cupped Holly's face in his hands

Holly looked into his eyes.

Mitch's voice was deep. 'I want you to know, this has been the best, the absolute best weekend I've had for as long as I can remember. Ever.'

Holly felt his lips reach hers and they shared a tender kiss – not the hungry type they'd had the day before, but what Holly considered the love type. *Love, now there's a word*, she thought as she pulled away and hugged Mitch, resting her head on his shoulder.

Pulling apart, they began the walk back to Rita's. Holly wondered what their relationship would be when they got back. As perfect as this weekend felt, she knew it was far from their real lives.

CHAPTER 29

*M*itch drew up in Lovelands' customer car park.

Holly leant over and kissed him on the cheek. 'Thanks for a great couple of days.'

He pulled her close and she felt his lips against hers, lingering, kissing her again. Pulling away, Holly opened the door and Trixy jumped out.

Mitch laughed. 'I have an early start tomorrow so you can keep her for the night of you like.'

Holly smiled. 'To be honest, I feel safer with her in the caravan.'

'Okay, but only if you're sure.'

Holly nodded. She got out of the pick-up, and put her rucksack on her back. 'Come on, girl.'

'See you soon.' Mitch smiled at her and she wanted to jump back in and kiss him all over again. She nodded and closed the pickup door. She waited, watching him drive away until he disappeared around the corner. Turning around she noticed Jaz's car, at the far end of the car park.

Trixy ran ahead of her towards the caravan. Holly stopped. Jaz sat on the caravan steps, as Holly neared she noticed the serious expression on her face.

Holly took her hand. 'Jaz, what's wrong? Have you split up with Julian?'

Jaz shook her head. 'It's Val.'

Holly felt dizzy. 'No!'

'She's had a stroke, a bad one.'

Holly put her palms to her cheeks. 'I should have been here. Is she going to get better?'

'They said to prepare for the worst.'

Holly fumbled for her keys, her hand shook as she unlocked the door of the caravan. They sat down and Jaz had her arm around Holly.

'Her sons were there,' Jaz said. 'They wouldn't have let you visit, anyway. There's nothing you could have done.'

'When can we see her?'

'Len said she's not conscious. They don't know yet whether her brain is functional.'

'Val would hate to be ...'

'I know.' Jaz stood up and put the kettle on. 'We've got to stay positive, hun. All we can do is wait. They said they won't know how bad it is until she comes around.'

'What if she doesn't wake up? I was off having a good time. I could have seen her again. I didn't tell her how much I love her. How much she means to me,' Holly sobbed, the tears running out of her eyes and nose.

Jaz pulled her up to standing and hugged her.

'I never get to say goodbye. Not to Mum, not to Dad and not to Val.'

'She's still here, hun. We need to be strong – we need to hope she'll pull through.'

Holly pulled sheets of kitchen paper from the roll on the worktop and wiped her eyes. They sat in silence for a while. Trixy jumped onto the seating, put her head on her paws, and stared at them, blinking, but remained quiet.

'How's Len?' Holly asked.

'Beside himself with worry. But the boys are with him.' Jaz said. 'I thought we could go over and see him this evening, maybe. I'll text Ben and find out.'

Holly nodded. 'I had such a great time away. I thought things had turned around.'

'They can, hun. They will.' Jaz rubbed her arm.

'Val's still got a lot of living to do. Eighty-two isn't old, is it? Not these days. I should have taken her to the doctors weeks ago. They might have picked it up. It's all my fault.'

'Holly, stop!' Jaz said.

Holly jumped.

'You can't go on, beating yourself up like this. It's awful, and I'm worried too. Val means everything to me as well. But she wouldn't want us to think this way, would she?'

Tears streamed down Holly's face. She knew Val wanted her to be happy, she knew Val loved her, through and through. But at that moment Holly felt overwhelmed with fear that she would never see her again.

She took a deep breath. 'You're right, Jaz.'

THREE DAYS LATER, Holly had not seen Mitch. She told herself she needed to focus on work, but in truth all she was doing was thinking about him. Remembering his kisses. Remembering how it felt when they made love. Remembering the perfection. But life was never that perfect and everyone she loved left her. She had to be strong and, if she saw him, she would crumble. She needed to be someone else, otherwise she would not be able to get through the wait – to see if Val would recover. Knowing she was in such a dark place, she wanted to preserve what they had in Croyde. The last thing she wanted was to taint what they had experienced over those couple of days away. No, it was better to put him off until she had calmed down.

Needing to check the sheds were ready for the farmers' market, Holly stepped out of the caravan and walked towards the huts then stopped when her phone rang. She fished it out of her cargo shorts. It was Jill. Hesitating she considered leaving it to go to voicemail, but answered it. *I have to face it,* she thought.

'I wanted to call, rather than send a letter,' Jill said. 'Now I don't want you to get upset. But there's a chance we'll have to go to court.'

Holly puffed out. 'What? I thought you said it would never come to that? That we needed to stand our ground.'

'Unfortunately, his cowboy solicitor has recruited a new guy. Peter James, I know him from old. I'm afraid he knows his stuff and plays hardball.'

'That's all I need.' Holly's bottom lip quivered. 'Are you saying I have to sell the land and give half to Tom?'

'Hopefully not, but we might need to make an agreement. Although it's taking months at the moment to be allocated a court date.'

'But I don't have months. I'm developing the nursery and hopefully will be receiving money from the Arts Council. I can't take the money and then sell up down the road. I need to sort this out within the next month. I need certainty.'

Holly's hand shook. She saw Joe lift his eyebrows. Realising she had raised her voice she turned around, speaking in a loud whisper. 'Isn't there something we can do?'

'You don't necessarily have to sell up. You could cut him in on the deal? Say you will rent his half of the land?'

'He owes me money. And I've told you. I know he's still got it.'

'And that will now form part of our dialogue with his team. We could offer twenty-five percent of the property with an understanding that he will rent it back to you on a twenty-year lease. There are all sorts of options.'

'I don't want an option that involves Tom in my life.' Her voice shook.

'You need to stay calm, Holly. Especially now.'

'I've got a farmers' market and a fair to hold. This will have to wait.'

'With Tom stating that you have a temper, you need to tread carefully.'

Holly counted to ten in her mind.

'Perhaps you should come into the office,' Jill said breaking the silence.

'I have so much on. I'll come in after the market. I'll probably have a clearer head by then.'

'I'll have everything ready for you to consider. I'll consult a conveyancer in the meantime.'

Holly ended the call.

'Hi, there.' She swung around – it was Mitch. 'I wondered if I could cook you something tonight?'

Holly tried to smile but she was too angry. If she told Mitch about Tom, she would lose it and start ranting. If he mentioned Val's name, she would be in floods of tears. She wanted her time with Mitch to be perfect, but at that moment there was no perfect and she would only trash it and ruin everything.

Mitch put his hand out. 'I wish you wouldn't shut me out, Holly.'

Don't cry, don't cry, she told herself. 'I'm not shutting you out. I have a few things to get through.'

'You're pushing me away.' Mitch rubbed the back of his neck. 'I thought we'd pulled down the barriers. I thought we'd got past this.'

Holly blushed. 'Well, some things I need to sort out in here.' She put a hand on her chest. 'On my own.'

'But we could do things together.'

Holly felt herself shaking. 'I'm quite capable.'

Mitch sighed. 'I'm not suggesting you're incapable, Holly. You're not the only one who's hurting. I've lost Sid, and Vanessa.' He looked into her eyes. 'Can't you see we're in the same boat? Why do you want to paddle alone?'

Holly felt hot tears threatening her eyes and her face reddened. *I can't cry in front of the staff,* she thought. Why was he piling on the pressure? She needed to be strong. She needed to get through the wait to see if Val would survive, a clear head to deal with the market and village fair, and strength to fight off Tom and his claim on her land. If she was to let her barriers down, she would be a total wreck. She did not want to be a weak, mess.

'Come on, Holly.' Mitch outstretched a hand.

Holly's bottom lip quivered; she knew if she spoke, she would only have a few words until her voice cracked. 'Please stop pressuring me, I don't need saving, I'm not Vanessa.' Holly heard the words echo in her head as if someone else had said them. She put her hand to her mouth as she studied Mitch's expression. It was if every feature on his face dropped an inch. He made no comment but whisked around.

'Mitch, I ...' Holly called out watching his back as he

strode away from her. *How could I have said that?* she thought as her lip trembled and she turned away, asking herself where the words had come from. Her whole face quivered until she got inside the caravan and let the tears stream down her face.

CHAPTER 30

*I*t was Thursday evening and everything was on track for the Saturday market day and fair. As Holly walked back to her caravan, her thoughts turned to Val. That morning, she had held her hand at her hospital bedside. Val looked drawn and weak but there was a distant sparkle in her eyes.

Holly caught her breath in her throat. The doctors were hopeful that she would recover but said another stroke could not be discounted, so they would need to keep her in hospital for some time and she might have to go to a nursing home. She could not imagine Val in a nursing home and told Len that she would attend any meetings with him about her future care. Val had helped to look after her as a child and she would return the favour.

Holly felt as if everything had rushed up in fast forward. Jaz had assured her that the stalls for the fair were all in hand. Holly felt uneasy, not having control of that side of the project but she had to admit, she would not have been able to cope without Jaz and Julian's help.

She went into the caravan and refilled the dog bowl with

wet food. Trixy wagged her tail as she wolfed it down. Gazing out of the caravan window towards Booth Farmhouse, Holly wished she could run down there and apologise properly. She had texted Mitch straight after her outburst. Saying sorry for the way she had hit out at him with the words she had regretted every moment since. He had been gracious but said she obviously needed some space. That was not what she had wanted to hear. She wanted him to rush over, demand hugs, demand kisses. Demand she let him into her life. She wanted him more than ever. *Why was I so cruel?* Holly imagined how great it would be to shut the door with Mitch inside and leave all her troubles outside. Like they had done in Croyde. *What's wrong with me?* she thought.

As she made a hot drink, she heard her mobile ding and her mood dropped further when she saw it was a text from Tom

I'm in the Eversley Arms. Can I come over to talk?

'That's all I need,' Holly said aloud putting her head in her hands. She took a deep breath and tapped out a reply.

Not a good idea, is it? Considering the court case?

The phone dinged again.

Maybe it can go away.

'I don't believe this.'

Trixy barked as Holly tapped out a reply.

Speak to Dawkins and Co. Good night.

Holly brushed her teeth and changed into her night-wear. Falling into a deep sleep, she dreamed of Tom and Grace. They were picking through her caravan, stealing the few possessions she had accumulated. Grace picked up a shell that Mitch had found for Holly on Croyde beach. 'I think I'll have that,' Tom said. 'No,' Holly cried out in her sleep. She heard Tom calling her name, 'Holly, Holly, Holly.'

Holly woke with a start, sweat covered her body and her hair stuck to her face.

'Holly, Holly.' Someone was rapping at the door. She could hear Tom's voice. 'I know you're in there.'

Trixy growled.

'You're joking.' Holly stomped to the door. She wrapped her arms around herself and shouted through the glass. 'Go away.'

'But we've got to talk. I've made a mistake. It's wrong, all wrong.'

Holly paused. *Is he really going to drop the case?* Taking Trixy she put her in the bedroom, she did not want Tom suing her for a dog bite on top of the divorce. She opened the door.

Tom walked in. 'Thanks, babe.'

'I don't think you should be calling me babe. And you stink of lager.' Holly's mouth felt dry. 'I'll put the kettle on and I'm going to change.' She remembered her dream. 'And don't touch anything.'

After putting the water on to boil Holly opened the bedroom door carefully, in case Trixy got out. Trixy jumped up and she petted her. 'Stay on the bed, girl – he'll be gone soon.' She pulled on jeans and returned to the main part of the caravan as the kettle clicked off.

'You've made it really homely in here, Holly. You make everything seem like home.'

Holly shook her head as she made Tom a strong black coffee. She placed his cup on the table.

Tom sat down and put his head in his hands. 'I miss you.'

'Miss me? What are you on about?'

'Exactly that, babe. I've been such a dick, running

around with Grace like that. It was a midlife crisis. She's young enough to be –'

'The child you don't want?' Holly shook her head.

'I felt pushed out by you. You were always busy.'

'We've already had this conversation, Tom, and I'm not going to accept any more of your put-downs.'

Tom stood up. 'Babe, I'm not here to put you down. I'm here 'cos I want us to get back together.'

'Back together? But what about Grace and the baby?'

'Eh?'

'Grace is pregnant, remember? You're setting up home together? Honestly, Tom, I knew you were irresponsible but this –'

'Oh. That. Her period was just a bit late.'

'And you didn't think to tell me that?' Holly stood up and walked away from Tom to the dining table.

'How could I? You've not been speaking to me.'

Holly spun around. 'You're supposed to be buying a place with her.'

'You seem to know a lot.'

'Just an assumption.'

Tom raked a hand through his hair. 'She's not you.'

'Clearly.'

'She's high maintenance.' He stood up and walked over to her.

Holly took a step back.

'I was only attracted to her because she reminded me of you. Of how you used to be when we first met. When you were young and happy.'

'Well, I'm sorry life dealt me a blow. So sorry my parents died.' Holly shook her head. 'Anyway, I've moved on.'

'I've heard you've been seeing that cockney.' Tom nodded his head towards the farm.

'You heard wrong, and my relationship status is none of your business.'

'You're still my wife and this is our land.'

'I've been over this before.'

'If we get back together, the whole thing will go away. I can help you build your art gallery. We can have a baby.'

Holly laughed. 'Are you for real?'

'And I might be able to help you financially.'

'How? You're supposed to be insolvent right? And you already owe me money.'

'Well, I might come into some.' Tom looked around the room and licked his lips.

'You have a new life and a new job, don't you? With Grace's dad, at Bunnings Motorhomes?'

'He's always breathing down my neck. And he wants me to buy into his business.'

'If you want out of your relationship with Grace and your job with David, don't use me as the excuse. I'm sorry life isn't as shiny as you thought it'd be. But forgive me for being a tiny bit unsympathetic. As I said, I've moved on and if you had an ounce of decency, you'd drop your claim on my land.'

'Our land, Holly. Our marriage, our history.'

'You've been hideous to me. I can't pretend none of this has happened and just go back to how we were.'

Tom walked back to the seating area, and sat down with his head in his hands as his shoulders quivered. Holly stared up to the ceiling. She could not even feel sorry for him. She wanted the court case to disappear and if there was a way out, she would take it. But stringing Tom along and pretending they would get back together was not an option.

She softened her voice as he wept. 'I don't want us to be

enemies, Tom, and I'd like the court case to go away. But you and me – it's not going to happen.'

Tom stood up and wiped the wet from his eyes on his sleeve. 'You bitch.' He pushed the mug off the table, spilling the coffee, which dripped onto Holly's rug.

Holly pointed at the door. 'I think you should leave.'

'You're gonna regret this. Get ready to say goodbye to your nursery. It's gone.' Tom rushed out of the caravan. He slammed the door, and it smashed with shattered glass flying everywhere.

Holly turned and shielded her face shaking all over. She wanted to run out, run down to Mitch's place and ask him to hold her, to tell her everything was going to be alright. But that was not an option, she had ruined it.

HOLLY WANDERED up Wells High Street. She had arranged an appointment with Jill to give a full account of Tom's visit. She also wanted to see if the divorce could be rushed through. Holly had taken pictures of the caravan door and left Joe back at the nursery repairing the damage. Any ammunition against Tom was a positive as far as she was concerned. Holly felt hardened, devoid of emotion, as if she'd wept her last reserve of tears the night before. Trixy trotted at her side, she was unsettled after Tom's visit and Holly did not want to leave her there with the noise of the door being fixed. She was surprised that Mitch had not asked for her back and realised that she should really return her.

She was twenty minutes early, so took a walk around the grounds of the Cathedral. The world seemed to be full of couples walking along holding hands, and kids swinging off the arms of their smiling parents. Why was her life not that simple? Someone to hold hands with, a nice little nine-to-five job, a family, a baby to hold, a blood relative to be close to. Family holidays to the coast? Croyde Bay popped into her mind and she pushed it aside. Deciding to shrug off her 'poor me' mood and get on with it.

Holly sat on a bench. Summer had definitely arrived. She loved this time of year, the relaxing feel of it. But she knew this summer would be full of tension. Maybe she should sell up and make her problems disappear — never to be seen again.

Back on the High Street, Holly considered enquiring with the estate agent the value of her land. She would have to do that anyway if she was going to make a settlement with Tom, no matter how small. As she neared the estate agent, she saw Mitch stride out. Moving back into a shop doorway she was thankful that Trixy, sniffing at something on the floor, had not noticed him. Waiting until he had gone quite a distance, she entered the estate agent's office.

'How can I help?' the woman sales assistant asked.

'I'm enquiring about selling my land. How quickly does land change hands these days?'

'Depends where it is and whether you put it up at a realistic price. Where is it?'

'Eversley.'

'That's odd, I was asked to value some land that way just now. Is something going on? There's not planning permission agreed for a new housing estate is there?'

Holly bit her lip – *so Mitch's selling up?* she thought. 'No. I own the nursery. There was a fire.'

'Oh, you must be from Lovelands. I was sorry to hear about that, I used to go over as a child with my parents.' Her voice softened.

Holly heard Trixy barking from outside, she hated being tied up.

'I can get someone to visit you tomorrow if you like?'

'I'll let you know.'

'Take my contact details.' She passed her a business card.

Holly put the card into her back pocket as she left the shop. She felt empty. That was that then, no point in even contemplating a reconciliation. Mitch was leaving and it would only ever have been Croyde, just Croyde.

CHAPTER 31

*H*olly stood inside one of the sheds that Joe had erected. Ethan had been over earlier for a coffee and given her posters with the designs he had amended. Following discussions she'd had with George the contractor, they'd had to make a few minor adjustments. Holly pinned the posters to the wall. Mitch had dropped her artwork up, leaving the small collection with Joe and, weather permitting, she would add the pieces to the shed the following day when the market opened.

Holly felt a little calmer since her most recent visit to Val. She had been propped up in the bed. She had moaned as Holly greeted her with a hug and a kiss. The doctor said it would be a while before her speech would come back but she looked animated as Holly told her about the goods to be sold at the market and about the fair. She had squeezed Val's hand, promising to take photographs to show her on her next visit.

Holly stepped back to study the plans she had pinned to the wall. The plans held her hopes and dreams and she wondered whether it had all been a waste of time. All this effort would be for nothing if Tom forced her to sell. Holly needed to get the settlement sorted with Tom, she could not wait for months on end. She knew Jill would not approve but she was sick of being at the beck and call of others. Her mind was clouded and needed to be clear. She had to meet him. But Holly did not want Tom to be prepared for her visit. In an effort to catch him off guard, she decided to try him at work. A voice in her head warned her not to go, but she was far from scared of Tom. He was like a spoilt child and she had to have it out with him. She called out to Joe and told him she was popping out.

HOLLY SWUNG her van into the car park of Bunning's Motorhomes. All was quiet. *Maybe they're shut?* she thought. Holly walked along the periphery of the building passing the showroom, in search of the offices. Holly heard Tom's voice and she walked towards it until she came to an open door.

'I'll book you in for a second viewing for Sunday and we can go over the financials.' Tom swung around in his chair; his mouth dropped as soon as he saw her. 'Okay, yes. Look forward to it, bye.' He replaced the receiver. 'Babe.' His spoke in a hushed voice. 'I'm glad you've come. Look, about the other night. I was bang out of order.' He ran a hand through his hair. 'Have you reconsidered?'

Holly walked in and crossed her arms. 'I'm here to settle this once and for all.'

'Look, why don't I come over to you later?'

'No, let's do this now.'

Tom stood up. 'I'll pay for the door.'

'Yes – you will.'

'We'll meet up this evening to discuss settling, maybe

over dinner? I guess we both want this done. Solicitors muddy the waters.'

Holly raised her eyebrows and stared at him. 'You're the one that appointed a solicitor in the first place.'

'It seemed the right thing to do at the time. I'm happy to accept thirty-five percent of the property and we'll call it quits on the money you invested in the hot tubs. To keep it out of the courts.'

Holly looked up to the ceiling shaking her head. She brought her gaze down slowly and it fell on the wall behind Tom's desk. She could not believe what she saw. 'What's that?' she said pointing to a painting.

Tom coughed. 'It's my portrait.'

'Yes, the one I painted of you.'

'For my birthday. It's mine, I never stole it.'

Holly clutched the desk. 'Trust me, I didn't want to keep it. But I would like to know how you acquired it?'

Tom's eyes darted from left to right and then back at Holly. 'I took it ages ago, to show to my folks. It's been in Newquay.'

'Don't lie to me. You got it the night of the fire, didn't you?' She threw her hands in the air. 'You set the nursery alight.'

'Woah, babe. Do you think I'm mad? Why would I do that when I'm entitled to half of it?'

'How did you find the painting in the dark? The electrics had blown.'

'I used my phone.'

'So now you're admitting to it, are you? You did get the painting that night?'

'What if I did? I never set the flippin' place on fire. You got it agreed, it was the electrics.'

Holly put her hands on her hips. 'How did you use the

torch on your phone when it had run out of charge? If I remember rightly you asked to borrow my charger and I refused.'

Tom paced the room.

Holly pointed at him. 'Come on, what did you do? Did you use a match?'

'No, it was that red candle from the porch. I left it in there. It must have fallen or something. It was a bloody accident okay?'

'You idiot. Do you realise what you've put me through?'

'Hey, I went through it too. Can you imagine how I felt when I heard about the fire? I thought I'd killed you. I drove over and you weren't there. There was no sign of you at the hospitals. And you weren't answering your phone. I thought you were in the morgue. It was an awful evening for me.'

'You are unbelievable.' Holly's whole body shook and her voice vibrated as she spoke. 'How does that compare to what I've been through? You've ruined my whole life.'

'You can't prove it was me. It could still have been an electrical fault. I'll say that the painting wasn't even in the studio.'

'Oh, I'll prove it alright.'

'There are no witnesses. The insurance has paid out. What's the big deal?'

'The big deal is, that you can get done for arson.'

'Only if I did it on purpose. It was an accident.'

'So you say. And I can prove you took the portrait that day because I logged all of my paintings with dated photographs.' Holly reached for her phone and brought up the pictures flashing through them one by one until she got to his portrait. 'There we are, the fourteenth of May.'

Tom leaned forward trying to grab the phone. Holly pulled her hand out of the way. 'It's on the cloud, brainbox.'

Tom walked towards the painting and lifted it off the wall. Holly quickly snapped a shot of him, with her phone.

'Another dated photo.' She paused as she tapped her phone, then looked at Tom. 'Uploaded.'

Tom walked towards her.

Holly watched his face twist. Then it changed, his eyes opened wide, as did his mouth. She heard Grace's voice behind her.

'Tommy, what's all the shouting about?'

'Why are you here?' Tom's face turned crimson.

'I was coming to talk about us getting back together. But you seem to be with your – wife.'

Holly spun around. 'Don't leave on my account.'

Grace pouted. 'Forget it, Tommy.' She left the office.

Holly swung back to Tom and crossed her arms. 'So you came back to me because you got dumped?' She laughed, then spoke slowly and quietly. 'You burned down my home, all the memories of my family are gone. You snuffed out everything I had. Call off the solicitor.'

'It was an accident.' Tom slumped into his chair and put his head in his hands. 'Honest, babe.'

Holly observed his cowering body.

'I lit the candle and forgot about it. Maybe it fell as I closed the door. I'd never have done it on purpose.' He looked up. 'You've got to believe me.'

Holly sighed. 'Save the excuses for the police. It's up to them to decide whether you're lying or not.'

Tom frowned. 'You wouldn't.'

'You ran off with another woman, you wanted out. I think it's probably for the best that the police are informed, don't you?'

Tom stood up. 'Look, I'll call my solicitor now.' He took his mobile phone out of his pocket.

Holly listened as he spoke to them, asking for his case to be withdrawn. 'Happy now?' he said as he slammed his mobile on the table.

'Nearly.' Holly turned and walked towards the door. 'There's just the matter of that money you owe me. I know you have eighty thousand in your savings account.'

Leaving Tom's office, she found Grace standing outside leaning against a wall, biting her thumb nail. Holly did not feel badly towards her, she had no energy for that. Grace looked up.

Holly smiled at her. 'You could do better. Much better.'

HOLLY'S LEGS trembled as she drove into the customer car park at Lovelands, wondering why she felt numb when she thought of Tom. Surely she should feel enraged. He had destroyed everything. Burned all of her memorabilia, the history of her parents and her ancestors. She could see the charred buildings rising up over the big fence they had erected. But the feeling that he would make no further claim against her property rubbed her anger away. At least it was her wreck, and it would stay hers. Her mobile rang. It was Jill.

'I have some amazing news.'

Holly did not intend to fill Jill in on what had happened.

'I have had communication from Tom's solicitor – he's pulling out.'

'That's what I was hoping you would say.'

'Have you been in contact with him?'

'He told me he was dropping it. I think his conscience got the better of him.'

'I will, of course, draw up papers for him to sign

confirming he will not revisit this in the future. Do you want me to sue him for my fees?'

'Hold fire on that. We'll wait and see if he returns my money. If I get it back, I'll settle your fees myself.'

Back at the caravan, Holly opened a bottle of wine and sat down, allowing herself to relax before Jaz turned up.

Later, Jaz listened whilst Holly filled her in on the events of the afternoon. She told Holly she was proud of her and what an absolute ballbreaker she was. Holly had laughed hysterically. *Thank goodness for Jaz,* she thought, as she felt her spirits rise.

CHAPTER 32

*H*olly woke at six, with a thumping headache, wishing she had not celebrated so hard the night before. Certainly not on the eve of the fair and farmers' market. Trixy jumped on the bed and licked her face. Jaz had spent the night and Holly could hear her showering, she sounded a lot brighter than Holly felt, singing an oldie they used to sing with Val as kids. *The sun has got his hat on.*

Peeking through the bedroom curtains, the sun did have his hat on, which Holly knew was great news for the day. Her phone dinged with a text; it was from Mitch she quickly opened it.

Good luck for today – see you shortly.

Holly smiled. With the court case out of the way and the land staying in her possession, she could see through the fog. After today was out of the way, she would arrange to have a chat with him. Apologise properly, maybe he would decide to stay at Booth Somerset rather than putting it on the market. She had time, selling a farm did not happen overnight. Maybe having a week or so to think about things had done her good because now she was certain – they belonged together.

THE SUN BEAT down as Holly and Joe walked the site. She had Trixy on a lead, trained or not, there would be too many different smells for the little dog to resist. Watching the farmers fill their respective sheds, and the fishmonger parking up his van, Holly scanned the area for Mitch. She spotted him as he assisted a couple of members of his staff arranging his wares. As usual, she felt the heat warm her cheeks at the sight of him. She could see he was busy so did not interrupt. Julie watered the pots dotted around for sale. Anne's husband was over at the petting zoo. He had agreed to oversee it for the day. Holly was touched at how many people were helping out for free, with the proceeds of the fair going to the arts hub fund.

'It's looking great, love,' Joe said. 'I'll get up to the top field now and take that scrap of a dog. Angela is looking forward to minding her for you.' Joe's wife had agreed to take care of Trixy at her sweet stall which was placed on the far edge of the field.

'Now be a good girl.' Holly handed the lead over to Joe. 'I'll get on and help Jaz and Julian with setting up the fair,' she said. 'Although they've recruited quite a team.'

Holly looked up the hill where a marquee had been erected the previous day. A couple of men emptied a Luton van full of tables they had borrowed from the village hall. Cars were parking on the field, with stall-holders unloading their goods. 'I can't believe how many people have got involved.'

'The whole village feels for you, love. And the fair has

created a lot of excitement over these past two weeks. Anyway, I'll get meself up there.'

'Thanks for all your help, Joe.' Holly gave him a brief hug,

Joe laughed. 'Good luck, love. It's gonna be a great day.'

After Joe and Trixy left, Holly nodded at a woman passing her, carrying a stack of wind chimes. Checking the list she had on her clip board, she could see everything was going to plan. *Is this my turning point?* she asked herself.

Looking up, Holly saw Jaz approaching, dressed in the nursery uniform of cerise polo and khaki shorts. She smiled, this was different to Jaz's usual clothes of dresses, suits and stilettos.

'I love you in uniform,' Holly said.

Jaz laughed. 'I'm too short in these boots, I need heels to give me height. But O-M-G, hun, today's gonna be mega.' She grabbed Holly around the waist and squeezed her tightly.

'How's it going up there?' Holly nodded to the field.

'Julian's collecting subs from each stall-holder and Noah is selling raffle tickets.'

'I'm so pleased Julian managed to find a cider farmer at this short notice. I'm hoping the alcohol will lead to impulse buys.'

'I've left them up there, so I can help with your meet and greet.'

Holly was pleased that Jaz had agreed to help show people around the property, she was excellent at sales, not pushy but very persuasive. Holly had sent email invitations to Trudy from the Arts Council and the local councillors, including Nina and David.

'Val will be so proud of you,' Jaz said, pulling her phone out and taking a picture of Holly. 'I'm taking pictures and video to show her like you asked.' She took a few more shots.

'Have you heard from Len? Is he coming?' Holly asked.

'No, but his son Ben is bringing the grandkids down.' Jaz's phone rang. 'I'll just take this,' she said.

Holly's stomach rumbled as the smell of bacon wafted over from the snack shack, as it sizzled on a portable burner. Anne spotted her looking over and waved. Holly's appetite had returned with a bang since Tom cancelled the court case.

She approached the shack. 'Bacon roll, please.'

'Same here.' She heard Mitch's voice from behind and swung around.

'Oh, hi,' she said brushing the hair out of her eyes.

'It looks like everything is going to plan?'

'Yes. I've had great news; Tom dropped his claim on my land.'

'Glad he saw sense.'

'Something like that,' Holly said as Anne handed her and Mitch a bacon roll each.

'That'll be two fifty,' Anne said to Mitch.

Holly laughed. 'Mitch's food is on the house.'

Mitch took the roll and bit into it. 'Amazing. These are gonna be a crowd-pleaser.'

Anne blushed.

Holly finished a mouthful. 'I've got a good feeling about today.'

'Yes,' Mitch said. 'It's going to bring loads in.'

Holly studied Mitch. There was a sadness in his eyes.

'I've left my staff, Jason and Emma in charge. I've spoken to all the farmers, they're set up and happy.'

'Great.' Holly longed to reach out to him and tell him how she felt. But it would have to wait until later.

'If they have any problems, they'll field their queries to me. So you only need to worry about issues on the nursery side.'

'Thanks.' Holly decided she would speak to Mitch that evening, without fail. She had to apologise properly. She could not help feeling responsible for the sadness in his eyes.

'I have to go, but I will be on the end of the phone should any problems arise.'

'Oh?' Holly said, disappointed Mitch would not be on site. 'Try and get back for the fair though. It's going to be amazing.'

'I'm sure it will. You've got everything under control here. So many people have stepped up. You've a great team around you.'

Holly looked around at the people milling about. She had felt isolated and lonely for months but now she was touched by the help and enthusiasm of the village. It felt as if everyone she knew was here. Ethan had turned up, bringing a crowd of their old college friends. Families from Eversley Burrows had arrived, including a few she knew from primary school. She turned back to Mitch, to tell him how much she appreciated his support, but he'd gone.

THE CUSTOMER CAR park was completely full after twenty minutes of opening. The guy on car park duty was directing visitors through the opening between the nursery and farm land as Mitch had agreed to use his scrub for overflow parking – rather than messing up Holly's spare grassy fields, which had been freshly cut for people to relax on. Jaz was at the gate, handing out leaflets and explaining what was on offer, giving Holly the heads up via text when any of the councillors arrived. Holly had spoken to a few of them already, including Nina, who was really enthusiastic. The excitement was starting to well up inside her.

Jaz texted to alert Holly that Trudy, the Arts Council representative had arrived with her husband and twin sons. Holly rushed over, wanting to show them around personally. After the introductions, Holly led the family to the shed, detailing the arts hub plans.

She pointed towards the blackened ruins. 'The tragic fire was caused by an electrical fault.' Holly would not be telling the wider public the truth she had learned from Tom. 'I lost my business, home and all my artwork.'

'That's awful,' Trudy's husband said. 'And whose paintings are these?'

'They're a couple of pieces I've painted since. And my landscape.'

'Oh yes, from the competition in Wells, I thought I'd seen it somewhere before. You have a real talent,' he said.

Holly blushed. 'Thank you. I was determined for something positive to come out of this, so I've drawn up these plans for an arts hub.'

Holly noted that Trudy's face seemed to light up as she spoke and her husband looked animated as she explained her proposals. Holly knew it would be a long road but this looked positive.

Trudy and her family went off in the direction of the fair. Holly turned to see David Bunning approach her, she was surprised he had shown up. His face was dark. *Oh no – not now*? she thought as she felt a panic start to rise, no doubt Grace had stuck her oar in, explaining how heartless, selfish and crazy Holly was. Grace may even have told him she was at his place of business yesterday, making trouble.

'I've been meaning to call you, Holly, to tell you – you

have my backing and that everyone's up for it. I wanted to let you know before today, so we could tell the representative from the Arts Council. I'm so sorry, I've been tied up with business issues, and council issues. Is Trudy here?'

'Yes, I've shown her around. She's up at the stalls. I thought you might not want to support me because of Tom and Grace.'

'Oh, that nonsense?' He shook his head. 'Grace is rather fickle. Love her to pieces but she does fall head over heels with the most unsuitable fellows, then loses interest. I'm sure she'll grow out of it. And I do hope she had nothing to do with the break-up of your marriage.'

'No, that was all Tom.'

'Enough of that, then. Let's go and find Trudy and tell her you have the Council's support.'

They headed to the field hosting the fair. The buzz of excitement was electric and her eyes threatened tears. She was touched by the number of people there, at Lovelands, on her property, having fun.

'You've done an amazing job.' David smiled at her.

They caught up with Trudy.

'Hello again, I'm David Bunning. We met at *The Beauty of Somerset,* awards evening.'

'Of course I remember you, David.' Trudy turned to them, and her husband took their boys towards the tombola.

'I wanted to let you know that we at Wells City Council fully support Holly's funding application.'

Trudy turned to Holly. 'I'm impressed with what you're doing for your local community. It's outstanding and I'll be giving your application my full support and, whilst I'm not meant to say this, your claim will definitely be approved in full. It's the best presentation I've seen in a long time.'

'Thank you so much. I don't know what to say. Really I don't.' Holly blinked her eyes rapidly.

'You don't have to say anything. You deserve it. You've worked really hard,' Trudy said.

David took them both by the arm. 'Let's celebrate. I'll have to treat you two ladies to something in the cider tent.'

Holly let David lead her away, but she looked over her shoulder. She was desperate to tell Mitch the good news.

Inside the packed cider tent, people were in jovial spirits — no doubt having sampled many of the ciders on offer.

'I hope you're all buying as well as tasting,' she called out.

Julian laughed. 'I am. I'll be placing an order of this one for the pub,' he said as he finished off his glass.

David got caught by another councillor and Trudy slipped away, presumably to find her family.

'Have you anything with a fizz in it?' Holly asked the cider maker. 'I'm celebrating.'

Jaz came up behind her. 'What happened with Trudy? I've been texting you. Have you got your funding?'

'Yes! Everyone here approves.'

The cider maker passed two small glasses to Holly and Jaz.

Jaz raised her glass. 'I'm pleased for you, hun, and so flippin' proud.'

They drank the sweet, fizzy cider, which brought a glaze to Holly's eyes.

Julian put his hand on Holly's shoulder. 'You're doing great things for our village.'

'Thanks for arranging the cider at the last minute. It's heaving in here5.' Holly placed her glass back on the make-shift bar.

Jaz pointed to a large man in front of a table. 'Jim from

Kelly's auction house is about to start the hub fund-raising auction. I managed to get a few local businesses to support it. We've got vouchers for restaurants, signed celeb photos, an entry into the caves over at Cheddar and all sorts.'

'I'm so grateful – I don't know what to say.' She gave Jaz a hug,

Holly heard Jim's voice testing the microphone and was filled with an overwhelming desire to see Mitch. A sense of urgency filled her. However, she could not leave the tent now, not when a fund-raising event was commencing for which she was the beneficiary.

The auction went well, especially as the cider flowed. There was a voucher for Sunday lunch at The Eversley Arms, a signed photo of a Wurzel who lived in a neighbouring village, a meal at a celebrity chef restaurant, tickets for local attractions and a voucher for the chippy on Eversley Burrows estate. At the end the mayor stood up, swaying slightly with cider and auctioned an off-the-cuff cream tea with her in Wells Cathedral. Holly could understand why Jim Kelly had a lifetime in the auction business as he certainly had a way of pushing the price up. Holly was called to the stage at the end and thanked everyone for coming.

Leaving the tent, Holly had only one thing on her mind, finding Mitch. She didn't want to wait until the evening. She felt an overwhelming sense of urgency, as she ran over to his shed in the market area, wondering whether he'd returned. He was not there, so she waited until one of his assistants had stopped serving a customer.

'Is Mitch about?' she asked.

'No, he was here for set up only,' the young woman said. 'He had to get off. But don't worry, everything's under control and we can call him if we have any problems. It's going great, isn't it?'

'Yes,' Holly smiled but her heart ached. It didn't look as if Mitch was coming back up for the fair. With the funding having been approved and Tom off her back, the tight knot which had inhabited her stomach had been untied and she felt free. The only strong feeling she had left was love and the need to apologise properly. *I must find him,* she thought.

Heading for the farm, Holly waved to people as she passed, not wanting to stop, as she darted between them. She needed to tell Mitch exactly how she felt. Glancing behind her she saw the villagers milling around her land, but all that seemed to matter, right now, in that moment, was Mitch. He was the person she wanted to share everything with. The person who made her feel human again because that was what she was feeling right now human with intense feelings. Laughing, she sped down the grassy slope her chest burned and she had a stitch but she felt free. She could not put it off any longer.

Stopping outside his home, she knocked on the farm-house back door. Silence. She spotted a solitary figure near the cow sheds. Three minutes later as she approached breathless, she could see it was not Mitch, it was his herdsman. Holly took a moment to catch her breath.

'Hey,' he said. 'You okay, love?'

Holly nodded. 'Where's Mitch?'

'He's gone already. Don't worry, he's left full instructions. He said he was going to drop them up to you. We'll still be supplying your market in the interim and he'll discuss it with the new owner to ensure it continues.' He smiled and looked up the hill. 'Looks like you've done a roaring trade.'

Holly stood in silence, trying to process what she had been told. 'New owner?'

'Mitch is going to consolidate everything in Essex. Not practical he says to have farms on opposite sides of the country. Lucky for us staff, the family have assured us it will be sold as a going concern.'

The knot returned to Holly's stomach.

The herdsman looked back up the hill. 'I'm surprised you didn't see him. He only left the sheds a short while ago. He said he was dropping something off to you, then he would be on the road.'

Holly turned and ran back up the hill. Her tired legs felt weak. She had not spotted Mitch's pick-up at the house. Maybe it was parked around the front and he was still loading it up? *Please let him still be here,* she thought. As she made her way back to the house. It was as if she was in one of her bad dreams, running through thick tar. Her muscles ached and slowed her down but she had to catch him. Holly stopped and put her hand up to shield the sun from her eyes and watched as she glimpsed Mitch's pick-up in the distance. It was to the right of her vision, gliding away from the caravan before disappearing around the bend as he drove out of Lovelands and out of her life.

The rest of the day went in a blur. Never had Holly put on such a brave face. She spoke to no-one on the matter, not even Jaz. Blocking from her thoughts the fact that Mitch was gone. She remained composed, as the staff and village helpers cheered when Jaz announced that they had raised well over five thousand pounds.

After the last person had left and her land was empty, Holly's chin trembled as she arrived back at the caravan with Trixy walking at heel. When she entered the caravan, there was a box on the dining table with a note stuck to it. Lifting the lid she found a file about the farmer's market and a pack of letters tied in string. The letters were those she had found in Sidney's desk, but were now all open. She picked up the note which Mitch had left her.

HOLLY,

I found these letters. I thought you might like to see them, it's our joint family history. Collect the painting of Ivy from the house when you are ready. I'll be in touch about the market. Don't worry, everything is under control. I've decided it's best for me to return to Essex and sell Booth Somerset. I will ensure the new owners buy into the market also, if that's what you wish. Look after Trixy, I can't take her with me as Sid's working dog is now in Essex and is too aggressive for Trixy. She loves you more than me anyway. I'll transfer money for her food and have left details of the pet insurance, which I have paid for in full for this year.

It's for the best. Mitch x

LATER, in bed with Trixy sleeping at her feet, Holly picked up the bundle of letters, reading how desperately Sidney had loved Ivy, realising that while the family feud was over, it appeared that a relationship between and a Booth and a Loveland was forever doomed.

CHAPTER 33

*T*he April morning blew a fresh breeze and Holly pulled her coat collar up as she walked along Wells High Street carrying her art folio. It had been ten months since the first farmers' market. Autumn, Christmas, Holly's birthday and a blanket of snow had been and gone. Val was back in her house and Holly had been helping out with her care. Rising early to pop over and help her wash and dress had become part of her daily routine and she had combined it with Trixy's walk. Jaz helped out in the evenings and Val had regained slow speech but it would be a long time before she would return to her usual chatty self.

The main nursery building was now rebuilt and filled with stock and an extension linked it with the old barn which was to house the arts hub. It was on schedule for the grand opening in a few weeks' time. Holly neared the Town Hall; many artists had shown an interest in using the hub. Now it was time to firm up the slots.

Once inside the meeting room, Holly opened her folio and retrieved the plans for the hub. She pinned them to an A-frame flip chart. The room was cold and she wondered whether it had been a good idea to hold the meeting here, but it was a great venue, size wise. Nina burst into the room wearing a long-sleeved electric blue dress and her dark wavy hair bounced off her shoulders.

'Holly, there you are.'

Holly was pleased to see Nina. As much as she had wound her up in the past, she was a great networker. Holly had seen more of her since Nina had got together with Ethan. They had met at the summer fair, having not seen each other since college, and had really hit it off. With Julian and Jaz also going strong, it seemed as if everyone was in love.

'It's a bit chilly,' Nina said, touching the old-fashioned cream radiators. 'The heating's kicking in, so it'll soon warm up.' She rubbed her hands together. 'Breakfast will arrive at nine. I've gone for plant based options as a lot of the arty types are well into the vegan revolution. Bear that in mind when talking about the farm next door.'

Holly blushed. 'I wasn't going to talk about ...'

'Oh, no, no of course not. Have you heard from Mitch?'

'No,' Holly said, standing away from the flip chart and looking at her plans, hoping Nina would not press her any further on the subject.

'It reminds me of college, doing all the arty stuff,' Nina sighed. 'I missed it when I went off to study business.'

'But it's served you well, you're a real success. *Something Special*, is the go-to place for brides for miles.'

'Yes, specialising was a good move.'

With Nina's help, Holly laid out pens, paper and an agenda for the prospective artists, who began flowing in at half eight.

First was James the potter, then Mandy who worked with textiles, Jackie who specialised in mosaic and sculpture, and finally Sarah with her knitting and crochet. Holly scanned the room; they were certainly a colourful bunch. Knits, tie dyes, denim, crushed velvet, scarves and boots. *A real mix of generations too,* she thought as she felt her palms sweat.

Nina put a hand on Holly's back. 'Do you want to start? I'll make notes for you.'

Holly smiled at Nina, she appreciated her help.

Holly stood up. 'Welcome. I know most of you attended the fair at Lovelands last year and saw the plans, but I wanted to refresh your memory and go over them again, in more detail. And to update you on the changes we've made. I'd also be grateful for any feedback you have.'

The briefing went well. The artists were attentive, asking questions and they appeared fully engaged. Holly felt a buzz of excitement. Was it just her? Or was it collective?

'I've been waiting for this type of venture for ages,' Jackie said.

'Me too,' Andrew added.

'My details are on the info pack, if you're still interested.'

'You're joking, right?' Mandy said gesturing around the room. 'We're all interested. This is amazing.'

'Definitely count me in,' Sarah said. 'And I have other contacts who would love to be invited.'

'I have spare information packs and leaflets if you want to take any.'

'I'll take a couple,' Jackie said, 'I know two others who would seriously consider this.'

Holly smiled. 'That's great. In the information pack is a calendar with time slots. If you could indicate any you're interested in, I'll plan a workshop rota. There are a few permanent spaces I can let out too, for anyone wanting a full-time space to work in. Obviously, they will be allocated on a first-come-first-served basis.'

'In that case, I'll have one,' Mandy said.

'The rates of hire are in the pack. Permanent areas have a set fee. Feel free to come over and I'll show you around, although please book this in advance as the contractors are still on site so I have to work around them.'

'Well that couldn't have gone any better,' Nina said to Holly after the artists had left.

'I thought it went well, too,' Holly said.

'The business model is great, I'm really impressed. And even with the not-for-profit strategy, you can still pay yourself a decent wage.'

'Oh, I do hope people will want to come – to join in and explore art.'

'They will, trust me. I've heard many people talking about it, and about you. You always were popular.' Nina opened her bag and put her pen and pad inside. 'I was jealous of you at college, with your perfect looks and lovely personality.'

'You're joking. Nina, you're beautiful.'

'Yes, beauty that takes me two hours to get right every morning. You could get out of bed after no sleep and still look great.'

Holly laughed. 'I doubt that very much.' She licked her lips and frowned. 'Nina, honestly, you're gorgeous. You always were, with or without make-up.'

'And here today, with these artists. You're the trendy crowd and I'm the outsider. They respect you so much.'

'You have people eating out of your hand at every meeting I attend,' Holly said.

'Nonsense.'

'No, really. People admire you.' Holly stepped forward

and wrapped her arms around Nina. She felt stiff but soon physically relaxed and hugged Holly back.

'I do try.'

'You're a perfectionist, Nina. Don't be so hard on yourself.'

HOLLY ARRIVED AT THE NURSERY. They had begun remodelling the car park to make full use of the space. This involved pulling back the brambles that had encroached on it over the years and laying pressed gravel to harden the surface, so it didn't kick up stones every time it was driven on. Holly skimmed the edge along the grass, taking her van close to the caravan. It was quiet. With the car park being resurfaced, they had decided to close for two days.

After dropping her folio at the caravan, Holly walked over to the now modern nursery building. It still had the original stone but had the addition of alpine-style wood and large glass windows. She waved at George who stood outside the arts hub building, chatting to a colleague as they drank coffee. The only boards up now were those surrounding her cottage.

Anne now ran the café, since Val was still in recovery. It was housed in the new extension linking the nursery with the old barn. She was singing away to the radio when Holly arrived. The café was open to serve the workers. Tea and coffee were free to them and they were sold food at a discount but Holly still made a profit as they bought food throughout the day.

Anne looked up and turned the radio down. 'Hi. love. How did it go?'

Trixy bounded from around the counter, jumping up at Holly.

Holly scooped the dog up, ruffling her fur. 'It went amazingly well. Fingers crossed, it'll be a success.'

'Hard work's done this, not luck.'

Holly nodded. 'True, we've all pulled together.' She placed Trixy on the ground and the little dog returned to her basket.

Holly looked at the cakes on display.

'Help yourself, love,' Anne said, pointing to the treats and snacks.

There were different cakes each day. Today's choice was, *Val's Victoria Sponge* or *Val's' Ginger Loaf*.

'I think a slice of ginger will hit the spot. I hope Val will be able to get over for the reopening.'

'She's making great progress,' Anne said as she passed Holly a mug of coffee.

'Yes, she gets a little better each time I see her.' Holly turned and scanned the room with her eyes. The rear café walls were covered with art work for sale, including a few pieces of her own. A small smile covered her face. 'It's all coming together.' She bit her lip, everything was perfect. All but one thing. As much as she fought it, her mind constantly flashed up images of Mitch.

CHAPTER 34

*M*itch rose early, it was still dark. He headed for the shower. He had moved back into his marital home, the part of his parent's house that he had shared with Vanessa. When he had left a year ago to look after Booth Somerset, it had felt as if he was running away and not facing up to it. Yes, Sid had needed him, so he would have gone anyway. But if the accident had not happened, Vanessa would have accompanied him. Winter had been tough; the wind had thrashed across the flat land with heavy rains flooding some of the fields. His father had been pleased for his help.

Mitch dried himself and pulled on his clothes. He was due to speak to Greg, the herdsman, in Somerset. They had a weekly call because Mitch still managed Booth Somerset remotely. His mother had co-ordinated the farmers' market during the remainder of the summer months. There had been some interest from prospective buyers when Booth Somerset had initially been placed on the market, but with continued economic uncertainties, it became apparent that the farming community were reluctant to take on new ventures.

Mitch put on his coat, opened the door and headed over to the sheep. His thoughts turned to Holly. The farmers' market had done well and he understood it would reconvene, next month. He felt bad about the way he had left Eversley, like a wounded animal – but things had not been right. He knew he should have gone over there to see her. Holly had invited Mitch to Eversley for the reopening of the nursery buildings, but he had to decline. It was lambing season and his parents were away on an extended holiday, celebrating his father's sixtieth. He'd explained to Holly in an email that he was tied to the farm during his parents' absence, although he guessed she would have thought it was an excuse. After a three-month adventure, his parents were due back and were currently travelling through France.

Mitch approached the lambing sheds where the young ewes were kept. The older sheep were left in the fields but the first-time pregnant ewes were kept in the shed in case they needed a helping hand. Also inside were those sheep expecting twins or triplets. They needed to eat well and had to be separated rather than left to fight for food with the rest of the flock. The ewes' wombs had been scanned so he knew exactly how many lambs each animal was expecting. By splitting them like this, he could monitor their feeding and nutrition. Mitch was all for managed farming. It not only made his life easier but it was better for the animals.

As he opened the shed door, Mitch was met with the noise of ferocious bleating. A lamb stood beside a motionless ewe. *Not another one,* he thought. This was the third ewe to die during labour that week. He guessed it might be a breeding issue, as the dead ewes were from the same bloodline. His father would have to consider that for the next breeding programme. Mitch did not intend to be involved with the lambing season the following year – he wanted to spread his wings. Maybe go into teaching and lecture at one of the agricultural colleges. Knowing it was time for a serious change in his life, he planned a visit to Cirencester Agricultural College about a vacancy they had for a lecturer.

Mitch extracted the colostrum from the dead sheep's teat using a tube and fed it to the orphan. He knew from experience that those nutrients were stronger than any man-made supplements.

'Now to get you adopted,' he said.

There was a first-time ewe who had given birth to a still-born the previous day and he had kept the poor lamb's skin before its body was disposed of. Mitch collected the skin and tied it around the new-born's neck. The ewe had been separated from the other sheep, so he took the lamb over to her, watching as they sat – one each side of the pen with the lamb bleating and the ewe looking on. Leaving them to it, he hoped they would bond. There was never a quiet moment during lambing season, and he went about the rest of his day.

Two days later, Mitch gave his parent's lounge and kitchen a clean through. His mother had texted and he was expecting them in half an hour.

He soon heard the throaty sound of his father's classic Range Rover and opened the front door.

His mother, rushed over, grabbing him for a hug. Stepping back, she gave him the once over. 'You look much better, Mitch. How do you feel?'

'Great, Mum. I think the last few months have done me good.'

His father, entered, looking frazzled and slapped him on the back. 'Good to see you, son.'

'I'll get your cases in.' Mitch fetched their luggage, noticing that they had a lot more than they had left with.

Mitch sat down in the lounge, his parents sitting on the sofa opposite.

His mother clutched her cup of tea. 'Nothing like a proper brew. So what's next, Mitch? Do you think you'll stay on?'

'I'd love to stay with you guys, but I was thinking of lecturing and am considering a position in Cirencester.'

'Really?'

'I might study a PHD alongside it.'

'Blimey, that's new,' his dad said.

'New is what I need.'

'What about Eversley? Had any thoughts there?' his mother asked, taking a sip of her drink.

Mitch pursed his lips. He was well aware of what she was getting at, but he was not going to discuss Holly with her.

She continued. 'We've not had much interest from anyone wanting to buy the farm – although it's starting to turn a profit, I see.'

'We'll have a board meeting about it,' his dad said. 'Might be worth keeping it on, rather than dropping the price.'

'Will you visit the farm now we're back? Someone needs to go over and do the staff reviews,' his mum added.

'I'm sure Greg can manage that. We could give him a promotion,' Mitch said.

'It'd be nice if you could promote him in person.' His mum peered over her mug as she sipped her tea.

Mitch took a deep breath.

'Maybe you should go for a week or so,' she continued. 'The farmers' market will be starting again soon, and we have a share in that remember? With Lovelands. You really need to meet with the other suppliers, to make sure they're still committed to it. There's only so much I can do on the phone.'

'Mother.'

'Sorry – I thought ...'

'I know what you were thinking.'

'Hope you're not match-making,' Mitch's dad said with his eyebrows raised.

Mitch stood up. 'You two relax. I'll get back down to the flock.'

As Mitch walked towards the lambs, he glanced at his phone. Eversley nagged at him. It had nagged at him for months. He wondered whether there was unfinished business there. Try as he might, he could never get Holly out of his mind. Maybe he should go to Eversley, one last time – just to make sure.

CHAPTER 35

*H*olly jumped out of bed and went to the kitchen area of the caravan. Pulling open the curtains, she smiled. Today was the official opening of Eversley Arts Hub. The artwork displayed in the new nursery building had already attracted attention. She had picked up a couple of commissions. A wedding gift for a couple over in Glastonbury and the other for a marketing business in Street. Not short of work, Holly had taken on new members of staff. The local sixth-form college had agreed to partner with her, so their students could be involved, both in the day-to-day jobs at the nursery, and also gaining experience with teaching younger kids and displaying their own work in the arts hub. Everything had fallen neatly into place.

Trixy yapped at her for her breakfast food. Holly watched her nose the dog bowl over the caravan's kitchen area. Whilst she loved her pet to bits, she was a constant reminder of Mitch. She opened the cupboard containing Trixy's food and filled the bowl.

Tom was now completely off the scene. He had eventually returned her money. Having split with Grace, he had tried to move himself back into the village circle but the gossips had made life difficult for him. She had mentioned nothing but had a pretty good idea that Jaz had spread the word. Holly had not gone too far out of her way to dispute any rumours about him, discovering that sometimes the Eversley grapevine could work in her favour. Taking on the role of village villain and being known as 'Arsonist Tom' had been too much for him and he had soon disappeared. Holly presumed he was back in Newquay with his parents. She knew the fire was an accident and was sure Tom regretted it. But that did not soften her thoughts towards him – he deserved the banishment.

There was a rap at the caravan door. Holly looked down at the pyjamas she was still wearing and squinted through the mottled glass to see who it was. Realising it was Jaz, she opened it.

Jaz beamed. 'I can't flippin' believe it, who'd have thought it would all be ready so quick?'

'I've been lucky to have such great people behind me. Such as you, Julian, the college, the Council, The Arts Council, the –'

'Cool it, chick. You're not picking up your local entrepreneur award just yet.'

Holly laughed, digging Jaz in the arm. 'Cheeky. Come inside.'

Once in the caravan, Jaz hugged Holly as a jealous Trixy jumped up at their legs.

'I'm so proud of you, hun.' Jaz leaned back. 'What time is everyone getting here?'

'The staff are due to arrive at nine. The gates are opening at eleven and the Mayor cuts the tape at noon.'

'Okay, I'll text Julian. He wants to be here. He's bringing Noah.'

'I've seen you doing the family thing, Jaz. It suits you.'

Jaz pulled a face. 'I don't think I'm mum material.'

'Rubbish, Noah is always laughing when you're around. You don't have to be his mum.'

Jaz shook her head.

Holly chose not to press her on the subject. 'Anyway, you've both been so good, helping me out.'

'Thanks for allowing us to.'

'What do you mean?'

'Not being funny, chick, but you used to want to do everything yourself. Sometimes it's nice for us to feel we can do something for you. You know – be useful.'

'You've always been there for me, since I was four.'

'I know, but it's nice to help organise things, to help in other ways. Other than being your bodyguard.'

Holly laughed. 'You still are that. But yes, I see what you mean. I guess I might have been a little bit of a control freak.'

Jaz raised her eyebrows. 'A little?'

Holly laughed. 'Okay, a lot. I think I must be mellowing in my old age.'

'Maybe with the hub ready, you can think about a social life.'

'With all this networking I've been doing, I feel like a social butterfly already.'

'I mean letting your hair down. Maybe a date or two?'

'Oh no, not that again.'

'I heard they haven't sold Booth Farm. They're going to keep it on.'

Holly switched the kettle on.

'I heard from Greg that Mitch might be coming over. They're going to do some recruitment and introduce that box scheme.' Jaz leaned on the worktop.

Holly took a couple of mugs out of the cupboard.

'And I assume they're carrying on with the farmers' market?'

'Yes, I'm in contact with his mum about that. She's really nice. I'd love to meet her. She's the business mind while Mitch's dad, is the technical guy, knows all about the sheep.'

'Does she mention Mitch?'

'She said he's been tied up with the lambing while they were off travelling.'

'So, she didn't mention if he was seeing anyone?'

Holly turned around. 'Of course not. Why would she? It's business correspondence, not pub talk.' Holly poured the hot water into the mugs over the tea bags.

'So, have you spoken to Mitch at all?'

'Jaz, if there was any Mitch contact, you'd be the first to know. I'm not keeping anything from you.' Holly put the soggy tea bags into her compost caddy.

Jaz took the milk out of the fridge and poured some into each cup. 'You may not have kept any facts from my attention but you defo avoid talking about him. I feel like you're fobbing me off if I mention the farm or his name.'

'That's because I don't really like talking about him. I spend so much of my day being reminded of him,' she said nodding at Trixy. 'I'm constantly pushing thoughts of him out of my head. It's automatic for me to change the subject.'

'Hun. I'm sorry, I didn't realise it was still that raw.'

'I guess I feel like I ruined it. That I pushed him away. If I had my time again …'

'It's not worth having regrets, chick. I mean he had loads of baggage – having lost his wife and all. It wasn't all your doing.'

'Maybe the timing was wrong. Although he could have made contact since and he hasn't. He could have messaged me instead of getting his mum to talk to me about the farm-ers' market.'

'He might think you don't want him to. Have you messaged him?'

'Not since I invited him to the nursery opening and he sent me back that short reply, saying he was too busy.' Holly took a sip of her tea then put it down. 'Anyway, today is a big day and I want it to be a happy one. I don't want to dwell on my non-existent love life, or Mitchell Booth. Today is a new beginning.'

'I'll drink to that.' Jaz tapped her mug against Holly's then took a sip of tea. 'You know what? I think I'm even more excited than I was for the fair last year, and that takes some beating.'

'Me too. There isn't a tonne of stress looming over my head like there was last summer.'

'That's true. Let's have the best day ever. Come on, chick. Get out of them PJ's. We've got work to do.'

HOLLY AND JAZ both wore the new Eversley Hub uniform, consisting of black top, purple fleece and khaki cargos. Trixy had a new dog coat displaying the hub emblem. A crowd was already growing in the car park, ready to walk in as soon as the gate was opened. Holly's nerves were kicking in. The local press had also arrived. She was pleased she had chosen a Saturday as there were many families there. Chil-dren always brought a sense of excitement.

'Pressure,' Holly said.

'Nonsense, hun. They're gonna love it.'

Trixy jumped up and down, Holly guessed she was picking up her nervous energy.

Holly opened the gate. As each person passed they

handed them a leaflet explaining the hub, including a new map of the nursery and all of the activities on display that day. There was an insert with a list of future bookable activities and events.

Once the first batch of customers passed, Jaz squeezed Holly's arm. 'You get inside, I'll do the meet and greet and text you when the Mayor arrives.'

Holly followed the stream of people towards the nursery, but stopped when she heard Jaz call her. Trixy also stopped, sniffing at the air.

'Holly. Hun?' Jaz's voice held a sense of urgency.

Holly turned, seeing Jaz staring at her, with eyebrows raised, pointing at the car park.

Holly recognised his walk first, the long strides. It was Mitch. Her heart thumped. Without thinking, she walked towards him. He was still some distance away when he spotted her and waved. Holly quickened her step and waved back. Mitch sped up, she started jogging, grinning as Trixy overtook her. As they neared each other, they both ran the last few paces. Mitch picked her up, swinging her around, with Trixy yapping in excitement. Holly tightened her arms around him and he lowered her to the ground, leaning back so she could see his face.

He laughed. 'I thought you'd turn me away.'

Holly blushed, moving her hair away from her eyes. 'I need all the customers I can get.'

Mitch pulled her close. 'I've missed you.'

Trixy jumped up at their legs, yapping in a high-pitched bark.

Mitch bent down and picked the little dog up. 'I missed you, too.' Trixy licked his face as he pulled her away. 'Woah, I'm sure you've put a stone on.'

'She's on a diet.'

'Of what? Sausages? She looks like a fattened lamb.'

Holly laughed, feeling the long-missed warmth from his presence.

Mitch returned Trixy to the ground. 'Well then, Holly Loveland, are you going to show me around?' He put his hand out and Holly held onto it, his touch sending tingles all over her body.

'So, are you here to check over the farm?'

'There's business to do over there, but that's not the reason I'm here.'

Holly felt Mitch squeeze her hand and she stopped. Facing him, she glanced up.

Stroking her face, his eyes met hers, questioning. She laid her hands on his chest and his warm mouth was soon upon hers. Aware of people walking past, she ignored them, not wanting the kiss to stop. A tender kiss that told her the reason Mitch was back in Somerset.

Mitch pulled away; his smile wide.

Holly blinked rapidly. 'I'm sorry that I –'

'Hey, there's plenty of time to talk. Show me this place you've created.' Mitch put his arm around her shoulders.

Jaz grinned at them when they reached the gate. 'Well, hello stranger. I won't ask you what brings you back to the village.' She winked at Holly. 'Here's a leaflet, sir. I'm sure your guide will show you all the interesting places.'

Mitch laughed. 'Thanks, Jaz. Great to see you again.'

Holly pulled Mitch up the path, as Trixy circled them. 'Trixy, heel. Please, heel.' Holly shook her head. 'She's not been like this for months.'

'That's obviously my fault then.'

'Absolutely.' Holly pointed towards the nursery. 'Here's the new building.'

'I hardly recognise it.'

'The café is in the new extension with a conservatory out back with extra seating. And along there.' Holly pointed. 'We've rendered the wall, where the artwork for sale is displayed.'

Holly led him into the buzzing café and smiled as he studied the array of paintings, tapestries and a couple of metal sculptures on shelves.

'Wow, there are some great pieces here. I take it it's not all your work?'

'No, I've sold most of mine already. The dragon is hanging up in a Chinese restaurant.'

'Nice.'

'The café and nursery have been up and running for a couple of months now. It's just the arts hub that's being opened today.'

'It looks like the café is proving popular.'

Holly nodded and watched the queue of people waiting to order drinks and cakes as Anne, and her new assistant, Koby, worked hard.

'Come this way.' Holly led Mitch through the café and into the main nursery building. She loved the earthy aroma, which always smelled like home to her.

'This is huge,' Mitch said looking around.

'Yes, there's a lot more space since the café has been moved. We've a greater variety of seeds, tools, house plants and indoor ornaments.' She pointed to the doors. 'Outside we've got our compost bags, outdoor plants, trees, the sheds and garden furniture.'

'You've not extended the footprint that much, but it seems much bigger with the extension and conservatory. I can see lots of people wanting to come over.'

'What time is it?'

Mitch looked at his mobile phone. 'Eleven forty-five.'

Holly glanced behind her; she could see Jaz bringing the Mayor over. 'Great, she's here. I need to gather everyone at the old barn. Or should I say the arts hub.' Holly felt a lump come into her throat. *Hold it together,* she told herself. 'I need to get everyone to congregate by the opening.'

'Right-o, I'll round them up like sheep,' Mitch said as Trixy trotted behind him.

The Mayor approached, wearing her full paraphernalia. 'Thanks so much for inviting me.'

Holly smiled. 'Thanks for coming. I know how busy you are.'

'What a great turn out you have. It could be well over a hundred.'

'All the leaflets are gone, so it's probably nearer three,' Jaz said.

STANDING on a platform that Joe had erected in front of the old barn, Holly tapped the microphone. She blinked every time the local press snapped a photo of her. The Mayor stood, at the barn door where Holly had earlier tied a yellow ribbon across its handles.

'One-two-three testing,' Holly said into the microphone as she looked into the crowd where she saw her staff amongst the sea of faces, including Anne's husband, who had Charlie the goat on a lead. Nina and Ethan, both wearing sunglasses, smiled up at her. Local business people had come along too, including Jim Kelly from the auction house. Many of her regulars had turned up with their kids clutching the free art-themed goody bags which Anne and Koby had handed out at the café. David Bunning and a few of the other councillors had arrived and Trudy was there representing the Art's Council. Ed, one of the farmers from the market, had brought his young family. Holly also beamed at Ruth, her aunt from Oldham who had popped over. She was staying at a cottage in Cheddar. Magda, Sid's carer was there too with her new client, who she brought to the café at least once a week. And her eyes found Len, pushing through the crowd to the front with Val in her wheelchair. They beamed at Holly as soon as they were in position. *Don't cry,* she told herself. Jaz stood to the left of Val with one hand on her shoulder, giving Holly the thumbs up as Julian stood next to her with Noah on his shoulders. And finally, her eyes rested on Mitch, wrestling to keep an excited Trixy under control.

'Come on,' Jaz shouted. 'Out with it.'

Holly laughed and snapped out of her reflective moment putting her business head back on. 'Thank you all for coming here today. I won't keep you long but I want to give some thanks before we let you in.' She swallowed, her mouth felt dry. 'I'd like to thank the Art's Council and the members of Wells City Council for their financial support. Without that, my vision would not have become a reality.'

Holly stepped back and clapped.

The crowd followed, accompanied by a few whoops.

She stepped forward to the mic again. 'There are also numerous people here to thank. Ethan for helping me with the plans and Nina with the promotion. My faithful staff and friends who stuck with me after the fire. All the villagers who came to the fair and continued to use our facilities, even when we were serving teas out of a shed, so that I could keep the business afloat. Julian, for being the big brother I never had. And Jaz, the best friend in the whole world, who keeps me sane. And I'm so pleased to be able to thank Mitchell Booth today. As the village grapevine knows there's been an historic feud between our families.'

Someone wolf whistled and the audience laughed.

'But Mitch literally saved my life when I was trapped in my burning cottage by calling the emergency services. And he gave me somewhere to live.' Holly pointed over the crowd towards the caravan. 'Without him, I may not even be standing here today. He's taught me what really matters.' Holly felt a lump appear in her throat. She didn't want this crumbling into a tearful Oscar-style speech so she stepped back and started clapping, which soon turned into group applause.

The photographer burst out a few more shots. She stood tall and beamed before returning to the mic. 'And finally, I'd like to thank the Mayor for accepting my invitation to open this event.'

Holly removed the microphone from its stand and stepped down the podium towards the Mayor as the crowd clapped.

The Mayor took the microphone. 'I'm honoured to support this project. Thank you, Holly, for improving the facilities of Eversley and providing this inspirational arts hub for Somerset. I now declare Holly's Hub open.' She cut the ribbon.

Holly smiled. *Holly's Hub?* It was actually called Eversley Arts Hub. She had named it after the village due to the help and support received from the locals. But as the doors opened and people streamed in, she guessed they would be calling it Holly's Hub for some time to come.

Holly watched as the visitors filed in. The artists were already at their work stations, showing their craft-making skills in practice, hoping to take bookings for their workshops. As Holly leaned on the door frame, she felt Mitch behind her snaking his arms around her waist and resting his head on her shoulder, with his mouth next to her ear.

'Congratulations, Holly Loveland,' he whispered.

She squeezed his hands as they watched the moving crowd. Holly raised her eyes to the far back wall and saw the large portrait of Ivy in her meadow which Sid had painted and felt a tear slide down her cheek. Smiling she brushed it away. Turning around she pecked Mitch on the cheek. 'Let's go and have a look around.'

VISITORS HAD FILTERED in and out of the arts hub for hours and by four o'clock there were still a few stragglers left as the artists packed away. They seemed pleased with the way the day had gone. Holly bade farewell to the last artist and she was alone in the barn, Mitch had been at the café helping Jaz, Anne and Koby clear up. Holly felt a smile spread across her face as she saw him approaching with Trixy who sat down, just inside the door, panting.

Mitch pulled Holly close. 'Jaz has taken the staff up to the pub, Julian's giving them drinks on the house. I said we'd follow.'

Holly felt his heart thud against her chest matching the beat of her own. 'I'm so pleased you came. It's been the best day.' She couldn't help the tears and didn't even try to stop them as they changed into a sob. Mitch held her tight, not saying a word, letting her cry. Pulling a pack of tissues from her pocket she wiped her eyes. 'Sorry, I don't know where that came from.'

Mitch brushed the hair out of her eyes. 'It's been a stressful year.'

Holly nodded. 'That thing I said. Telling you to stop trying to save me because I wasn't Vanessa, I've regretted it every second since. I've wanted to ask you to forgive me. It was a truly awful thing for me to say.'

'You hit a nerve. But as they say – the truth hurts. I was trying to compensate for not saving Vanessa.' He shook his head. 'I don't need to forgive you, Holly, or anyone else. What I need to do is somehow forgive myself.'

Holly gave Mitch a squeeze. After a while she looked up at him. 'So we're good?'

Mitch laughed. 'Yes, really good. I feel like I've come home.'

'Really?' Holly asked.

'As soon as I saw you I wanted to stay and – assuming you're up for it?'

'Up for it?' Holly stepped back and put her hands on her hips.

Mitch chuckled. 'I'm not known for my romancing words – I'm not exactly Shakespeare.'

'Well, as it happens, Mr Booth. I am up for it,' Holly said and moved forward, kissing him tenderly on the lips. He took her in his arms, holding her tightly.

After a while Mitch pulled away. 'Let's get that drink.' He took Holly by the hand and led her along the path as Trixy followed. 'So when are you rebuilding the cottage?'

'I'm all out of funds, I'm afraid. I'll be in that caravan for some years to come.'

'Maybe I can help. You have the property – I'll buy the materials.'

'Oh, Mr Booth, you're not after my land, are you?'

'Ms Loveland, I can assure you, I'm after a lot more than your land. Maybe you'd like to stay at the farmhouse with me while we rebuild the cottage?'

They walked hand in hand to the pub with Trixy bounding ahead, knowing that whatever life threw at them, they'd be together.

A NOTE FROM SUZANNE.

Thank you very much for reading Chasing Dreams in Eversley Village. Do you want more? Would you like an invitation to Holly and Mitch's wedding? Why not try the next book which is all about Holly's best friend, Jaz.

Jaz's career has gone from strength to strength and she has been working in Cheshire, selling high performance cars to high performing football players. But her life is turned upside down when she is called back to Somerset after her estranged mother falls ill. She not only has to face her past, but she has to face her feelings for Julian, the man she left behind.

REVIEWS ARE REALLY helpful to an author so please leave one if you have a few moments.

PLEASE VISIT www.suzannefox.co.uk to join my mailing list.

ACKNOWLEDGMENTS

I started this novel way back in 2018 when I wrote the first three chapters as part of my Open University degree with the help of my tutor, Rosemary Dun who helped some more, after I joined a couple of her short courses. I also had help from Jenny Kane in her 'novel in a year' course. And help from an anonymous author through the Romantic Novelists' Association's new writer's scheme, who gave it two read throughs. And Alison Knight who has edited it. And my lovely beta readers Callie Hill, Claire O'Connor, Jenny Treasure and Shell Rice Mutimer, who will always know this book under its working title of 'Holly's Hub'. I mainly publish cozy mysteries under a pen name, however wanted to publish this novel, so turned it into a trilogy and have other ideas in the pipeline for this genre.

Thanks also goes to the rest of my friends in the writing community, to my husband, the insurance broker for giving me advice on the matter and for putting up with me tapping away at the keyboard 24/7.

Made in United States
North Haven, CT
26 September 2025

80142016R00199